# Ba[...]

Singl[...]
it[...]

# *Nine* MONTHS

Leonie and Vivien will have to make it on their own.

But Giles and Ross have made up their minds that in

# *Nine* MONTHS

baby will make three!

*By Request*

**Charlotte Lamb** was born in London in time for World War II, and spent most of the war moving from relative to relative to escape bombing. Educated at a convent, she married a journalist, and has five children. The family lives in the Isle of Man. During the more than twenty years that Charlotte Lamb has been writing for Mills & Boon over 50 million copies of her books have been sold in over 100 international markets. She remains one of our best loved authors by readers around the world.

**Miranda Lee** is an Australian, living near Sydney. Born and raised in the bush, she was boarding-school educated and briefly pursued a classical music career before moving to Sydney and embracing the world of computers. Happily married, with three daughters, she began writing when family commitments kept her at home. She likes to create stories that are believable, modern, fast-paced and sexy. Her interests include reading meaty sagas, doing word puzzles, gambling and going to the movies. Since her career started with Mills & Boon in 1990, Miranda Lee has become one of our most prolific and popular authors.

# Nine MONTHS

**FORBIDDEN FRUIT**
by Charlotte Lamb

**SIMPLY IRRESISTIBLE**
by Miranda Lee

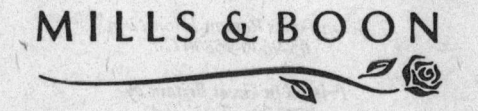

MILLS & BOON

**DID YOU PURCHASE THIS BOOK WITHOUT A COVER?**
If you did, you should be aware it is **stolen property** as it was reported *unsold and destroyed* by a retailer. Neither the author nor the publisher has received any payment for this book.

*All the characters in this book have no existence outside the imagination of the author, and have no relation whatsoever to anyone bearing the same name or names. They are not even distantly inspired by any individual known or unknown to the author, and all the incidents are pure invention.*

*All rights reserved including the right of reproduction in whole or in part in any form. This edition published by arrangement with Harlequin Enterprises II B.V. The text of this publication or any part thereof may not be reproduced or transmitted in any form or by any means, electronic or mechanical, including photocopying, recording, storage in an information retrieval system, or otherwise, without the written permission of the publisher.*

*This book is sold subject to the condition that it shall not, by way of trade or otherwise, be lent, resold, hired out or otherwise circulated without the prior consent of the publisher in any form of binding or cover other than that in which it is published and without a similar condition including this condition being imposed on the subsequent purchaser.*

*MILLS & BOON, the Rose Device and By Request are trademarks of the publisher.*
*Harlequin Mills & Boon Limited,*
*Eton House, 18-24 Paradise Road, Richmond, Surrey, TW9 1SR*

*Forbidden Fruit and Simply Irresistible were first published in separate, single volumes by Mills & Boon Limited.*
*Forbidden Fruit in 1991 and Simply Irresistible in 1993.*

*Forbidden Fruit* © Charlotte Lamb 1991
*Simply Irresistible* © Miranda Lee 1993

ISBN 0 263 79835 6

*Set in Times Roman 11 on 12 pt*
*05-9606-96800 C*

***Printed in Great Britain by***
***BPC Paperbacks Ltd***

# FORBIDDEN FRUIT
by Charlotte Lamb

# CHAPTER ONE

LEONIE craned her neck to catch sight of herself in the mirror, and caught her breath, her lips parting in an audible gasp. She didn't recognise the slender girl in the floating white dress; it was a stranger standing there. Oh, she knew the silvery fair hair which she often wished less fine, the oval face it framed, the skin she always felt was too pale, the widely spaced dark blue eyes. Her familiar features looked back at her, sure enough; and yet there was a disorientating sense of unfamiliarity. Could a dress make that much difference?

'That isn't me!' she thought aloud, and Angela impatiently clicked her tongue.

'Stand still, or I won't be able to get the hem straight!'

'Sorry!' Leonie obediently lapsed back into her previous posture, looking out through the window into a cold blue sky. It was early spring; a chill wind lashed the trees along the London street, but there were daffodils braving the wintry afternoon and pink sprays of blossom breaking out on the almond tree's black boughs.

'So Malcolm's away for three more days?' asked Angela, deftly inserting a final pin in the hem and leaning back to assess the result.

She had insisted that the dress should be her wedding present to the bride, even refusing to let Leonie pay for the beautiful and expensive materials, the silk, ribbon and lace. The style was romantic in the extreme; extravagantly medieval, a high-necked, long-sleeved gown which made the girl in it look like the heroine of a fairy-story come to life.

Leonie knew that Angela's work was so good that she had a long waiting list of clients, to whom she charged very high rates.

'It's too generous of you!' she had protested when Angela first said she was going to make the wedding dress as her present to the bride, but Angela had simply brushed the words aside with a shake of the head.

'Don't argue, I've made up my mind!' she had said firmly. Angela prided herself on being down to earth. Warm-hearted she might be, but she hated to be emotional.

Leonie's mouth curved in a smile now. 'Yes, Malcolm gets back on Thursday.'

'He goes away a lot, doesn't he?'

Leonie's smile faltered. 'Lately he does, yes. He never used to, but I think his brother is deliberately sending him on all these selling trips to keep him away from me.' Her blue eyes were shadowed now, and she looked down at her friend unhappily. 'If they could stop Malcolm marrying me, they would, you know. They don't think I'm good enough for him.'

Angela bristled indignantly, and stood up, her face flushed. 'Are they still being standoffish with you? Who do they think they are? Royalty?'

Leonie gave a husky laugh. 'I wouldn't be surprised! They are very wealthy, Angela. The firm has been making paper at Kent Warlock Mills since the nineteenth century, and their home is much older than that, although I think they bought it about fifty years ago. They haven't always lived at Warlock House, but Mrs Kent comes from a very old family. She grew up in a castle somewhere in Scotland.'

Angela snorted, unimpressed. 'That doesn't give her the right to look down on you! I've no time for snobs.'

Angela was always very forthright; a short, determined brunette with fierce brown eyes and lots of energy. She and Leonie were opposites in many ways and yet they had been friends since they were at school, perhaps because something vulnerable in Leonie's nature made Angela feel she needed someone to look after her and tell her what to do, and Angela was good at that.

Nobody was ever going to get the chance of ordering Angela about, of course, which was why, when she started work, her passion for dressmaking had quite naturally led to her setting up in business on her own. She was successful from the start, and she was her own boss. The job enabled her to work from home, independently, doing as much, or as little, each day, as she chose.

'I can understand Mrs Kent's being disappointed that Malcolm isn't marrying someone from her own background,' Leonie said soberly, trying to be fair, and Angela made impatient noises.

'Someone with money, you mean!'

'I really don't think it is just a question of money. They wanted Malcolm to marry a different sort of girl. Someone from their world, someone whose family they know. I'm just a secretary from an ordinary family.'

'They should be glad Malcolm has found someone so pretty and nice,' Angela said aggressively, and Leonie smiled at her.

'Thanks. Oh, I expect they'll get used to the idea of me. I'll do my best to fit in, and, after all, Malcolm and I have known each other for nine months; they must realise we're both serious. It isn't a spur of the moment impulse—we know what we're doing. I only hope they come to the wedding...'

Angela looked shocked. 'You mean, they might not come?'

'Malcolm says they will, but they haven't answered the invitations my mother sent them.'

'Well, if they don't come they aren't worth bothering about. This is going to be your big day, so don't let them spoil it for you! Once you and Malcolm are married they'll soon come round, wait and see.'

'Do you think so?' Leonie's delicate face lit up, and Angela nodded firmly.

'Of course. There is one thing you can always be sure about with rich people—they're realists. Once you're Malcolm's wife they'll come to terms with the idea.' She caught sight of the clock on the mantelshelf, and gave a groan. 'Look at the time! I've got to meet Jack in the West End at six—we're going to a party. I haven't got time to take the dress home first. I'll have to leave it here, and pick it up tomorrow morning—but guard it with your life. I want it to be perfect on the day!'

'You don't need to worry.'

'But I do!' Angela began hurrying to the door, but lingered, her anxious eyes on the dress. 'Maybe I should stay and help you take it off?'

'I can do it!'

'Well, OK, but... you will be extra careful, especially with the zip?'

'Of course!'

'And don't, whatever you do, let Malcolm see it; it's unlucky!'

'I won't be seeing him!'

'No, of course not.' Angela still couldn't tear herself away. 'And put it back inside the cover before you hang it up!' she reminded her from the door.

'I know!' Leonie laughed and made pushing gestures. 'Go on! I can manage!'

Laughing, Angela said, 'OK. Bye, then, see you tomorrow!' She vanished, the front door of the little flat slammed, and Leonie turned slowly to stare once again at her own reflection, able to do so, this time, at her leisure. She was thrilled with her dress and the way it made her look—she couldn't wait for Malcolm to see it. She had so badly wanted to look really special on their wedding-day, and Angela's clever fingers were going to make that dream come true. Nobody else would ever have had precisely this style of dress, since Angela had designed it for her, a unique, one-off wedding dress for her day in a lifetime.

This was how she had dreamt of looking—so why did she feel strange, unfamiliar?

A frown knit her brows. She was passionately in love with Malcolm—it couldn't be any doubts about him—but she had to face it. Her wedding-day was not going to be all bliss, nor could she be certain about her future life with the man she loved, which was why her moods, for weeks, had swung wildly between deep happiness and a troubled uneasiness. Oh, not about Malcolm, or their feelings for each other—but about his family's hostility, and how that might affect their relationship.

From the very beginning the Kent family had made no secret of their shock, and their dislike of the girl Malcolm had taken home to meet them one hot July evening. She remembered it as if it had been yesterday. There had been thunderstorms rumbling somewhere in the distance, across the rolling wheatfields in the Essex farmland surrounding Warlock House. The sky had been an ominous colour; heavy with cloud, an occasional flash of lightning splitting the horizon. Midges had hummed under the heavy green branches of the trees in the beautifully kept gardens, and the air had been humid.

Leonie had noticed all that, anxiously, and then had been struck dumb by the magnificence of Malcolm's home, a large Queen Anne house built of red brick and stone, set in parkland. The interior matched the beauty and grace of the façade: golden oak panelling, polished woodblock floors, gleaming antique furniture and flowers everywhere, scenting the rooms. She had become so nervous by the time she met Malcolm's family that she was trembling as she shook hands with Mrs Kent, a slim, elegant woman with silvered dark hair. Leonie knew she had been widowed for some five years, and was over sixty, but she certainly did not look it.

Face to face, Leonie had shakily smiled, but been given no smile in reply. Mrs Kent had merely looked Leonie up and down, her thin brows rising in cold disdain.

Meeting those dagger-sharp grey eyes, Leonie had hurriedly turned away to shake hands with Malcolm's elder brother, Giles, only to face the same animosity, the same icily level gaze, and to recognise with a sinking heart that there was no welcome for her in that house.

In the ensuing weeks they had made sure that she met some of the girls Malcolm might have married if he had not met her. They were much the same, all of them: rich, pretty, arrogant, fitting in perfectly with the world Malcolm's family inhabited. The Kent family wanted her to feel inferior and out of place, and Leonie was so shy and unsure of herself that she was an easy target.

One autumn evening she had stood alone at a garden barbecue at the Kent house, miserably watching Malcolm dancing with another girl, who had clung to him, her body sinuously moving in rhythm with his, her arms tightly clasping his neck. Leonie had felt like crying, but she had gritted her teeth and pretended to smile. After all, Malcolm had chosen her, hadn't he? He had not asked any of these other girls to marry him!

'Enjoying yourself?' Giles Kent had asked in a dry, sarcastic voice, suddenly joining her, and she had started, her body tense as she'd looked up at him. He rarely spoke to her, but when from time to time they did meet she always felt wary and tense in his company.

'Yes, thank you,' she had lied, and his mouth had twisted wryly.

'You don't look as if you are.'

'I can't help the way I look!' she had retorted, stung, and he had smiled with an odd sort of irony.

'No, I suppose you can't.' His grey eyes had flicked over her, and for no reason she could explain she had felt her skin burning. His face still held hostility, but for that second she had seen something else in his glance, a sensual awareness of her that had made her blush.

He had laughed at her hot colour. 'Did you think I hadn't noticed the way you look?' he'd softly mocked. 'I'm sure men always do. You're lovely, and I can't blame Malcolm for wanting you. I wouldn't say no, myself, if an offer was made.'

She would have been insulted if she had not been so startled. It was the last thing she had expected from Giles Kent, that sort of remark. She'd almost believed she was imagining the whole thing; hallucinating.

Then he had put out his hand and touched her neck, softly, lightly, his fingertips stroking downwards from her ear to her bare shoulder, and she had felt a shudder run right through her. The brief touch had had an intimacy that had shaken her like an earthquake. She had leapt backwards, eyes huge in her burning face, and a second later Malcolm had been there, frowning, looking at his elder brother with suspicion.

'What's going on? What are you up to, Giles?'

Coolly, Giles had drawled, 'I was making a pass at your girlfriend.'

She hadn't known where to look. Why was he acting this way? Was he trying to cause trouble? Insulting her? Trying to come between her and Malcolm? She could not believe he really felt any attraction; he had always been so icily hostile to her in the past.

Malcolm had stared at him, dark red colour rising in his face. 'Oh, you were, were you?'

The brothers had faced each other, their bodies tense as if they might come to blows any minute, and Leonie had been frightened. 'Stop it! Please, stop it!' she had cried, turning white. Malcolm had given her a quick, concerned look, and relaxed a little, grimacing.

'OK, darling, don't look so upset! I won't punch him in the nose, although he deserves it.'

'Let's go, Malcolm,' she had muttered, careful not to look at Giles.

Malcolm hadn't been ready to leave yet, though. He was too angry. 'Of course,' he'd said furiously, 'I might have known he would, sooner or later. He's used to women falling over themselves to get his attention; he probably thought he could have you with one snap of his fingers.'

Giles had stood there impassively, his face totally without expression, but every line of it taut, his bones locked in tense concentration.

Malcolm had laughed shortly. 'That's what you thought, isn't it, Giles? Well, you won't get anywhere with her—you can't stop our wedding that way! And you can tell Mother that she won't get anywhere with her delaying tactics, either. I'm not interested in any other girls, so tell her to stop pushing them at me. Whether she likes it or not, I love Leonie, and she loves me, and we are getting married, so you and Mother had better get used to the idea.'

Leonie had felt her heart turn over. At that moment she had really begun to believe she and Malcolm could be happy together, that it wasn't just an impossible dream. She had always been afraid that his family would lure him away from her, that his feelings for her would not last, but as he'd smiled down at her at that moment she had been so happy that she had almost burst into tears.

Remembering that evening, the smoky firelit garden, the music and laughter in the background, Giles Kent watching her with those remote grey eyes, and Malcolm smiling at her with love and reassurance, she sighed, a little smile curving her mouth. They were going to be happy. Whatever anyone said or did, in just a few days they would get married, and they would start to build a wonderful life together.

Dreamily, she turned away from the mirror and began to unhook the neck of her dress. A zip ran all the way down to the waist, at the back, but first she had to open the high neck. As she freed the hook she heard the doorbell begin to ring, and grinned to herself.

It was probably Angela, having changed her mind about leaving the precious dress here overnight. Leonie held her long skirts carefully in both hands, to lift the hem off the floor, and made her way to the front door.

Half laughing, she opened it, ready to tease her friend. It wasn't Angela outside, though. It was a tall man in a dark suit. Giles Kent! Leonie's smile died; she stiffened at the first sight of him, her blue eyes startled.

'Oh. It's you,' she muttered, looking away immediately. It troubled her, as always, to meet his cool stare. He had known her for months now, but she was beginning to think that he would never like her, and yet at the same time she was always conscious of that underlying awareness of her, which he had first let her glimpse that day at the barbecue, an awareness matched inside herself, in spite of herself. It was far from being simple attraction; it was too complex for that; a disturbing mixture of hostility and a physical response, which she resisted angrily. She did not want to be conscious of that tall, lean body. She disliked the man intensely! Why on earth should she nevertheless feel this quiver of sensual attention whenever she saw him? She could only think that her dislike was so intense that it triggered off a chemical reaction that was far too much like desire.

She hoped he wasn't aware of her secret feelings, but something in those mocking grey eyes usually made her uneasily suspect he was. Not today, though. She frowned. Today, he was even more hostile than usual. He was frowning heavily, his mouth tightly controlled. Why was he looking at her like that? What was he doing here if he disliked her so much? Through her lashes she noted inconsequentially that he was wearing a black tie. Maybe he had been to a funeral? That would explain his grim expression—but not what he was doing here, visiting her. He had never been to her flat before. Why was he here now?

'What do you want?' she asked edgily.

He didn't answer; the sight of her in her wedding dress seemed to have stupefied him. That would have been the last thing he'd expected—to have her open the door to him in her wedding dress. No doubt he wondered why on earth she was wearing it!

'I was having a fitting,' she stumblingly explained.

'Oh, I see.' He seemed to wrench his stare from her, scowling, as though he hated the sight of her in the lace and silk dress.

He probably did. It must remind him that any day now she would be his sister-in-law, one of his family. Like his mother, Giles Kent did not think she was good enough for that.

'Are you alone?' he asked tersely, looking past her into the flat. Did he wonder if Malcolm was there? No, of course, he knew his brother was abroad on the firm's business, in Switzerland.

'Yes,' she admitted warily, wondering if she should refuse to let him enter her flat. Would it be wise to be alone with him? Malcolm had warned her, after that incident at the barbecue, not to trust his brother, never to let Giles near her. 'He's ruthless with women,' he had told her. 'Giles is ruthless with business, the family, everyone, but especially with women.'

Why was he here, when he knew his brother was away? She bit her lip, wondering what to do. 'Angela... the friend who is making my dress has just gone out,' she hurriedly said, rather flushed. 'But she should be back some time soon...'

He nodded again, but absently. 'May I come in?' He didn't wait for an answer. He stepped forward, and she had to let him pass. She wished she knew why he was here—she couldn't believe this was a casual, friendly visit. Had he come to ask her to give Malcolm up? To persuade? Or to threaten? The latter, probably; Giles Kent gave off an air of threat most of the time, and that was what she could expect from him.

Leonie felt stupid in the long, elaborately romantic dress and would have gone to take it off, except that she did not want to encourage Giles Kent to stay any longer than necessary. He made her far too nervous.

'Have you got any brandy?' he asked abruptly, swinging to face her suddenly, and she couldn't stop herself visibly flinching.

'B... brandy?' She looked rather wildly around the sitting-room, shaking her head. 'Sorry, I'm afraid... I don't drink, you see. I don't keep spirits in the flat. There is some white wine in the fridge, for dinner when Malcolm gets back——'

'He won't be back!' Giles Kent interrupted, his voice harsh, and she stared at him in some confusion, her brow furrowed.

'Is this trip taking longer than expected?'

Suspicion raced through her—were they trying to keep Malcolm abroad as long as possible, still hoping to separate them?

Giles didn't answer. Instead, he suddenly took her shoulders and pushed her backwards on to a chair. She was too surprised to struggle, her body pliant in his grip for a second. He looked so odd that he frightened her. He was going to make another pass at her, after all. Her heart beat suffocatingly, and she tried to think what to do. This time they were alone and she didn't know if she could handle him; he was so much stronger, a tall, hard, lean man whose body could dominate hers without much effort.

He bent over her, his face inches away, a disturbing mask of bone out of which grey eyes watched her frowningly.

'Please, don't...' she stammered, trembling, too scared even to be angry, but then he interrupted her, his voice rough.

'Leonie, listen... God, I don't know how to say this... there's no painless way of doing it—if I could, I would, but... best to be quick, get it over.' He took a long breath. 'He's been killed.'

Leonie stared at him, blank-faced, not yet understanding. 'Who are you talking about?'

'Malcolm,' Giles said. 'Malcolm is dead.'

The breath seemed to leave her body. Her heart seemed to stop beating. She didn't make a sound, just sat there, staring.

Giles talked on in that angry voice, the words like bullets aimed at her, or fate, or maybe even himself. 'This morning—he was killed this morning. On the ski slopes. He came down too fast, collided with someone and was killed instantly, a head injury, a glancing blow from the other man's ski as they fell together. A one in a million chance, they say. A stupid accident, need not have happened if he had been thinking what he was doing...'

Leonie hadn't moved, hadn't given a sign of life since he said that first sentence. She was still hearing it. 'He's dead.' The words repeated in her head while she sat staring at Giles; face deathly white, blue eyes wide and dark and fixed, like the eyes of a china doll, not the eyes of a living girl. He's dead. He's dead. He is dead, the words crashed and beat inside her, but she didn't believe them, she couldn't bear to believe them.

'They rang me from Zurich,' Giles said. 'Our clients out there heard the news first, and got in touch with me, a couple of hours ago.'

Her eyes flickered then; a deadlier pallor creeping into her face. Malcolm had been dead for hours. While she had laughed and talked, and tried on her wedding dress, Malcolm had been dead in the cold white snow, and she hadn't known.

'I had to break it to my mother first,' Giles said, and there was the faintest note of apology in his voice, or recognition of her claim to have heard sooner. His mouth twisted with a sort of bitterness. 'She took it badly, of course. He was always her favourite. We had to get her a doctor. He gave her a sedative; she's sleeping now.'

Leonie wasn't listening. Her eyes had a fixed, strained look. 'No,' she said suddenly. 'It can't be true. He's on a business trip. He didn't go skiing. You're lying to me. You and your family...you hate me...you've always hated me...' Her voice rose hysterically and she got up, pushing Giles out of the way so angrily that it was like a blow. 'You're lying; I don't believe he's dead!'

Giles grabbed her and she struggled wildly. 'Let go of me! Don't you touch me!'

'Be still, then,' he said through his teeth. 'You're acting crazily. You have to believe it; it's the truth, Leonie. I wouldn't lie about something like this; you know it's true... don't try to pretend it isn't, you'll just go mad.'

She swayed, her eyes closing, and let him push her back on to the chair.

'He shouldn't have been on the ski slopes,' Giles said. He crouched down in front of her and took both her icy hands. He rubbed them slowly, methodically, sending a little wave of warmth through the frozen fingers.

She didn't try to pull them away, because she wasn't really aware what he was doing. She was trying not to believe what he was saying to her. Malcolm couldn't be dead... ten minutes ago she had been looking forward to her wedding, life had been crammed with promise, she had been so happy—and now...

The words echoed in her head again. He is dead. He is dead. She couldn't bear to believe it. If it was true her whole life was over, she was looking into an abyss, into nothing, for ever and ever.

'He should have been in Zurich, but he went off skiing for the weekend, cancelling two business meetings, important ones. Utterly typical,' Giles said curtly. 'He was always going off like that, forgetting the work, just off looking for some fun...'

She got angry then and pushed him away, shaking her head. 'No! Shut up. Don't talk about him! You hated him, too; you hated both of us.' She struggled to her feet again, although he tried to stop her. 'Get your hands off me! Don't touch me!' she muttered thickly, sounding almost drunk.

'You're in shock,' Giles said roughly.

'Leave me alone!' She tried to walk away and fell over the long, flowing skirts of the dress, angrily tearing at it. 'I have to get this off... got to get it off...!' She couldn't bear to wear it, she couldn't bear to feel it against her skin. Her mind brought back the memory of her reflection in the mirror a little while ago. A smiling bride; all white lace and satin. 'Must get it off!' she groaned, straining to reach the zip, and Giles came up behind her. She felt the brush of his cool fingers on her skin and shivered. Then the zip slid down and the dress fell apart, leaving her smooth, pale back bare.

She let the dress slip to the floor and stepped out of it, wearing nothing but a lacy white bra and panties. It didn't even occur to her that Giles was watching her; she wasn't even aware of him.

Kicking her wedding dress aside, she walked like an automaton towards her bedroom. Giles somehow got there first, although she hadn't seen him pass her. He met her, a dressing-gown in his hands.

'Put this on; you'll catch cold.'

She tried to walk past. 'Leave me alone!'

'Leonie, for God's sake!' he muttered hoarsely, his eyes fixed on her averted face.

'Just go away! I don't want you near me!' she whispered.

His mouth indented, but he didn't leave. He took hold of her as if she were a doll, manhandled her forcibly into the dressing-gown.

She resisted, but Giles got his way, of course. He always did—Malcolm had often said so. Giles had not wanted her in the Kent family, and he was getting his own way there. His brother was dead, and she would never be his sister-in-law.

'I hope you're satisfied,' she said bitterly. 'This is what you wanted, isn't it—to stop him marrying me? And now he won't. You must be very happy.'

'Hate me as much as you like; at least that's a healthy emotion,' he said drily. 'But it won't bring Malcolm back to life if you get sick, so I want you to go and lie down now and try to sleep.'

She didn't answer. What did it matter? Nothing in the world mattered now. Malcolm was dead. Malcolm was dead. Thinking it, repeating it, did not make it seem any more possible, any more believable.

He tied the belt of the dressing-gown around her waist, staring down at her white face. 'Is there someone I can call? Your mother? Shall I ring her and ask her to come?'

'I don't want anyone.'

'You shouldn't be alone. You must have someone with you, to look after you. I can't stay, or I would, but I must get back to my mother; she'll need me there when she wakes up. Let me call your mother—what's her number?'

'I don't want her.'

'A friend, then?' he patiently insisted. 'The one who was making your dress? Did you say she was coming back soon? I'll call her, shall I?'

'No. Don't call anyone,' she whispered with the last of her energy. 'I just want to be alone.' She couldn't start believing in what he had told her, start bearing it, accepting it, until he had gone and she was alone, away from watching eyes and listening ears. 'Please, go away and leave me alone.'

'Look...' Giles Kent began quite gently, but Leonie had had enough. She saw the darkness opening out in front of her and fell forward into it.

When she recovered consciousness, she was in bed, the duvet piled over her, the curtains drawn and the bedroom dark and silent. For a second she blankly did not remember what had happened, and then she did, and, thinking she was alone, she opened her mouth to let out a primal cry; wordless, a groan of agony.

At that somebody moved in the room. Her head twisted on the pillow, her cry bitten off as she stared. The dark shape of a man stood by the window, outlined by a faint glow from a street-lamp outside. He came towards her, bent to look at her, and she saw it was Giles Kent. He had not gone, he was still here.

'I've rung your mother, she should be here within an hour,' he said quietly. 'I'll stay until she gets here. Is there anything I can get you? Some tea? Milk?'

'No,' she said hoarsely. 'I don't want anything, I don't want anyone... I don't want you here...'

'I understand,' he said in that low voice. 'But you're in shock. You shouldn't be alone. A cup of hot tea would help, you know. Let me make one for you.'

Anything to get rid of him, she thought wildly. 'Yes, yes, I'll have tea, then...'

'Good girl,' he said, almost smiling. 'I won't be a moment...'

He went out, closing the door behind him, and she lay there in the bed, her body still icy cold and shivering in spite of the warmth of the duvet. She was alone now, she could cry, but she couldn't, there were no tears, just a terrible anguish eating away at her.

She closed her eyes and saw Malcolm's face; smiling, that teasing, charming smile which made him so irresistible. He had his family colouring; dark hair, pale eyes, height and a slim figure, but in Malcolm they somehow made a different pattern. He was less daunting than his elder brother, much better looking and more light-hearted; a little spoilt, perhaps, by his mother, as Giles had said, but Leonie could understand her spoiling him— Malcolm must have been an adorable little boy. He had often told her Giles was jealous of him, but he had laughed about it, found it funny, even secretly been pleased about it.

Leonie had always felt that Malcolm wasn't yet fully grown up—his mother's partiality had kept a boyishness in him—but she had been sure he would grow out of that once they were married, when they had children of their own.

Now they never would, she thought with a pang of grief that shook her body physically, and that was when the tears began pouring down her face. Shaking with sobs, she couldn't stop them once they had begun, and when the bedroom door opened she had to roll hurriedly on to her face and hide them from Giles.

She heard him put a cup down on her bedside table, and lay still, stifling her sobs and wrenched breathing in her pillow, hoping he would think she was asleep and go away.

He stood there for a second, watching her and listening, then he said quietly, 'I'll be in your sitting-room if you need me. Drink your tea, Leonie, don't let it get cold.'

When he had gone again she sat up, her sobs silenced now but the tears still running down her face. She had always hoped to make friends with Giles and his mother, and his older sister, Linda, who was married, with two children, and lived in Devon, but they had kept their distance and now that, too, was something that would never happen, although Giles was being kind to her, kinder than he had ever been before.

He must be in a state of shock, too, she thought, wiping a hand over her wet eyes and face. When he first arrived she had felt he was angry, and grief took that form sometimes, especially when it came like a blow, out of the blue, and this had, for both of them, for all of them. They might not have liked her, but she had always known that the Kent family were very close, a real family, full of affection, not like her own family, which was why she had longed to become part of them one day, why she had gone on hoping that they would accept her in the end.

Giles had sent for her mother, and Martha would come, naturally. She always did what she knew the world viewed as 'the right thing'; she would be wearing black. She always had a little black dress for every occasion—black was elegant and sophisticated and suited her. She would be muted and sad, but Leonie knew she would get no comfort, or even understanding, from her mother. She wished Giles had not sent for her.

## CHAPTER TWO

Two months later, Leonie was stretched out on a beach in Italy, her head shaded by a striped umbrella, her body gleaming with oil and already beginning to take on a pale tan. Angela sat on a beach mattress beside her, painting her toenails a warm shade of pink and occasionally yawning because they had been up late last night at a disco held in their hotel, and had then been awoken early by the splashing and giggling of children leaping into the hotel swimming-pool.

'I shall need a holiday to recover from this!' Angela moaned, and Leonie gave a wry little smile.

'It was your idea to come here!'

'How was I to know this hotel was a whirlpool of mad activity from dawn until the early hours of the morning? It was a good idea at the time; we both needed to get away, didn't we?'

'Yes.'

'You have enjoyed it, haven't you?' Angela asked with an anxious little frown, and Leonie gave her a sideways look, smiling a reassurance.

'You know I have... it's magical...'

She stared at the shimmering blue sea, the sky arching above it for what seemed an endless distance, and sighed. Magical was the only word she could think of to describe this landscape, especially in the mornings, when the sea and sky seemed newborn, a miracle of changing colours and echoing vistas. For the first couple of days after they had arrived, she had hardly noticed their beauty; she had just plodded obediently with Angela from hotel to beach and back again, as blind to everything around her as she had been ever since Giles Kent had told her Malcolm was dead. Then, slowly, the loveliness of sea and sky had penetrated the ice which had walled her in for weeks, and her eyes had opened on to a new world.

'A holiday—that's what we need,' Angela had said in the flat one rainy May morning. It had been a Saturday, and neither of them had been working.

Leonie had come to dread weekends; she could face life during the week, when she could keep her mind on her work, surrounded by the buzz of busy colleagues, but when she was alone her mood always darkened, and she couldn't stop her thoughts from wandering.

She hadn't said anything to Angela, but she had not needed to—Angela had guessed, or noticed, and had taken to popping in at weekends to keep her company or talk her into coming out.

That morning, Angela had stood by the window looking out over wet gardens full of bedraggled spring flowers; tulips and wallflowers and white lilac. Opposite stretched a vista of wet London roofs. Leonie had been obsessively doing a jigsaw puzzle at the table; it had two thousand pieces and was fiendishly difficult, if not impossible. She had started it the day after Malcolm was buried and so far she had barely done a quarter of it, although she worked at it lethargically during any spare time she had. It gave her something to do.

'Somewhere sunny and foreign,' Angela had said, turning to watch her.

Leonie had carefully fitted an oddly shaped piece of blue sky into the outer rim of the puzzle, then looked up, staring at the grey sky behind Angela's head, realising for the first time that it was raining, and had been raining for days. 'We don't seem to have seen the sun much lately,' she'd flatly agreed.

'So? Shall we do it?' Angela had challenged. 'Come on. Let's walk round to that travel agent in Wilberforce Street and pick up some brochures. It will be fun just looking at them.'

They hadn't needed brochures. The travel agent had told them that there was a fortnight on offer, beginning two weeks later, at a reduced price because it had been under-booked, in Italy, at a lively resort on the Adriatic coast. When he'd shown them a picture of the hotel, and told them the overall cost, Angela had looked eagerly at her.

'What do you think? Shall we? It's a terrific bargain.'

Leonie had hesitated just for a second, but then she had thought of getting away from everything familiar, everything that reminded her of Malcolm, and she had made up her mind.

'Yes, let's go.'

Now they had been here a week and she was very glad she had come. She couldn't say she was happier, exactly; only that she had begun to believe it was possible to be happy again one day. She had begun to lift her head and look about her and notice the world again, and for that much she was very grateful to Angela.

Smiling, her friend relaxed again, screwed the top back on to her bottle of nail varnish, and lay down beside her, closing her eyes. 'Mmm... this is the life. I could stay here, doing nothing but sunbathe, all year round, couldn't you?'

'I wouldn't go so far as to say that! I've an idea it might get boring after a while.'

'Maybe.' Angela stretched again, but her nature was not suited to idleness, and after five minutes' silence she shifted restlessly, turned on to her side and asked, 'Shall we go on this trip this afternoon to Ravenna, to see the Byzantine church?'

Leonie laughed outright at that. 'If you want to! I would quite like to see it, although I don't know much about Byzantine churches. It will make a change from lying on the beach or looking at the shops.'

'That's what I thought,' Angela admitted, caught her friend's amused grin and grinned back. 'Well, we have done a lot of sunbathing!'

The hotel organised a weekly coach trip to the ancient town of Ravenna, an hour's drive away—it was a popular event. When they went to buy their tickets, the girls were told they were lucky to get the last two available, and the coach was already crowded by the time they arrived. They weren't able to sit next to each other. Angela found herself sitting next to a very chatty lady in her late seventies, and Leonie had to sit down next to a skinny young man in denim shorts and a T-shirt, who had already spent a lot of time staring at her in the hotel restaurant.

Delighted, he made the most of his opportunity to get to know her, telling her in a rush that his name was Adrian, he was a trainee architect, and lived with his parents in Sheffield, before going on to ask her endless questions. Where did she live? Did she live alone or with her family? Was Angela her friend or her sister? Where did she work? Oh, a solicitor's office—how interesting; did she like her job?

Leonie kept her replies short and as uninformative as possible, but then he became more personal, shifting closer to her so that his knee touched hers and she could smell the overpowering scent of his manly aftershave.

'I've been dying to get to know you, Leonie... that's a lovely name; I never met anyone called Leonie before. I expect you realised I've been watching you—you're far and away the prettiest girl in the hotel, in the whole town, come to that... but I suppose you've got a boyfriend?'

Leonie was spared having to answer that one, her throat hurting and her face pale under her light tan, because at that moment to her relief they drove up to San Vitale, the Byzantine cathedral in Ravenna, and everyone started exclaiming and staring out of the windows.

'Oh, we're here!' Adrian said, his attention mercifully distracted. 'I'm longing to see the mosaics here; they're the most famous in the Byzantine world, you know.'

'No, I didn't,' admitted Leonie, and he looked round at her with the eagerness of an expert given a chance to educate.

'Really? Oh, yes; in a lot of Byzantine churches the mosaics were defaced or even destroyed centuries ago, especially in places where the Moslems conquered a city, but here in Ravenna they have been kept in marvellous condition, although they date back to the sixth century, and you'll see amazing portraits of the Emperor Justinian and his wife, Theodora. Have you heard about her? The story is that she was once a prostitute, or at least a highly paid courtesan, before she married the emperor—although I don't know how true that is...but...'

As they got off the coach with everyone else Adrian talked on and on in Leonie's ear, stunning her into silence and making Angela give her an amazed and laughing grin. Leonie hurried to catch up with their party, hoping that once the official guide had taken over Adrian would stop talking, but he shadowed her throughout the visit, giving her his own version of the history of Ravenna, until the irritated guide came over and asked him to be quiet while he was in the cathedral.

Then Adrian did lapse into silence, and a few moments later Leonie managed to slip away while Adrian's attention was fixed on the mosaics.

She wandered out into the dazzling Italian sunshine and decided to look at the local shops to see if she could find a present for her mother. It might placate Martha if she could find something really special; an elegant sweater or a handsome leather bag, both items for which Italy was famous.

Martha Priestley loved clothes and wore them well. Strangers often took Martha for a woman in her late thirties, but, of course, she was a good ten years older than she looked, although she hated admitting it, which was one reason why she had insisted that, from an early age, Leonie should not call her Mother, or Mummy, but should use her first name. Martha loved it if new acquaintances took them for sisters. She hadn't much wanted a child at all, Leonie had soon realised, but Martha positively hated having a grown-up daughter.

'I was a mere child when I was married,' she always said plaintively. She had, in fact, been eighteen when she was married to Leonie's father, and nineteen when Leonie was born, but somehow she made it sound as if she had been a child in school uniform.

If her audience knew Leonie was her daughter, Martha would add with a wistful sigh, 'And then what did he do but die, leaving me alone in the world, with a baby...'

If the audience was a man, who didn't know she had a child, Leonie suspected that her mother did not mention her. It wasn't necessary, because from an early age Leonie had not lived with her mother. After the death of her father, when she was nine,

Leonie had been sent to stay with her father's mother, Granny Priestley, down in Hampshire, and there she had stayed until her grandmother died during Leonie's last year at school.

It had not been an unhappy childhood: Leonie had loved her grandmother and known that she, in turn, was loved and needed by a lonely old woman whose husband and only son were dead. It had, in some ways, been idyllic, living in the country, in a village, near the sea and the forest, with ponies to ride and lots of friends at school.

Leonie didn't bear her mother a grievance; she understood that a child did not fit in with the sort of life Martha Priestley wanted and worked hard to achieve for herself.

Now she had a very smart dress shop, and lived in the flat above. She had a circle of like-minded friends, and several male admirers, although she apparently didn't want to marry again. She had found marriage disappointing, and preferred the endless excitement of courtship to the routine which succeeded a wedding.

She was a very attractive woman—her hair more or less the same shade as Leonie's, but worn in a fine chignon, drawn back to reveal the exquisite bone-structure of her face. Her eyes were paler than her daughter's: a blue close to grey, cold and slightly hard. She relentlessly dieted, and had a wand-like figure. She wore classic clothes, which never went out of fashion, cost a great deal but lasted for years, and suited her perfectly, her cold English beauty at home in black or good tweeds, in pastel twin sets and pearls or in the elegance of Paris designs from Chanel or Dior.

Leonie had grown up seeing very little of her. Indeed, they had only really got to know each other after Leonie got engaged. That was when Leonie really began to understand her mother, and see her clearly, and she had not much liked what she saw.

Malcolm's family was very rich, had a lovely home and moved in social circles Martha had always longed to join—Leonie's news had made her mother very happy. She had begun to plan the wedding at once: it was going to be the social event of the year, if Martha had anything to do with it, and she spared no expense, insisting on making all the arrangements herself.

Malcolm's death had wrecked all those plans, and Martha had been white when she'd arrived at her daughter's flat that day. White, not with grief, but with rage. Leonie would never forget what she had said. 'I've spent a fortune, and all for nothing...will his family help me pay the bills?' And later, in a sudden outburst, 'How could he be so reckless? Skiing, just before the wedding...why did you let him go there alone? You should have gone. It wouldn't have happened if you had been there.'

Remembering the sharp, cold voice, Leonie closed her eyes. Ever since her mother had said it she hadn't been able to help wondering...was it true? If she had insisted on going along with Malcolm would he be alive today?

She felt people watching her, and made herself walk on, looking straight ahead. A second later she saw a man sitting at a table in a street café on the other side of the road; their eyes met, and Leonie stopped dead, trembling.

It couldn't be. She was imagining it. A shiver ran down her spine, in spite of the hot Italian sun. Giles Kent? Here?

He got up and strode over to her, looking more casual than she had ever seen him; his cream trousers and open-necked caramel-coloured shirt elegantly relaxed. Designer holiday wear, Leonie thought wildly. She might have expected it from him. He was always perfectly dressed for every occasion.

'What on earth are you doing in Ravenna?' he demanded sharply, as though suspecting her of following him around.

'I'm on holiday,' she snapped back. 'What are *you* doing here?'

'A business trip,' he said in that curt voice, and she winced, turning pale. It had always been Malcolm who went on these overseas selling trips—that had been the major part of his job; he had been good at talking people into buying the company's products. He had had such charm and warmth; people always liked him, and he could probably have sold anything.

'The new sales manager has just gone down with flu, so I had to take over some of his work,' said Giles, and she felt grief pour through her like smoke through a burning house.

Malcolm was dead; there was someone else doing his job now, life had to go on without him. It hurt. She couldn't stop the tears welling up in her eyes.

Giles watched her with a frown. Her tears probably embarrassed him; they were embarrassing her. 'Sorry, sorry,' she whispered, turning as if to run away, but Giles moved too and she cannoned into him, her face coming up against his chest. Before she could back, his arm came round her and held her there, his fingers briefly closing over the back of her head in a soothing movement while he murmured wordlessly.

'Ssh...'

She stood there, face buried, wanting to let go completely and cry out all the misery of the past weeks, but she wouldn't let herself do that, not with Giles Kent, of all people.

She pulled herself together and straightened up. 'I'm OK now, thanks,' she muttered, grateful for his kindness, and surprised by it because she knew how hostile he had been from the minute his brother had taken her home. Like his mother, he had never thought she was good enough to marry into his family.

'You don't look it!' Giles brutally told her. 'You should sit down for a while.' He propelled her towards the table at which he had been sitting and drew out a chair. Leonie sat down in the shade of a yellow-striped parasol. He was a very overbearing man, she thought as he sat down opposite. She watched his hard face with some perplexity. Even his kindness had a touch of tyranny.

A waiter arrived. 'Coffee?' asked Giles, and she nodded.

'Yes, thank you.'

When the waiter left there was a fraught little silence; Leonie wished Giles wouldn't watch her like that. There was something so male about that tough face, those hard grey eyes, that it made her conscious of being a woman, and that was not an awareness she wanted any more, especially not from him.

'So, why are you here?' he asked quietly, and huskily she repeated,

'On holiday.'

'In Ravenna?' he queried with lifted eyebrows, because although Ravenna attracted many tourists it was not a holiday town.

'No,' she said. 'We're staying at Rimini, having a seaside holiday; sunbathing and swimming. We came to Ravenna on a coach trip.'

'We?' he questioned sharply.

'I'm with Angela, the friend who made my...' She broke off, biting her lip, suddenly remembering that day he'd come to tell her Malcolm was dead and she'd stood there in her wedding dress, her life torn apart as she'd listened.

Giles watched her, his brows together; she wondered if he was remembering, too. What had he thought when she'd begun acting like a crazy woman? She had tried to forget everything about that day, but seeing him again had triggered off the memories—had she really pulled off her wedding dress and kicked it away?

She had been almost out of her mind, she had not cared then what he thought, but suddenly a hot flush swept up her face. She couldn't meet his eyes. She would never have behaved like that normally, stripping off her clothes in front of Giles Kent, of all men!

'Your wedding dress?' he murmured drily, and she knew he remembered. She was afraid of what he might say next, so she began to stammer disconnected words.

'Yes... that beautiful dress... what a terrible... terrible way to treat... something made with such loving care; Angela took such trouble with it... she must have been upset when she saw what had happened to it.'

Leonie broke off suddenly, remembering how delighted she had been just minutes before—staring happily at her reflection in the mirror. The dress had been pure magic, she had loved it; and then Giles had arrived with his bitter news, and she had feverishly pulled off her lovely dress and left it in a heap on the floor. She had never seen it again. Angela must have taken it away with her when she'd come next morning, but she had not said anything, and Leonie had never been able to ask her about the dress. She had wanted to forget everything that had happened that day.

'I'm sure she understood,' Giles said quietly.

Leonie nodded. 'She's my oldest friend; we were at school together. It was her idea to come to Italy—the weather has been so bad in England lately, nothing but endless rain, and Angela felt she had to get some sun. She loves beach life. I think she would be perfectly contented to lie in the sun all day.'

She was chattering stupidly—she didn't really know what she was saying to him—but he made her nervous; she didn't know what he was thinking as he watched her with that thoughtful gaze. He had always been her enemy, he had been dead set against her marriage to his brother, but he no longer seemed so angrily hostile. Well, why should he be now? She was no threat to him and his family any more.

'What about you?' he asked. 'Do you like beach life? Are you happy, lying in the sun all day?'

'Well, it has been a restful week,' she admitted.

'Even though you're so pale I can see you're getting a tan,' he observed, running his glance down over her face, throat and shoulders, and she turned pink again, hoping he had forgotten all about seeing her half naked.

His grey eyes held mockery. 'Maybe I should take another day off and spend it on the beach, too?' he drawled, watching the confusion in her face.

Was he flirting with her? Leonie found it oddly hard to breathe, and was relieved when the waiter arrived at that moment with their coffees. She managed a smile and a shy, *'Grazie!'* She hadn't known a word of Italian until she came here, but now she was beginning to speak a little of the language, enough to communicate with waiters and shopkeepers.

The waiter smiled, said something polite, which she did not understand, and went away. Leonie felt Giles Kent's wry gaze on her but self-consciously didn't meet his eyes. She picked up the small cup instead and gratefully sipped the black liquid it held. Italian coffees rarely seemed the same twice; sometimes she was given a frothy milky coffee, other times a tiny cup of almost lethally strong coffee arrived, and she was only now beginning to sort out what to order.

'Do you speak Italian?' Giles asked, and she shook her head.

'I've picked up a few words, that's all. Do you?'

'Yes,' he said, and she might have expected it. Malcolm had once said that Giles was good at everything; whether at work or play, he'd said, Giles was so successful that he was terrifying.

Malcolm's secretary had interrupted, grimacing, 'You can say that again! He makes me nervous every time he walks into my office!'

'That's because of your guilty conscience, Joanne!' Malcolm had said. 'You're afraid he'll find out how little work you ever do!'

Everyone had laughed, but Leonie had taken the other girl seriously. She could imagine how unnerving it could be to have Giles Kent suddenly walk into your office.

Giles didn't have Malcolm's looks, or charm, of course. He didn't have Malcolm's light touch, either. He didn't chat cheerfully to people who worked for him, make jokes, talk as if he were one of them.

He wasn't exactly popular with the firm's employees. They respected, even admired him, but they made no secret of the fact that they were afraid of him. They certainly did not grin as soon as they saw him, the way they did when they saw Malcolm.

'Are you in Ravenna to sell paper to a client?' she asked him politely, without caring much, but making conversation.

'No, I'm here for the day, too. Of course, I'm not with a coach party...'

'Of course not,' she said with a faint irony that made him look sharply at her. She could not imagine Giles joining a coach party on a day's outing.

'I'm driving myself,' was all he said, though. 'I flew over, naturally, and then I hired a car so that I could get around without needing to use public transport or hire taxis all the time. I prefer to drive myself. I've always wanted to see Ravenna, and since I was only a couple of hours' drive away I decided to fit a visit into my schedule, and I must say it has been worth it.'

She was grateful for a neutral subject to talk to him about, and eagerly said, 'Yes, the Byzantine mosaics are marvellous, aren't they?'

'Breathtaking,' he agreed, and opened a glossy handbook on the table between them, pointing to a photograph of the mosaic portrait of the Emperor Justinian. 'I've often seen photographs of the mosaics here, but to see them in real life gave them a whole new dimension.'

Leonie bent over the handbook, her pale hair falling forward until it almost touched Giles's hand. 'Did you buy that here? The one I got didn't have such terrific photos in it.'

He bent forward, too, brushing her hair back so that he could see the photograph, too. Leonie's head lifted at once, nervously. She was intensely aware of his touch. His face was only inches away; she saw the grain of his skin, his thick black lashes, his tough cheekbones, the curl of his hard mouth. It was an impressive face from a distance, but close to it was even more so. Malcolm had had charm and light-hearted good looks, but Giles Kent had a strength and unshakeable purpose, which one could read in every line of that face.

'Yes, I bought it here,' he said brusquely, his grey eyes so close that she could see every detail of them, the very pale iris, flecked at the rim with tiny yellow rays, the jet black pupil.

The shock of looking into his eyes froze her; she couldn't say a word, and they sat there staring at each other in a sort of trance, the hot Italian sun pouring down, the busy sounds of the town all around them, yet for that instant neither of them was aware of their surroundings. Leonie didn't know what Giles was thinking, nor what she was thinking herself, but she felt the rapid, wild beat of her pulse in her throat, was deafened by the beat of it in her ears.

What on earth was wrong with her? It must be the sun, she thought, her mouth dry. It was making her dizzy.

# FORBIDDEN FRUIT

It was Angela who broke the spell. She rushed up, crossly chattering as she came.

'Oh, there you are! I've been looking all over the place for you. Why did you vanish like that? You might have said you were going! The last I saw of you, you were with that thin boy, what's-his-name, in the cathedral. I saw him chatting you up, so I thought I'd be tactful and fade away, and then you vanished, and he was on his own. I asked him where you were, and he didn't know, and I couldn't see you anywhere. You scared the life out of me. I thought you might have got lost.'

'No, I——' Leonie began, but Angela cut her short more cheerfully.

'No, you just wandered off in a dream, as usual! I should have known. Oh, well...come on, I want to get some shopping done before we have to get on the coach.'

'OK,' Leonie said, finishing her coffee hurriedly.

Only then did Angela give the man sitting opposite Leonie a curious, half-suspicious look.

A second later she recognised him, her eyes opening wide, her jaw dropping.

'Hello,' Giles said with dry amusement.

'You...you're...aren't you...?' stammered Angela, for once almost speechless, and Giles nodded, smiling crookedly.

'That's right. You have a good memory. I'm Giles Kent—and you're Leonie's friend, Angela, aren't you?'

'That's right,' Angela said, giving Leonie a stunned look that still managed to fizz with curiosity. What was going on here? her stare asked. What was he doing here? And why hadn't Leonie told her he was going to turn up?

Giles stood up and drew out a chair, gesturing politely. 'Sit down, have some coffee—I'll call the waiter.'

Leonie stood up in a hurry. 'No, we must go. Thank you for the coffee; enjoy the rest of your trip.'

'Enjoy the rest of your holiday,' he said, staying on his feet.

'Thanks,' she said, not quite meeting his eyes because she was suddenly very self-conscious. She slid a hand through Angela's arm and pulled her away, walking fast and not looking back.

Only when they were out of earshot did Angela demand, 'Well? What on earth is going on? What is he doing here, and how did he know you were in Ravenna?'

Halting in front of a shop window to look at some silk blouses, Leonie said, 'He didn't know. We met by sheer chance.'

'Oh, come off it!' Angela said drily. 'That is too big a coincidence.'

'It's true. He's in Italy on a sales trip and he just happened to come to Ravenna because he's always wanted to see the Byzantine remains here. I remember Malcolm saying that Giles was keen on history and was always going off sightseeing when he was abroad.' Leonie walked on, deciding the silk blouses were too expensive for her.

'I still think it's a massive coincidence that he turned up here while we were here,' Angela said. 'Maybe he was keeping an eye on you?'

Startled, Leonie did a double-take, frowning at her friend. 'Why on earth should he do that?'

'Well, you were almost his sister-in-law—maybe he feels responsible for you?'

Leonie laughed shortly. 'No chance! He doesn't even like me, and he's very glad I'm not going to be his sister-in-law, believe me!'

Angela made a face. 'A pity you aren't. You could have arranged a blind date for me and him.'

Leonie frowned. 'You must be joking!'

'I think he's very sexy,' insisted Angela.

The sun was beating on the top of Leonie's head like a gong; her ears buzzed and she began to feel strangely cold. She swayed, feeling sweat break out on her forehead, and from a long way off heard Angela exclaim, 'Leonie... You aren't going to faint, are you?'

'No,' Leonie whispered, a strange roaring in her ears, and then the next thing she knew was that she was lying on the ground with people standing all round her, staring down at her. Her bewildered eyes roamed the faces and at last found Angela.

Angela anxiously said, 'You fainted—how do you feel now? You're so pale. Are you OK? We'll get a doctor when I can manage to make someone understand what is wanted.' She looked round the circle of staring, curious Italian faces. 'A doctor? Please, a doctor? Oh, what is that in Italian? Oh, I wish I spoke the language...'

As she spoke, someone pushed through the crowd, which parted, almost melted, instinctively before his arrogant assurance and his rapid, insistent Italian.

Leonie looked up at him dazedly, and gave a gasp of horrified shock as she recognised Giles. What was he doing here? She had imagined he would be well on his way by now. She tried to struggle upright, but before she could move he was beside her, one arm going round her waist, the other suddenly behind her knees, lifting her off her feet as if she were a child.

'Oh,' she broke out, blushing to her hairline. 'Put me down, Giles! I'm perfectly OK.'

'Is that why you fainted?' he enquired curtly. 'My car is parked over there; we'll drive to the nearest doctor and find out what's wrong.'

The crowd watched, beaming, enjoying the drama as Leonie wriggled, shaking her head so that her long blonde hair spilled like molten sunshine over the sleeve of his jacket.

'Good idea,' Angela said cheerfully, moving into his angle of vision and smiling. 'I expect someone in that chemist's shop over there could tell us where to find a doctor's surgery.'

Giles gave a brusque nod. 'Will you go and ask them while I'm putting Leonie into my car?'

'Well, my Italian is non-existent,' Angela said. 'What do I say to them?'

He gave her a brief Italian phrase to say. 'Get them to write the address down, too,' he commanded, and Angela gave a military salute, pulling a wry face.

'Yes, sir!'

He half smiled at the mockery, then began to walk away while Angela hurried off to the chemist.

The crowd watched all of them with evident fascination. It was better than a circus, all this exciting drama; they only wished they knew precisely what was going on between these three foreigners. If only they would start speaking Italian so that everyone could follow what was said.

'There's no need to bother a doctor,' Leonie said huskily, but Giles took no notice, his long strides covering the distance to his parked car in no time.

She looked up at him through her lashes and saw his face from a strange angle; the chiselled planes of his face, the taut jaw, the surprising warmth and passionate potential of that hard mouth. Her heart began beating very fast again, and she felt almost sick. It made her breathless to be this close to him, able to see the graining of his face, the rhythmic beat of a pulse in his throat under that tanned skin, and her own reactions were terrifying the life out of her. How could you feel such a violent physical sensation and yet dislike the man touching you?

He must put her down soon; she couldn't bear being this close to him.

'Giles, please,' she whispered, and he looked down at her pausing beside his car, his dark head arrogantly tilted.

'Giles,' she pleaded, her lower lip trembling at the cool way he stared down at her. 'Please, put me down; I don't need a doctor, I'm not ill, I'm fine now. It was just the heat, and I think the coach trip made me feel rather sick, and then walking around the cathedral... but I'll be OK now.'

'You ought to see a doctor!' he merely said.

She was as flushed now as she had been white when she had first recovered consciousness. Held in his arms like this, how could she fight these disturbing responses to his touch, his nearness?

'Well, I don't want to!' she muttered crossly. 'Stop bullying me! You're always trying to push me around, and I hate it!'

He lowered her into the front passenger-seat of his car. 'Then if you won't see a doctor I'll drive you back to your hotel in Rimini.'

'There's no need for you to go out of your way! I can go back on the coach with everybody else.'

He bent down and caught her face in his hand, pushed it back and stared frowningly down at her, his eyes glittering like dark stars.

'Why are you so obstinate?'

'Why are you?' she said, deeply aware that he was staring down at her mouth. She wanted to scream at him: stop it! Stop looking at me like that. You don't know what you're doing to me! But she couldn't say anything, of course, or even hint that he was having this bewildering effect on her. It was probably all in her own fevered imagination, this intense awareness of him. He didn't even like her; he never had.

'I'm being sensible; you aren't,' he said curtly. 'Look, I'll drive you back to make sure you don't faint again, and when we get back to the hotel I'm going to insist you see a doctor.'

Leonie didn't bother to argue any more because Angela was running towards them.

'They gave me a list of local doctors,' she panted, holding out a printed sheet which held telephone numbers and addresses. 'I think the nearest one is——'

Giles interrupted. 'Leonie prefers to go back to Rimini and see a doctor there. I'll take her in my car, to save waiting around for this coach to start back.'

'Oh, that's great,' Angela said cheerfully. 'I'll hop into the back, shall I?'

Through her lowered lashes Leonie saw Giles frown, but Angela didn't wait for him to answer; a moment later she was in the back seat of the car and after a brief pause Giles got behind the wheel and switched on the engine.

Leonie leaned back, her eyes closed, hoping Giles wouldn't speak again until they reached Rimini. Angela was rattling on from the back, telling him about their holiday, asking about his work, asking about his mother's health. Giles answered coolly, politely, but Leonie sensed that his mind was on something else. Secretly she watched his hands on the wheel; they moved with such certainty and long-fingered deftness. Giles was a very confident man; she wished she had his certainty about himself and life. Her gaze flicked down sideways to observe the rest of his body; he was strongly built, yet graceful, with that deep chest, slim waist, and long legs.

Angela kept talking about how sexy he was; maybe that was why she, herself, couldn't apparently think about anything else?

Her face burned as she suddenly realised that while she had been assessing his body he had been watching her do so.

His brow lifted mockingly. 'Well?' he murmured, his voice so low that only she heard.

Leonie pretended not to have heard, though. Hot-faced, she turned her head away and stared out of the window without answering. She was furious when she heard Giles laugh. What on earth must he be thinking?

She didn't look his way again and stayed silent, but it was an enormous relief to drive up to their Rimini hotel some time later. Giles came round to help her out of the car, and she muttered a hurried thank you, but refused point-blank to see a doctor, in spite of everything Giles said.

'I told you, I fainted because of the heat,' she said firmly. 'I don't want to see some foreign doctor; he probably wouldn't understand a word I said, and I certainly wouldn't understand him, so just forget it, will you?'

'Well, at least promise me that if you feel ill again you'll get a doctor at once!' he said impatiently, and she promised, her fingers crossed behind her back.

'I'd better be on my way,' Giles said.

'Oh, stay for dinner!' invited Angela eagerly, but after a brief glance at Leonie's shuttered and averted face Giles coldly said he couldn't stay any longer, he had to get up early in the morning.

'Thank you very much for your help,' Leonie said rather distantly, knowing that Angela was pulling faces at her behind his back, silently ordering her to plead with him not to go yet.

He nodded, his mouth wry and crooked, then he had gone, and Angela burst out crossly, 'Why were you so offhand with him? If you'd asked him I'm sure he would have stayed for dinner!'

'I didn't want him to. I'm going to bed early!'

'You may be!' Angela said, her eyes accusing. 'I'm not! I may never get another chance to seduce him!'

'Sorry about that!' Leonie said insincerely, walking away towards the lift. 'But I'm going to bed now.'

It wasn't until she was back in England that she went to see a doctor, and then the suspicion that had begun to grow in her mind was finally confirmed.

She was pregnant.

## CHAPTER THREE

'OH, LEONIE! What on earth are you going to do?' Angela said, looking aghast.

'Have it,' Leonie said, her face obstinate.

'But have you thought...? It will be so difficult, bringing up a baby alone!'

'Yes, of course I know that, but I'll manage, somehow. It will be worth it, to have Malcolm's baby!'

Angela blew her nose and looked fierce, then said, 'Do you think they'll let you go on working in your office until you have the baby?'

'I hope so,' Leonie said, but her voice was not confident. The head of the legal firm she worked for was a very old-fashioned man in his late sixties, and she suspected he would be taken aback when he discovered that she was going to have a child.

'Well, they can't sack you for it!' Angela said belligerently. 'Not in this day and age!'

Leonie wasn't too sure about that, her blue eyes rueful because she had already been over this argument, mentally, with herself, and she couldn't decide what might happen when her boss found out. 'For the moment, I'm not telling anyone at the firm,' she admitted. 'Mr Rawlings is as blind as a bat, and the others may not notice for a while, so

I should have time to look about for another job.' She sighed. 'And somewhere to live.'

Angela was frowning. 'Won't you be able to stay on in this flat? They can't turn you out because you've had a baby! That's inhuman. There is plenty of room here.'

'Yes, but in my tenancy agreement it says that I cannot have pets or children in the flat—these flats are meant for single people; that's why they're so tiny.'

Angela bit her lip. 'Oh. But is it binding? I mean, you could fight them...'

'I'd lose. I haven't worked for a solicitor for years without finding out quite a bit about the law, and I signed that agreement, knowing what it meant.'

'But what will you do? I wish I could help, but you know there simply wouldn't be room for anyone else in my flat.' Angela's was a studio flat; one very spacious room which served her as bedroom, kitchen and sitting-room, and in which she also worked at her dressmaking, plus a tiny bathroom.

'Of course there wouldn't, although it's nice of you even to think about it!' Leonie said, smiling at her friend gratefully. 'Oh, don't worry, I'll find somewhere, Angela. I'm a good secretary, I'll get good references from Mr Rawlings if he does want me to leave my job—and, you know, even if he says I can stay on, I may have to go because London rents are so high. I doubt if I could afford them if I had a baby to keep, too. I'll have to find someone to look after the baby while I work, and that will cost money, so I may have to leave London.'

'Leave London?' Angela sounded absolutely horrified. A Londoner born and bred, she couldn't imagine living anywhere else, and her expression was that of someone hearing that a friend had been condemned to exile from everything safe and beloved. 'But you won't know anyone—all your friends are in London! I think it would be a mistake to move to a strange place just when you're going to need support, Leonie. Don't even think of it.' Angela broke off. 'Unless... do you mean you're going to live with your mother?'

Leonie gave her a wry look, shaking her head. 'That wouldn't please my mother! She isn't really family-orientated, you know. She never wanted me when I was a child; she won't want me around now that I have a baby of my own.'

'Does she know?' Angela watched pink colour creep up Leonie's face and her blue eyes darken.

'Not yet. I'm waiting for the right moment to break it to her.' Leonie gave her a rueful look. 'If I told her now she would try to browbeat me into getting rid of the baby while it is still possible, and I don't want that, so I won't tell her until I have to.'

Nodding, Angela vaguely murmured, 'Probably wise...' Then she said with hesitation, 'What about Malcolm's family? Couldn't they help? After all, this is his baby, and if he was alive it would be his responsibility, and the Kents are a rich family—they could easily afford to help you...'

'No!' Leonie said, turning dark red, her voice shaking with anger and determination.

Angela stared, looking amazed. 'But why not? Surely... after all, it will be Mrs Kent's grandchild!'

'No, I don't even want them to know about it!'

'You can't be serious!' gasped Angela. 'You don't even mean to tell them you're having Malcolm's baby?'

'No.' Leonie pushed back her fine silvery hair, leaving her delicate profile exposed, and for the first time Angela could see a resemblance between her and her mother. Leonie's face might have a fragile bone-structure, but it was set, determined, and it had a strength Angela had never noticed in it before.

'But why not?' Angela couldn't understand Leonie's attitude at all.

Leonie's blue eyes glittered with hostility. 'They didn't want me in their family. They didn't even answer the invitations to the wedding; they probably wouldn't have come. Oh, Giles Kent has been quite kind to me since...' Her voice quivered and she bit down on her lower lip, then took a deep breath and went on, 'Since Malcolm died... When he came to tell me, that day, he was a bit brutal at first, but when he saw I was knocked sideways by it he started being quite kind, and then in Italy, when I walked into him in the street, he was almost nice...'

'He's certainly sexy,' said Angela, grinning. 'I wouldn't say no to a date with Giles Kent!'

Leonie gave her a startled frown. 'You must be crazy! Sexy is the last word I'd apply to Giles Kent!'

'It isn't me that's crazy! It's you. And blind, too! He's got all that power and money...they're potent aphrodisiacs, for a start!'

'Well, you're welcome to him,' Leonie said flatly. 'But I don't want anything to do with him, or any of them.'

'But they have lots of money——'

'That's why I'm not telling them! They might try to take the baby away from me.'

'They couldn't do that!'

'I think they might—after all, they could obviously give the baby a luxurious home, whereas I'm going to have a hard struggle to manage...'

'But isn't that exactly why you are going to need their help? I'm sure they wouldn't try to take the baby away—but they might give you an allowance which would make all the difference!'

'I don't want their money.'

'Oh, but Leonie...'

Face stubborn, Leonie said, 'Please, Angela, drop the subject! I've made up my mind about this. I am not going to tell the Kent family anything, and don't you tell anyone, either. Promise.'

Angela reluctantly promised. Sighing, she asked, 'So, if you aren't going to live with your mother, where are you going to live?'

They spent the next hour discussing possibilities: trying to think of some part of the country where Leonie could get a job, find someone to look after the baby while she worked, but still afford to rent a flat. It was a dispiriting and fruitless discussion.

A month later Leonie began to notice people giving her a second look, their eyes startled and disbelieving at first. She went a little pink, and waited for a comment, but perhaps nobody liked to say anything, since she had not dropped any hints and they weren't sure they were not imagining things. Then people started standing in huddles, whispering, until she appeared, when they would hurriedly spring apart and disappear in all directions without meeting her eyes.

After a few days of this, her boss gruffly asked her to come into his office one morning, and, after clearing his throat a few times and fiddling with the papers on his desk, muttered, 'Miss Priestley, I am sorry to have to ask you this, it is very embarrassing for both of us, but...there is some gossip in the office... I am told that people think...that...'

Leonie was sorry for him, he was finding it so hard to get the question out, so she answered it without his needing to ask.

'Yes, I am going to have a baby, Mr Rawlings,' she said quietly.

He let out a long sigh. 'Oh, dear. I...I am very sorry to hear that...'

'I am not sorry to be having it, Mr Rawlings,' Leonie said at once, her voice husky. 'I was happy when I knew; it will be some compensation for losing Malcolm, to have his child.'

Mr Rawlings picked up a pencil and doodled on a sheet of paper without looking at her. 'I have every sympathy, of course, and we are not so behind the times that we take a moral attitude, I assure you... but how will you manage to go on working after the child arrives?'

'If I can find someone to take care of it until I get home each evening...' she began, and he looked at her at last, kindly, with pity.

'You couldn't possibly afford a full-time nanny on your salary, Miss Priestley. My daughter has a baby and still works, but quite a sizeable chunk of what she earns goes to pay the nanny. If she weren't married she would never be able to manage. I think you aren't being very realistic. But, if you can make some arrangement of the sort, of course you can keep your job, and we will allow you the usual maternity leave. I will get an agency secretary in until you can come back, but please let me know well in advance whether or not you will definitely be coming back. If you are not able to make some arrangement for the child to be cared for full-time, you can always carry on working here in another capacity, perhaps part-time, or work flexible hours to enable you to spend time with your baby.'

She was grateful that he was allowing her to stay on in her job until the birth; that gave her a useful breathing-space. At least he wasn't telling her to go at once. She had suspected he might. His office was highly respectable and dealt with some very wealthy, often quite elderly, and at times narrow-minded clients. This might be the end of the twentieth century, but she often thought that some of their clients were not aware of that fact.

'Thank you, Mr Rawlings; I promise to let you know, well in advance, what arrangements I've been able to make,' she said.

She was just as fortunate in the agents who represented the owner of her flat. They at once pointed out that she could not be permitted to have a baby living in the flat, but agreed with some sympathy that she could stay on until after the birth, so she had a breathing-space during which she was sure she would come up with something.

She started hunting for another flat at once, but London prices were so high, and landlords tended not to want unmarried mothers as tenants unless they could afford massive rents. She still had two and a half months before the birth, but time was passing so quickly.

The last person to find out that she was going to have a baby was the one she might have told first if her mother had been different. Leonie had not seen her since her angry, resentful reaction to Malcolm's death, but, when Leonie was a little more than six months pregnant, her mother arrived at the flat one Saturday afternoon without warning.

Leonie opened the door and her mother froze on the spot, staring fixedly, her cold eyes opening wide in shock.

'You had better come in,' Leonie said wearily, holding the door and standing to one side to let her pass.

Her mother walked into the flat, Leonie closed the door and followed her into the sitting-room, waiting for the storm to break over her head.

Swinging to face Leonie, Martha let her pale blue eyes flick down over her, her nostrils flaring in anger and distaste. 'When is it due?' she asked, and, when Leonie had answered that, at once asked icily, 'It is Malcolm Kent's, I presume?'

Hot coins of red in her face, Leonie snapped back, 'Yes, it is!'

Martha's lips thinned. 'I thought you had more brains than to let this happen to you! I can see why you stayed away and never said a word to me about it! Well, at least his family can afford to support you, that is one mercy!'

Leonie looked aside, biting the inside of her lip.

Martha's eyes narrowed and she sharply asked, 'They are going to help you, aren't they?'

Leonie took a long breath. 'I don't want to involve them——'

'Don't be ridiculous!' Martha interrupted. 'What did they say when you told them? Didn't they offer to——?'

'I didn't!' Leonie said shortly.

'What?' Martha was red with anger now. 'Are you telling me that they don't know? You stupid girl! Of course you must tell them. They have plenty of money, and you have a right to some of it. I'll speak to them if you're so proud that you can't bring yourself to!'

'Don't you dare!' Leonie desperately burst out, for once having the courage to contradict her mother to her face.

Martha Priestley looked disbelievingly at her, stiffening, and for once wordless. 'Stay out of it,'

Leonie went on less fiercely. 'I want nothing more to do with Malcolm's family. They hate me; they didn't want me when Malcolm was alive, and I'm not going begging to them. I would rather live on welfare than ask them for a penny.'

She hadn't silenced her mother, of course. Martha was shaking with rage, and she had a lot to say, firing the words at her daughter like bullets.

'You can't afford to be so high-minded! And neither can I! You know very well I wanted to ask the Kent family to help me pay the bills I was left with for that wedding. Some things could be cancelled—the reception and the church, the wedding cars, the flowers... but a lot of things still had to be paid for. The invitations, the cake, that real lace veil you were going to wear... the accessories, your white shoes, your trousseau... oh, I know it was my present to you, but the bill was enormous! And then there was my own dress...'

She caught Leonie's eye and flushed angrily, although her daughter hadn't said a word. 'Well,' Martha defended herself sharply, 'I had to have something special; I didn't want the Kents to think their son was marrying into a poor family. I had a dress made by a famous designer, and I couldn't hand it back, I had to pay for it—I would never have bought anything so expensive for myself; I only ordered it for your wedding. I have always been very careful with money, and, let me tell you, I hated running up debts of that sort, and I couldn't see why the Kents, with all their wealth, should not have been asked to help. After all, it would have been their son's wedding as much as yours, and I was extravagant only because I wanted to make sure the wedding was a grand affair, an occasion to which all the Kent family and friends could come with pride.'

'I know,' Leonie said unhappily, wishing she would stop talking about it. Her own anxieties over her pregnancy had somehow eased her pain over Malcolm's death; it wasn't that she had forgotten him or that she missed him less—indeed, she often thought of him when she thought of her baby—but she had so many other problems on her mind, and time kept ticking by like a racing clock. In a few months now she would be having her baby, and she needed to get her life sorted out first.

'I don't think you do!' Martha snapped at her. 'I did not, in fact, ask the Kents for help, in the end, because you became almost frantic when I spoke to you about it. But that meant that I was left to bear the burden of that debt, when in my opinion the Kents might have offered to help me! And if you think that I am going to help you carry the cost of Malcolm Kent's baby, you are very much mistaken!'

'I didn't ask you to help!' Leonie said, on the point of tears. 'I'm sorry if you got into debt on my behalf; I wish I had the money to pay you back now, and one day when I do have some money I will pay you, but I'm not asking you for money now, or for help, or... or anything... I'll manage, somehow.'

Martha stared at her, breathing hard, her cold blue eyes like marble, her fine-boned face clenched in fury. Leonie flinched, afraid of what she might be going to say, but her mother simply walked past her and slammed out of the flat.

On a Saturday Leonie did the shopping and the housework, so she was able to push the thought of her mother to the back of her head while she concentrated on her usual weekend routine. She found it rather more tiring at the moment, of course, so she didn't try to rush about, but took it slowly and easily.

She ate a light salad lunch once her work was finished, and then lay down for an hour, but she had no sooner closed her eyes than the doorbell rang, and she sighed and trudged back up the corridor.

She expected Angela, who often dropped in on a Saturday afternoon for a chat or a cup of tea, but when Leonie opened the front door she was appalled to find herself looking into the cold grey eyes of Giles Kent.

She couldn't get a word out, flinching in alarm, waiting for his first reaction to the sight of her, but as she stared at him she realised that he already knew she was pregnant. His face didn't register shock or incredulity; he ran one brief glance over her heavy body and then he took a step forward, into the flat, forcing her to step back out of his way.

Leonie's mind was racing. He had known before she'd opened the door. Someone had told him! My mother! she thought bleakly. It has to be my mother; she was the only one who would have done it. In spite of everything I said to her—oh, how could she?

And *what* did she say to him exactly? What did she ask him to do? Leonie's hands screwed up into tight little balls of tension and misery. Martha had asked for money, for some financial arrangement, of course—that was why she did it. Money has always been what mattered most to her. I told her I didn't want anything from the Kents; I told her exactly how I felt... how could she?

'You're not looking well,' Giles said abruptly, and she gave him an incredulous look.

'You may not have noticed, but——'

'You're pregnant, I know; I am quite observant enough to notice that, I assure you,' he said with a dry intonation. 'But I've always understood that pregnant women looked radiantly healthy, and you are very pale and listless. Are you taking care of yourself?'

'Yes, thank you,' she said in a mock-submissive voice, and he half smiled, a quick crook of the mouth before his lips straightened again.

'Sit down,' he ordered in that peremptory way of his, gesturing to a chair, and Leonie, with a sigh of resignation, obeyed, saving her energy for whatever argument might be going to follow. She was determined not to let the Kent family interfere in her life, but she suspected Giles was not going to give in easily.

Once she was seated, Giles sat down, too, near by, leaning forward, his black hair lit with a halo of the autumnal sunlight filtering down behind him, through a plane tree in the street outside. His face was half in shadow as he stared at her; she couldn't guess what he thought about her situation, but then Giles Kent could, when he chose, always hide what he was thinking.

'Your mother rang me,' Giles told her without a flicker of expression, and a wave of hot colour swept up Leonie's face.

Angrily, she burst out, 'I suspected she had when I saw you outside, but she did that without my permission. I told her not to get in touch with your family!'

'I know, she mentioned that,' Giles said, with dry irony. 'It was a very frank conversation.'

Leonie winced, embarrassment in her eyes as she looked down. 'If she asked you for money, please forget it——'

'She didn't ask me for money,' he interrupted curtly. 'Well, not directly. Of course, she did point out how difficult life was going to be for you when you had the baby. She explained that she wanted to help you, but she had financial problems of her own at the moment. She explained that there was a large debt she had incurred because the wedding had had to be cancelled.'

'Oh, no!' Leonie said, biting her lower lip. She looked up then, her darkened lashes flicking against her pale cheek. 'I'm sorry...'

'Why should you be?' Giles coolly returned. 'I blame myself for letting her get into debt. It should have occurred to me long ago that there might be a financial problem. I imagined Malcolm would have seen to it that the wedding expenses were not left to your mother to pay—she is a widow living on a small income, and I can see it must be difficult for her. I'll deal with her problem immediately. I only wish I had thought of it before, but...' He paused, frowning, his mouth incisive. 'But I had other things on my mind, I'm afraid.'

Leonie watched him, her dark blue eyes sensitive to the tension in his face. She could guess what he was thinking about. Her own grief at the loss of Malcolm was mirrored in the Kent family; she had not forgotten how Malcolm's mother must have felt these past months and she had often regretted that the dislike Mrs Kent felt towards her meant she was unable to give her the comfort and support she must have needed.

'How is your mother?' she asked gently, and Giles looked up, his gaze flicking across the room to her again.

'She has been in a state of deep depression for months.'

'I'm sorry,' Leonie murmured.

He nodded. 'From the look of you, so have you!'

She didn't answer that, and he went on, 'She is finding it hard to come to terms with Malcolm's death; he was always her favourite child—I suppose mothers always feel a soft spot for their youngest, and Malcolm had a lot of charm. It hit her very hard, and she won't accept professional help, she won't see a therapist or even talk about her feelings, which might help. Bottling it all up inside herself just makes the situation worse, her grief is feeding on itself—I've become increasingly worried about her.'

'I can quite understand why she doesn't want to see a psychiatrist, or talk about it,' Leonie thought aloud with sympathy. Mrs Kent was a woman of great pride; she would hate the idea of confiding her innermost feelings to anyone, especially to a stranger, and Leonie imagined that she would equally dislike the idea of having analysis. She would probably think that it was shameful, and would be afraid of her friends finding out, of being talked about, even laughed at.

'You and my mother have more in common than she realises,' Giles said, staring narrow-eyed at her, and she flushed, her look startled. Before she had time to think about that remark, Giles went on, 'I have been at my wits' end, trying to think of a way to get through to her; nothing I could do seemed to help. When your mother rang me today it was like a gift from heaven—I realised at once what it would mean. This is going to snap my mother out of her depression; this baby is going to give her something to live for. It will be like giving Malcolm back to her. So you don't need to worry any more, or agonise about ways and means of coping on your own, Leonie. From now on, you can leave everything to us.'

# CHAPTER FOUR

THAT was what Leonie had been afraid of, what she had dreaded, and she burst out anxiously, angrily, 'No! I don't care what my mother told you, she wasn't talking for me. I may have problems, but they are my own business, nobody else's, and I can deal with them. This baby is mine, and I want it, I'm keeping it—I can take care of it myself without any help from my mother, or you, or anybody. I'm certainly not giving it up.'

Giles's eyes narrowed and hardened, and she reacted instinctively to the threat of his stare, in a flare of fear, her dark blue eyes wide and strained, stumbling to her feet with the ungainly movement of a pregnant woman, her body heavier than she ever remembered until she tried to move fast.

'Be careful!' Giles said roughly, and suddenly there he was, next to her, his arm around her, supporting her. 'You shouldn't have got up so suddenly! You have to take care of yourself now, for the baby's sake.'

'I'm OK, thank you!' she muttered, stiffening as she became aware of the warmth of his skin, the firmness of bone and muscle under that. His hands pressed into her back, his fingers splayed, each pressing down into her own flesh.

It was a long time since she had been in anyone's arms, held close; the human contact was tempting, the comfort one she often longed for in the dark hours of the night when she was alone and aching with loneliness and need. She tried to be strong and brave, but sometimes she broke down. It was only human to need to be held, to be close to another living body—but she mustn't give in to that need, let him go on holding her and stroking that warm hand up and down her back.

It might become a habit; she might come to need it, need him. After all, this wasn't even the first time she had broken down and he had been there to help her. It disturbed her to remember that when they met in Ravenna she had cried in his arms, and now she was close to doing so again, the tears only just held back. It wasn't wise; after all, he might seem gentle and kindly now, but she mustn't forget the cold hostility he had shown her right up until his brother had died.

He had only become kinder because she was no longer any threat to himself or his family—so what did that tell her about him? Giles Kent was a man whose head ruled his life. He coolly decided how to deal with everyone around him, for reasons which had nothing to do with his emotions—if he had any emotions they were never allowed to show, or to influence how he behaved. It would be folly to forget that, especially now that everything had changed again.

'You don't look very OK to me,' Giles said drily, his mouth moving close to her hair, stirring the delicate silvery strands with his breath. 'You may not want our help, Leonie, but it's obvious you need it.'

She had something he wanted; she was carrying his brother's child, the baby he felt might make his mother happy again—and Giles wanted it. Malcolm had often said with a mixture of wry admiration and faint resentment that Giles was relentless in pursuit of what he wanted; he had a powerful will, a tenacity of purpose. That was what made him so good at running the family business, Malcolm had said, grimacing as though he'd wished he were cut from the same stuff. Malcolm had been a warm, lovable human being, though, not a man of iron.

No, Giles was not made of iron; his metal was altogether more invulnerable—that was what made him such a dangerous enemy to make. You couldn't get through his defences, he was impervious, and he was always determined to have his own way. Leonie knew that if she refused to do what he wanted he would stop smiling at her, being gentle and protective—she would see his icy enmity show through again.

But she wasn't afraid of Giles—she had too much to lose if she weakened—so she pulled away and faced him defiantly, her chin up. 'I *can* take care of myself—and the baby, too! I've always taken care of myself, since I left school, and I'll manage somehow, now that there will be two of us. My mother managed to bring me up all on her own.' Her eyes moved away from his face, and she frowned, remembering her childhood, her own bewilderment and loneliness. Well, she wouldn't send her baby away, whatever happened, however hard it might be to keep it. At all costs, she wouldn't repeat the mistakes her mother had made. Somehow, she would manage to keep her baby with her.

His eyes were bitingly ironic, his voice brusque. 'Do you really want your baby to grow up the way you did?'

She drew a startled breath, looking up into his eyes. She had never confided in him, ever told him anything about her lonely childhood. How did he know all about that? Malcolm? Or had he had her background investigated as soon as he'd discovered that his brother meant to marry her?

'I'll make sure my baby is happy,' she said firmly, lifting her chin, defiance in her blue eyes.

'You'll have to go out to work, and that means you won't be with the baby very much, you know that,' Giles said, his black brows heavy.

'I've thought it all out,' she insisted. 'Plenty of other women manage, and so shall I. As long as my baby knows I love it, and want it, everything will work out in the end.'

His hard mouth parted impatiently, to snap out some disbelieving reply, but she spoke first, angrily.

'Look, this baby is my problem, and I'll solve it somehow; I'll manage. I'm sure you only mean to be kind, but I'd really rather you didn't.' Before he could go on arguing, she rushed on, 'I'm sorry about your mother. I would have been to see her before if I had thought she wanted to see me—it would have helped me to talk to her, you know. After all, we're both grieving for Malcolm, we both miss him badly. But I knew she wouldn't want to see me; I suppose I would have reminded her that she and Malcolm had been arguing for weeks before he was killed. It must be hard for her to remember that, but I'm sure Malcolm wouldn't want her to blame herself, I'm sure he has forgiven her. And... well, if she wants to see the baby when it has been born, she'll be very welcome to come and see us any time she likes, or I'll bring the baby to visit her, but only if it is understood that my baby stays with me.'

Giles had decided to change his tactics now. Instead of being domineering and trying to force her to do as he demanded, he tried a soothing voice, a smile that held some of Malcolm's charm.

'Of course it will!' he assured her, pretending to look surprised. 'You didn't think I wanted to take it away from you, did you? Of course I don't. I wouldn't dream of it.'

She wasn't convinced, though. How could she trust him, knowing the ways in which he and his mother had tried to stop her marrying Malcolm?

'Well, I'm glad about that,' she said, the defiance still glittering in her blue eyes. 'As long as you understand how I feel about everything.'

There was an impatient, obstinate look about him, and she didn't want him arguing any more so she gave a deliberate yawn. 'I don't want to be rude, but I was just going to take a nap when you arrived... so if you don't mind...?'

He gave her a searching look and nodded. 'Yes, you look pretty drained. Anxiety is no good for a woman in your condition, Leonie...you don't need all that tension...'

'It isn't an illness, you know! I'm going through a perfectly healthy, natural process; it hasn't turned me into a helpless invalid,' she muttered, walking to the front door and pointedly opening it.

He took the hint, shrugging, but paused before leaving and studied her flushed face. 'Malcolm would want us to do what we can to take care of you,' he said, and that really was below the belt. She gave him a furious look.

'I don't remember you being so concerned about Malcolm's feelings when he was alive!'

His jawline tightened and he frowned blackly. 'Maybe I've learnt a lot since the day my brother died,' he said in a low, harsh voice, and then he walked away and Leonie bit her lip, staring after him and feeling ashamed and guilty.

When she talked to Angela later, she wasn't surprised by her friend's reaction—Angela made it quite clear that she thought she was mad, and ought to accept whatever the Kent family wanted to give her.

'After all, the baby will be one of their family,' said Angela forcefully, 'Even though you and Malcolm hadn't got around to marrying yet. You would have done if Malcolm hadn't been killed, so you're entitled to a claim on the Kents. You know very well it is going to be tough, bringing up a baby without any help from anyone. You haven't got anywhere to live after the baby is born, you may not even have a job... what are you going to do if you turn down the offer Giles Kent made you?'

'I don't know,' Leonie said wearily. 'Don't bully me, Angela. I got enough of that from Giles Kent.'

'You mean you know I'm making sense!' Angela said drily, but she didn't go on trying to convince Leonie; she merely shrugged and started to talk about her new boyfriend, Andrew.

Her last one, Jack, had recently been transferred by his firm to another part of the country. He had suggested that they kept in touch, wrote, saw each other whenever possible, but Angela had shaken her head. She was far too practical not to see the pitfalls ahead. 'It would never work,' she had said to him bluntly. 'I couldn't bear to live anywhere but London, and I couldn't afford to travel back and forth to see you all the time. It would soon drive us both mad. Better to split up now, and stay friends. If you're ever in London, give me a ring, but if you find someone else, date her with my blessing, because, frankly, I shall do the same.'

Angela was very independent; she had her life worked out and running smoothly, she could take care of herself and was ambitious for the future. Although she loved men's company, she had never yet felt she could not live without any one of them, but there was something new in the way she talked about her latest boyfriend, a young doctor at a London teaching hospital. Leonie wasn't sure what was different—a touch of breathlessness? A flush on her cheeks? A brightness in the eyes?

'When am I going to meet Andrew?' Leonie asked her curiously, and Angela promised to give a little supper party in her flat one evening soon.

'You'll like Andrew,' she assured her, adding, 'We'll just have a few people. There isn't room for more than a dozen. Something simple to cook and serve... a paella, or pasta... they can help themselves in the kitchen and then sit down on the floor to eat. Some garlic bread! Fruit... and wine... Perfect.'

'Can I opt out of sitting on the floor to eat?' Leonie wryly asked. 'I may get down there, but I'm not sure I shall be able to get back up again!'

Angela looked down at her heavy body and laughed. 'Sorry, stupid of me! Of course you can sit on a chair.'

She continued to plan aloud, 'I'll ask people to bring a bottle of something, too. Whatever they can afford, preferably wine.'

'I'll help you with the food,' offered Leonie, glad to have something to keep her mind off her own problems.

It wasn't as if she could do much about them as yet. She still had nine weeks to go before the baby arrived, she was sure she would find somewhere to live before then, and the local health clinic had given her the names of several women who might agree to take care of the baby while she went on working. Leonie had met two of them and liked them, but until the baby had actually arrived she felt she couldn't make any firm arrangements. She would get six weeks' leave after the birth, which meant that she wouldn't have to make a final decision for over three months.

In one way that was a relief, but in another the uncertainty was worrying and unsettling. She didn't know what the future held, she didn't know if she could cope, and her pregnancy meant that she was often tired—her life was a mess.

Angela's party was something to look forward to, and she enjoyed helping her get ready for it. They cooked a huge paella, which they then covered with silver foil and kept hot in a low oven, they prepared bowls of salad, and Leonie made an enormous chocolate mousse, which was popped into the fridge an hour before the guests arrived.

Angela had bought a few bottles of red and white wine to start the party off, and was hoping everyone would bring a bottle too, to keep things going with a swing.

The first to arrive was Andrew, and Angela greeted him with flushed excitement, especially when she saw what he was carrying under each arm—two bottles of champagne!

'Very extravagant of you, but marvellous! You're a love!' she said, throwing her arms around his neck and kissing him.

Leonie liked him on sight; he was tall and skinny with dark brown hair and hazel eyes, not good-looking exactly, but with such a warm smile that nobody could help smiling back.

'This is Leonie,' Angela said casually, waving a hand at her. 'You remember, I told you about her?'

Leonie flushed—what had Angela told him? She didn't much like the thought that Angela had been gossiping about her to someone she hadn't even met.

She met his hazel eyes uncertainly, and Andrew gave her a friendly grin, offering his hand. 'Hi, I'm Andrew, and judging from your wary expression you're doing just what I'm doing—wishing you knew just what she has been saying!'

Leonie laughed, relaxing. 'Something like that!'

'Oh, don't be so silly, the pair of you,' said Angela. 'There's the doorbell again—I'll go and open the door while you open the champagne, Andrew. Leonie, find some suitable glasses!'

'She loves to give orders, doesn't she?' Andrew teasingly asked, but Angela just rushed off to let in the new arrivals, who were also carrying bottles, to Angela's delight and relief.

The room was soon crowded with people and humming with voices, and it was several hours before Leonie ran into Andrew again. She was carrying a tray of clean glasses from the kitchenette, where she had just washed and dried them, and Andrew gave her a sharp look, took the tray from her and handed it to another girl, asking her to take them over to the man in charge of pouring out drinks.

'As for you, you are to sit down and stay down,' Andrew told Leonie firmly. He looked behind her and calmly said to some people lounging around on the sofa, 'Would you mind getting off there? Leonie needs to put her feet up.'

They scrambled up at once. 'Sure, Doc!'

'Oh, no, really...' Leonie began to protest, but Andrew manoeuvred her backwards and down on to the sofa.

'Feet up!' he ordered, and with a flushed face she obeyed, frowning a little because she hated being the centre of attention, and everyone was watching them.

'You aren't going to have the baby any minute, are you?' asked someone.

'Certainly not,' said Andrew. 'But she has been on her feet for far too long, and has done far too much this evening. Now it's someone else's turn to fetch and carry.'

People drifted away, probably afraid they would be asked to do some work, and Andrew sat down on the end of the sofa, lifting Leonie's feet on to his lap, and, to her embarrassed amazement, taking off her shoes.

'Angela says you're looking for somewhere cheap to live after the baby is born,' he said as he almost absent-mindedly began to massage one of her feet, his long fingers deft and soothing.

She nodded, grimacing. 'Which is like looking for gold-dust in the street!'

He laughed. 'Don't I know it! When we were all students it was hopeless finding anywhere cheap to live if we couldn't live in at the hospital doctors quarters. Look, are you determined to find somewhere around here? I mean, would you consider moving out of London?'

She looked quickly at him, her heart leaping. 'Why? I mean, yes... I mean, I'd consider anything... you don't mean you know somewhere... somewhere I might be able to afford?'

He hesitated, his face wry. 'Well, don't get your hopes up too high—it is just an idea, it might not be possible. It's just that... well... my mother doesn't usually take lodgers, but my father died five months ago, and she is living alone in their house, and she might consider letting you move into part of the house.'

Leonie drew a sharp, excited breath and he shook his head at her. 'I said, don't get too hopeful. I haven't spoken to her. It only occurred to me this evening. I have to go and visit my mother tomorrow; she's lonely on her own, she's always ringing me up and begging me to come and see her, and I was wondering about the future because I can't keep driving back and forth, but she is too old to get a job, or move...'

'How old is she?' asked Leonie.

'Sixty-four,' said Andrew. 'Frankly, I don't know what to do—I don't seem to have any spare time any more. If I'm not working I'm driving to see my mother. Angela is getting quite bad-tempered about it, and, I must admit, I am, too—I'd like at least a few hours for my own life every week. On the other hand, I feel I have to do something to help my mother. She needs company, something to take her mind off her own troubles.'

'Where does she live?'

'Deepest Essex—a village some miles from the Thames estuary, near Burnham,' he said. 'That's the problem. If you kept your job here it would mean hours of travelling, but I'm sure you could get a job somewhere down there. Of course, I can't speak for my mother. I know she is thinking of letting the flat—the rent would be a help for her. But she would have to see you and make up her own mind.'

'Of course,' Leonie said eagerly.

'Would you like me to talk to her, ask if she'll see you?'

'Yes, please!' How could he doubt it?

He smiled at her, reading her expression while his long fingers still kept busy massaging her feet. It was an amazingly soothing feeling, and she loved it. 'OK, then,' he said. 'I'll talk to her. When could you go there? Could you come down with me on Saturday morning?'

'Yes, of course!' Leonie breathed. She would have agreed to any arrangement, and somehow got the time off, but Saturday would, undoubtedly, be the easiest day to go. It wouldn't involve asking permission of her boss, or having to work overtime to make up for the time lost.

Angela suddenly arrived beside the sofa, eyeing them coldly. 'What are you two up to? You've been whispering away in this corner for hours—what are you talking about?' Then before they could answer she asked even more crossly, 'And are you some kind of foot fetishist, Andrew? Why have you got Leonie's feet on your lap; why are you sitting there stroking and fondling them? Goodness knows what people are thinking!'

'Who cares what people think?' Andrew asked lightly, obviously resenting Angela's suspicions, and Leonie looked from one to the other, very upset at the thought of causing trouble between them.

'Angie, don't be silly! Andrew was only being kind,' she hurriedly said, removing her feet from Andrew's hands and swinging her legs down to the floor.

'Oh, kind is he?' Angela asked with a cynical expression.

'Yes!' Leonie was very pink. 'Oh, come on...look at me! I'm the size of a baby elephant at the moment—you couldn't suspect Andrew of fancying me in my condition!'

Angela didn't look too sure about that.

'Anyway,' Leonie said, 'He may have found me a flat...isn't that wonderful! And he was giving my feet a massage because...'

She broke off, not knowing quite why Andrew had been massaging her feet, and it was Andrew who solemnly explained.

'Her ankles had swollen up with all this trudging about with trays of food and drink, Angel. She shouldn't have been on her feet for such a long time—she should take better care of herself, and rest more, until the baby arrives.'

'Hmm...' Angela said, not quite a hundred per cent convinced, but deciding to let that one go. 'And what is all this about a flat? What flat? Where?'

When Andrew told her she made a face. 'But it will mean leaving London...going away from all her friends...me, for instance...She's a Londoner; she won't like it in the country. And I'll miss her.'

Leonie smiled affectionately at her. 'I'll miss you, too, Angela, and all my friends—but I think I am going to have to leave London, you know. It's the only way I can make this situation work.'

'Not the only way,' Angela said drily. 'There is always Giles Kent.'

'I wouldn't even consider accepting any help from him!' Leonie said with angry force, and the other two fell silent, watching her.

Andrew rang next evening to say that his mother had agreed to meet her and discuss the possibility of Leonie's moving into the flat.

'But nothing is decided yet, remember,' Andrew stressed. 'If my mother feels you two could get on, she may agree, but on the other hand she may not be able to face sharing her home with a stranger. I'll pick you up on Saturday morning at ten, and drive you down to meet her. She suggests we all have lunch together—she enjoys cooking and giving hospitality. We'll arrive there at around midday, have lunch, then you two can talk while I go for a walk. There's a train back in the late afternoon, and I'll drive you to the station to catch it.'

Leonie was very nervous about meeting Andrew's mother, but she need not have been. Mrs Colpitt was as warm and friendly as her son; a small, grey-haired, energetic woman Leonie found it very easy to talk to and easy to like.

'It would be nice to have some company,' she said frankly. 'Some days I don't see another living soul, unless I walk down to the village shop and talk to Mrs Dawlish, or a neighbour. But this flat is self-contained; you'll have your own front door—come and look at it now, see what you think.'

It was a cosy little flat; Leonie would have her own kitchen and a tiny sitting-room cum dining-room, and bedroom and a diminutive bathroom.

'It's wonderful,' she said, and, within half an hour, it was all settled. Leonie would move into the flat in three weeks' time. Her maternity leave began then, so she would not need to look for a new job for some months and could take time to settle into the flat, and into the village. She would have to change doctors and make a new arrangement with the local maternity hospital, Andrew pointed out as he drove her to the station later that day.

'It's vital to do that as soon as possible, as they may well be fully booked already!' he warned.

She nodded soberly. 'I'll make sure to do that at once, then.'

On the platform she turned to him and said gratefully, 'I don't know how to thank you, Andrew. You don't know how worried I've been; I really didn't know how I was going to cope—and now everything is so different suddenly, all because of you.'

A faint flush in his face, he said gruffly, 'That's OK, it was just an idea I had...glad it's worked out...'

Leonie stood on tiptoe and kissed him quickly, on the cheek, as the train roared into the station. 'Thank you,' she whispered, then turned and climbed into the nearest carriage and settled in a window-seat, waving to Andrew as the train began to move again.

On the Sunday morning she got up late and had a light breakfast, then sat down to write a list of everything she must do before she moved. She had got into the habit of thinking she had plenty of time to arrange everything, but suddenly there were only three more weeks before she left London and her job, and all the familiar places and faces. Her life was about to change drastically forever, she thought, staring down at the sheet of paper on which she had written her list.

A little shiver ran down her spine. She felt scared for an instant, facing the unknown future. Then she lifted her chin and sat up straight. She would cope. She had been telling herself that for months now. She could cope—with anything. And she would.

The doorbell jangled and she jumped. Who could that be? Angela, she thought, relaxing and smiling as she got heavily to her feet and made her way to the door, one hand supporting her back. She had tried to ring Angela last night, to tell her what had been decided, but Angela had been at the theatre and hadn't got back until late, by which time Leonie had been asleep for ages. She went to bed early these days, although her sleep was often patchy, since she kept waking up and then going to sleep again during the night.

Opening the door, she began cheerfully, 'Andrew is a darling! It's all arranged...' Then her voice died away as she stared into Giles Kent's hard grey eyes.

'What is?' he asked curtly, frowning, and Leonie bit her lip, so taken aback that she couldn't help stammering.

'Oh, I thought you were Angela.'

'As you see, I'm not,' he said drily. 'What is all arranged? Are you going out today?'

'No, but...' Her voice trailed away uneasily, she flushed, and his black brows rose sharply.

'But what? You're making me very curious.' He took a step forward and Leonie reluctantly had to stand back and let him enter her flat, although she didn't feel strong enough to confront Giles Kent this morning.

He wandered into the flat, and Leonie closed the front door, hurriedly thinking—should she tell him she planned to leave London and move into the country? She wasn't sure she wanted him to know anything about her life; she wanted to make a clean break and get away from him and all the unhappy memories he brought back.

When she followed him into the sitting-room she realised she did not need to make that decision anyway. He had picked up her list and was studying it, his brows together.

Suddenly swinging round to face her, he bit out, 'What is all this?'

'I've found a new flat,' she said huskily. 'I'm moving in there in three weeks' time, when I begin my maternity leave, and I was just making a list of all the things I have to do first.'

'Where is this new flat?' Giles demanded, and, before she could answer that, added in an icy voice, 'And who the hell is Andrew?'

## CHAPTER FIVE

LEONIE was confused into flushing and stammering. 'H...he...it...it's his flat!'

Giles stiffened, his eyes narrowing on her. 'His flat?' he repeated in a deep, harsh voice. 'Are you telling me you're moving in with this man?'

'No!' she denied, going quite crimson. 'Of course not! You're confusing me! What I meant was that the flat was Andrew's...'

'What's his surname?' Giles bit out.

'Colpitt,' she said crossly, wishing he would stop talking to her in that hostile voice. She always felt as if she were on the witness stand and he was a prosecuting counsel who did not believe a word she said. Even now, his hard face had a disbelieving look. 'Andrew Colpitt,' she expanded. 'The flat is his, but he isn't living in it at the moment. He is a doctor; he lives in at a London hospital where he works.'

'Is that where you met him?' Giles flicked a glance over her heavily pregnant body, frowning. 'Is he your maternity doctor?'

'No, we were introduced by a friend, who had told Andrew I had a problem finding somewhere to live, so he offered to let me take over his flat for a while, until I can find somewhere of my own. He doesn't use it at the moment. You see, the flat is in Essex, right on the far side of Essex, near the Thames estuary, between Malden and Burnham——'

'That's barely twenty miles from us,' Giles interrupted, and she hadn't thought of that until that moment.

'I suppose it is,' she said, taken aback. She had only visited his home a few times, and had no happy memories of Warlock House, although it was a very handsome building set among lovely gardens, and the Essex countryside surrounding it was beautiful. Malcolm had adored his home, but she had never felt welcome, or at home, there. How odd that she hadn't realised how close to it she would be if she moved down to Andrew's village! Or perhaps it wasn't odd at all. Maybe she had deliberately blanked out the realisation that she would be so close to Warlock House?

'What about your job?' asked Giles. 'Surely you won't commute from there?'

She shook her head. 'No, of course not—that's what I was trying to explain—why Andrew doesn't use the flat: it's too far for him to be able to commute back and forth, but that won't matter to me because I start my maternity leave shortly, so I won't be working for quite some time, anyway.'

'Of course,' said Giles slowly.

'I could have stayed here until the baby had arrived, but I'd have to find a flat somewhere else after that, so when Andrew offered to let me have his flat while he isn't using it, I jumped at it.'

Giles was watching her with a black frown. 'And what about when he does want to use it?' he asked, his mouth crooked with cynicism. 'Or hadn't you thought of that? Don't tell me his offer is just altruistic, because I don't believe it. What if he arrives one day and expects to move back in? What will you do then?'

'You don't understand! Oh, I haven't explained this very well,' Leonie began, and Giles interrupted coldly,

'I think I'm getting the picture!'

'No, you're not!' she snapped, glaring at him. 'You're just jumping to all the wrong conclusions. Deliberately. You like insulting me. You want to believe the worst of me, you always have!'

His frown deepened and the hard eyes were ice floes. 'I'm stating the obvious. I offered my help, and you turned me down—but you're taking this man's help. Why? Is he an old friend?'

She bit her lip, hesitated, then had to be honest and shook her head. 'But that has nothing to do with it,' she muttered, and Giles smiled icily.

'No? So, how long have you known him?'

'A... a little while,' she said, her eyes avoiding his, not liking to say she had only met Andrew a week ago.

'A little while? How long is that? A few months?' His eyes intently read her expressions. 'A few weeks?' Leonie didn't answer, didn't look at him, and he added scathingly, 'but you are accepting his help, when you turned down mine?'

'That's different,' she said, suddenly very angry, her blue eyes moving to his taut face, her chin lifted in defiance. 'I would rather die than take anything from you or your family! You know why. And what I do is none of your business—I don't know what makes you think you have the right to cross-question me as if I were in the witness box and you were the prosecution lawyer. Or the judge! Yes, you think you're entitled to sit in judgement on me, don't you? I've always felt that that was what you were doing.'

Her voice had risen; she was trembling with a peculiar, volatile mixture of feelings: she was nervous because she was telling Giles what she thought of him, she was angry, as always when she thought of the way he and his family had treated her, and she felt a hurt resentment because he always thought the worst of her.

'You shouldn't get so upset—it must be bad for the baby,' was all Giles said, and that made her want to scream.

'Oh, go away!' she threw at him furiously, very flushed. 'I don't want you in my life. Will you stop turning up out of the blue? We have nothing to say to each other, we never have had. We don't like each other, and I never want to see you again.'

That, at least, finally hit home. She saw his grey eyes flash like summer lightning, brilliant and dangerous. A dark flush invaded his face, too. His mouth was tightly reined, and he barely parted his lips to snap back at her. 'That's too bad, because you're going to have to see me again! I've been consulting my lawyers——'

'Lawyers!' she muttered, paling.

'Yes, and we had a very useful discussion,' Giles said with an angry sort of triumph, watching the alarm in her eyes. 'Malcolm left a will, you know. He made it before he even met you, but it is still valid, and it names me as his executor, which, you must realise, means that I take charge of all legal matters arising from his affairs. He didn't leave a fortune, but he did leave quite a large sum, and, of course, he also leaves a share of the family estate. That would have passed to me, but, after a good deal of consideration, our lawyers believe that your child will have a perfectly valid claim on his or her father's estate...'

'I'm not going to claim anything!' Leonie protested, but Giles overrode her, his tone insistent.

'A claim, which, as the child's uncle, as well as the executor of the estate, I shall certainly see is admitted, whether you like it or not. Malcolm's child isn't going to be cheated out of his or her rights. In any case, sooner or later this matter would have to be cleared up. You may not want the money, but when the child comes of age I've no doubt he or she will take a very different view, and it will be much easier to sort it out now.'

Angrily, Leonie said, 'Well, I can't stop you, I suppose, but I don't want any of the money. Put it in a trust fund or something.'

'We could do that; indeed, that is undoubtedly what will be done, since the child is not yet even born,' Giles agreed blandly, and something in his tone disturbed her. 'Which, of course, raises other important questions.'

'What?' she warily asked, every nerve in her body prickling with a sense of danger.

'Custody and access,' said Giles, and she went white.

'What?'

'Well, obviously, as executor of my brother's estate I would also be executor of the trust fund which would be set up for his child, and that would make me legal guardian of his child, the heir to that estate,' Giles said in a calm, reasonable voice which was like a knife twisting inside her.

'Malcolm didn't make you the baby's guardian; he didn't even know I was having a child...' she cried, her mouth dry.

'No,' agreed Giles coolly, smiling. 'Naturally, he did not, but if he had known he was going to be a father, and if he had had second sight and realised he was going to die, I am certain he would have made provision for me to be the child's guardian, just as he made me the executor of his will— Malcolm trusted me. He knew I would look after his interests, and, since the child is in a sense part of his estate, as the main beneficiary of it, especially since you insist that the money is put into a trust fund, which I shall have to administer for the child, I shall obviously become the child's legal guardian.'

'No!' Leonie whispered, her legs shaking under her so that she had to sit down on the nearest chair.

Giles hurriedly crossed the room. 'Are you OK? You aren't going to faint, are you?'

She shook her head, closing her eyes against the penetrating probe of those grey eyes.

'Can I get you anything? A cup of tea? Brandy?' he asked, sounding husky.

'C... could you get me a drink of water?' she asked shakily, and he went at once, returning a second later with a glass which he pushed into her hand, his cool fingers closing around her own to help her lift the glass to her mouth, as if she were a child.

Leonie drank thirstily, keeping her eyes closed yet very conscious of him beside her, his long, lean body a physical and mental threat she could not face for the moment. Perhaps he would go away if he believed she was ill?

When she stopped drinking, he removed the glass and stood up, but only to say, 'How do you feel now?'

'I would like to lie down for an hour, so if you don't mind leaving...?' Leonie said softly.

There was a silence, then he said drily, 'Can we finish our discussion first? I think you should be aware of the legal steps I'm taking.'

'Legal steps?' she repeated, her eyes flying open.

She was surprised to find him still so close. He stared down at her, his grey eyes cool and determined. 'I intend to become the child's legal guardian, by virtue of being my brother's executor, and I am sure the law will uphold my claim.'

'I'm the baby's mother!' she denied fiercely, and he smiled, a faint twist of the mouth which had no humour in it.

'You have no money and no home of your own, you will shortly have no job, and you will have to live on state benefit. And, even if you get another job after the birth, you will earn very little, and you will have to leave the child with someone else.'

She stared at him bleakly, unable to contradict any of that, and he nodded at her.

'Yes, it is all true, isn't it? I, on the other hand, have a great deal of money, and can offer my brother's child a wonderful future, the sort of life he or she would have had if Malcolm had lived and married you.'

'Money isn't everything. I shall love my baby, and I shall make a good home for it,' she muttered, tears at the back of her eyes.

'I'm sure you would try, but it would be hard, for both of you, and it doesn't have to be! You are being stubborn and selfish.'

'Selfish!' Leonie broke out, hating him.

'What else can one call it? You aren't thinking about what is best for the baby, you're only concerned with your own ego. You resent me because I didn't want you to marry my brother, so you are refusing to let me help, even though that means your child will suffer.'

She bit down into her lip, unable to argue about that.

Giles watched her for a moment in silence, then said coolly, 'Now, we can go to court to argue this out, but I assure you that I would win.'

She stared at him dumbly, believing it. Giles always won. Hadn't Malcolm told her that, over and over again? He always won, and he would win this time. She could feel that he was already winning. She simply did not know how to argue with him.

'I am not disputing your right, as the child's mother, to have custody,' he said after a pause to see if she would speak. 'But I feel that it may be necessary to register an equal right, legally, as its guardian, to determine the place of its abode, its education, and so on—and to make sure of access, visiting rights, for myself and my mother.'

'I've already said that your mother can see the baby!' Leonie protested, disturbed by all this talk about law and rights. Was he moving towards claiming the child, taking it away from her? Could he do that? She must see a lawyer herself, at once—but how on earth was she to afford one? She would go to the Citizen's Advice Bureau and ask them for help. She might be able to get a lawyer's opinion under the legal aid system. She bitterly wished she knew more about such things, but she had never had to worry about the law before.

'Ah, but it is always wise to have these things in writing, in a form of legal, contractual agreement,' said Giles. 'You might change your mind later, or deny you had ever promised that.'

'I wouldn't!'

He shrugged. 'All the same, we would like it in black and white. And there's another thing—the child can inherit Malcolm's estate, but it will not carry his name, and that makes my mother unhappy. She wants the baby to be a Kent.'

Leonie hesitated, sighing. 'Well, I did think of that—and I would like Malcolm's baby to have Malcolm's surname, but it could be embarrassing if we had different surnames.'

'That's true,' said Giles, 'but there is a way round that.'

She looked up at him blankly. 'Oh?'

'Yes,' he said without expression. 'You could marry me before the baby is born, and then it will, legally, take the Kent name.'

She stood there, frozen on the spot, staring at him and not really sure whether it had been a joke or not, or even whether she had heard him correctly.

'That isn't funny!' she whispered at last.

'It wasn't meant to be!'

'You can't be serious.' She knew he couldn't mean it. He hadn't wanted her to marry his brother—he certainly wouldn't dream of marrying her himself.

'Very serious,' Giles said in that cool, level voice which sounded so matter-of-fact that somehow it made her feel more and more as if she were trapped in a weird, surrealist dream—or a nightmare. 'You see, it wouldn't really be good enough to simply register the baby under the surname Kent,' Giles added. 'My mother is afraid about the future—if you married someone else, for instance!'

'I wouldn't——' she began, and he spoke over her, his tone hard.

'You may say that now, but you're very young, you'll get over Malcolm's death and you'll meet someone else. This doctor, for instance...Dr Colpitt...I've no doubt he must be interested in you, or he wouldn't have been so generous in offering to let you use his flat.'

'He isn't interested in me at all!' Leonie denied immediately, but Giles again spoke over her, his voice harsh.

'Perhaps you simply haven't realised how he feels yet! And, even if you aren't interested in Dr Colpitt, there will be someone one day. You're beautiful, and you're very feminine. You aren't cut out for the single life, even if you do have a child. You'll marry sooner or later, and your new husband might insist that the baby take his name, might refuse us access, might even try to get his hands on the baby's money. We have to protect our rights, and those of the child.'

'You're crazy!' Leonie burst out, and Giles suddenly laughed, startling her even more.

'On the contrary, I'm talking sound common sense,' he drawled. 'We are not going to allow you to marry someone else and give Malcolm's child into the control of a stranger. And, as there isn't much time left before the birth, I suggest we get married in a register office as soon as possible.'

Leonie was gasping like a landed fish. Breathlessly, she managed to gulp out, 'I've never heard anything so——'

'I'll make all the necessary arrangements,' Giles interrupted her splutterings.

'You must be out of your mind!'

'I suggest we only invite close family to attend. Your mother. Mine. My sister and her family. No friends, not even your pal Angela.'

Leonie shouted at him, since he didn't appear to have heard her until now. 'Listen to me, will you? I am not going to marry you!'

'Any preference as to the location?' he calmly enquired. 'London? That would probably be best; it would arouse less interest than it might if we got married in Essex, near my home. We don't want a lot of gossip and people turning up to stare.'

'I don't believe this is happening,' Leonie said to the ceiling.

'Oh, by the way, I shall require you to sign a pre-marital contract,' said Giles casually. 'Quite common, these days, I assure you, but under these very unusual circumstances I must protect myself, you understand——'

'I won't marry you!' Leonie yelled.

'And of course I shall have the legal documents referring to Malcolm's child drawn up at the same time, so that there is no legal confusion later as to whose child it is...'

Leonie got up and said through almost closed lips, very quietly and firmly, 'I am moving out of this flat and going away, and whatever you say or do won't make any difference—I am not marrying you, I won't even see you again if I can help it, and you are going to have to take me to court to get access to my baby, because after this I am going to fight you, whatever it costs me.'

'It will cost you your child!' Giles icily promised, and she stood there, appalled, staring back at him.

'You couldn't——'

'I would,' he said, and she believed him. A wave of chill shock flowed up over her whole body. She was trapped. He had spelt it out for her now—whatever she tried to do, wherever she turned, or tried to run, he would stop her, he would force her to do as he and his family wished. She was carrying his brother's child, and he meant to control it—and her. It was his nature to impose control, he understood only too well how to do it, and he terrified her.

'You will marry me,' he said, and she felt so threatened that she turned to run away like a scared child, not even knowing where she was going or what she meant to do.

Not that it mattered much what she intended, because Giles caught her before she had got very far. His hands fastened on her shoulders and dragged her round to face him.

'Get your hands off me!' she shakily threw at him. 'I wouldn't marry you if you were the last man in the world! I hate you!'

For a second he was very still, staring down at her, his face locked in a taut mask she couldn't read until she suddenly saw that his grey eyes glittered with anger, his mouth was hard with temper. A shudder of dismay and foreboding went through her.

'That's too bad,' he said through his teeth. 'Because, hate me or not, you are going to marry me, Leonie, so you had better get used to the idea.'

'No,' she whispered, her eyes held hypnotically by the power of his demanding stare. 'I couldn't marry you! I can't even bear it when you touch me!'

As soon as the words left her lips she wished she could call them back; she knew it had been a stupid, reckless thing to say, and his expression underlined her own instincts.

'Can't you? Well, let's see, shall we?' he bit out, and her nerves leapt at the furious flash of his icy grey eyes.

His head began to lower towards her, and she cried out in shock and alarm, 'No! Don't...'

His mouth took hers with driving force and her head went back under the insistence of that demand. She fought him, twisting and turning in his arms, but he pulled her closer, the warmth of his body touching her from breast to thigh, his hands moving on her, up and down her back, under her hair, caressing her nape, her throat, her breasts. She couldn't breathe, she was trembling violently, heat mounting inside her as his exploration of her body became more and more intimate, his kiss deeper and more urgent.

She hadn't expected to feel this way; she was so appalled by her own physical reaction that she couldn't go on fighting him. Her body was swamped by an intense desire, her eyes closed, her hands went flat against him, touching his body and feeling the warmth of him through his clothes, beating up into her palms and through her own body until they were almost one being, the rhythm of their lives merging in a fierce, heavy beat. Her back arched as she yielded limply, swaying against him like a flower too heavy to stand upright. Her lips parted, trembling, under the hot pressure of his kiss.

When Giles finally lifted his head she was almost fainting, but she felt him looking down at her, the power of his will forcing her lids to flutter upwards.

He stared into her eyes and she stared back helplessly, for a second unable to think because passion had drowned out everything else in her head.

She thought for that instant that Giles looked as shaken as she felt, and her trembling intensified, her bones seemed to have turned to jelly. Was he feeling like this? What was happening to them?

Then his eyes flicked down, noting the tremors in her body, he frowned, and his mouth twisted. He looked up again, into her eyes, and gave her a mocking little smile. 'What were you saying?'

She felt her skin burning and looked away, hating him, but now hating herself, too. How could she have let him do that to her? He had deliberately set out to shame and humiliate her, show her that if he chose to exert the sex appeal Angela had kept talking about she wouldn't be able to resist him, and she had let him prove his point.

She pulled herself together somehow and managed a husky defiance. 'Just because I couldn't fight you doesn't mean I enjoyed it! I didn't! I hated every minute of it and if you ever lay a hand on me again I'll kill you!'

A dark flush invaded his face, too. His brows met, his grey eyes threatened.

'You will marry me, though!' he told her curtly. 'Or take the consequences, and, I assure you, Leonie, I will win. I always do.'

She believed him, and fell silent. What option did she have? She was going to be forced into this marriage, whether she liked it or not.

'You can't!' Angela said, her face shocked and incredulous. 'You've always said how much you hated the man! Now you're saying you're going to... Oh, I don't believe it. It's crazy! You can't marry him!'

'You were the one who said I should go to him for help!' Leonie muttered in grim amusement, although why she should find it funny that Angela was so shaken she did not know. There was nothing amusing about any of this—Angela was right: it was crazy to even consider marrying Giles Kent.

Crossly Angela snapped, 'You know what I meant! I still think the Kent family ought to help you. The baby is Malcolm's too, even if you weren't actually married yet. You were going to be, and I'm sure you could make some sort of legal claim on them—and heaven knows they have enough money! They wouldn't miss it if they made some sort of financial settlement on you. They could afford to be generous.'

'The money is the whole point,' Leonie said bitterly. 'You're right, I would have a good legal claim on them. They have found out that the baby would be entitled to claim its father's share of the family money. That's what their lawyers have told them, and it's scared the life out of them.'

Angela grew flushed with excitement, her lips parting in a gasp. 'But that's marvellous! You won't have any more worries if——'

'You don't understand!' Leonie interrupted brusquely. 'They have no intention of settling money on me—and, in fact, I told him I didn't even want their money, but he doesn't believe me, doesn't trust me. He says I may say that now, but how do they know I won't change my mind later? Anyway, they're going to set up a trust fund for the baby, and he is going to be the executor of it, because Malcolm's will made him his executor.'

Angela's frown deepened. 'Well, that's good, isn't it? You know that's what Malcolm would have wanted. You can't resent Malcolm's baby inheriting his father's money?'

'No, of course I don't!'

'Then...' Angela looked bewildered. 'You've lost me. You said Giles was blackmailing you into marrying him! Now you say he agrees that the baby should inherit Malcolm's share of the business.'

'I've just explained—it will all go into a trust fund for the baby, and Giles intends to manage the fund. But he's afraid that I may marry someone who will come along, one day, and try to take over running the fund as the child's stepfather. He wants to make quite sure that can never happen, so he is marrying me himself to get control of my baby and keep the money in the Kent family.'

Angela's eyes rounded, and she chewed on her lower lip thoughtfully, a calculating expression in her face. 'Well, it makes sense, I suppose.'

'To a computer!' Leonie spat, infuriated. 'Or to a man with all the emotions of a computer!'

Angela shrugged, eyeing her with curiosity. 'Don't do it if you really hate him that much! After all, he can't force you to marry him!'

'He can,' said Leonie.

Angela laughed scornfully. 'Not in this day and age. What is he going to do? Drag you to the altar?'

'Start legal proceedings to take the baby away as soon as it is born,' said Leonie.

Angela gasped. 'You're kidding!'

'That's what he threatens. He would ask for custody on the grounds that the baby is the heir to a large trust fund, and I am not in a position to bring it up properly.'

'He would never get a court to agree!'

Leonie smiled wearily. 'Well, maybe not. But what if he did? These things do happen. Rich people can afford top barristers, they can manipulate the system. And, let's face it, the Kent family can offer the baby far more than I can, in a material sense. He pointed out that I'd have to go out to work, leaving the baby with someone else, and I wouldn't have much money, especially as I refuse to take any from him, and I can't afford a very nice flat, or even a full-time, properly qualified nanny. Oh, thousands of unmarried mothers do manage to look after a baby and have a job, but nobody says it's easy, and a court might feel that it would be in the baby's best interests for it to live with its grandmother.'

Angela was sober now. She grimaced. 'Yes, I see what you mean!'

'I must get in touch with Andrew and explain, and apologise!' Leonie said on a long sigh. 'He has been so kind, and his mother was, too. I would have loved to live in that flat. Oh, why is life so... so unpredictable? Why do things keep happening to me like this? So suddenly, I mean, out of the blue. Just when I think I've finally worked something out, got my life into shape—wham! Fate hits me with something I couldn't possibly expect. Just when I was going to marry Malcolm...' Her voice broke. She bit down on her lower lip, gesturing, tears in her eyes. 'Oh, you know... it all blew up in my face!' She ran a hand over her eyes. 'And now this. One minute everything seemed to be falling into place so nicely... all my worries dealt with... and I felt so marvellous for a while, thinking I was going to be moving down there, able to relax for a while before the baby came, have my baby peacefully and take my time looking for a job near by—and then fate sees to it that it all blows up in my face again.'

'You mean Giles Kent sees to it!' Angela said drily.

Leonie nodded grimly, getting up out of her chair with some difficulty, her hand on her aching back. She hadn't slept much the night before; partly because she had been lying awake anxiously thinking about what Giles had said to her, and partly because the baby had been very lively, kicking violently all night. Even before it was born, she had the feeling this baby was going to be a typical Kent: obstinate, overbearing, determined to get its own way.

'I think he only decided to marry me after I'd told him I was moving into Andrew's flat,' she muttered. 'He suspected I might be getting involved with Andrew, and he wouldn't believe me when I told him I wasn't romantically involved with anyone.' She smoothed a hand down over her heavy body, looking down at it with a rueful expression. 'As if it were likely! What man would look twice at me when I look like a barrage balloon?'

Angela didn't answer the rhetorical question. Instead, she said with sudden interest, 'What are you going to wear?'

Leonie laughed shortly, giving her a wry, impatient, but affectionate look, because it was so typical of Angela to be distracted by thoughts of clothes.

'That's the last thing on my mind! Nobody will be dressing up, anyway. If anybody comes!'

'I'll come!' Angela said indignantly. 'And I'll be dressing up, you can bet on it!'

'I'm sorry, I can't invite you—Giles says no friends,' Leonie told her apologetically. 'Just family, and as few of them as possible. But you wouldn't want to go, anyway—you won't be missing much. This isn't a real wedding, Angela. It is just a sham; a legal arrangement. I get the feeling he wants to be able to get out of it as easily as possible later, so he's making sure not too many people know about it.'

'Well, he isn't stopping me from turning up to see you get married,' Angela muttered, scowling. 'What's he going to do afterwards? Hide you somewhere until after the baby has been born?'

Leonie went pale. She hadn't thought about 'afterwards' yet. Now she did, and she did not like what she suspected the future might hold for her. Questions crowded into her head, and while she was thinking about the answers Angela began to ask the questions aloud, in her practical, direct way.

'Where are you going to live, for instance? At Warlock House? With that old gorgon of a mother? And what do you mean... not a real wedding? Are you saying you won't be living as man and wife?'

Leonie didn't know, she could only shake her head helplessly and shrug.

Angela gazed at her disbelievingly. 'You're out of your skull if you go through with this!' she told her, and she was right, thought Leonie.

She must be mad to be marrying a man who not only did not love her, but didn't even like her. In fact, she had often felt he hated her. There was a darkness behind Giles Kent's grey eyes; something fierce and angry and threatening. It had been there from the beginning. She had always been aware of it; a taut thread had stretched between them whenever they were together, a consciousness, one of the other, which frightened her. She had been able to cope so long as she did not see too much of him—but she went into panic every time she thought of becoming his wife, being alone with him, at his mercy.

# CHAPTER SIX

THEY were married three weeks later, in a brief civil ceremony, which was over so fast that Leonie both at the time and afterwards felt as if it had been a dream.

It was all so functional, so banal. She wore a cream wool two-piece suit. Giles wore grey. Neither of them smiled. Their voices murmured in the quiet room, and they went through the motions as commanded without even looking at each other.

Behind them, in a row, sat a handful of people. His mother, his sister and her husband, Leonie's mother, Angela and Andrew. There were so few of them in the room that Leonie could actually hear them all breathing, even above the sound of rain.

It seemed very apt that it should be raining. London in the rain had such a bleak look, depressed and depressing—the grey-blue slate roofs of tall office blocks opposite shone wet, bare wintry trees bowed in resignation before the attack of the wind, and there was a sound of tyres on wet roads, the running of water in gutters. People huddled in doorways, ran for buses, hurried along the slippery pavements hunched in their coats.

There was no wedding reception. Giles had ruled that that would be pointless, in the circumstances. He whisked her away without allowing her to exchange more than a few stiff words with anyone, and she was glad about that, even while she resented his high-handed assumption that he merely had to give an order for her to meekly obey.

'What dreadful weather, isn't it?' his sister, Linda, said, trying not to stare at her. They had not met since before Malcolm's death, and, although she knew Linda had been told she was pregnant, it was obviously still a shock to actually see the evidence of it.

'Were the roads difficult on your way here?' Leonie asked without caring whether Linda answered or not. What else was there to say? Anything that was really on their minds had to be left unsaid as too dangerous.

She had said something to Mrs Kent, but she had hardly known what she was saying. Mrs Kent had answered her, but their eyes had never met. Perhaps they had both been thinking about that other wedding-day, which had never happened? It would all have been so different on that day. Not a brief, muttered exchange in a shabby London office, between people dressed as if for a day at work, but a sacred ritual, with everything that that meant— a bride in white, a church, the peal of an organ, crowds of smiling wedding guests, a groom waiting at an altar, faith, hope and love exchanged along with the rings they gave each other.

How could she have met Malcolm's mother's eyes when they were both remembering what might have been?

Yet Leonie had been very aware of the older woman's pallor and the fact that she was horribly thin. She had never been anything but slim, an elegant woman with a good figure. Now she was fleshless, and as tense as a tightened bow. Malcolm's death had drained his mother, too, of life; had depleted her, left her looking some ten years older.

Angela had come to hug her, half crying, and Leonie had tried not to cry, too, hurriedly turning to shake Andrew's hand.

He made some conventionally polite remark, and she said, 'Thank you,' huskily.

Leonie had been too angry to talk to her own mother, whose triumphant glitter she had seen out of the corner of her eye as she'd walked into the room. Martha was tense, too, but with excitement, exaltation. She was there to watch her daughter marry into a very rich family, and she was walking on air.

She looked superb, of course; her pale hair in a French pleat at the back of her head, her face perfectly made-up, her slender body sheathed in coral silk, her small, thin feet in shoes that matched that shade exactly. She wore a tiny white silk hat perched on the top of her head, a fine veil falling over her eyes, giving her an air of mystery.

Leonie wondered how much the elegant clothes had cost her. A small fortune, no doubt, and Giles was probably going to have to foot the bill. Martha would make sure of that. It was humiliating, and Leonie almost hated her mother at that moment.

'We're leaving now,' Giles had said, though, before she had had to decide whether or not to publicly ignore her mother, and a moment later she found herself walking away, his hand under her elbow, steering her.

A sleek grey limousine had been waiting at the kerb, outside. Giles had helped her into the back, slid into the seat beside her. Then they were moving away, through the softly falling rain, through the grey London streets, and Leonie had leaned back, closing her eyes wearily, glad to escape from the necessity to be polite, to talk, to smile, to pretend.

Giles sat beside her, an apparently relaxed figure; a tall, lean man in a smoothly tailored suit, a white carnation in his buttonhole the only evidence that they had been married. He didn't say anything; she barely heard him breathing.

After a few moments she opened her eyes again and gave him a quick, nervous, sidelong look.

'Where are we going?'

'Home,' Giles said, and she had a confused moment of uncertainty about what he meant.

'Home?' she repeated, her voice rising to a question.

'Warlock,' he said, and she couldn't help an instinctive shudder. Warlock House might mean home to him, but she had been unhappy there on her few visits. She had been forced to recognise that Malcolm's family were hostile to her, rejected her, and at some level of her mind she had begun to feel that the house itself rejected her.

Giles frowned, his body half turned towards her, his cold eyes stripping her face of privacy, invading her mind, understanding what she was thinking in a way she found increasingly disturbing.

'It *is* your home now,' he said curtly.

There was anger in his voice, in his face, and she knew why. Giles resented having had to marry her, he hated the idea of bringing her, of all people, home to Warlock as his bride.

She shook her head, her face paler than ever inside its frame of fine silvery hair. 'No. I'll never feel I belong there, or that it is my home. How could I? I'm not really your wife. Our marriage was a crazy piece of legal fiction; it isn't real!'

'Don't deceive yourself!' Giles snarled, brows heavy and black over those icy grey eyes. 'Or anybody else! Don't give anyone any wrong ideas. That guy Colpitt, for instance—I saw the way he looked at you, and the way you almost burst into tears when he was holding your hand. If he so much as shows up at Warlock, I'll set the dogs on him. Just remember this... our marriage is very real, and you not only are my wife, you are going to stay my wife unless, or until, I say otherwise!'

A flood of startled, incredulous pink washed up her face. 'What are you talking about? Andrew?' Her voice broke down into a husky, embarrassed stammer. 'He isn't my... we aren't...'

'Not yet?' sneered Giles coldly, then without warning caught hold of her chin in his long fingers, tipped her head back, and stared down into her wide dark blue eyes.

'He's another guy like Malcolm, isn't he? Easy on the eye, easy to like—a charmer.'

She was startled, incredulous. 'Andrew's nothing like Malcolm!' How could he think he was? 'Malcolm was much better looking, and very different in character,' she denied. There was much more to it than that, though. 'Andrew... well, he's serious... a very caring man...' She didn't want to seem to be criticising Malcolm, especially to Giles, but he had been light-hearted and at times even a little selfish. Andrew was probably a much better man, although he was not as lovable as Malcolm had been.

Giles looked angrily into her eyes, seeming to dive down into them, read the mind behind them. 'You still think about him?' he bit out, and she went white again.

'Damn you! This isn't the time and place to talk about Malcolm!' she muttered.

He shrugged and let go of her. 'No. You're right. Well, remember what I said—if I find Dr Colpitt near you again I won't be so gentlemanly next time.'

She shrank away from him into the corner of the limousine and stared out of the window as they drove east, through London's grimy suburbs, each mile taking them closer to the flat Essex countryside.

What he had just said had shown her suddenly that her memories of Malcolm had changed in some inexplicable, subtle way. Her love for him hadn't so much ended as faded, like a photograph left in the light, the edges blurring, the sharpness softening. She thought of him far less; days passed without Malcolm entering her thoughts, although when he did she still felt a sadness, but without the incredulous, piercing pain, the ache she had once felt.

That was why she had gone white when Giles had asked her if she still thought of Malcolm. It had shaken her to realise she could do so without wanting to cry—when for so long she had dreamt of him and woken in tears. She couldn't have borne it for Giles to know, to read the admission in her face. Her anger had been defensive; ashamed.

She bit her lip, watching the thinning ranks of grey houses at the edge of London as they sped along a motorway leading towards the coast.

Malcolm had only been dead for seven months! Shame washed through her and she closed her eyes. She had believed her heart was broken the day Giles had told her his brother was dead. How could she get over his death this soon? Was that all love meant? Seven months and you forgot?

'Are you OK?' Giles spoke quietly, but he still made her start in shock, her eyes flying open.

She looked round at him. 'What?'

He was pale. He looked into her dark blue eyes, frowning. 'I was afraid you might be feeling ill. You don't look well.'

She relaxed slightly, seeing that his fit of harsh temper was over. He was a strange man and she did not understand him, but when he spoke gently like this she felt she might actually learn to like him.

'I'm a little tired, that's all,' she huskily said. 'It was a bit of an ordeal, after all, the ceremony and so on.'

He nodded. 'Of course. And I'm sorry if I upset you; it was stupid of me to start an argument over nothing. I was feeling rather tense myself, I suppose.'

She gave a faint sigh of relief. 'I understand. It has been a difficult day for both of us.'

They finished the drive to Warlock House in a friendlier silence, each staring out of the window at the countryside they passed through. Essex was not one of the most beautiful counties of England; it was flat and heavily built up in places, but in some of the older villages there were interesting houses and churches; white wood steeples, decorated plastering on house walls, black and white frame houses.

As they drove along narrow, winding, hedge-lined lanes and came within sight of Warlock House, Leonie began to get nervous. Every visit she had made to this house had been fraught and uneasy. She didn't know if she could bear to live there, under the same roof as Giles and his mother, even if it was only for a few months.

She was feeling confused about that now. The marriage had happened so quickly; she hadn't seen much of Giles in the past few weeks and they hadn't talked much about what was to happen after the wedding. What he had said had given her the distinct impression that after the birth of the baby they would make some arrangement—an annulment, maybe, or at any rate a legal separation. He would obviously be the baby's guardian, but she would have custody of her child, and she had vaguely had an idea that she would find a flat, a job, as she had planned before, and someone to look after the baby.

She certainly did not think of the marriage as a real one; as she had said to Giles just now, it was a legal fiction, meant to give Giles more power as the executor of Malcolm's will. She had agreed because of the blackmail Giles had threatened her with, but she had gone through with it without believing in what she was doing.

She didn't feel like a married woman; she didn't feel as if Giles was her husband.

She gave him a startled, confused look sideways. He was staring straight ahead, himself wrapped in thought, his black brows knit, his jawline taut.

For the first time Leonie realised the fact—the man beside her was her husband!

At that instant Giles turned to look at her, as if becoming aware that she was watching him, and Leonie felt hot colour wash up her face.

For a second they stared into each other's eyes, and she heard her own heart beating, fast and loud, echoing in her ears like the sea in a shell, then Giles glanced away and said flatly, 'We're here.'

As the car pulled up outside the house a man hurriedly emerged, buttoning up his black jacket. He opened the door and solicitously, as if she were an invalid, helped Leonie to descend, a polite smile on his thin face.

'Welcome home, madam.'

Leonie murmured a husky, 'Thank you.' She didn't know who he was, and hadn't seen him before.

He flicked an uncertain sideways glance at Giles as he joined them, and she uneasily wondered just what Giles had told people about her and their marriage. Her condition was so obvious; she knew it must be arousing a lot of gossip, and her embarrassment made her flush to her hairline.

'This is George,' said Giles, standing close to her, a frown knitting his brows. 'He and his wife are running the house for us now. Is Marjorie waiting inside, George?'

'Yes, sir.'

'Good. Then come and meet her, Leonie.' Giles put a hand under her elbow and steered her towards the front door.

She went reluctantly. Warlock House had always overawed her. She walked into it now with a sensation of disbelief; after Malcolm's death she had never expected to see it again, yet here she was walking into the house as the wife of Giles Kent himself.

At least his mother wasn't here. She was spending the next week with her daughter, so Leonie would be given a short breathing-space, a little time to get accustomed to living in this house with Giles as her husband.

She swallowed, giving him another sidelong look of confused incredulity. Her husband? Giles Kent?

It made her feel odd to think about it, so she made herself think about her new mother-in-law instead. She was hoping Mrs Kent was less hostile towards her now, but she wasn't yet sure. Only time would tell.

She hadn't seen enough of her new mother-in-law over the past month or so to be able to guess whether or not they were going to get on together. It all depended on how Mrs Kent felt about the baby. If Giles was right, she would be ready to make Leonie welcome for the baby's sake. If he was wrong about his mother's feelings, life was going to be impossible in this house.

'Ah! There you are, Marjorie!' Giles said as a woman hurried towards them from the back of the panelled hall, and Leonie started, turning her attention back to the present.

George's wife, Marjorie, was a woman in her forties, fair and flushed, rather short, but wiry, with lively blue eyes. She very carefully did not notice Leonie's obvious condition, smiling at her and beginning to talk at once in a breathless voice. 'Oh, I'm sorry I wasn't there to welcome you, but I was upstairs, putting the finishing touches to your room, when I heard the car coming up the drive.'

'Not at all,' Leonie shyly murmured, shaking hands.

Marjorie gave Giles an uncertain look. 'I hope everything went off OK? I mean, I hope it was a nice wedding.' She was stammering now, looking confused under Giles's ironic gaze. 'And congratulations... best wishes for the future...'

'Thank you, Marjorie, that's very kind,' Giles said drily. 'Now, would you show my wife her room? She is tired and would like a rest before lunch.' He glanced down at Leonie. 'I'll see you down here in half an hour, OK?'

'Yes,' she said in a low voice, turning to follow the housekeeper towards the staircase.

Giles had promised her that their marriage would be one in name only; they would not share a room. She was relieved to find he was keeping his word, but at the same time it embarrassed her that everyone should know they were sleeping apart. But in her condition that probably wouldn't surprise anyone! After all, she would have the baby very soon, a matter of a few weeks now!

She gave Marjorie a secret glance, biting her inner lip. What was the other woman really thinking? Leonie was glad she did not know.

Marjorie flung open a door and stood back, smiling. Leonie walked into the room and gave a spontaneous cry of pleasure. 'Oh, it's lovely!'

Marjorie beamed. 'I'm glad you like it.'

It was obvious she had taken trouble over the room; it was immaculate and smelt of roses, a large vase of pink ones which stood on a bedside table next to a glass bowl of fruit. The décor was light and spring-like, green and cream; the antique oak furniture, mostly from the end of the last century, in the art nouveau style, was golden in colour and so highly polished that you could see the room reflected in it.

'Your bathroom is through this door,' Marjorie said, and Leonie looked into the matching room beyond, that too decorated in cream and green; the deep-piled cream carpet identical to that in the bedroom, the green and cream chintz curtains the same, too. Thick, fluffy cream towels, embroidered in dark green with the initial 'K' for Kent, hung over a heated towel-rail. On shelving behind the bath stood rows of jars and bottles full of expensive lotions and bath oils, and the air was scented with perfume.

'What a nice deep bath—and a shower cubicle, too!' she said politely.

'And this is Mr Giles's room,' Marjorie said with a little smile, opening another door.

Leonie felt herself blush and didn't look into the other room, turning away, wishing Marjorie would go now and leave her alone.

As if picking that up, Marjorie said, 'Is there anything I can get you? A cup of tea? Some milk?'

'No, thank you.' Leonie just wanted a little privacy.

'Well, I'll be off, then—I'll turn down the bed for you first.' Before Leonie could protest she deftly stripped the green and cream chintz cover, which matched the curtains, from the bed, and turned down the sheet. 'I'll draw the curtains, too, shall I?' she said, straightening.

'No, please don't,' Leonie said, staring at the window and watching as sunlight shone through the clouds in the sky. The rain had stopped now; the clouds were blowing away. Leonie did not want to shut out the sun; it made her feel less bleak and depressed to see it.

'OK, then, have a nice rest,' said Marjorie cheerfully. The door closed behind her and Leonie was alone. She stood in the middle of the room, looking around, feeling lost and bewildered, and very much afraid.

This was her home now. She stared into the dressing-table mirror, her dark blue eyes enormous, incredulous. This wasn't happening, it couldn't be. She was not here, in Warlock House, Malcolm's home, as the wife of his brother.

Giles couldn't be her husband. He hated her, he always had; he had not wanted her to marry his brother, he had not wanted her to join his family. Yet she was here now, in this house, and she was his wife.

She put both of her cold, trembling hands to her face, her fingers exploring the delicate bones of her cheeks, temples, jaw. In the mirror the reflection did the same.

She still didn't believe it. She wished someone would tell her it was only a strange, terrifying dream, from which at any moment she would awake. None of this was real, including herself. She did not know that face she saw in the mirror, the face her fingers had touched. It couldn't be her, standing here, in this room; she did not know that girl with the huge, frightened eyes and white face, the strangely distorted body.

Turning away, she lay down on the bed and closed her eyes, but she couldn't sleep or even lie still; she kept twisting about, sighing. She couldn't stop thinking, yet her thoughts kept dissolving like wraiths vanishing into a mist; she had lost all sense of reality. She was like a leaf being carried helplessly on a strong flood towards... what?

She turned over on to her side heavily, and her arm flew out and hit something which crashed to the floor with a noise like splintering glass. With a cry of shock, she sat up to see what she had knocked down.

As she did so, Giles strode into the room from his own. 'Are you OK?' he demanded harshly.

'I'm sorry, I've broken a glass!' she said, swinging her legs to the floor to stand up.

Giles grabbed her by the shoulders and pushed her back on to the bed, kneeling on it beside her, holding her down.

'Are you crazy? You could cut your foot open on that broken glass!'

She was trembling stupidly. 'I...I didn't think...'

'No, that's the trouble, you never do,' he muttered, staring down at her, and she looked back at him, her mouth dry. A strange confusion swept over her. She couldn't stop watching him, the strong face, the grey eyes which no longer looked cold, that mouth which had such passion in the hard, firm lines of it.

'The glass must be swept up before someone treads on it,' Giles said in a deep, husky voice.

'Yes,' she whispered. She must stop staring, stop thinking like this—what on earth was wrong with her? Her heart was beating heavily, fiercely, inside her, crashing against her ribs so hard that it made her almost sick.

Giles stared back at her, his skin flushed and taut, like her own. His eyes had a savage glitter, and she knew this time that it was not rage, it was the same primitive, physical reaction sweeping through her. He wanted her, in the same way she wanted him. He was staring at her mouth, and she felt her lips part and burn, and was terrified.

She drew an audible breath. 'We'd better call Marjorie!' she said loudly, and saw his eyes blink, his head snap back.

He let go of her and stood up beside the bed, avoiding the broken glass.

'Yes,' he said, in a rough, low voice, picked up the phone, and spoke into it, but she was so distraught that she didn't hear what he said.

He put the phone down, and said brusquely, 'She'll be up in a moment.' His mouth twisted in cold, sardonic mockery then, and he added, 'So you can stop shaking—you're quite safe!'

Turning on his heel, he walked out, and Leonie lay there, on the point of tears. Living in the same house as Giles was going to be like living on the edge of a volcano. How on earth was she going to survive it?

When she got up for lunch, though, Giles was politely distant, treating her like a visitor, almost a stranger. Leonie gratefully accepted his lead, talking small talk, avoiding all contact with him, trying never to meet his eyes.

When she went back to her room an hour later, he opened the door for her, a sardonic look in his face.

'Going to sleep for a while? Pleasant dreams.'

Leonie pretended not to hear any undertones in that comment, and stayed upstairs all afternoon. Dinner was a repeat of lunch: they talked politely and remotely and parted in the same way.

The pattern was set. Each day they had breakfast together, then went for a drive for an hour or two, exploring the countryside in that part of Essex. They returned in time for lunch, and then Giles insisted that she take a long rest on the bed in her room. At dusk they had drinks in the lounge before a light dinner, after which they listened to music or watched TV before Leonie went to bed early.

Giles treated her with cool courtesy and concern, and they talked quietly over meals, during their drives, in the evenings, getting to know each other a little better each day. He often surprised her; they had more in common than she had ever suspected—liked the same books, same music, same films. There was always something for them to talk easily about, at least. Sometimes, though, their eyes would meet and she would flush and look quickly away, but never before she had seen his mouth go crooked, and those cold grey eyes mock her.

He knew what he could do to her now, and she was disturbed by that expression in his eyes. She was glad she did not know what he was thinking. She knew now that he wanted her, but did he still bitterly resent having been forced to marry her? Did he still hate her?

By the end of that week, Leonie was almost eager to see Mrs Kent return. She was still nervous about her mother-in-law, but she hoped life would be a little easier if she was not always alone with Giles. He could then stop pretending that this was a real honeymoon, and go back to work, and perhaps she might feel less tense and edgy.

Mrs Kent arrived late on a cold, windy afternoon, complained of a headache after her long drive home, and went straight to bed.

In the morning, Giles left for the office early, before Leonie was up, and so Leonie faced her mother-in-law alone over breakfast.

Mrs Kent arrived after Leonie had eaten, paused in the doorway as though startled to see her, then muttered, 'Good morning,' and sat down opposite her at the table. She poured herself some orange juice, sipped it, took a slice of toast and spread a thin layer of marmalade on it in silence.

Leonie felt her spirits sink. Was this how it was to be? Grim silence? Hostility? Isolation? She did not know how she was going to stand it.

Then Mrs Kent looked up and gave her a quick look, frowning. 'Leonie...' she began, and then sighed, breaking off.

'Yes?' Leonie met her eyes, her own gaze pleading. She could not live in this house if both Giles and his mother were to be her enemies.

'Leonie,' Mrs Kent began again, then abruptly held out both her thin hands, which were trembling. 'My dear, don't look at me like that; you make me so ashamed... I wasn't kind to you; I wish I had been—you and Malcolm might have got married right away, and he wouldn't have gone skiing, and...' She broke off again, her lip quivering, her lashes wet with tears. 'Oh, but what's the use of wishing? You can't turn back the clock.' The tears began to trickle down her white cheeks.

'Please, don't... don't cry...' Leonie whispered, horrified, and Mrs Kent let go of her to run one hand over her own face, scrubbing away the tearstains.

'No, you're right—we mustn't cry over what we can't change,' she said in a husky voice. 'We have the future to think about. That is what matters now. The baby. His baby. When Giles told me, it was like a miracle—I'd been so unhappy, and then to hear that there was going to be a baby, Malcolm's baby. Oh, it changed everything. I've got something to live for again.' She pulled out a handkerchief and blew her nose, then managed a watery smile. 'If it is a boy, Leonie, you will call him Malcolm, won't you?'

'Yes, I mean to,' Leonie agreed, but she felt a shiver of odd uneasiness. Mrs Kent was an obsessive woman, and that made Leonie a little frightened.

What if Mrs Kent became too possessive over the baby? Tried to take it over completely? Leonie was not aggressive, her nature was too gentle for that, but if her mother-in-law became a threat she was determined that she would not back down. This was her baby, and she was not giving it up to anybody.

Two days later, she was taking a walk around the garden before lunch when she stopped with a gasp, her hand going to her back.

It couldn't be the baby coming! It wasn't due for ten days. The stabbing sensation subsided. She waited, gingerly massaging her back, but the pain seemed to have stopped. A false alarm? Slowly she began to walk back to the house, took off her coat and went to wash before lunch.

Another pain hit her as she turned on the taps. This time she was sure what it was, and, wincing, she looked at her watch. Well, it wasn't going to happen for a while, the pains were too far apart, but she had to face it: the baby was definitely on the way.

She decided not to say anything to her mother-in-law for the moment. She would eat her lunch first and wait until the pains were coming at much closer intervals. No point, yet, in alerting the maternity hospital in which she was going to have the baby. They would not want to see her until a much later stage.

Leonie had been afraid she would panic when the time came, but oddly enough she felt very calm and relaxed. She ate a light lunch of fruit and an omelette, then lay down on her bed, glad to be alone so that nobody should realise what was happening, and she could ride the pains without an audience. They were not very severe yet, and she found it helped to practise her breathing lessons.

It was four hours later that she finally decided it was time to admit she was in labour. Mrs Kent was the one who panicked. She began to shake, turning pale; could hardly dial the number of the hospital to warn them Leonie was on her way, and her voice broke as she called for George to drive Leonie there at once.

'I'm coming too!' she said, helping Leonie out of her chair. 'You'll want some support!'

The baby was born at nine o'clock that night, a boy weighing six pounds exactly, and it wasn't Mrs Kent who was there at the moment when Malcolm's son emerged into the world. In fact, she hadn't even been allowed to be present during labour. The ward sister firmly explained that only fathers were permitted to be present.

'This is my grandson!' Mrs Kent protested, scarlet with rage

'We don't know yet whether it is a boy or a girl, do we?' said the sister sharply. 'I'm sorry, but I cannot bend the rules for you or anybody else. Fathers only. This is a hospital, not a game show. I can't have my labour-room full of relatives!'

Mrs Kent looked as if she did not believe her ears, and Leonie had been horrified by the gathering storm, but she never knew what happened next because a nurse appeared at that moment and discreetly led her from the waiting-room into the labour ward.

So it was Giles who told Leonie she had a son. He arrived an hour after Leonie was wheeled into the labour-room, and was there throughout the birth, to her startled surprise. She had not expected it of him. It did not seem to be his scene.

When he first walked in, he looked so formal and elegant, wearing one of his dark grey pin-striped city suits, a cream silk shirt, and a dove-grey silk tie. He looked totally out of place, and she had stared at him almost angrily, her forehead beaded with sweat, her hair dishevelled, half inclined to ask him to go away, for heaven's sake, because she knew she looked terrible and she did not want him to see her looking this way.

'Are you the husband?' the midwife asked him, her eyes fascinated.

'Yes, what can I do to help?' Giles answered coolly, and then to Leonie's disbelief he took off his jacket and tight-fitting waistcoat, undid his tie and shed it, opened his shirt collar, rolled up his shirt-sleeves and took over from the busy young midwife, who was delivering another baby in a neighbouring cubicle.

Giles wiped her sweating face with a cool, moist sponge, talked soothingly to her in between the spasms of pain which came with each contraction, and when the pain began again helped her count down her breathing.

It was Giles who held her hand during the final stages, and Giles who said quietly at last, 'You have a son, Leonie, a wonderful little boy.'

She was lying there, exhausted by that final push and already on the dark verge of sleep, her eyes shut, but they opened at the sound of Giles's voice, her lashes fluttering against her cheeks. She looked around the cubicle eagerly. 'A boy? Where is he? I want to see him.'

'You will later, but he's gone to the nursery for tonight,' the midwife said, and Leonie frowned, suddenly afraid.

'Why so soon? Why didn't you let me see him? Is there something wrong? Tell me——'.

'He's perfect; there's nothing wrong at all,' Giles said quickly.

'Perfectly normal procedure,' said the midwife. 'You're tired and the baby is slightly premature, and we thought we would tuck him up in the nursery right away so that you could get some rest.'

'But I haven't even seen him!' protested Leonie. 'Bring him back.'

'Wait until you're in bed in the ward,' said the midwife calmly. 'Then we'll see.'

Giles bent down and said soothingly, 'I saw him, and, I promise you, he's fine; he has masses of hair, already jet black, and he's going to be tall, I think; his legs look very long—he's a real Kent.'

'Just like his father,' said the young midwife, smiling at Giles. He was the sort of father she liked to have at her births; he was capable and useful, he had taken a lot of her work off her hands, kept his wife happy and stable until the time when her own expertise was really needed. Not to mention that he was very good to look at! Dark, like his son, she thought; tall and long-limbed, and had a charming smile when he wasn't too absorbed in his wife to turn it in the midwife's direction!

Leonie met Giles's eyes and read the mocking irony in them. The midwife was looking at him, but both of them thought of Malcolm. But he smiled at her, his cool mouth twisting.

'Yes,' he said. 'He is just like his father.'

# CHAPTER SEVEN

A WEEK before Christmas that year, Leonie woke up early out of a very deep sleep and at once lifted her head, listening for some sound from Mal. He slept next door, in the old nursery, which had been redecorated while she was in hospital—a surprise present from Mrs Kent, whose passionate enchantment with her grandson needed expression.

Each time she had come to see them she had brought armfuls of toys and clothes for baby Malcolm, and flowers, magazines and books for Leonie. When they got back to Warlock House it was to find a uniformed nanny waiting in the nursery, which had been painted glossy white, then stencilled with animals in pastel shades—pink and blue and yellow and green.

Leonie had protested, 'I don't want him to have a nanny! I want to look after him myself!'

Earnestly, Mrs Kent had soothed, 'Of course you do, my dear, and of course you will, but babies are a twenty-four-hour responsibility, and, take my word for it, you'll be glad to have help with him. My children had a nanny. Nanny Grant—such a nice woman; she was with me for years, even after Malcolm grew up and went off to boarding-school. She had no family, you see. This was her only home by then. She was such a comfort to me after my husband died. We sat and talked for hours, about the children when they were small. She loved them, too—we shared them. I was very fond of her. I missed her when she died.'

'I remember Malcolm talking about her,' Leonie had admitted, and Mrs Kent had smiled a little mistily at her. Since the birth of her grandson she no longer seemed to be on the verge of tears every time anyone mentioned her dead son, but her love for Malcolm was as deep as ever.

'Well, my dear, Malcolm was the baby, the youngest, so she clung on to him longest.' Mrs Kent had sighed. 'I suppose she spoilt him. Well, we both did. But Nanny Grant really loved babies, and when I was interviewing girls to take care of Mal the thing I wanted to be sure about was that they loved babies.'

'This girl, Susan Brown, is highly trained,' Giles had intervened in a coldly remote voice. 'Whether she loves babies or not, she has been to a good training college, and she seemed very level-headed and sensible to me. You can trust her with the baby, Leonie—and, as to your not wanting a nanny, let me remind you, you were planning to leave him with someone else while you went back to work, so I don't see why you are making all this fuss.'

She had flushed angrily. 'I wanted to spend as much time as possible with him, too! I didn't intend to hand him over to a nanny all the time!'

'You're free to make whatever arrangements you wish with Susan Brown,' Giles had shrugged. 'She will want time off, you know; she won't be employed on a twenty-four-hour, seven days a week basis. I'm sure she will be only too happy to let you take care of the baby whenever you choose. I agreed that she should have weekends off, anyway, although she is ready to make a special arrangement should you need to go away at any time. It would only be a question of overtime. She will work a five-day week, in other words, and she would have free time during the day, plus some evenings off, but I've left it to you to make final arrangements with her about time off during the week.'

'It seems you've arranged everything!' Leonie had muttered crossly.

'You'll like her, my dear; she's a very nice girl,' Mrs Kent had coaxed. 'I'm quite sure you'll be pleased with her.'

Leonie had liked Susan, luckily; it would have been hard not to like her. Fresh-complexioned, with curly blonde hair and calm blue eyes, Susan had a warm and friendly nature, and, above all, it was obvious from the start that she was enthralled with Mal. Leonie could not help liking someone who adored her baby.

They had talked over cups of coffee later that day and come to a very amicable and flexible agreement to share Mal, for the moment. Leonie would look after him in the mornings, Susan in the afternoons, and they would take it in turns to be on call during the evening and night. If Leonie wanted to go out in the morning, or Susan wanted to go out in the afternoon, that would be worked out between them.

'And when I start work we'll draw up a schedule acceptable to both of us,' Leonie had promised, and Susan had given her a surprised stare.

'Will you be going back to work, then?'

'Probably,' Leonie said defensively. 'But I'm not sure when, yet.'

'What sort of work do you do? Something exciting?'

'I was a secretary.'

'Oh,' said Susan, frowning. 'To someone important? Was it a highly paid job?' She was clearly baffled, especially when Leonie shook her head.

'It was nothing special, and I didn't earn that much, no.'

Susan pulled a face.

'Why are you looking at me like that?' Leonie asked, laughing.

Bluntly, Susan said, 'Well, if I was you, I'd much rather stay at home. I mean—you've got this marvellous house, and a lovely baby, and an absolutely terrific husband.'

Leonie flushed. 'I like my independence!'

She had a sneaking feeling Susan was right, though. It would be only too easy to forget about finding a job, settle down to enjoy the comforts of this luxurious home and the joy of her little boy.

But she couldn't get too accustomed to this life. One day she was going to have to leave. After all, her marriage was not a real one and might end at any time.

So she started reading the job advertisements in the local paper, getting some idea of the sort of work available. There were few good jobs on offer; this was a largely rural area. Any good office job meant a long drive to a nearby town.

There was some seasonal work as Christmas approached, but none of it was secretarial. Maybe in the New Year there would be more work around? she thought, turning over in bed, since she couldn't hear a sound from the nursery.

Mal was already living in a routine, waking, eating and sleeping regularly so that one could plan one's day more easily. Last night Susan had been to a party and had returned in the early hours, so she would be sleeping late, and Leonie was looking after Mal herself until midday, when Susan would take over.

She would get up in another five minutes and see to him, but first she stretched and yawned, her body warm and at ease under the covers.

She was wearing a gift Giles had given her while she was in hospital—a boxed set of exquisite nightwear, all matching: a nightdress, tiny bed-jacket, pyjamas and robe in pure silk, white, but with the monogram 'K' embroidered on them in black, and they had the simplicity of sheer elegance. They were designer-made, the label inside them carried a Paris name recognisable all over the world, and they must have cost a fortune.

He had handed the silver-wrapped box to her while one of the nurses watched, fascinated. Her hands rather shaky with surprise and nerves, Leonie had unwrapped the present, and stammered her thank-you, blushing.

'I look forward to seeing you wearing them,' Giles had drawled in that light, mocking tone which always made her so edgy with him.

The nurse watching them had giggled, but Leonie had kept her head down, pretending to admire the cut of the nightdress, but all the time fiercely aware of Giles watching her.

She had put the box away unopened when she had returned from the hospital, never intending to wear any of the contents, but the housekeeper, Marjorie, had come across the box and put all the lovely garments into a chest of drawers.

'They'll be ruined if you leave them in that box!' she had told Leonie, who had been glad Marjorie had not mentioned it in front of Giles.

Last night, coming to bed, she had found the nightdress laid out on her bed. She had stared down at it, grimacing. Marjorie strikes again! she had thought irritably, and had been inclined to put the nightdress away again, but that would have been to make it all seem too important, so she had worn it in bed last night.

A sudden sound made her jump and sit up again, the narrow straps of the nightdress sliding down over her shoulders, leaving them bare.

It was not Mal crying. It was someone opening her bedroom door.

She looked across the room, and through the half-light of the wintry dawn she saw Giles silhouetted in the doorway, and her nerves thudded in shock.

'Good, you're awake!' he said with what sounded to her like soft menace.

Leonie watched him in breathless suspension as he closed the door and began to walk towards her, his long, lean body shrouded in a black silk dressing-gown over matching pyjamas.

'What do you want?' she whispered, looking away from him because the way he was staring at her made her intensely conscious that her nightdress left most of her shoulders and breasts bare. She grabbed the sheet and pulled it up to hide herself.

He stopped beside the bed, and her eyes hurriedly flicked up to him in time to see his brows swooping upwards in mocking irony. 'It isn't so much what *I* want,' he drawled. 'Not just at the moment. It's what *he* wants...'

For a second she didn't understand. She had been so busy trying not to look at him that she had not seen that he was carrying the baby in his arms.

She went scarlet. 'Oh...yes, of course,' she stammered.

Why had she been such a fool? Now Giles knew that she had jumped to that wild conclusion, had had the crazy idea that he had come into her room to make some sort of pass at her, when all he was doing was bringing the baby to her. She wished the earth would open up and swallow her!

'I imagine he wants his breakfast,' Giles said in that cool, mocking voice.

'Yes, of course,' she said again huskily, wishing he would just hand Mal to her and go away. 'Did he wake you up? Sorry... I didn't hear him crying.'

'He wasn't yelling, just gurgling to himself, and chewing his fingers in a hungry way, but I must have been more wide awake than you are,' Giles said, then amazed her by adding, 'I changed his nappy in the nursery, and washed and changed him.'

'Oh,' she said, stunned. 'Oh, thank you, that... that's very kind.'

'I enjoyed looking after him,' Giles said gravely. 'Well, now all you have to do is feed him.'

On cue, Mal began to cry, screwing his little black head round to glare accusingly at her, and Giles laughed.

'And I don't think he's in a mood to wait much longer.'

To her horror, he promptly sat down on the side of her bed and handed Mal to her.

She looked down as the baby turned into her body, hunting for her nipple, nuzzling the smooth silk of her nightgown. At once, the milk began to rise, her breasts rounding, full and aching in readiness for that little mouth.

Giles watched her hesitate, and his mouth twisted ironically. 'I saw him at your breast the day he was born, remember?' he mocked, then, leaning over, he deftly undid the two buttons on the front of her nightdress.

Leonie was too shocked to move; she could scarcely breathe. His hand slid inside and she shuddered as she felt his fingers curl round her full breast, pushing back the silk still partially covering it.

She could hear him breathing audibly, thickly; he was staring down at her naked breast, face flushed, his grey eyes brilliant, the pupils glittering like jet, while his fingers were moving rhythmically, stroking the warm flesh, the hard nipple. Leonie closed her eyes, trembling, feeling deep inside her body a convulsive clutch of erotic excitement. It was so long since a man had touched her like that. She couldn't help the wild shiver of pleasure, the heat and ache of aroused desire between her thighs.

Then Mal began to cry again, louder this time, and the spell was broken. Leonie's eyes flew open, and she tensed, burning with shame.

Oh, God, what had she been about to do? What had he been about to do?

Giles laughed shortly, his hand falling from her breast. 'You'd better feed him before he screams the house down!' He got up and walked out so fast that she barely had time to realise he had gone before the door slammed. Like an automaton, Leonie put Mal to the breast, and felt him begin to suck hungrily.

She sat there while the baby fed, staring at nothing, stunned by a sudden realisation. She had wanted Giles badly just now; so badly that she was still shuddering with that need, but that was not what had shocked her.

I'm in love with him! she thought incredulously, and closed her eyes, a groan wrenched out of her.

It couldn't be true! She had been ready to admit, for some time now, that she was attracted to him, even though her common sense told her it would be madness to let Giles suspect that, because he was more than capable of taking advantage of the way she felt, but love... no, she couldn't be in love with him!

It was too late, though, to tell herself that. From the instant that she first admitted her feelings, they began to grow, raging through her like a forest fire running out of control, devouring everything in its path.

How had it happened, though? When had it happened? How long had she felt like this? When had she stopped loving Malcolm and begun to feel like this about Giles?

She tried to conjure up Malcolm's face, to remember how much she had loved him. But Malcolm had been fading from her day by day for months now, withdrawing gently into a past which seemed ever more distant. It would soon be a year since he'd died, and she no longer felt the stab of pain or of passion. Malcolm was someone whose memory she would always cherish, he was the father of her child, but she no longer mourned bitterly for him. She had gradually stopped thinking about him; for her he had gone forever. There was a gulf between them now—she was on one side, alive, and Malcolm was on the other side of that abyss, and no longer in the same world as herself.

She would never forget him entirely, of course; she had loved him too much for that, but her love had become a gentle affection and her grief had become a quiet sadness, a resigned acceptance. She was alive, and she was a passionate woman; she needed an answering passion.

Oh, but from Giles, of all people? she thought, her face burning. Until this moment she had never felt an emotion she could not handle. She had never felt threatened by her own feelings, driven and torn in all directions. Her thoughts swirled like the dark centre of a maelstrom. She could not drag herself out of that chaos, back to safety.

She kept remembering the sensuality of his hands, the tormenting promise of his mouth, and she was dry-mouthed from the intensity of her own excitement.

She didn't want to admit it, but the truth kept forcing itself on her. If Mal hadn't been between them, if Mal hadn't begun to cry when he did, they would have made love.

Reminded of him, she looked down at his flushed face and dark head. He had finished feeding and was half asleep, head heavy against her arm.

She smiled involuntarily. He was so sweet when he was like this—sated, content, angelic.

She did up her nightdress with slow and careful fingers, so as not to disturb him, and lay back, keeping his small body in the crook of her arm, while she wondered how on earth she was going to face Giles after this.

He must know how close she had come to giving in to him, and he was an opportunist. She shuddered to think what he might be planning next. It had been understood between them that their marriage was not a real one; merely a legal fiction meant to ensure the Kent family's rights over her son. Giles needed not imagine that he had any rights over her, too!

It was another hour before she went downstairs, leaving baby Mal fast asleep in his swinging crib in the white-painted nursery. Leonie had dressed casually, in jeans and a fine blue cashmere sweater, her blonde hair tied up with blue ribbon and swinging in a pony-tail behind her head.

Giles was reading a newspaper over the breakfast table, although he had finished his breakfast. He was casually dressed, too, because this was a Sunday and he was not going to work. He wore a jade-green shirt, and over that a black sweater, with black denims, but managed to look as if dressed by a top French designer, which she suspected he might have been! His casual wear was often designer fashion; when he dressed for the City he wore classic, expensive English tailoring.

When she walked into the room he lowered the paper and studied her wryly, his brows lifting.

'You look about fifteen! Retreating into your teens, Leonie?' he drawled. 'It won't do you any good, you know. You can't escape from life; it has a nasty habit of catching up with you sooner or later.'

'You're being too clever for me!' she said coldly, sitting down at the table opposite him and pouring herself coffee.

He laughed. 'Oh, I think you know what I'm talking about. You'd like life to be as simple as ABC, wouldn't you? Malcolm was simple—he was glamorous and charming and he made you feel like a princess in a fairy-story. You're only happy thinking in stereotypes, so you cast me as the wicked brother because I was too blunt in saying that I didn't think you and Malcolm would be happy together. I was just the tyrant who was trying to stop your marriage to Malcolm, and you still see me the same way, don't you?'

She was not going to be dragged into a discussion on those lines, so she got up without answering him, without even giving him as much as a look, and made herself some toast in the electric toaster standing on the sideboard.

Still silent, she went back to the table, spread the toast with a thin layer of butter and marmalade and bit into it, although she was not at all hungry.

Watching her, Giles drily murmured, 'From your expression, I gather you're in a bad mood this morning! Feeling guilty, by any chance?'

She felt her cheeks burn. 'I have nothing to feel guilty about!'

He laughed. 'Oh, I agree—but you don't, do you? You're still trying to stay faithful to Malcolm's memory, but this morning in your bedroom you forgot all about him for a minute——'

'Shut up!' She got up, very flushed and angry, her chair falling over. 'I'm not staying here to listen to this!'

Giles got to his feet, too, flinging down his paper. 'Oh, sit down again and eat your breakfast. I'm going—you can stop trembling and looking so stricken.'

He walked to the door and she slowly sat down again, her hand shaking as she reached for her coffee-cup. Giles paused, glancing over his shoulder, his face impassive once more.

'Oh, by the way, we're going to a Christmas party tonight, given by my godfather, Lord Cairnmore. It won't be a large party, but everyone there will know me, so I want you to make a good impression. Wear something special.'

She resented the peremptory tone.

'Don't you give me orders!' she threw back at him, glaring across the room. 'I'm not one of your possessions, or a servant—and I'm not dressing to please you, or impress your friends! I'm not going to this party with you.'

He turned glittering eyes on her. 'You will go!'

Her dark blue eyes were spitting fire. 'You can't make me!'

'Can't I?' He laughed and his tone was light, but it was still a challenge and she faced it, her chin up, very flushed and defiant. He wasn't taking her seriously, and it was time he did.

'No, you can't!'

'Do you want to bet?' he mocked.

'I mean it, Giles!' she said angrily.

'And so do I,' he said through his teeth. 'Now, stop being silly, Leonie. This party is being given for us. My godfather wants to meet you, he wants to introduce you to our friends. Our wedding was very private, none of them were invited; they're curious. Good heavens, Leonie—every one of them will expect my wife to be there!'

'Stop calling me your wife!' she muttered, wildness in her veins. She knew she was provoking another scene and it was folly, but she couldn't stop.

'That's what you are!' Giles snarled as his temper flared higher. 'You're my wife. My *wife*, Leonie! Start believing it, because it's a fact!'

His face was darkening with anger, and she was glad. She hoped he would lose his temper. Why should he stay in control of himself when she had lost all command of herself and her emotions?

He took a long, threatening stride back towards her, and she leapt to her feet again and faced him, bristling.

'I'm not really your wife, this isn't a real marriage, it's just a legal fiction for Mal's sake.'

'Never mind Mal—leave him out of this,' Giles said curtly.

'How can I? He's the only reason I let you talk me into that phoney wedding, and why you insisted on marrying me, too!'

'Oh, there were other reasons, believe me, Leonie!' he said mockingly, and was suddenly too close for comfort, his grey eyes glittering down at her.

'What other reasons?' she whispered breathlessly, and then could have bitten her tongue out. How could she have been such a fool as to ask that? This was a game Giles Kent had played often in the past, but she was a clumsy newcomer to sophistication; he was running rings around her.

His smile taunted, gleaming with amusement. 'Do you want me to show you again? Come back upstairs and I'll be glad to.'

She slapped his face as hard as she could, and felt him rock on his heels in shock. He looked at her in icy fury, mouth tight, a white line around it, jaw set, eyes violent.

'Don't ever strike me again, Leonie. Next time, I might hit you back!'

'That would be better than having you kiss me!' she flung at him, and saw the rage in his face with a sense of reckless satisfaction in having got under his skin. He wasn't quite so cool now!

For a moment she didn't know what he would do next—he looked so angry that she felt her heart beating in her very throat—but then they both heard Marjorie coming towards the door, her footsteps echoing on the wood-block flooring in the hall.

Giles glanced at the door and stiffened, a cold mask coming down over his face again. 'Listen,' he said harshly, 'you had better be ready for this party tonight, or I will personally come up to your room and dress you, and then carry you downstairs over my shoulder if I have to! And don't think I don't mean it. Because, I assure you, I do. You are my wife and not in name only. If you want to force a showdown between us that's up to you, but, I promise you, you won't enjoy what happens.'

# CHAPTER EIGHT

ALL that day Leonie swung between one mood and another: one moment determined to defy him, the next deciding that discretion might be the better part of valour. She stayed close to her mother-in-law as much as she could to keep Giles at bay, but it did not stop him watching her, those grey eyes of his gleaming with mockery and warning. He had meant it, she could be sure of that.

At half-past six, after they had all watched the TV news, he glanced at his watch and got up. 'Time to take a shower and get dressed for the party, Leonie,' he drawled.

His mother smiled, her fingers busily knitting a sweater for the baby. 'Of course, I'd forgotten Cairnmore's party. I'm sure you'll enjoy that, Leonie. He's such a kind man.'

'Are you coming?' Leonie asked hopefully, but her mother-in-law shook her head.

'No, my dear, I was invited, but I'd rather have an early night.'

'Come along, Leonie,' Giles murmured, his fingers curling round her arm and fastening into an iron bracelet.

She couldn't struggle, not in front of his mother. She had to let him steer her out of the room, but when the door shut behind them and they were at the foot of the stairs she tugged free, glaring.

'Don't manhandle me!'

'I wouldn't need to if you didn't keep arguing!'

Marjorie appeared, carrying a tray towards the dining-room to lay the dinner table for Mrs Kent. She gave them a puzzled, surprised look. Leonie forced a stiff smile, and walked up the stairs with Giles behind her. She couldn't fight him with Marjorie watching them.

Hurrying into her bedroom a moment later, she quickly slammed the door and tried to lock it, but the key had gone.

She stood, staring, and heard Giles on the other side of the door, his voice amused. 'I'll come and find you when I'm ready—you've got about half an hour, Leonie!'

He walked on along the corridor, and she backed, forehead corrugated, wondering what to do— should she give in, or refuse to go to this party?

How dared he remove the key from her bedroom door? How dared he threaten her? Who did he think he was?

She heard his shower running, and looked at her watch. Time was rushing past; she had to make up her mind.

But she knew she had. She was too scared of a scene in this house, with her mother-in-law and the servants listening. Giles knew that, damn him.

She threw open her wardrobe and looked at her clothes. What was she going to wear? She didn't have many clothes which were suitable for a smart party. All the women there tonight were going to be dressed to kill.

Then her eye fell on one dress she had not worn for many months. She couldn't have got into it while she was pregnant. Malcolm had chosen it, picked it out for her to wear at a party they had gone to just over a year ago. She had felt very self-conscious in it, and had only worn it that once, although it had made quite a stir at the party. But it had been Malcolm's favourite dress and he had constantly urged her to wear it, without success. A sexy black satin, it was skin-tight, hugging her body from her breasts down to her knees but leaving much of the rest of her bare: her arms, her shoulders, her throat and the beginning of her breasts. She knew it made men stare, but she had never been the sort of girl who enjoyed that sort of attention.

An angry little smile curled her lips. Giles wanted her to 'impress' his friends, did he?

She pulled out the black dress and held it up against herself, staring at her reflection in the long mirror in the wardrobe door, then she laid the dress over her bed and went to have a shower.

Giles opened her door some half an hour later and stopped in his tracks, his eyes narrowing and his jawline tight.

She pretended to ignore him, her attention given to a wayward strand of blonde hair which kept trying to curl the wrong way, but of course she was tensely waiting for his reaction to the way she looked.

Curtly, he suddenly snapped, 'Oh, no!'

'What?' Leonie asked, all innocence.

'I'm not taking you, looking like that!' he grated, and she swung to face him, blue eyes wide and mock-surprised.

'What do you mean?'

'You know perfectly well what I mean,' Giles said through his teeth.

'Don't you like the way I look?' she murmured, smoothing a hand down over the clinging black satin.

His eyes followed the movement of her hand, down over her swelling breasts, the small waist and rounded hips, and she heard the intake of his breath, saw the flare of his nostrils, the glitter of those hard grey eyes. 'Be careful, or I'll show you just how much!' he muttered thickly, and suddenly Leonie couldn't breathe.

Giles watched the colour creep up her face, and he laughed. 'And there isn't time for that!'

Leonie couldn't think of any answer for that, but he didn't wait for her to answer him, anyway; he looked at his watch, and grimaced. 'There isn't time for you to change into something more suitable, either!'

'You told me to put on my best dress!' she snapped. 'Well, this is it! It was Malcolm's favourite, anyway.'

A long silence followed, charged with an intensity she felt in every nerve of her body, then Giles swung on his heel and walked out, saying over his shoulder, 'We're going to be late if we don't hurry.'

She picked up her short evening coat, a quilted black velvet lined with silk, slid into it, collected her matching black velvet evening bag, and followed him more slowly, getting cold feet now that she was on her way to the party.

His wealthy, snobbish friends were going to stare at her in disbelief, their respectability outraged by the very sight of her. She felt her heart sink. Why had she done it? Oh, she had told herself she was putting on the black dress to annoy Giles, but that hadn't been true.

She knew she had been kidding herself. The truth was, she had wanted to see that look on his face; it excited her to excite him, and that was stupid, that was crazy, because it was dangerous.

She was in his power. Wasn't that bad enough? Why had she put ideas into his head by dressing this way tonight? She had never liked living dangerously, she wasn't the sort of girl who enjoyed walking a tightrope, and the last thing in the world she wanted was to attract Giles. Wasn't it?

She bit her lip, shivering. Well, wasn't it? she asked herself angrily, and the question echoed inside her head without any answer coming back.

What *is* the matter with me? she thought. What is going on? She looked down the stairs to where Giles waited for her, a tall man, his face hard, his body lean and powerful in his formal black evening suit, and felt almost sick with nerves and a strange yearning.

Oh, no, she thought: I'm not really falling in love with him, am I? That really would be insanity. I can't let it happen.

She almost turned and fled back up to the safety of her room, but at that instant Mrs Kent came out to say goodbye to them, her eyes widening at the sight of Leonie in the very provocative dress.

Heaven knew what she thought, but she didn't make any comment, just said, 'Have a lovely evening, both of you!'

Leonie managed a shy smile before Giles took her by the arm and steered her out of the house into the waiting car. George was driving them, so that Giles could drink at the party. With another pair of ears attentive to everything they said, they were almost silent during the drive, which only lasted ten minutes, anyway.

There was a line of cars turning into the great wrought-iron gates leading into the park around Cairn House. George slotted into place at the end of the procession, and they made their way at a funereal pace, their wheels grating on the gravelled drive. Looking out of the windows, Leonie saw little of the parkland; a dim outline of a tree here, the white blur of a grazing sheep there.

'What time shall I pick you up, sir?' asked George as he opened the car door for them in front of the elegant portico of the large white eighteenth-century house, which was one of the loveliest stately homes in Essex.

'Eleven-thirty, unless I ring to change the time,' Giles said.

Leonie was staring up at Cairn House, which was floodlit, giving something of the effect of moonlight on the perfectly proportioned façade of the building. She had seen it from the road as she'd driven past, but she had never been able to see it close up, and, of course, she had never been inside. It was wonderful, she thought, transfixed. She had always thought Warlock House was beautiful, but this was in another league altogether. It was a work of art.

George drove on, and Giles and Leonie turned towards the steps leading up to the portico, under which waited Lord Cairnmore himself, a grizzled, upright figure in evening dress, his silver hair gleaming in the darkness.

Giles put a hand under her elbow and led her up to meet his godfather, who smiled down at her with a mixture of curiosity and admiration.

'This is Leonie, sir,' Giles said, and the old man held out his hand.

'Leonie. I am very pleased to meet you at last. I wish I could have been at your wedding, but unluckily I was abroad. I hope you and Giles are going to be very happy, my dear.'

She murmured, 'Thank you,' shyly, and he smiled again.

'You know, this is a very elusive fox you've managed to corner! A lot of pretty girls have hunted him in the past without success, and everyone was incredulous when they heard that he was getting married at last—but one look at you makes it very clear why you pulled it off where they failed! Every man here tonight is going to envy him. I do myself! Giles, I hope you know what a lucky fellow you are?'

'I do indeed,' Giles drawled.

Leonie liked Lord Cairnmore; there were lines of humour and kindliness in his face, but there was strength there, too.

'I hope I'm going to see a lot of you in the future, Leonie,' he said, and she smiled up at him, surprised and relieved that he was being so welcoming. She had not expected this warmth.

'Thank you, Lord Cairnmore.'

'Call me Harry,' he said.

'Stop flirting with my wife, sir!' Giles said, looking wryly amused.

'Was I?' The older man pretended surprise, then grinned at him. 'Sorry about that, Giles! But that's something you are going to have to get used to, I'm afraid. You shouldn't have married someone this gorgeous if you didn't want other men to look at her!'

'Looking is OK,' Giles drawled, sliding his arm around Leonie's waist in a proprietorial, possessive gesture. 'So long as they don't go any further than that!'

Lord Cairnmore laughed loudly. 'Going to be a jealous husband, are you, Giles? Well, why not? Why not? Don't blame you. Take her inside and get her a drink. I'll see you later.'

He turned to welcome some new arrivals, and Leonie and Giles moved on into the candlelit hall, fragrant with bowls and great vases of flowers, where they were welcomed by Lord Cairnmore's elder daughter, Jess Cutler, whose husband, Neil Cutler, was a famous polo player and horse breeder.

Leonie had seen photos of Jess Cutler in the Press often enough to recognise her at sight. A woman of around forty, Mrs Cutler was herself reputed to be one of the best riders in England, and she certainly had a face like a horse, a well-bred horse, with a long, thin nose and high forehead, straight brown mane and enormous, staring eyes.

After shaking hands with Leonie, to whom she said very little, she talked to Giles about mutual friends, braying with laughter now and then.

Suddenly, she said, 'Can't believe it, you know. You, of all people, getting married! I tell you, Neil almost burst into tears. He thinks it is a terrible waste, he says. He did say he was going to ask you to let him have your little black book, so that he could console all your old flames, but, if he asks you, you had better not say yes, or I'll be after you!'

Giles laughed. 'Don't worry, I won't let him have it!'

'I should hope not,' she said in her loud, assured, arrogant voice, then glanced at Leonie before saying, 'Which reminds me, I'd better warn you: Steff is here.'

Leonie stiffened, her face going blank, mask-like, while behind that her mind was busy working out what Mrs Cutler meant.

Steff? Who was Steff? Then it dawned—Mrs Cutler must mean Stephanie Ibbotson, a vivacious redhead Giles had been dating around the time Malcolm first took Leonie home to meet his family.

Stephanie Ibbotson might be designing gardens for wealthy clients at the moment, but she had been a photographer at one time, and had once been a photographic model herself, when she was about eighteen. She had never quite hit the heights in any of her careers, but she did have a genius for self-publicity, which meant that she was well known in spite of not being a huge success.

'I didn't know she was a friend of yours, Jess,' Giles drawled, his expression bland. If the news that Stephanie Ibbotson was here worried him, he certainly did not show it by so much as a flicker.

'I wouldn't call her a friend,' Jess Cutler said with faint hauteur. 'She's designing a garden for me. You know Neil inherited a manor house over the border in Suffolk from a cousin last year? Place hadn't been touched for years; garden gone to seed, house worse. We had to wait all this time to get possession—you know how the lawyers drag their feet on these things. Anyway, we couldn't possibly move in, of course, not with the place the way it was, so I got a good architect and builder to do the house, and Steff to do the garden for me.'

'She's very talented,' Giles murmured, and Leonie shot him a glance.

In what direction? she wondered acidly, and then caught his eye and hurriedly looked away, hoping he had not read her expression. She did not want him to think she was jealous. She wasn't, of course. Not in the least.

'Oh, she's doing a wonderful job! Transforming the place! Of course, gardens take time, but already you can see it's going to be absolutely fabulous.' Jess looked past Giles into a panelled reception hall behind him. 'And speak of the devil, there she is!'

Leonie and Giles followed her glance, both of them immediately recognising the young man talking to Stephanie Ibbotson.

'I told her to bring someone and she turned up with a good-looking young doctor,' said Jess, laughing. 'It gives a whole new meaning to the words private medicine, doesn't it?'

Neither of them laughed, but Jess was oblivious to their stiff expressions. Her eyes flicked past them and her face lit up. 'Gerry, darling—wonderful that you could come!'

She darted off to greet the newcomer with outstretched hands. It was no surprise that he should be another of the horsy fraternity; a bluff man in his thirties with a fresh complexion, hard face and casual manner.

Giles said coldly, 'The guy with Steff is the fellow who came to the wedding, isn't it? Andrew something or other. The one who offered you a flat?'

Leonie nodded, frowning. 'I can't understand what *he* is doing here!' she thought aloud.

'Did you expect him to stay faithful to you forever?' Giles asked with a sting in his voice, and she flushed.

'Andrew was never involved with me—it was Angela he was seeing!'

Giles looked at her sharply, frowning. 'Angela?'

'Yes.' Leonie was feeling guilty because she had forgotten all about Angela since the birth of baby Malcolm. So much had happened, she had had so much on her mind. 'I should have rung or written,' she said regretfully. 'She came to see me and Mal while I was in hospital, but since then I haven't seen her. I kept meaning to get in touch with her, but there was always so much to do. Maybe she and Andrew have split up? I do hope not; he's so nice, and Angela was really serious about him.'

'From the way Steff is gazing up at him, I'd hazard a guess that she's pretty serious about him, too,' Giles said with a sort of venom, and Leonie wondered if he was jealous. Which of them had ended their relationship—Giles or Stephanie Ibbotson? How did he really feel about her? Leonie's heart sank as she stared across the room at the other girl. Stephanie Ibbotson was beautiful, so vibrant with that red hair and vivid green eyes, her figure dynamic and sexy in a jade-green silk dress. She made Leonie feel colourless and boring.

'That seems to bother you,' Giles said in a clipped way.

Starting, Leonie looked up at him, stammering. 'What? No...I...why should it? I just didn't think Andrew was the type to switch girlfriends every few weeks.'

Giles bit out irritably, 'You don't know who broke it off—him or your friend Angela. She has had quite a few men in her life, hasn't she? She isn't the faithful type, exactly.'

Frowning, Leonie said, 'You don't know her well enough to say something like that!'

'Malcolm talked about her a couple of times. I got a pretty clear idea of what she was like.'

'Angela has been unlucky with her men,' Leonie muttered. 'She always seems to pick the wrong ones.'

'That's a classic pattern with men and women,' Giles said, drily, and she wasn't sure exactly what he meant by that. There was something in his expression that made her feel he was not just talking about Angela. He had always made it plain that he thought she was the wrong girl for Malcolm—was he obliquely saying so, again?

She met his eyes angrily, reacting more to what she thought he might be hinting at than to what he had actually said. 'Why are you always so censorious? What makes you an expert on the subject? And don't say anything against Angela—she's my best friend, I've known her since we were at school together!'

Giles laughed suddenly, his face relaxing. 'Oh, I'm up against the freemasonry of women, am I? Oh, well, I won't say another word. Angela is perfect, of course.'

Leonie bit her lip, then laughed, too.

They stood there, smiling at each other; and Leonie felt a strange happiness flooding through her; she felt weightless, as if she could float, and as free as a bird. She could almost believe that if she tried she would be able to fly. She could not ever remember being this happy for a very long time, and that was amazing, that was incredible, because it meant that Giles had made her happy simply by smiling at her, and that might be frightening if she let herself dwell on it. Was he becoming that important to her?

'Leonie?' a startled voice said beside them a moment later, and with a wrench she tore her eyes away from Giles and turned to look at the other man who had come up to them.

'Oh... Andrew...' she stammered, her voice husky and unsteady because she was still reverberating with the wild happiness she had felt when Giles had smiled at her.

'I can't believe my eyes!' Andrew said, gazing at the way the skin-tight black satin dress followed every curve of her body. He grinned wryly. 'Sorry if I'm staring, but the last time I saw you you looked so different.'

'I was seven months pregnant at the time!' she said lightly.

'So you were!' Andrew laughed, then caught sight of the black scowl Giles wore, and stopped smiling. 'Congratulations on your son,' he said quickly, changing the subject. 'I heard all about him from Angela.'

Leonie gave him an uncertain glance, wondering whether or not to ask the obvious question. 'How is she? I haven't seen her for ages.'

'Neither have I,' Andrew said, grimacing. 'She got a job working with some film crew, making costumes, and went off to Spain for three months to work out there. I had a few postcards and phone calls at first, then nothing, so I don't know if I'll ever see her again.'

Leonie impulsively took his hand, squeezing it warmly. 'I'm sorry, Andrew. Angela has always... well...' She didn't know quite how to phrase it, but Andrew grimaced and bluntly said it for her.

'She's fickle, you mean? Yes, I've realised that now. I did think we had something special, and I was knocked for six for a few weeks, but I'm getting over it now. I've met this terrific girl...' He grinned, and Leonie laughed.

'Oh, I am glad,' she said, and he put an arm around her, hugging her in a brotherly way.

'You're so sweet, Leonie!'

There was a rustle of silk next to them a second later, and then Stephanie Ibbotson drawled, 'Giles, what *is* going on here? Are you going to let every man in the place make love to your wife?'

'You think I should knock your new boyfriend down?' Giles enquired blandly.

Stephanie laughed, looking far from amused. 'Darling, how primitive and thrilling—I believe you would!'

'And you're right,' he said through tight lips.

Stephanie ran a hand up and down his arm, feeling his muscles. 'I do love dangerous men!' she cooed, and Leonie's teeth met. She did not like Stephanie Ibbotson.

'No,' Stephanie said, sounding reluctant. 'No, don't spoil the party, Giles. I'm sure Andrew is going to be a good boy now, aren't you, Andrew, darling?'

Andrew gave her a faintly uncertain smile. He was not the ultra-sophisticated type and wasn't sure how to take her idea of a joke.

'Oh, come on, Steff! You don't really think I was making a pass at Leonie?' he muttered, darkly flushed. 'Honestly!'

'Well, what's sauce for the goose is certainly allowed to the gander,' Stephanie said with a smouldering look, put her arms around Giles's neck, swayed closer until their bodies touched, and kissed him on the mouth, lingeringly.

His hand automatically came up to grip her waist, and Leonie felt a stab of pain so sharp and fierce that it took her breath away. Shaken, she thought, I'm a fool; he's the last man to fall in love with, and it is crazy to feel this jealousy because he doesn't care a jot for me, he only married me to keep control of his brother's child, his brother's share of the family estate. I must not love him.

But how did you stop? To say 'stop' to love was like trying to float instead of falling after you had jumped out of an aeroplane without a parachute. You might be able to manage that for a little while, but sooner or later gravity triumphed and you plummeted, like Icarus, falling out of a blue sky after flying too high.

'Behave yourself, Steff!' Giles drawled, and Leonie reluctantly looked back to see him holding Stephanie at arm's length, his hands grasping her shoulders.

Stephanie looked at him through half-closed, flirtatious, cat-like eyes, and Leonie watched bleakly, hating her.

'Darling, you're still the sexiest man I know!' the other woman purred, her red mouth curving in feline satisfaction, the cat after it had swallowed the cream.

Andrew had stiffened and was pale. Frowning, he turned away and walked off. Steff looked after him, her mouth quirking.

'Oh, dear, someone is sulking!'

There was a smear of that vivid lipstick on Giles's mouth. Leonie looked at it with distaste. Giles met her eyes, no doubt read her expression, and pushed Stephanie away. Pulling out a handkerchief, he wiped his mouth, but she knew she would not so easily be able to erase the memory of seeing Stephanie in his arms. Oh, she had always known that he had had affairs; Malcolm had laughingly almost boasted about it. He was quite proud of his elder brother's success with women. But now Leonie had seen him with one of his women, and it hurt.

'You had better go after your new plaything if you don't want someone else to grab him,' Giles said to Steff, and Leonie wondered if it hurt him to see her with Andrew, with any other man.

How did he really feel about Steff? Pain twisted inside her like a dagger, and she had to close her lips tightly to stop a cry of agony escaping.

'He's very cute,' Stephanie said with a wry smile. 'See you later, Giles; have fun.'

She ignored Leonie and walked away. Giles gave Leonie a searching stare.

'Still in a bad mood? Well, come and meet some of my friends, and try to be polite, and smile, for heaven's sake!'

She didn't argue—she was too busy fighting with the pain in her chest. Obediently, she followed him, a fixed smile on her pale face, hoping he would not notice her misery.

The rest of the party seemed to pass in a strange dream-like fashion; she talked to people without really knowing what she was saying or who they were, sipped champagne, nibbled desultorily at the elegant food from the buffet table, although she did not really want any, and throughout it all felt totally unreal.

Giles introduced her to a string of his friends, and she liked a number of them very much. Some were polite, some warm and friendly, others, though, were neither, and she didn't miss the curiosity in people's faces when they talked to her.

Everyone knew, of course, that she and Giles had got married just weeks before she'd had a baby, and it was obvious that guests at the party were whispering about it in every corner. She was conscious of being watched, edgily aware of scandalised or fascinated stares, of a mixture of disapproval, dislike and envy.

She coped with all that by withdrawing behind a wall; pretending not to care or even be aware of those reactions, just smiled and made small talk without allowing anyone to really reach her. She hoped she was convincing most of them, but knew she had not fooled Giles, who kept giving her a piercing stare, frowning.

She had not fooled Andrew, either, it seemed. 'You don't look happy,' he said some time during the evening.

'Don't I?' She laughed with a tang of bitterness, wishing he were not so sharp-eyed. 'Well, I've had a difficult year, I suppose.'

'I know you have, Leonie,' Andrew said gently. 'It must have been an enormous strain, coping with everything that's happened. I only hope this marriage of yours isn't going to make things worse.'

'Angela talks too much!' she said with a grimace.

He laughed. 'Doesn't she, though? I'm sorry if you mind my knowing.'

He had a sympathetic face, a lovely smile. 'No, I don't really mind,' Leonie said, smiling back. 'And there are good things to balance out the bad; I've got a lovely baby, and I'm healthy—what more can I ask?'

'If there is ever anything I can do...' Andrew offered, and she gave him a grateful look.

'Thank you, you're very kind, Andrew.'

At that moment, Giles came up to them and said curtly, 'We ought to be on our way. Didn't you say you wanted to get back to feed the baby?'

'Is he still on night feeds?' asked Andrew with professional interest, and Leonie smilingly shook her head.

'Mostly he sleeps right through to the six o'clock morning feed, but sometimes he's hungrier than usual, and wakes up during the night. That happens less and less often, though, thank heavens. I can usually count on an unbroken night's sleep.'

'He sounds like the perfect baby,' Andrew said with amusement. 'I must meet this paragon!'

'Next time you're driving down to visit your mother, drop in and see us!' Leonie impulsively invited.

'Are we leaving now or not?' Giles bit out before Andrew could answer that. He caught her arm and began to walk away, pulling her with him without giving her time to say goodnight to Andrew.

He only paused *en route* for the front door to say a few words to his godfather. 'Wonderful party—we had a great time. Afraid we must leave now, our car will be waiting outside. Thank you for inviting us.'

'Glad you enjoyed yourself, my boy,' Lord Cairnmore said with something like irony. 'I wasn't sure you had.' Giles scowled, and his godfather grinned, then said, 'Leonie, a pleasure to meet you, and I shall be over soon to look at the latest addition to the Kent family.'

She smiled warmly at him. 'I'll look forward to seeing you, Lord Cairnmore.'

'Harry,' he reminded, leaning down to kiss her on the cheek.

'Goodnight, sir,' Giles said in that sharp, curt voice, jerking her away and striding out of the house. The winter night was cold. There was no cloud cover, the stars were fixed and bright overhead, but Leonie had no time to look up and admire them. George was waiting; they got into the car and a moment later were driving back to Warlock House.

She sat staring out of the window. Giles looked at her as if he hated her—and she was crazy about him. Why was life such hell?

# CHAPTER NINE

MRS KENT was in bed by the time they got back to Warlock House, and most of the rooms were dark. Leonie turned at once towards the stairs, saying over her shoulder as she began to climb them, 'I'm tired—I'll check on Mal, and if he's asleep I'll go straight to bed, I think.'

Giles didn't answer; he strode into the sitting-room, where a faint amber light glowed from one of the table lamps. She faintly heard the chink of a decanter, then the sound of something being poured into a glass. Hadn't he had enough to drink at the party? Not that he seemed to be drunk, but she already knew him well enough to realise that he had a hard head and could drink quite a lot without showing it.

Leonie paused outside the nursery door, listening. She had left Susan in charge of baby Malcolm, but there was no sign of her. She slept in a room on the other side of the nursery, but after being up so late the night before Susan was probably fast asleep, and might well have slept through any crying from the baby.

Softly opening the door, Leonie tiptoed in and listened before approaching the swinging cradle in which baby Malcolm slept. She did not put on the light, but she could see quite well by the light from the corridor outside. He was curled round, one tiny hand flung out, palm upward, his face flushed with sleep, his breathing almost silent. Leonie was tempted to bend down and kiss him, but that would wake him, so after a moment she crept out again and closed the door without making a sound. With any luck he might sleep until morning.

In her own room, she kicked off her high heels and yawned, realising only then how sleepy she was, stretched and reached for the zip on the skin-tight black dress. Getting out of it was almost as tough as getting into it! You needed to be something of a contortionist.

She hadn't been able to lock her door because Giles still had the key, but before she got into bed she would put a chair under the handle to make sure the door could not be opened from the outside. Not that she was afraid of him! She had lived here for some months now, and Giles had never once tried to come into this room.

The zip slid down, she peeled the dress off and carefully hung it up in her wardrobe, then sat down on the edge of her bed to take off her stockings. She was wearing a black silk French basque corselet which pushed up her breasts and pulled in her small waist even further, giving her an hourglass figure. It ended above the thigh with a flurry of richly decorated black lace, very sexy against her white skin.

Her stockings were black, too, very sheer and fine. She didn't get time to take them off. The door opened and Giles walked in while she was sitting there, one knee lifted so that she could unhook her suspenders.

Giles didn't say anything, he just stood there, staring, and her heart beat so heavily that she almost thought she was going to faint.

'Get out of my room!' she whispered.

'So *this* is what was under that sexy black dress!' he merely said.

'Get out!' she said again, trying to sound angry but afraid she sounded more scared.

'I've been wondering all evening,' was all he said, looming over her in a way that made her even more nervous. 'I'd bet a lot of other men have been, too. I saw them watching you, their eyes popping out of their heads, every damn one of them imagining what was underneath that dress.'

She couldn't shout at him, for fear of waking baby Mal. Very flushed, she muttered furiously, 'That's enough! Go away.'

'Not yet,' he drawled. 'Not before we've had a talk.'

'At this hour?' She didn't know what he was doing in here, why he was tormenting her like this, but she was trying not to look as worried as she felt in case it made him more dangerous. 'It's very late, after all,' she said in a tone she forced to sound polite. 'Whatever you want to say can wait.'

'No, it can't,' he bit out.

'Look,' she snapped back, 'I was getting ready for bed.'

'So I see,' he drawled, and his grey eyes wandered over her barely clothed figure with a mocking insolence that made her want to hit him. How dared he look at her like that?

'And we've got nothing to talk about!' she defiantly threw at him.

'You know that isn't true, Leonie,' Giles murmured, and then to her shock and disbelief he knelt down in front of her.

She looked down at him, her dark blue eyes enormous, their pupils dilated and as black as jet.

'Here I am, at your feet,' Giles said with light mockery, and then, while she was still off balance from that remark, his hand lifted to touch her thigh.

Leonie gave an audible intake of breath, stiffening. 'What do you think you're doing?'

'You can see what I'm doing.' Giles slowly began to undo her suspenders, his fingers cool as they brushed against her skin. A shudder of aroused excitement went through her, although she could have kicked herself for responding like that.

'Stop that!' she whispered to cover how she really felt.

He gave her a glinting look from under his lashes, his mouth wickedly amused. 'You want them off, don't you? Weren't you taking them off when I arrived?' He was peeling one stocking down now, taking his time, and she was beginning to tremble violently.

'But I prefer to do it myself!'

He laughed mockingly. 'Ah, but I'll enjoy doing it far more!'

Her skin burned; she couldn't think of anything to say, and while she was trying to pull herself together Giles was deftly busy.

One stocking was completely off, and he began to remove the other one, his fingertips sending a shudder through her as they touched her inner thigh in intimate contact.

'You have terrific legs,' he said, staring down at them. 'Nice slim ankles, pretty feet, and such smooth skin.'

The other stocking was off, her legs were bare, and he was stroking them, from thigh to calf, sending shivers down her spine. She pulled her foot out of his hand and stood up, not knowing quite how to get him to leave.

He got to his feet, too, and, before she could get away, caught hold of her bare shoulders, forcing her round to face him, their bodies almost touching.

He was still in his evening suit; the grave formality made him look even taller, and was in strange contrast to her own half-naked informality, in the black basque. It was like a scene from some impressionist painting; sensuous, suggestive. Leonie found it disturbing, yet exciting, too, and that bothered her even more.

'Let go of me!' she protested, struggling.

'Not until we've had that talk!'

'We can talk tomorrow.'

'I've waited long enough as it is,' Giles said angrily, his face tightening. 'And tonight I realised I couldn't afford to wait any longer, or it may be too late.'

She looked up at him puzzled, frowning. 'What are you talking about?'

'What do you think I'm talking about, for heaven's sake? This sham of a marriage, Leonie!'

She turned cold, faint, miserably wondering if Giles was about to suggest it was time they separated, time this meaningless marriage was finished.

She swallowed, lifting her chin. 'OK, I'll leave whenever you say the word, and we can be divorced, or the marriage annulled, or whatever you like, but I'm taking Mal with me; I am *not* leaving him with you!'

'There will be no divorce,' he snarled, scowling. 'No divorce, no annulment—and you aren't going anywhere. You are my wife, and you are staying right here with me.'

She looked up at him blindly, too dazed to take in what he had said. 'But... then... I don't understand. What did you want to say to me?'

He laughed shortly, then his arm went round her, his hand flattened against her bare back, forcing her towards him until their bodies merged.

'Just that! It's time you realised you *are* my wife, and this is going to be a real marriage.'

As he muttered the words, she felt him unzip her basque, felt it give way and begin to slide down, and she gave a choked gasp.

'Don't!'

Her mind was in turmoil. What was happening? Had she given herself away tonight? Had he guessed she had fallen in love with him? He must have done, or else he would not be doing this, he wouldn't be here now, trying to make love to her!

A bitterness made her close her eyes briefly. He was a ruthless opportunist. How could he? He had suddenly seen how she felt, and was taking advantage of it without caring what that might do to her.

Her certainly wasn't in love with her. She had seen the cold anger in his eyes when he'd looked at her tonight at that party. It was the same look she had seen so many times in the past, from the very beginning, when they'd first met, when his brother had brought her home and told his family he was going to marry her.

Giles had looked at her so icily that day that it had been like a slap in the face—and from time to time since then she had seen that look again. Giles hated her. If he made love to her it would be in contempt, to hurt and punish her, and Leonie couldn't bear the idea of letting him touch her in such a mood.

It would destroy her if he did. She would have another bitter memory to add to all the others, the hurts and humiliations he had given her in the past, but this time she would loathe and despise herself, too, for giving in to him and her own stupid feelings for him.

'Don't,' she kept saying more and more angrily, trying to fight him off, trying to get away, but he was stronger, she couldn't stop him. The basque finally fell to the floor and then she was naked in his arms, shaking from head to foot, and in tears.

'I won't... Let go... I hate you,' she groaned.

'That's too bad,' Giles muttered. 'Because I'm not letting you go, Leonie! I've run out of patience.' He bent his head, and wild shock waves hit her as his mouth caressed her bare shoulder. She couldn't get away, but she couldn't bear him to see her face, read her expression, guess what he was doing to her. With a low moan she buried her head against his shirt and stopped fighting, her body quivering under the silken glide of his fingers on her skin, an exploration of her body which sent waves of heat and helpless need crashing through her.

Suddenly, his hand curled around her chin and lifted her head, forced it back until she had to look up, with a sense of shock so violent that it was like an earthquake, into his grey eyes. She had thought she knew him quite well by now, but tonight he was a stranger, his face carved into strange planes, mouth wide and sensuous, eyes glittering, his face taut with desire.

Leonie stared back, transfixed, like a rabbit hypnotised by a snake. Her heart turned over heavily, she caught her breath, shaking. Whether he hated her or not, still, there was no question about it: he wanted her, and the thought made her weaker, her legs almost gave way and she clutched at him to support herself.

'Giles, don't...'

'Nothing is going to stop me now,' he bit out. 'I've got to the end of my tether. I've waited long enough. It feels like a lifetime, not just a year. After

Malcolm died, of course, I knew it was far too soon to even think about it...'

She froze, staring. 'What?' What had he just said? After Malcolm died? What did he mean, too soon to think about it? About what?

He didn't give her a chance to ask; he was talking fast, his face full of force. 'I told myself I'd wait a few months before getting in touch again, but when your mother told me you had gone to Italy on holiday I decided to take the risk of following you out there...'

'What?' she said again, incredulously, and saw a dark flush crawl up his face.

His voice deepened, roughened. 'Yes. I followed you. I could have sent someone else—there was no need for me to go myself—on that sales trip, but the fact that it was coming up just when you were over there seemed like an omen. I couldn't pass up the chance, so I went, and when I got to your hotel they told me you were out that day, on a trip to Ravenna, so I followed you there, and saw you, and although you were friendlier than you had ever been before you cried on my shoulder and it was obvious you were still grieving for Malcolm, I was being a fool, wasting my time, so I didn't hang around.'

She was so stunned by hearing that it had been no coincidence that he had turned up in Ravenna when he did that she couldn't think of anything to say and just stared at him.

He shifted restlessly, his mouth faintly sulky. He didn't like admitting all this—it was humiliating to confess his feelings—but he set his jaw obstinately, and ground out, 'So I flew back home, telling myself it was far too soon, and I settled down to wait as patiently as I could. I thought I'd give it another six months, and try again.' He laughed curtly. 'And then I found out you were pregnant! My God, that was a shock!' His mouth twisted. 'If Malcolm had known he would have laughed himself sick.'

She winced, watching him uneasily and seeing the glitter of jealousy in his grey eyes.

'I was shaken to the depths,' he said harshly. 'I couldn't help feeling as if Malcolm was reaching out of the grave, claiming you. I was actually jealous of my own brother, even after he was dead!'

Giles ran a rough hand over his face, sighing. 'I didn't know what to do about myself, but when the first reaction died down I realised I still loved you just as much, and wanted you, and the baby was part of you, so I was going to love it, too. I saw that the baby would change everything—for one thing, it gave me an excuse for seeing you and keeping in touch. I realised that the baby might be the bridge I had been looking for—a way of building common ground between us.'

She was bewildered; he was making her see the last year in a very different light and she wasn't sure how much of what he said she should believe.

'Of course, all my threats about being his guardian, taking him away from you, were moonshine! I could never have got any court to accept my claims, and I knew it——'

'You made all that up!' she gasped.

'I wanted you so desperately I would have said anything,' he admitted thickly. 'I didn't really expect you to fall for it; any lawyer would have told you I was talking rubbish, and no court would have taken your child away from you, or made me his guardian while you were alive, but I was thinking on my feet, anything to keep in touch with you and the baby, especially after you said you were moving in with Andrew Colpitt...'

She flushed crossly. 'I didn't say anything of the kind! That flat belonged to Andrew's mother; it was meant for him, but he didn't use it at the time because he lived in London, and as he was dating Angela he offered it to me! I keep telling you this—there was never anything between me and Andrew.'

He grimaced. 'OK, maybe there wasn't, but that doesn't mean he didn't fancy you. I've seen the way he looks at you, and I know what is on his mind. I ought to! It's always on my mind when I'm looking at you!'

Her eyes fell, and he sighed impatiently. 'Don't look that way! I've finished with lies and pretences, Leonie. From now on, I'm going to say what I really feel, even if you don't like it.'

'Frankly,' she said in a husky voice, 'I'm finding it hard to believe all this! You haven't given me any idea that you...'

She couldn't hold his eyes and looked down again, whispering, 'That you... liked me...'

'Liked you? My God, I've spent most of my waking hours trying to keep my hands off you!'

Her face burned. 'I felt it made you furious just to look at me!'

'It did,' he said curtly. 'I was going crazy with frustration—of course I was angry! I had to wait so long, month after month...'

She was trembling at the emotion in his voice—if only she could believe him! If Giles loved her they could be happy, this marriage would be a real one at last. But what if he was lying?

'And since you had the baby,' he said bleakly, 'I've been afraid to move too fast, in case I drove you away altogether, but tonight I realised I was being a fool. I had to stand there and watch you flirting with other men——'

'I wasn't!'

He turned dark, angry eyes on her. 'Whatever you call it, I am not watching you smiling at Andrew Colpitt like that again!'

'Are you sure you weren't jealous because he was with Steff?' she threw at him, out of her own jealousy, and he stared at her, his brows dragging together.

'Jealous over Steff?' He gave a short laugh. 'You're crazy. If I had ever been serious about Steff we wouldn't have broken up. I ended it because I knew it wasn't deep enough to matter, and it wasn't fair to her to go on seeing her when I knew I would never feel any different.'

Leonie couldn't stop the long sigh she gave, her body trembling in his arms.

Giles watched her intently. 'Leonie?' he asked with husky eagerness. 'Were you...did you mind...about Steff and me? Did it matter?'

She looked down, her lashes flickering against her flushed cheeks, and couldn't get out a word.

'Darling,' Giles said hoarsely, and kissed her neck, her cheek, her mouth, quick, brushing kisses which made her head swim. She still wasn't sure what was happening—what had he called her?

'Darling,' he said again, his voice shaky, and she looked up at him, her dark blue eyes searching his face for clues, for a sign that he meant it, that he wasn't just using the word lightly.

He picked her up in his arms and carried her to the bed, laying her on it tenderly, as if she were made of china and might break. As he knelt beside her on the bed, his hand smoothed her fine silvery hair back from her face.

'I've waited so long for this,' he whispered thickly. 'I'm half scared to touch you in case I wake up and find I was only dreaming. I've had this dream too many times; it can't be really happening at last.'

He softly stroked one finger down her face; over her forehead, nose, cheek, mouth, jaw, gazing all the time into her eyes. 'You're beautiful,' he said. 'So lovely that you took my breath away the first time I saw you—one look and I was crazy to have you. God, if only I'd met you first, instead of Malcolm, I used to think, but I knew I was being a fool, because it was obvious you didn't even like me.'

It was true, she thought, frowning. She hadn't liked him, even before they'd met. Malcolm had told her so much about his elder brother that turned her against him. Had that been deliberate? she wondered for the first time. Had Malcolm wanted to make them enemies?

Whether he had or did not, he hadn't lied, though, had he? He had said Giles didn't approve of his dating her, and that had been true, especially after Giles met her, on his own admission.

She had known Giles was angry; she hadn't guessed why, but she had picked up those vibrations in him, and resented them. Oh, she had told herself she would go out of her way to make friends with both Giles and Mrs Kent, but underneath that she had already been arming herself for conflict—and that had been what she'd met. Outright war.

Gently, she said, 'You didn't make it easy for me to like you, did you? You and your mother made it crystal-clear that I wasn't wanted!'

'Oh, you were wanted!' he muttered, his eyes dark with a mixture of passion and laughter.

His hands moving downward, he caressed her tenderly, looked at her body with an intensity that made her bones turn to water.

'That was the trouble!' he said thickly. 'I wanted you like hell, but I couldn't show it, I had to hide it, and it was driving me crazy. It hurt. I was too jealous to think straight. I couldn't let you guess how I felt, so I went to the other extreme, and was nasty to you whenever I saw you.'

'Yes, you were,' she said, smiling, and he gave her a look that made her catch her breath, then his head swooped down and his mouth took hers.

She kissed him back, her eyes closing and her arms going round his neck, and the hunger blazed up in both of them before she knew it. She clung, her hands clenching on his back, and Giles groaned against her yielding, parting lips.

'I love you. God, I love you.'

Happiness overwhelmed her—she felt as if she were floating, her body weightless, a radiance of light around her. It was like nothing she had ever felt before; it was like being in heaven, and she barely managed to get out a husky answer.

'I love you, Giles.'

He stiffened. 'Don't say it just because you know I want you to...'

'I fell in love with you weeks ago,' she said. 'I was horrified, I thought I must be out of my mind, falling for you when I was sure you hated me. I think I must have been in love with you before I married you—that was really why I said yes, not just because you blackmailed me.'

'I was desperate,' he said, his eyes grimly contrite. 'I'm so sorry, my love. I was afraid you would go off with someone else, afraid I would never get the chance to change your mind about me—I was talking wildly, I didn't know what I was saying, I made up any crazy threat to get you to marry me. If you had talked to a lawyer you would soon have realised what a fairy-tale I was spinning you. But even if it had been legally possible I wouldn't have taken Mal away from you, I swear it. But I'm sorry I frightened and upset you; it was a rotten way of trying to get what I wanted, and I'd deserve it if you refused to forgive me.'

'Yes, you would,' she said with wry irony because she knew he might say that he knew he deserved it, but he was still banking on her forgiving him.

He looked uncertain, reading her expression, and his own eyes wavering. 'Leonie? Are you very angry?'

She pretended to think about it. 'You would have to swear you'd never do anything like that to me again——'

'I swear,' he said, too quickly, but his face was drawn with anxiety and she had to relent, smiling at him.

'Well, I suppose I can't help myself—I love you too much to stay angry with you for long.'

His arms convulsively clutched her closer, he began kissing her wildly, her eyes, her cheeks, her hair, her neck, her mouth.

'Leonie, I love you ... Leonie ... my darling ...'

She unbuttoned his shirt and began to tug it free of his trousers, and he breathed as if he had run a gruelling race, his face darkly flushed. Desire burnt high in both of them, their bodies moving restlessly against each other, their hands touching and caressing.

Giles shed his clothes in a fevered rush, and they kissed, bodies entwined, naked and warm on the bed—and then they heard the baby crying, and lay still, heads raised, listening.

'No,' Giles muttered, grimacing. 'Not now, Mal, for heaven's sake!' but the crying got louder, more determined, and Leonie giggled helplessly.

'He isn't going to stop!'

'Maybe Susan will hear him?' Giles suggested hopefully. 'Isn't it her turn to get up, anyway?'

'Yes, but after her late night yesterday she's probably sleeping like a log.' Leonie shifted reluctantly, sighing. 'I shall have to go!'

'Must you?' Giles groaned, kissing her bare shoulder. 'Let him cry! He may go off to sleep again if you leave him.'

'And he may just yell louder, and wake your mother!' Leonie gently detached herself from his possessive arms, and slid off the bed. She put on her dressing-gown and tied the belt firmly before she went to the nursery. She hadn't expected Giles to join her, but he did, a few minutes later, also in a dressing-gown, his tousled hair brushed down smoothly again.

She was sitting on a low chair, feeding the baby, and Giles quietly came over and knelt beside her, watching with every sign of fascination.

She smiled at him, touched by something in his face, a gentleness, a warmth, that was not for her alone, but for the baby in her arms. She had wondered if Giles might ever come to resent her love for his brother's child, but the look in his eyes was reassuring.

He put out a tender hand to touch the baby's hair, stroking it back from the perspiring little forehead, and Mal swivelled his eyes to look at Giles, then shut his eyes again and concentrated on his food, his small pink fingers possessively patting the warm swell of his mother's breast.

'I'm sorry he picked the wrong moment, Giles!' Leonie whispered.

'That's OK,' he said, his eyes passionate, as he bent to kiss the white breast at which the baby fed. 'I can wait. I've waited a long time for you, Leonie. I can wait another half an hour.'

If he could be patient, so could she—but it was the longest half-hour of Leonie's life.

# SIMPLY IRRESISTIBLE
by Miranda Lee

# CHAPTER ONE

'WE'VE been accused of doing too many heavy stories lately,' Mervyn announced to his underlings seated around the oval table. 'From now on, one of the four segments we tape for each week's show is going to be in a lighter vein.'

Vivien looked up from where she was doodling on her note-pad, a sinking feeling in her stomach. As the last reporter to join the *Across Australia* team—not to mention the only woman—she just *knew* who would be assigned these 'lighter-veined' stories.

She hadn't long come off a *Candid Camera* style programme, and while it had been a huge success, she'd been relieved to finally have the chance to work on a television show that was more intellectually stimulating. At twenty-five going on twenty-six, she felt she was old enough to be taken seriously.

Ah, well, she sighed. One step forward and two steps backwards...

'And what constitutes lighter-veined?' demanded a male voice from across the table.

Vivien glanced over at Bob, widely known as Robert J. Overhill, their hard-hitting political reporter who wouldn't know 'lighter-veined' if it hit him in the left eye. Thirtyish, but already going bald and running to fat, he conducted every interview as a personal war out of which he *had* to emerge the victor. He had a sharp, incisive mind, but the personality of a spoilt little boy.

'I'm not sure myself yet,' Mervyn returned. 'This directive has just come down from the great white chief himself. I've only had time to think up a try-out idea to be screened on Sunday week. Ever heard of Wallaby Creek?' he queried with a wry grin on his intelligent face.

They all shook their heads.

'It's a small town out in north-western New South Wales just this side of Bourke, but off the main highway. Once a year, in the middle of November, it's where the Outback Shearers' Association hold their Bachelors' and Spinsters' Ball.'

Everyone rolled their eyes as the penny dropped. There'd been a current affairs programme done on a similar B & S Ball a couple of years before, which had depicted the event as a drunken orgy filled with loutish yobbos and female desperadoes. The only claim to dubious fame the event seemed to have was that no girl went home a virgin.

Vivien chuckled to herself at the thought that, from what she had seen, not too many virgins had gone to that particular ball in the first place.

'I'm so glad you find the idea an amusing one, Viv,' her producer directed straight at her, 'since you'll be handling it. The ball's this Saturday night. That gives you three days to get yourself organised and out there. Now I'm not interested in any serious message in this story. Just a fun piece. Froth and bubble. Right?'

Vivien diplomatically kept her chagrin to herself. 'Right,' she said, and threw a bright smile around the table at all the smug male faces smirking at her.

It never ceased to amaze her, the pleasure men got from seeing women supposedly put in their places in the workplace, but she had always found the best line of defence was to be agreeable, rather than militant. She defused any antagonism with feminine charm, then counter-attacked by always giving her very best, doing such a damn good job—even with froth and bubble—that her male colleagues had to give her some credit.

'I hear they drink pretty heavily at those balls,' Bob said in a mocking tone. 'We might have to send out a search party of trackers to find Viv the next day. You know what she's like after a couple of glasses. Whew...' He whistled and waved his hand in front of his face, as though he was suddenly very hot.

Vivien sighed while the others laughed. Would she *never* live down the channel's Christmas party last year? How was she to know that someone had spiked the supposedly non-alcoholic fruit punch with vodka? She was always so careful when it came to drinking, ever since she'd discovered several years before at her first university party that anything more than two glasses of the mildest concoction turned her from a quietly spoken, serious-minded girl into a flamboyant exhibitionist, not to mention a rather outrageous flirt.

Luckily for Vivien on that first occasion, her girlfriend had dragged her home before she got herself into any serious trouble. But her hangover the next morning, plus the stark memory of her silly and potentially dangerous behaviour, had made her very careful with alcohol from that moment on.

The incident at last year's Christmas party had hardly been her fault. Vivien groaned silently as she recalled how, once the alcohol took effect, she'd actually climbed up on this very table and danced a wild tango, complete with a rose in her mouth.

Earl had been furious with her, dragging her down and taking her home post-haste. He'd hardly spoken to her for a week. It had taken much longer for the people at work to stop making pointed remarks over the incident. Now, her acid-tongued colleague had brought it up again. Still, Vivien knew the worst thing she could do would be to react visibly.

'Worried you might miss out on something, Bob?' she countered with a light laugh.

'Hardly,' he scowled. 'I like my women a touch less aggressive.'

'Cut it out, Bob,' Mervyn intervened before the situation flared out of hand. 'Oh, and Viv, I can only let you have a single-man crew. You like working that way anyway, don't you?'

'I'll get Irving,' she said. Irving was a peach to work with, a whiz with camera and sound. A witty companion, too.

But the best part about Irving was that he wasn't a womaniser and never tried to chat her up. In his late twenties, he had a steady girlfriend who adored him and whom he adored back. Fidelity was his middle name. Definitely Vivien's type of man.

'It goes without saying that you'll both have to drive out. *And* in the same car,' Mervyn went on. 'You know how tight things have been since they cut our budget again. I rang the one and only hotel in Wallaby Creek to see if they had any vacancies and, luckily enough, they did. Seems the proprietor is refusing to house any revellers for the ball after a couple of his rooms were almost wrecked last year. Might I suggest you don't leave any valuable equipment in the car that night after you've retired? OK?'

'Sure thing, boss,' Vivien agreed. Maybe it wouldn't be so bad, she decided philosophically. She'd always wanted to drive out west for a look-see, having never been beyond the Blue Mountains. Not that she secretly hankered for a country lifestyle. Vivien was a Sydney girl. Born and bred. She couldn't see herself giving up the vibrant hustle and bustle of city life for wide-open spaces, dust and flies.

Not only that, but it would give her something to do this weekend, since Earl didn't want her to fly down to visit him. *Once again*, she reminded herself with a jab of dismay.

'Well, off you go, madam,' her boss announced before depression could take hold. 'Grab Irving before he's booked up elsewhere. That man's in high demand.'

'Right.' She smiled, and stood up.

'Phone call for you, Vivien,' the main receptionist called out to her as she passed through the foyer area on her way back to her office. 'I'll switch it back to your desk now. That is where you're heading, isn't it? It's STD, by the way. Your boyfriend.'

Vivien's heart skipped a beat. *Earl*? Ringing her during working hours? That wasn't like him at all...

She hurried along the corridor towards the office she shared with her three fellow *Across Australia* reporters, her heart pounding with sudden nerves.

Somehow she just knew this phone call didn't mean what she so desperately hoped it meant, that Earl wanted to say sorry for the way he'd been behaving, that he was missing her as much as she was missing him. Perhaps he'd finally given up trying to make her suffer for not dropping her career and following him to Melbourne the second he got his promotion and transfer six weeks ago.

Her heart twisted as she recalled the awful argument they'd had when he'd come home that night and made his impossible demand. She'd tried explaining that if she just quit on the spot she'd be committing professional suicide. But he hadn't been prepared to listen, his relentlessly cold logic being that if she loved him she would do what *he* wanted, what was best for *him*. If she wanted to marry him and have his children, then *her* career was irrelevant.

Although he had always shown chauvinistic tendencies, his stubborn selfishness in this matter had startled then infuriated her. She had dug in her heels and stayed in Sydney. Nevertheless, she had still been prepared to compromise, promising to look for a position in Melbourne in the New Year, which had been only three months away. To which idea Earl had sulkily agreed.

To begin with, Vivien had flown to Melbourne every weekend to be with him. These visits, however, had not been a great success, with the old argument inevitably flaring about her throwing in her job and staying with him. After three weeks of these bittersweet reunions, Earl had started finding reasons for her not to come, saying he was busy with one thing and another. Which perhaps he was... But underneath, Vivien believed he'd been exacting a type of revenge on her, being petty in a way he'd never been before.

She swept into the empty office and over to her corner, sending papers flying as she slid on to the corner of her desk and snatched up the receiver.

'Hello?' she said breathlessly.

'Vivien? That is you, isn't it?' Earl drawled in a voice she scarcely recognised.

Taken aback, she was lost for words for a moment. Where on earth had he got that accent from? He sounded like an upper-class snob, yet he was from a working-class background, just like herself.

'Oh—er—yes, it's me,' she finally blurted out.

His laugh had the most peculiarly dry note to it. 'You sound rattled. Have I caught you doing things you shouldn't be doing with all those men you work with?'

Now *that* was just like Earl. Jealous as sin.

She suppressed an unhappy sigh. He didn't have to be jealous. She'd never given him a moment's doubt over her loyalty from the moment she'd fallen in love with him two years before. Hadn't she even gone against her principles and agreed to live with him when he postponed their plans to marry till he was thirty?

'Don't be silly, darling,' she cajoled. 'You know you're the only man for me.'

'Do I? I'm not so sure, Vivien. And *you're* the one who's been silly. *Very* silly.'

Vivien was chilled by the tone in his voice.

'If you'd just come with me when I asked you to,' he continued peevishly, 'none of this would have happened.'

'None of w—what would have happened?' she asked, a sick feeling starting in the pit of her stomach.

'We'd probably be married by now,' he raved on, totally ignoring her tremulous question. 'The chairman of the bank down here likes his executives suitably spoused. You would have been perfect for the role of my wife, Vivien, with your personality and looks. But *no*! You had to have your own career as well, didn't you? You had to be liberated! Well, consider yourself liberated, my sweet. Set free, free of everything, including me.'

Vivien thought she made a choking, gasping sound. But perhaps she didn't.

'Besides, I've met someone else,' he pronounced with a bald cruelty that took her breath away. 'She's the daughter of a well-connected businessman down here. Not as stunning-looking as you, I admit. But then, not many women are,' he added caustically. 'But she's prepared to be a full-time wife, to devote herself entirely to *me*!'

Shock was sending Vivien's head into a spin. She wanted to drop the phone. Run. Anything. This couldn't be happening to her. Earl *couldn't* be telling her he'd found someone else, some woman he was going to *marry*?

Somehow she gathered herself with a strength that was perhaps only illusory. But she clung to it all the same.

'Earl,' she said with a quiet desperation, 'I love you. And I know you love me. Don't do this to us...not...not for the sake of ambition.'

'Ambition?' he scoffed. 'You *dare* talk to me of ambition? You, who put your career ahead of your so-called love for me? Don't make me laugh, sweetheart. Actually, I consider myself lucky to be getting out from under this...*obsession* I had for you. Any man would find it hard to give you up. But I'm cured now. I've kicked the habit. And I have my methadone at hand.' He laughed. 'Name of Amelia.'

Vivien was dimly aware that she was now in danger of cracking up on the spot. The hand that was clutching the receiver to her ear was going cold, shivers reverberating up her arm. She tried to speak, but couldn't.

'I'll be up this Saturday to get the rest of my things,' Earl continued callously. 'I'd like you to be conspicuously absent. Visit your folks or something. Oh, for pity's sake, say something, Vivien! You're beginning to bore me with this frozen silence routine. It's positively childish. You must have known the writing was on the wall once you refused to come with me.'

'I...I would have come,' she said in an emotionally devastated voice, 'if I'd known this would happen. Earl, please...I *love* you——'

'No, you bloody well don't,' he shot back nastily. 'No more than I loved you. I can see now it was only lust. I'm surprised it lasted as long as it did.'

Only lust?

Her face flamed with humiliation and hurt. She couldn't count the number of times sex hadn't been all that good for her. She'd merely pretended. For *his* sake. For his infernal male pride!

'No come-backs?' he jeered. 'Fine. I don't want to argue, either. After all, there's nothing really to argue about. You made your choice, Vivien. Now you can damned well live with it!' And he slammed down the phone.

She stared down at the dead receiver, her mind reeling as the reality of the situation hit her.

Earl was gone from her life.

Not just temporarily.

Forever.

All her plans for the future—shattered.

There would be no marriage to him. No children by him. No nothing.

Tears welled up behind her eyes and she might have buried her face in her hands and sobbed her heart out had not Robert J. Overhill appeared in the doorway of the office at that precise moment. Luckily his sharp eyes didn't go to her pale, shaken face. They zeroed in on her long, shapely legs dangling over the desk corner.

For the first time Vivien understood Bob's vicious attitude towards her. He *did* fancy her, her crime being that she didn't fancy him back.

With a desperate burst of pride she kept the tears at bay. 'Well!' She jumped to her feet and plastered a bright smile on her face. 'I'd better stop this lounging about and get to work. You wouldn't know where Irving might be, would you?'

'Haven't a clue.' Bob shrugged, his narrowed eyes travelling slowly back up her body.

'I'll try the canteen,' she said breezily.

'You do that.'

He remained standing in the narrow doorway so that she had to turn sideways and brush past him to leave the room, her full breasts connecting with his arm.

But she said, 'Excuse me,' airily as though it didn't matter, and hurried up the corridor, hiding the shudder that ran deeply through her. All of a sudden, she hated men. The whole breed. For they were indeed hateful creatures, she decided. Hateful! Incapable of true love. Incapable of caring. All they thought about or wanted was sex.

But then she remembered her father. Her sweet, kind, loving father. And her two older brothers. Both good men with stable, secure marriages and happy wives and families. Even Irving was loyal and true,

**SIMPLY IRRESISTIBLE** 15

and *he* was in the television industry, hardly a hotbed of faithfulness. Was she asking for too much to want that kind of man for herself?

'Oh, Irving!' she called out, spotting the man himself leaving the canteen.

He spun round and smiled at her. 'What's up, Doc?'

'Got a job for you.'

'Thank the lord it's you and not Bob. I've had politicians up to here!' And he drew a line across his throat. 'So where are we off to this time?'

'Ever heard of Wallaby Creek?'

# CHAPTER TWO

The Wallaby Creek hotel was typical of hotels found in bush towns throughout Australia.

It was two-storeyed and quite roomy, sporting a corrugated-iron roof—painted green—and wooden verandas all around, the upper one with iron lacework railings—painted cream. It sat on the inevitable corner, so that any patrons who cared to wander out from their upstairs room on to the adjoining veranda would be guaranteed a splendid view of the main street below and an unimpeded panorama for miles around.

Vivien was standing on this veranda at six on the following Saturday evening, wiping the perspiration from her neck and looking out in awe at the incredible scene still taking shape before her eyes.

When she and Irving had driven into the small, dusty town the previous evening, tired and hot from the day-long trip west, they'd wondered where the ball would be held, since, at first glance, Wallaby Creek consisted of little else but this hotel, a few ancient houses, a general store and two garages.

They'd asked the hotel proprietor, a jolly soul named Bert, if there was a hall they'd missed. He'd given a good belly-laugh and told them no, no hall, then refused to answer their next query as to where the venue for the ball would be.

'Just you wait and see,' he'd chuckled. 'Come tomorrow afternoon, you won't recognise this place.'

He'd been right. In the short space of a few hours, the sleepy hollow of Wallaby Creek had been transformed.

First, heavy-transport vehicles accompanied by utilities filled with men had descended on the place like a plague of locusts, and within a short while a marquee that would have done the Russian circus proud had mushroomed in a nearby paddock. Next came the dance-floor, square slabs of wooden decking that fitted together like giant parquet.

A car park was then marked out with portable fences, its size showing that they were anticipating an exceptionally large turn-out. This expectation was reinforced by the two long lines of porta-loos that stretched out on either side of the marquee, one marked 'Chicks', the other 'Blokes'.

Refreshment vans had rolled into town all day, with everything from meat pies to champagne to kegs of beer. Two enormous barbecues had been set up on either side of the front entrance to the marquee, complete with a multitude of plastic tables and chairs, not to mention plastic glasses and cutlery. Lessons had been learnt, it seemed, from accidents in previous years. Real glass was out!

Vivien had been kept busy all day, interviewing all sorts of people, from the members of the organising committee to the volunteers who helped put the venue together to the people who hoped to make a quick buck out of hot dogs or steak sandwiches or what have you.

She was amazed at the distance some of the men had travelled, though it had been patiently explained to her that Wallaby Creek was fairly central to most of the sheep properties around this section of New

South Wales and country people were used to covering vast distances for their entertainment. Every unmarried jackeroo, rouseabout, stockhand and shearer in a three-hundred-kilometre radius would be in attendance tonight, she was assured, together with a sprinkling of station owners and other assorted B & S Ball fans. Apparently a few carloads of young ladies even drove out from Sydney for such occasions, in search of a man.

If Vivien hadn't been so depressed inside, she might have been caught up in the general air of excited anticipation that seemed to be pervading everyone. But she couldn't even get up enough enthusiasm to start getting ready. Instead, she lingered outside, leaning on the old iron railing, staring at the horizon, which was bathed in the bold reds and golds of an outback sunset.

But she was blind to the raw, rich beauty of the land, her mind back in her flat in Sydney, where at this very moment Earl was probably taking away every single reminder she had of him. When she went back, it would almost be as though he had never existed.

Only he *had* existed, she moaned silently. And would continue to exist in her mind and heart for a long, long time.

Vivien's hands lifted to wipe moisture away from her eyes.

Damn, she thought abruptly. I can't possibly be crying again. There can't be any tears left! Angry with herself, she spun away and strode inside into the hotel room. 'No more,' she muttered, and swept up the towels off the bed for a quick visit to the bathroom. 'No more!'

SIMPLY IRRESISTIBLE 19

And she didn't cry any more. But she still suffered, her heart heavy in her chest at having thought about Earl again, her normally sparkling eyes flat and dull as she went about transforming herself as astonishingly and speedily as Wallaby Creek had been.

By five to seven, the miracle was almost complete. Gone were the pale blue cotton trousers and simple white shirt she'd been wearing all day, replaced by a strapless ball-gown and matching bolero in a deep purple taffeta. Down was her thick black hair, dancing around her shoulders and face in soft, glossy waves. On had gone her night-time make-up, dramatic and bold, putting a high blush of colour across her smooth alabaster cheeks, turning her already striking brown eyes into even darker pools of exotic mystery, emphasising her sensually wide mouth with a coating of shimmering violet gloss.

At last Vivien stood back to give herself a cynical appraisal in the old dressing-table mirror. Now who are you trying to look so sensational for, you fool? And she shook her head at herself in mockery.

Still, the dressy dress was a must, since all patrons of the ball were required to wear formal clothes. And one did look insipid on television at night unless well made up.

There was a rapid knocking on her door. 'Viv? Are you ready?' Irving asked.

'Coming,' she said brusquely, and, slipping her bare feet into high-heeled black sandals, she swept from the room.

By ten the ball was in full swing, the heavy-metal band that had been brought up from Sydney blaring out its strident beat to a packed throng of energetic dancers. Vivien squeezed a path between the heaving, weaving bodies with her microphone and cameraman in tow, doing fleeting interviews as she went, as well as a general commentary that she probably wouldn't use except as a basis for her final voice-over.

Most of the merry-makers were co-operative and tolerant, and when she remarked to one group that some of the young people's 'formal' gear was not of the best quality she'd been laughingly told that 'experienced' B & S Ball attendees always purchased their tuxes and gowns from second-hand clothing establishments.

'Otherwise their good clothes might get ruined!' One young man winked.

'How?' she asked.

They all looked at her as though she'd just descended from Mars.

'In the creek, of course! Don't you city folks have creeks down in Sydney?'

'Er—well . . .' Hard to explain that one didn't go swimming in the Parramatta or St. George's River. Too much pollution. 'We do have the harbour,' she tried.

'Not as good as our creek,' someone said, and they all laughed knowingly.

They were still laughing as she moved on.

'I'm getting hot and tired, Viv,' Irving said shortly before eleven. 'I could do with a bite to eat and a cool drink.'

It was indeed becoming stuffy in the marquee and Vivien herself fancied a breath of fresh air. 'OK. Meet me back here, near the band, at midnight,' she suggested.

'Will do. Here. Give me the mike.' He rolled up the cord, slung it over his shoulder with his camera, and in seconds had disappeared, swallowed up by the throng.

Suddenly, despite being in the middle of a mêlée, Vivien felt incredibly lonely. With a weary sigh she glanced around, waffling over which of the various exits she would make for, and it was as her eyes were skating over the bobbing heads of dancers that she got the shock of her life.

For there was Earl, leaning against one of the tent poles, looking very elegant in a black evening suit, bow-tie and all.

She gasped, her view of him obscured for a moment. But when the intervening couples moved out of the way again she realised it wasn't Earl at all, but a man with a face and hair so similar to Earl's that it was scary.

She couldn't help staring at him, and as she stared his eyes slowly turned, drawn no doubt by her intense scrutiny. And then he was looking right at her.

The breath was punched from her lungs. God, but he was the spitting image of Earl! Facially, at least.

Perhaps she should have looked away, now that he was aware of her regard. But she couldn't seem to. It was as though she were hypnotised by this man's uncanny resemblance to the man who had been her lover for the past two years.

A frown formed on his handsome face as they exchanged stares, an oddly troubled frown. It struck Vivien that perhaps he thought he was getting the come-on and was embarrassed by her none too subtle stare.

But if he was, why didn't he just look away?

Suddenly, he moved—destroying his almost apparition-like quality—his spine straightening, his shoulders squaring inside his black dinner-jacket. His eyes never left her.

He was walking now, moving inexorably towards her, the gyrating crowd parting before him like the Red Sea had for Moses. Closer, he was still incredibly like Earl. The way his thick brown hair swept across his forehead from a side parting. The wide, sensuous mouth. And that damned dimple in the middle of a similarly strong square-cut jaw.

But he was taller and leaner than Earl. And his eyes weren't grey. They were a light ice-blue. They were also compellingly fixed on her as he loomed closer and closer.

Vivien's big brown eyes flicked over his elegant dinner suit. No second-hand rubbish for him, she thought, and swallowed nervously. Jackets didn't fit like that unless they were individually tailored. Of course, he was no callow youth either. He had to be at least thirty.

He stopped right in front of her, a slow and vaguely sardonic smile coming to his face. 'Care to dance?' he asked in a voice like dark chocolate.

'D-dance?' She blinked up at him, thrown by how amazingly similar that lop-sided, lazy smile was to Earl's.

His smile grew wider, thankfully destroying the likeness. 'Yes, dance. You know...two people with arms around each other, moving in unison.'

She blushed under his teasing, which rattled her even more than his looks. Good grief, she *never* blushed, having achieved a measure of fame around the channel for her sophisticated composure, her ability never to be thrown by anything or anyone. Which was perhaps why everyone had been so surprised by the wildly mad exhibition she had made of herself at that Christmas party.

'I...yes...all right,' she answered, her mind in chaos, her heart pounding away in her chest like a jackhammer.

He swept her smoothly into his arms and away on to the dance-floor, and once again there seemed to be miraculous room for him. She felt light as a feather in his arms. 'I don't disco,' he murmured, pulling her to him and pressing soft lips into her hair. 'I like my women close.'

'Oh,' was all she could manage in reply.

*Good lord*, she thought. What am I *doing*? I should have said no. He *had* to have got the wrong idea from my none too subtle staring, not to mention my tongue-tied schoolgirl reaction to his invitation.

Make your apologies and extricate yourself before things get awkward here, she advised herself.

Yet she stayed right where she was and said absolutely nothing, aware of little but the pounding of her heart and the feeling of excitement that was racing through her veins.

Somehow Earl's double invented a dance to the primitive beat of the music, even though it was more a rhythmic swaying than any real movement across the floor. People swirled back around them, shutting them in, making Vivien feel suddenly tight-chested and claustrophic. Someone knocked into them and her partner pulled her even closer, flattening her breasts against the hard wall of his chest.

'Put your arms up around my neck,' he murmured. 'You'll be less of a target that way.'

True, she thought breathlessly. I'll also probably cease to exist as a separate entity, because if I get any closer I'll have become part of *you*!

But she did as he suggested, amazed at herself for her easy acquiescence. The whole situation had a weird, supernatural feel to it, from the man's uncanny likeness to Earl to her out-of-character reactions to him.

Or maybe they were *in* character, she thought dazedly. Maybe her body was simply responding to the same physical chemistry she felt when she was with Earl. Her responses were not really for this man. They were merely for a face, the face of the man she loved.

A moan of dismay punched which sounded more sensual than desolate from her throat and clearly gave her partner even more of the right—or wrong—idea.

'You feel it too, don't you?' he rasped, one of his hands sliding up under her bolero to trace erotic circles over her naked shoulder blades. 'Incredible...'

She tensed in his arms, appalled yet fascinated by her own arousal. She couldn't seem to gather the courage or common sense to pull away, to put a stop to what was happening between them. When he bent his head to kiss her neck, a betraying shiver of pleasure rippled through her. He groaned, opening his mouth to suckle softly at her flesh.

A compulsive wave of desire broke the last of her control and her fingers began to steal up into his silky, thick hair, fingertips pressing into his scalp.

'God...' he muttered against her neck.

The mindless depth of arousal in his voice plus an abrupt appreciation of where they actually were acted like a cold sponge on Vivien, snapping her back to reality.

'Dear heaven,' she cried, and, shuddering with shame, wrenched away from him.

He stared down at her, smouldering blue eyes still glazed with passion.

Her left hand fluttered up to agitatedly touch her neck where his mouth had been. The skin felt hot and wet and rough. There had to be a red mark. 'You shouldn't have done that,' she burst out. 'I...I didn't like it.'

A chill came into his eyes. 'Didn't you?'

'No, of...of course not!' she denied, her demeanour as flustered as his was now composed.

His eyes narrowed, his top lip curling with a type of sardonic contempt. 'So,' he said with a dry laugh, 'you're nothing but a tease. How ironic. How bloody ironic.'

For a moment she stared back up at him, confused by his words. But then she was angry. 'No, I'm *not*!' she retorted, chin lifting defiantly. 'And there's no need to swear!'

But when she went to whirl away his hand shot out to grab her arm, spinning her back into his body. 'Then *why*?' he flung at her in a low, husky voice. 'Why look at me the way you did? Why let me go that far before you stopped me?'

What could she say? I don't know? Maybe it wasn't *you* I was letting do that. Maybe it wasn't *you* I was wanting.

And yet...

She stared into the depths of the eyes, looking for answers, but finding only more confusion. For suddenly Earl was the furthest thing from her mind.

'You...you wouldn't understand,' she muttered.

'Wouldn't I? Try me.' And he gathered her forcefully back into his arms.

She gaped up at him. But before she could voice any bewildered protest he urged her back into their rocking, rolling rhythm, his hold firm, his eyes stubborn. 'Start explaining.'

For a second, her hands pushed at his immutable shoulders. But it was like trying to push a brick wall down with a feather.

'I deserve an explanation,' he said with maddening logic. 'So stop that nonsense and give me one.'

She glared up at him, knowing she should demand he let go of her, should tell him he had no right to use his superior male strength to enforce his will. Yet all she wanted was to close her eyes and melt back into him. It was incredible!

'I don't think I'm asking too much, do you?' he went on, disarming her with a wry but warm smile.

She groaned in defeat, her forehead tipping forwards on to his rock-hard chest. When he actually picked up her arms and put them around his neck, she glanced up at him, then wished she hadn't. He was too overwhelmingly close and too disturbingly attractive to her.

'So tell me,' he murmured. 'Why did you stare at me the way you did?'

Vivien tried to think of a plausible lie, but couldn't. How could she explain something she didn't fully understand herself? With considerable reluctance, she was forced to embrace the part she *could* grasp. 'When I first saw you I thought you were someone else. You... you look a lot like someone I know. *Used* to know,' she amended.

'An old boyfriend?'

'Sort of.'

He pulled back slightly and gave her a penetrating look. 'Would you like to be more specific?'

She sighed. 'Ex-lover, then.'

'How ex is ex? A week? A month? A year?'

'Three days. *No*.' She laughed bitterly. 'Three *weeks*. Maybe even longer. I just didn't know till three days ago.'

He stopped dancing. There was a strange stillness about his body.

'I see,' he finally exhaled, and began to move again. 'What about later?' he resumed casually enough. 'When we started to dance? What's your excuse for that?'

'I can't explain it,' she choked out.

'Neither can I,' he said, the hand on her waist lifting to hold the back of her head with surprising tenderness, forcing her face to nestle under his chin. 'I've never felt anything like it. Yet I don't even know your name.'

'Vivien,' she whispered, her lips dangerously close to his throat.

'Vivien what?'

'Roberts.'

'Mine's Ross. Ross Everton.'

'Are... are you a shearer?' she asked, trying desperately to get their conversation on to safe, neutral territory. Anything to defuse the physical tension still enveloping her.

'I *can* shear. But it's not my main job.'

She pulled her mouth away from his neck and looked up. 'Which is?'

'I manage a sheep station.'

'I would have thought you were an owner.'

He arched one of his eyebrows. 'Why's that?'

'You don't sound like a shearer or a jackeroo.' Which he didn't. He sounded very well educated.

He laughed. 'And what are they supposed to sound like? I'll have you know we had a jackeroo on our place last year who was the son of an English lord.'

'*Our* place? I thought you said you managed.'

'I do. My father's property. For the moment, that is.'

'You sound as if it's only a temporary arrangement.'

A black cloud passed over those piercing blue eyes. 'Dad had a serious stroke last month. The doctors say his chances of having another fatal one are high.'

'Oh. I . . . I'm sorry.'

'It's all right. You couldn't have known.'

There was a short, sharp silence between them.

'So tell me, Vivien Roberts,' he said abruptly. 'What television programme are you representing here tonight? No, don't bother asking. I spotted you earlier doing your stuff. Is it *Country Wide*? The *Investigators*, maybe? As you can see, we country folk can watch any station we like as long as it's the ABC.'

She laughed, and felt her tension lessen. 'Sorry, but I'm from a disgusting commercial station and the show's called *Across Australia*. And if you tell me you've never heard of it I'll be mortified.'

'I've heard of it,' he admitted, 'but never seen it. Do you think I'd forget you, if I had?'

Her stomach flipped over at the intensity he managed to put into what should have been a casual compliment.

'Ross,' she began hesitantly, 'this . . . this attraction between us. It can't go anywhere.'

Again she felt that stilling in his body. 'Why not?'

'It... it wouldn't be fair to you.'

'In what way?'

What could she say? *Because you're not just* like *the man I've loved and lost. You're almost his mirror image. I'd never know if what I felt for you was real or not. Besides, you're from a different world from me, a world I would never fit into or want to fit into.*

'I'm still in love with Earl,' she said, thinking that should answer all arguments.

Ross was irritatingly silent for ages before saying, 'I presume Earl is the man I remind you of, your ex-lover?'

'Yes,' was her reluctant admission.

His laugh sounded odd. 'Even more ironic. Tell me honestly, Vivien, if dear Earl walked back into your life this minute would you take him back?'

'Never!'

'That sounded promisingly bitter. Didn't he love you?'

'I thought he did. Apparently not, however. He's moved to Melbourne and found someone else.'

'I presume you're from Sydney, then?'

'You presume right.'

'And you're going to take your broken heart and enter a convent, is that it?'

Startled, she stared up at him. There was a mocking light in his eyes.

'Very funny,' she bit out.

'Yes, it would be. Somehow I don't think the woman I held in my arms a few minutes back would make a very good nun.'

She might have wrenched herself out of his arms and stalked away at that point if they hadn't been interrupted by a third party, a good-looking young man who tapped Ross on the shoulder with one hand while he held a can of beer in the other. By the look of him, it hadn't been his first drink of the night.

'Well, well, well,' he drawled with a drunken slur. 'I thought you were supposed to be here to watch over me, big brother. But *I've* been watching *you*. What would our dear father think of his God-like first son if I told him you spent this evening so differently from the rest of us mortal men, trying to get into some woman's knickers?'

Vivien gasped, then gasped again when Ross's fist flew out, connecting with his brother's chin. For a second, the young man merely looked shocked, swaying back and forth on his heels. But then his bloodshot eyes rolled back into his head and he tipped backwards, his fall broken by the quick reflexes of the man he'd just insulted.

'Well, don't just stand there, Vivien,' Ross grated out, looking up from where he was bent over his brother, hands hooked under his armpits. 'Pick up his feet and help me get the silly idiot out into some fresh air!'

# CHAPTER THREE

NO ONE seemed particularly concerned as Ross and Vivien carted the unconscious young man through the crowd towards the front exit.

'Too much to drink, eh?' was the only comment they received.

Vivien began to think one could murder someone here tonight and get away with it, by saying the corpse was 'dead' drunk as it was carried off for disposal.'

'For a lightly built young man, he's darned heavy,' she complained once they made it out of the marquee and tried to prop him up in one of the plastic chairs. Vivien frowned as his head flopped forwards on to his chest. 'Do you think he'll be all right, Ross? Perhaps you hit him too hard.'

Ross made a scowling sound. 'He's lucky I didn't break his damned neck!'

'Why? He was only telling the truth.'

He flashed her a dry look. 'You do have a poor opinion of men at the moment, don't you? Look, if it was just casual sex I was after, I could have my pick of a hundred willing females here tonight. I certainly wouldn't attempt to seduce a sophisticated city broad who probably knows more counter-moves than a chess champion. Here, you pat his cheek while I get him a glass of water. But don't bat those long eyelashes at him if he comes round,' he added sarcastically over his shoulder as he strode off. 'He might get the idea you fancy him!'

31

She squirmed inside, a guilty blush warming her cheeks. But she busied herself doing as he'd asked, trying to awaken the slumped body in the chair. Tapping cheeks didn't work so she started rubbing hands. His head jerked back and two bloodshot blue eyes fluttered open just as Ross returned with a couple of glasses in his hands.

'Wha—what hit me?' his brother groaned, then clutched at his chin.

'What in hell do you think?' Ross snapped. 'Here, drink this water and sober up a bit.' He turned to face Vivien. 'This is for you,' he said, and pressed a fluted plastic glass of champagne into her hands. 'Your reward for helping me with lunkhead, here. I didn't think water would be your style.'

'Oh, but I... no, really, I...' She tried to give him back the glass, which brought a scoff of disbelief from his lips. 'Good God, what do you think this is, a ploy to get you drunk so that I can have my wicked way with you? Hell, honey, you have got tickets on yourself.'

Vivien stiffened with instant pique. She lifted the champagne and downed it all in one swallow, rebelliously enjoying every bubbly drop, at the same time reminding herself ruefully not to touch another single mouthful that night. She plonked the empty glass down on the littered table near by and looked Ross straight in the eye. 'Even if I were plastered,' she stated boldly, 'I wouldn't let you touch me!'

The young man sprawled in the plastic chair gave a guffaw of laughter. 'Geez, looks like the legendary Ross Everton must have lost his touch! Isn't she falling down on her knees, begging for your body, like every girl you give the eye to?'

Ross swung on his brother as though he was about to hit him again. 'Gavin, I'm *warning* you!'

'Warning me about what, big brother? What more could you possibly do to me? You've got it all now, everything I've ever wanted.' He struggled to his feet and managed to put a determined look on to his weakly handsome face. 'Let me warn *you*, brother, dear,' he blustered. 'Watch your back, because one day it's going to be *me* taking something that's *yours*! You mark my words.' And he lurched off back into the marquee, colliding with several people on the way.

'Will he be all right?' Vivien asked, worried.

'Tonight, you mean? I hope so. God knows why he has to get so damned drunk on these occasions. When he drinks to excess, he goes crazy.'

He's not the only one, Vivien thought, eyeing the empty champagne glass with a degree of concern. *I* don't even need to go to excess. My troubles start around glass number three.

She looked back at Ross, who was rubbing his temple with an agitated forefinger. She forgot about being annoyed with his earlier remarks, seeing only a human being weighed down with problems. And her heart went out to him.

But along with the sympathy she felt a certain amount of curiosity. Was his brother being sarcastic when he'd referred to him as legendary? And legendary in what way, for goodness' sake? His sexual prowess? Vivien's gaze skated over Ross's macho build. He was certainly virile-looking enough to be a womaniser.

There were other questions too teasing at her female curiosity. 'What did Gavin mean,' she asked in the end, 'when he said you've got everything he ever wanted?'

Ross shrugged. 'Who knows? The management of the property, maybe. Or Dad's good opinion. He thinks Gavin's an irresponsible fool. Though Gavin can only blame himself if Dad thinks that. He keeps acting like one. Last year, at this ball, he drove the utility into the creek and nearly drowned. You'd think by twenty-five he'd have started to grow up.'

'Twenty-*five*? He doesn't seem that old.'

'He *looks* his age. He just doesn't act it.'

'Is that why you came along tonight? To see he didn't do it again?'

He nodded. 'I don't think Dad needs any more stress right now.'

Vivien was impressed with his warm concern for his father. 'And your mother?' she queried. 'How's she coping with your father's stroke?' One of Vivien's uncles had had a stroke a couple of years previously and her aunt had almost had a nervous breakdown coping with his agonisingly slow recuperation.

'Mum's dead,' came the brusque reply. 'There's just Dad, Gavin and me.'

'Oh...'

'Yes, I know,' he muttered, and frowned in the direction of the marquee. 'You're sorry and I'm sorry. More than you'll ever know.' His head snapped back to give her a long, thoughtful look.

She squirmed under his intense gaze, especially when his eyes dropped to inspect her considerable cleavage, which the bolero wasn't designed to hide.

'Well,' he sighed at last, eyes lifting back to her face, 'I'd better go and check up on Gavin before he picks a fight with someone else, someone who won't know to pull his punches. Goodbye, Vivien Roberts. Time for you to go back to your world and me to mine.'

He went to move away, but couldn't seem to drag his eyes from her. 'Hell, but you're one beautiful woman. A man would have to be mad to get mixed up with you anyway. Still, I'd like to have a little more to remember than a mere dance!'

Before she realised what he had in mind, he pulled her into his arms and kissed her, his mouth grinding down on hers, his teeth hard. Only for the briefest second did his lips force hers apart, his tongue plunging forward with a single impassioned thrust before he tore his mouth away. Without looking at her again, he spun round and strode off, back into the marquee.

She stared after him, the back of her hand against her mouth. She wasn't at all aware of Irving coming to stand beside her, not till he spoke.

'Hey, Viv, what was that all about? Who *was* that guy?'

Vivien blinked and turned to focus dazedly on her colleague. 'What did you say, Irving?'

He frowned at her. 'Get with it, Viv. It's not like you to go round kissing strange blokes then looking as if you're on cloud nine. Aren't you supposed to be living with some chap back in Sydney? You're not getting swept up with the atmosphere of this Roman orgy, are you?'

She gathered herself with a bitter laugh. 'Not likely. And I'm not living with anyone any more, Irving. He tossed me over for someone else.'

Irving looked surprised. 'What is he, a flaming idiot?'

Vivien's smile was wry. 'That's sweet of you, Irving. But no, Earl's not an idiot. He's a banker.'

Since Irving didn't socialise at the channel, he had never actually met Earl. Vivien only knew as much about Irving as she did because they had worked together before and he was quite a chatterer on the job.

Irving chuckled. 'Well, a banker's not much different from an idiot, judging by the state of the economy. You're probably well rid of him. But that doesn't mean you should encourage any of the males here tonight, sweetheart. They're all tanked up and ready to fly, yet most of them don't have a flight plan. It's gung-ho and away they go! You should see them out behind the marquee.' He rolled his eyes expressively. 'No. Come to think of it, *don't* go and see. Not unless you want to research a programme on the more adventurous positions from the *Kama Sutra*!'

Vivien was astonished. 'That bad, is it? I thought everything was fairly low-key, by city standards.'

'Gracious, girl! Where have you been this last half-hour? Things are really hotting up around here.'

'*Really*?' She wasn't sure whether to believe him or not. Irving's sense of humour included exaggeration.

He nodded sagely. 'Really. The only safe place now is *inside* the marquee, but, judging by the exodus to the nether regions down by the infamous creek, that'll be empty soon except for the band. Which reminds me—you haven't interviewed them yet. Maybe you could do that during their next break.'

'Good idea.'

Vivien, re-entering the marquee, doubted that it would empty as Irving predicted, for there was still a huge crowd of fans standing around the band, clapping and singing, as well as dozens of couples dancing. She and Irving took up positions behind the bandstand to wait for the music to stop.

It didn't seem in a hurry to, one number following another. Vivien spotted Ross's tall head once, very briefly, and the sighting agitated her. She didn't want to think about him any more. She certainly didn't want to think about that disturbing kiss. It had sent sensations down to her toes that not even the longest, most sensuous kiss of Earl's could do, which was all very confusing.

Don't think about either of them, she kept telling herself. It's crazy. Futile. *Stupid*!

But to no avail. She couldn't seem to stop. She especially couldn't get her mind off Ross. He intrigued her, whether she wanted him to or not!

'Another glass of champagne?' a low male voice suddenly whispered in her ear.

She jumped and spun round, knocking an arm in the process and spilling some of the champagne Ross was holding.

'Oh, dear, I'm so sorry!' she gasped.

'So am I,' he said, and smiled with apologetic sincerity at her. 'I shouldn't have kissed you like that. Forgive me?'

She looked up into his quite beautiful blue eyes and felt a real churning in her stomach. It threw her into even more confusion.

'Oh, for Pete's sake, forgive him,' Irving drawled from beside her. 'And give me that damned mike. This band looks as if it's going to keep playing till the year 2000. I think I'll go off and take some sneaky bits down at the creek, all by myself. You go and do some flying, Viv. You deserve it if you've been banking all this time.'

'What did he mean by that?' Ross asked once he'd moved off.

'A private joke,' Vivien said, and struggled to smother a mad chuckle. Not since Earl's ghastly phone call had she felt like laughing about their breakup. And in truth, her perverse humour didn't last for long. Thinking about Earl only served to remind her that what she was feeling for Ross couldn't be real. It was an aberration. A cruel joke of nature.

'Have I said something wrong, Vivien? You look...distressed, all of a sudden.'

She gazed searchingly up into his handsome face, clinging to the various differences from Earl. But his features began to blur together and it was a few seconds before she realised tears had swum into her eyes.

'Here, drink this,' Ross urged, and pressed the plastic glass into her hands. 'It'll make you feel better.'

She hesitated, blinking madly till she had control of herself, all the while staring down into the glass, which was about three-quarters full. Perhaps it *would* make her feel better. Less uptight. Less wretched. There was no real danger. This drink wouldn't even bring her up to her two-glass limit.

'To absent bastards,' she toasted, holding the glass up briefly before quaffing the champagne down. 'Now, where's the fireplace?' she said, putting a forced smile on her face.

'*Fireplace*?'

'To smash the glass into. Oh, I can't,' she sighed, examining the glass in mock disappointment. 'It's plastic.' She looked up and flashed Ross what she thought was her most winning smile. Little did she know how brittle it looked, and how heartbreakingly vulnerable were her eyes.

'So is your Earl,' he murmured, 'if he let a girl like you get away.'

Vivien's whole throat contracted as an instant lump claimed it. 'I . . . I wish you wouldn't say things like that.'

'Why? Don't you believe me?' he asked gently.

'Does anyone believe in their own worth after rejection?'

'I should hope so.'

She gave him a bitter look. 'Then you haven't ever been rejected, Ross Everton. Perhaps if you had, you'd know how I feel. And how your brother feels.'

Vivien saw she had struck a nerve with her statement, and regretted it immediately. Ross might not be a saint, but she couldn't see him deliberately hurting his younger brother. Gavin was indeed a fool, trying to blame someone else for the consequences of his own stupid and irresponsible behaviour.

Before she could formulate an apology, Ross spoke.

'Gavin's passed out in the back of his station wagon. From past experience, he'll sleep till morning. Which leaves me free to enjoy the rest of the evening. I thought that perhaps you might . . .' He hesitated, his eyes searching hers as though trying to gauge her reaction in advance.

'Might what?' she probed, heart fluttering.

'Go for a walk with me.'

'W—where?' she asked, feeling a jab of real alarm. Not so much at his invitation, but at the funny tingling feeling that was spreading over her skin. And now she detected a slight muzziness in her head.

She frowned down at the empty glass in her hands. Perhaps the champagne had been a particularly potent brew... Or maybe on her empty stomach the alcohol had gone to her head, almost as if it had been shot straight into her veins.

Ross shrugged. 'Not many places to go. Down towards the creek, I suppose. It's a couple of hundred yards beyond the back of the marquee.'

'Irving said I wasn't to go down there,' she said with a dry laugh, though inwardly frowning at how hot she felt all of a sudden. Her palms were clammy, too.

There was no doubt about it. The alcohol had hit her system hard. A walk in some fresh air would probably be the quickest way to sober her up, but she wasn't ignorant of the dangers such a walk presented.

She lifted firm eyes. 'Just a walk, Ross?'

He settled equally firm eyes back on her. 'I'm not about to make promises I won't keep. You're a very lovely and desirable woman, Vivien. I'm likely to try kissing you again, and I won't be in such a hurry this time.'

His eyes dropped to her mouth and she gasped, stunned by the shock of desire that charged through her.

Don't go with him, common sense warned.

Before she could open her mouth to decline he took her free hand quite forcibly and started pulling her behind the bandstand. 'There's a flap in the tent we can squeeze through back here,' he urged. 'We'll go through the car park and down to the creek, but well away from the other carousers.'

Vivien quickly found herself outside, any further argument dying on her lips when the fresh air hit her flushed face. She breathed in deeply, sighing with relief as her head started to clear. 'Oh, that *is* better.'

'I was certainly getting stuffy in there,' Ross agreed. 'It's a warm night.'

'Is it ever anything else but warm in this neck of the woods?' She laughed.

'Too right it is. Some nights it's positively freezing. Come on. It'll be very pleasant down by the creek.' He took her hand again, which brought a sharp look from Vivien.

He smiled at her warning glare and quite deliberately lifted her hand to his mouth, kissing each fingertip before turning her hand over and pressing her palm to his mouth. Her eyes widened when his lips opened and she felt his tongue start tracing erotic circles over her skin.

One small part of her brain kept telling her to yank her hand away. The rest was dazed into compliance with the sheer sensual pleasure of it all.

'You... you shouldn't be doing that,' she husked at last.

He lifted his mouth away, but kept her hand firmly in his grasp. 'Why?' Dragging her to him, he dropped her hand to cup her face, all the while staring down into her startled brown eyes. 'You're a free agent, aren't you? Why shouldn't I kiss you? Why shouldn't you kiss me?'

'Because...'

His mouth was coming closer to hers and her heart was going mad.

'Because——' she tried again.

'Because nothing,' he growled, and claimed her parted lips, his arms sweeping round her back in an embrace as confining as a strait-jacket.

When he released her a couple of minutes later, Vivien was in a state of shock. When he put his arm around her shoulder and started leading her through the car park in the direction of the creek, she was still not capable of speech.

Had Earl been able to arouse her so completely and totally with just a kiss? she was thinking dazedly. She didn't think so. When he'd made love to her, most of the time her desire had just been reaching a suitable pitch as he was finishing. Yet here... tonight... with Ross...

Perhaps she *was* tipsier than she realised. Alcohol did have a way of blasting her inhibitions to pieces.

'Are you always this silent when a man kisses you?' Ross murmured into her ear. He stopped then and turned to press her up against one of the parked cars, taking her mouth once more in another devastating kiss. She was struggling for air by the time he let her go, her heart going at fifty to the dozen. She was also blisteringly aware of Ross's arousal pressing against her. With great difficulty she ignored the excitement his desire inflamed in her, concentrating instead on the implication of what she was doing.

Truly, she could not let this continue. It wasn't fair to him. And, quite frankly, not to herself. She had never felt such desire, such excitement. In a minute or two, she wouldn't be able to stop even if she wanted to.

'Ross,' she said shakily as she tried to push him away, 'we have to stop this. We're both getting....excited, and I...I don't go in for one-night stands.'

'Neither do I,' he grated, stubbornly refusing to let her go.

'Ross, try to be sensible,' she argued, her stomach fluttering wildly. 'You're country. I'm city. After tonight we won't ever see each other again. I'm very attracted to you, but...' She shook her head, and carefully omitted to add anything about his physical resemblance to her ex-lover.

'Those problems are not insurmountable,' he said. 'Vivien, this doesn't have to stop at tonight. I often come down to Sydney to visit Dad in hospital and——'

She placed three fingers across his mouth and shook her head again, her eyes truly regretful. 'No, Ross. It won't work. Believe me when I tell you that. And please,' she groaned when he took her hand and started kissing it again, 'don't keep trying to seduce me. I... I'm only human and you're a very sexy man. But I don't really want you.'

He stopped kissing her palm then, lifting his head to peer down at her with thoughtful eyes. 'I don't think you know what you want, Vivien,' he said tautly.

'I know I don't want to act cheaply,' she countered, cheeks flaming under his reproving gaze.

His smile was odd as he dropped her hand. 'A woman like you would never be cheap.'

'Are you being sarcastic?' she flared.

He seemed genuinely taken aback. 'Not at all.'

'Oh... I thought——'

'You think too much,' he said softly, laying such a gentle hand against her cheek that she almost burst into tears.

She swallowed the lump in her throat and lifted a proud chin. 'Better to think tonight than to wake up pregnant in the morning.'

His surprised, 'You're not on the Pill?' brought an instant flush. For of course she was. Earl had adamantly refused to take responsibility for contraception right from the start of their affair, claiming it was in *her* interests that she took charge of such matters. *She* would be the one left with an unwanted baby. Vivien could see now that it was just another example of Earl's selfishness.

'Actually, yes, I am,' she admitted. 'But there are *other* concerns besides pregnancy these days.'

'Not with me there aren't,' he bit out.

She viewed this statement with some cynicism. 'Really?' Her eyes flicked over his very male and very attractive body. 'I wouldn't have taken you for the celibate type, Ross.' His brother had implied just the opposite, Vivien remembered ruefully.

'One doesn't have to be celibate to be careful.'

'And would you have been careful tonight if I'd given you the go-ahead?' she challenged.

A slash of red burnt a guilty path across his cheeks. 'This was different,' he muttered, and lifted both hands to rake agitatedly through his hair.

Her laugh was scornful. 'I don't see how.'

His blue eyes glittered dangerously as they swung back to her. 'Then you're a fool, Vivien Roberts. A damned fool!'

For a second, she thought he was going to grab her and kiss her again. But he didn't. Instead, his mouth creased back into the strangest smile. It was both bitter and self-mocking. 'Look, let's walk, shall we? That's what you obviously came out here for. And don't worry your pretty little head. I won't lay a single finger on you unless I get a gold-edged invitation.'

## SIMPLY IRRESISTIBLE 45

He set off at a solid pace through the rows of cars, Vivien trailing disconsolately behind him. For she knew in the deepest dungeons of her mind, in the place reserved for unmentionable truths, that she didn't want Ross to lay a *single* finger on her. She wanted *all* his fingers, and *both* his hands. She wanted every wonderfully virile part of him.

## CHAPTER FOUR

'CAN you slow down a bit?' she complained when the distance between them became ridiculous.

Ross had long left the car park and was almost at the tree-lined creek, while she was still halfway across the intervening paddock. If she'd tried to keep up with him she'd probably have fallen down one of the rabbit holes hidden in the grass. She'd already tripped a few times over rocks and logs and the like. Lord knew what her high heels looked like by now.

He stopped abruptly and threw a black look over his shoulder. Moonlight slanted across the angles of his face and she caught her breath as, for the first time, she saw little resemblance to Earl. His features suddenly looked leaner, harder, stronger. Yet they still did the most disturbing things to her stomach.

She slowed to a crawl as she approached, her eyes searching the ice-blue of his, trying to make sense of what she kept feeling for this man, even now, when he no longer reminded her so much of Earl. She couldn't even cling to the belief that she was tipsy, for the brisk walk had totally cleared her head.

His eyes changed as she stared up at him, at first to bewilderment, then to a wary watchfulness, and finally to one of intuitive speculation. They narrowed as they raked over her, his scrutiny becoming explicitly sexual as it lingered on specific areas of her body.

A wave of sheer sensual weakness washed through Vivien and she swayed towards him. 'Ross, I... I——'

He didn't wait for the gilt-edged invitation. He simply read her body language and scooped her hard against him, kissing her till she was totally breathless. 'God, I want you,' he rasped against her softly swollen mouth. 'I'll go mad if I don't have you. Don't say no...'

She said absolutely nothing as he lifted her up into his arms, carrying her with huge strides to the creek bank, where he lowered her on to the soft grass under a weeping willow. But her eyes were wide, her mind in chaos, her heart beating frantically in her chest.

'I won't ever hurt you, Vivien,' he whispered soothingly, and lay down beside her, bending over to kiss her, softly now, almost reverently.

Dimly she heard the sounds of distant revellers, their shouting and laughter. But even that receded as Ross's hand found her breast.

'You're so beautiful,' he muttered, and, pushing back the taffeta, he bent his mouth to the hardened peak.

Vivien closed her eyes and held his head at her breast, trying to take in the intensity of feeling that was welling up inside her. Briefly she remembered all that had happened to her over the last few days, and for a second she felt overwhelmed with guilt. She wasn't in love with Ross, couldn't possibly be. No more than he could be in love with her.

A tortured whimper broke from her lips.

'What's the matter, sweetheart?' Ross said gently, and returned to sip at her mouth. 'Tell me...'

'Oh, Ross,' she cried, her eyes fluttering open, raw pain in their depths. But as they gazed into his brilliant blue eyes, which were glittering above her with the most incredible passion in their depths, the most seductive yearning, she melted. He wanted her. He *really* wanted her. Not like Earl. Earl had never *really* wanted her.

An obsession. That's what he'd called his feelings for her. An obsession... An unhealthy, an unwanted need, one to be fought against, to be got over like something nasty and repulsive.

What she saw in Ross's eyes wasn't anything like that. It was normal and natural and quite beautiful.

She trembled as she clasped him close. 'Say that you love me,' she whispered. 'That's all I ask.'

He lifted his head to stare down at her, blue eyes startled.

'Oh, you don't have to mean it,' she cried, and clung to him. 'Just say it!'

A darkly troubled frown gathered on his brow and for a long, long moment he just looked at her. But then his hands came up to cradle her face and he gazed at her with such tenderness that she felt totally shattered. 'I love you, Vivien. I really, truly love you...'

She shuddered her despair at demanding such a pretence, but could no more deny the need to hear them than the need Ross was evoking within her woman's body.

'Show me,' she groaned. 'Make me forget everything but here... and now...'

At the first slightly vague moments of consciousness, Vivien was aware of nothing but a very fuzzy head and a throat as dry as the Simpson Desert. Her eyes blinked open to glance around her hotel room, and straight away she remembered.

With chest immediately constricted, she rolled over and stared at Ross beside her, flat on his back, sound asleep, his naked chest rising and falling in the deep and even breathing of the exhausted.

Rounded eyes went from him to the floor beside the bed, where her beautiful taffeta dress was lying in a sodden heap. Her black lace panties were still hanging from the arm-rest of the chair in the corner where Ross had carelessly tossed them. Her bolero and shoes, she recalled, were still down beside the creek.

Oh, my God, she moaned silently, the night before rushing back in Technicolor. How could I have behaved so... so outrageously? To have let Ross make love to me on the river-bank was bad enough. But what about later?

Her face flamed as guilt and shame consumed her.

She should never have allowed him to talk her into going skinny-dipping in the moonlit creek afterwards. Naked, he was even more insidiously attractive than he'd been in his dashing dinner suit, his body all brown and lean and hard.

Vivien had been fascinated by the feel of his well-honed muscles. She'd touched him innocently enough at first, holding on to his shoulders to stop herself from tiring as she trod water in the deep. But her hands hadn't stayed on his shoulders for long. They had begun to wander. Once she had started exploring his body, one thing had quickly led to another and, before she knew it, Ross was urging her into the shallows, where he'd taken her again right then and there in the water.

Afterwards, he had carried her limp body back on to the bank where he'd dressed her as best he could, then carried her back to the hotel. Vivien could still remember the look on the hotel proprietor's face when Ross had carried her past his desk and up the stairs.

By this time her conscience had begun to raise its damning head, but Ross managed to ram it back down with more drugging kisses in her room, more knowing caresses. Before she knew it, he was undressing her again and urging her to further amazing new heights of sensuality.

Vivien blushed furiously to think of her abandoned response to his lovemaking.

*I have to get out of here. Fast. I couldn't possibly face him. I'd die! God, I even made him say he* loved *me!*

She cringed in horror, then even more so as she recalled how after the last time here on the bed she'd actually wept. With the sheer intensity of her pleasure, not distress. Ross's lovemaking had seemed to possess not just her body but her very soul, taking her to a level of emotional and physical satisfaction she had never known before.

At least...that was how it had *seemed* at the time...

Looking back now, Vivien realised it couldn't *possibly* have been as marvellous an experience as she kept imagining. Certainly not in any emotional sense. Ross was simply a very skilled lover, knowing just what buttons to push, what words to say to make a woman melt. After all, she'd only asked him to say he loved her once, but he'd told her over and over. There were times when a more naïve woman might have believed he really *did* love her—he sounded and looked so sincere!

She darted a quick glance over at his face, at his softly parted lips. And shuddered. There wasn't a single inch of her flesh that those lips hadn't passed over at some time during the night.

Once again, she felt heat invade her face. Not to mention other parts of her body.

Thank God the bathroom is down the hall, Vivien thought shakily. I'll get my things together and slip out of this room and be gone before he opens a single one of those incredible blue eyes of his. For if I wait, I'm not sure what might happen...

A few minutes later she was knocking on Irving's door. He looked decidedly bleary as he opened it wearing nothing but striped boxer shorts.

'Viv?' He yawned. 'What are you doing up? I thought you'd be out of it for hours.' He gave her a slow, sly grin. 'Bert informed me that you were escorted back to your room at some ungodly hour by someone he called the "legendary Ross Everton". I presume he was the handsome hunk you were with earlier in the night. Did he—er—cure you of the banker?'

Vivien coloured fiercely, though her whirling mind was puzzling again over that word 'legendary'. Legendary in what way? Her colour increased when she realised it probably meant Ross's reputation with women. No doubt she had just spent the night with a very well-known local stud. Why, even his own brother had suggested Ross was a real ladies' man, with an infallible success rate.

Squashing down a mad mixture of dismay and mortification, Vivien gave Irving one of her most quelling 'shut-up-and-listen' looks. 'I need to be out of here five minutes ago, Irving. Do you think you can get a rustle on?'

'What's the emergency?'

'Shall we just say I don't want to see a certain "legendary" person when he finally wakes up?'

Irving pursed his lips and nodded slowly. 'Mornings after can be a tad sticky.'

'I would have used another word, like *humiliating*! You and I know this is not like me at all, Irving. I'm quietly appalled at myself.'

'You're only human, love. Don't be too hard on yourself. We all let our hair down occasionally.'

'Yes, well, I'd appreciate it if this particular hair-letting-down didn't get around the channel. Not all my colleagues are as good a friend as you, Irving.'

'Mum's the word.'

'Thanks. Look, I'll fix up the hotel bill and meet you at the car as soon as possible.'

'I'll be there before you are.'

Irving dropped Vivien outside her block of flats at seven that evening. She carried her overnight bag wearily up the two flights of stairs, where she inserted the key into the door numbered nine. She pushed the door open and walked in, switching on the light and kicking the door shut behind her in one movement.

Her mouth gaped open as she looked around the living-room in stunned disbelief. Because it was empty!

Well, not exactly empty. The phone was sitting on the carpet against the far wall, and three drooping pot plants huddled in a corner. Gone were the lounge and dining suites, the cocktail cabinet, the coffee-table, the television, the sound system and the oak sideboard, along with everything that had been on or in them. The walls were bare too, pale rectangles showing where various paintings had been hanging.

Vivien dropped the overnight bag at her feet and walked numbly into the kitchen. A dazed search revealed that she was still the proud owner of some odd pieces of chipped crockery and some assorted cutlery. The toaster was the only appliance still in residence, probably because it had been a second-hand one, given to them by her mother. The fridge was there too. But it had come with the flat. Vivien approached the two bedrooms with a growing sense of despair.

The main bedroom was starkly empty, except for her side of the built-in wardrobes. The guest bedroom shocked her in reverse, because it actually contained a single bed complete with linen.

'Oh, thanks a lot, Earl,' she muttered before slumping down on the side of the bed and dissolving into tears.

Five minutes later she was striding back into the living-room and angrily snatching the phone up from the floor. But then she hesitated, and finally dropped the receiver back down into its cradle.

There was no point in ringing Earl. Absolutely no point. For she hadn't paid for a single one of the items he'd taken from their flat. When she'd moved in, Earl, the financial wizard, had suggested *she* pay for the food each week while *he* paid for any other goods they needed. Over the eighteen months he'd bought quite a bit, but she'd also forked out a lot of cash on entertaining Earl's business acquaintances. He always liked the best in food and wine.

Now she wondered with increasing bitterness if he'd known all along how their affair would end and had arranged things so that he'd finish up with all the material possessions she'd assumed they co-owned.

A fair-minded person would have split everything fifty-fifty. To do what Earl had done was not only cruel. It also underlined that all he'd thrown at her over the telephone was true. He had never loved her. He'd simply used her. She'd been his housekeeper and his whore! And he'd got them both cheap!

But then she *was* cheap, wasn't she? she berated herself savagely. Only cheap women went to bed with a man within an hour or two of meeting him, without any real thought of his feelings, without caring where it led, without...

'Oh, my God!' she gasped aloud, and, with the adrenalin of a sudden shock shooting through her body, Vivien raced over to where she had dropped her bag. She reefed open the zip. But her fumbling fingers couldn't find what she was looking for. Yet they had to be here. They *had* to!

A frantic glance at her watch told her it was almost eight, thirteen hours after she usually took her pill. In the end she tipped the whole contents of the bag out on to the floor and they were were!

Snaffling them up, she pressed Sunday's pill through the foil and swallowed it. But all the while her doctor's warnings went round and round in her mind.

'This is a very low-dosage pill, Vivien, and *must* be taken within the same hourly span each day. To deviate by too long could be disastrous.'

The enormity of this particular disaster did not escape Vivien. She sank down into a sitting position on the carpet and hugged herself around the knees, rocking backwards and forwards in pained distress.

'Oh, no,' she wailed. 'Please, God...not that...I couldn't bear it...'

Vivien might have given herself up to total despair at that moment if the phone hadn't rung just then, forcing her to pull herself together.

'Yes?' she answered, emotion making her voice tight and angry. If it was Earl ringing he was going to be very, very sorry he had.

'Vivien? Is there something wrong?'

Vivien closed her eyes tight. Her mother... Her loving but very intuitive mother.

She gathered every resource she had. 'No, Mum. Everything's fine.'

'Are you sure?'

'Yes. Positive.' Smiles in her voice.

'I hope so.' Wariness in her mother's.

'What were you ringing up about, Mum?'

Vivien's mother was never one to ring for idle gossip. There was always a specific reason behind the call.

'Well, next Sunday week's your father's birthday, as you know, and I was planning a family dinner for him, and I was hoping you would come this time, now that Earl's in Melbourne. That man never seems to like you going to family gatherings,' her soft-hearted mother finished as accusingly as she could manage.

'Of course I'll be there,' she reassured, ignoring the gibe about Earl. Not that it wasn't true, come to think of it. Earl had never wanted to share her with her family.

She sighed. Perhaps in a fortnight's time she'd feel up to telling her mother about their breakup. Though, of course, in a fortnight's time she'd probably also be on the verge of a nervous breakdown, worrying if she was pregnant or not. God, what was to become of her?

'Do you want me to bring anything beside a present?' she asked. 'Some wine, maybe?'

'Only your sweet self, darling.'

The 'darling' almost did it. Tears swam into Vivien's eyes and her chin began to quiver. 'Oh, goodness, there's someone at the door, Mum. Must go. See you Sunday week about noon, OK?'

She just managed to hang up before she collapsed into a screaming heap on the floor, crying her eyes out.

# CHAPTER FIVE

'I'M SORRY, Viv,' Mervyn said without any real apology in his voice. 'But that's the way it is. *Across Australia* has received another cut in budget and I have to trim staff. I've decided to do it on a last-on, first-to-go basis.'

'I see,' was Vivien's controlled reply. She knew there was no point in mentioning that fan mail suggested she was one of the show's most popular reporters. Mervyn was a man's man. He also never went back on a decision, once he'd made it.

'There's nothing else going at the channel?' she asked, trying to maintain a civil politeness in the face of her bitter disappointment. 'No empty slots anywhere?'

'I'm sorry, Viv,' he said once more. 'But you know how things are...'

What could she possibly say? If the quality of her work had not swayed him then no other argument would. Besides, she had too much pride to beg.

'Personnel has already made up your cheque,' he went on matter-of-factly when she remained stubbornly silent. 'You can pick it up at Reception.'

Now Vivien *was* shocked. Shocked and hurt. She propelled herself up from the chair on to shaky legs. 'But I'm supposed to get a month's notice,' she argued. 'My contract states that——'

'Your contract also states,' Mervyn overrode curtly, 'that you can receive a month's extra pay in lieu of notice. That's what we've decided to do in your case. For security reasons,' he finished brusquely.

She sucked in a startled breath. 'What on earth does that mean? What security reasons?'

'Come, now, Viv, it wouldn't be the first time that a disgruntled employee worked out their time here, all the while relaying our ideas to our opposition.'

'But...but you *know* I wouldn't do any such thing!'

His shrug was indifferent, his eyes hard and uncompromising. 'I don't make the policies around here, Viv. I only enforce them. If I hear of anything going I'll let you know.' With that, he extended a cold hand.

Vivien took it limply, turning on stunned legs before walking shakily from the room. This isn't happening to me, she told herself over and over. I'm in some sort of horrible nightmare.

In the space of a few short days, she had lost Earl, and now her job...

'Viv?' the receptionist asked after she'd been standing in front of the desk staring into space for quite some time. 'Are you all right?'

Vivien composed herself with great difficulty, covering her inner turmoil with a bland smile. 'Just wool-gathering. I was told there would be a letter for me here...'

Vivien walked around the flat in a daze. She still couldn't believe what had happened back at the channel. When she'd arrived at work that morning, she'd thought Mervyn had wanted to talk to her to see how the segment at Wallaby Creek had gone over the weekend. Instead, she'd been summarily retrenched.

How ironic, she thought with rising bitterness. She had virtually lost Earl because of that job. And now... the job was no more.

Tears threatened. But she blinked them away. She was fed up with crying, and totally fed up with life! What had she ever done to deserve to be dumped like that—first by the man she loved, then by an employer to whom she had given nothing but her best? It was unfair and unjust and downright unAustralian!

Well, I'll just have to get another job, she realised with a resurgence of spirit. A *better* job!

Such as what? the voice of grim logic piped up. All the channels are laying off people right, left and centre. Unemployment's at a record high.

'I'll find something,' she determined out loud, and marched into the kitchen, where she put on the kettle to make herself some coffee.

And what if you're pregnant? another little voice inserted quietly.

Vivien's stomach tightened.

'I can't be,' she whispered despairingly. 'That would be too much. Simply too much. Dear God, please don't do that to me as well. *Please...*'

Vivien was just reaching for a cup and saucer when the front doorbell rang. Frowning, she clattered the crockery on to the kitchen counter and glanced at her watch. 'Now who on earth could that be at four fifty-three on a Monday afternoon?' she muttered.

The bell ran again. Quite insistently.

'All right, all right, I'm coming!'

Vivien felt a vague disquiet as she went to open the door. Most of her acquaintances and friends would still be at work. Who could it possibly be?

'Ross!' she gasped aloud at first sight of him, her heart leaping with... what?

He stood there, dressed in blue jeans and a white T-shirt, a plastic carrier-bag in his left hand and a wry smile on his face.

'Vivien,' he greeted smoothly.

For a few seconds neither of them said anything further. Ross's clear blue eyes lanced her startled face before travelling down then up her figure-fitting pink and black suit. By the time his gaze returned to their point of origin Vivien was aware that her heart was thudding erratically in her chest. A fierce blush was also staining her cheeks.

Embarrassment warred with a surprisingly intense pleasure over his reappearance in her life. My God, he'd actually followed her all this way! Perhaps he didn't look at the other night as a one-night stand after all. Perhaps he really cared about her.

And perhaps not, the bitter voice of experience intervened, stilling the flutterings in her heart.

'What... what are you doing here?' she asked warily.

He shrugged. 'I had to come to Sydney to visit my father and I thought you might like the things you left behind.' He held out the plastic bag.

Her dismay was sharp. So! He hadn't followed her at all. Not really. She wasn't deceived by his excuse for dropping by. The way he'd looked at her just now was not the look of a man who'd only come to return something. Vivien knew the score. Ross was going to be in town anyway and thought he might have another sampling of what she'd given him so easily the other night.

Her disappointment quickly fuelled a very real anger. She snatched the plastic bag without looking inside, tossing it behind the door. She didn't want to see her ruined bolero and shoes, not needing any more reminders of her disgusting behaviour the other night. Ross's presence on her doorstep was reminder enough.

'How kind of you,' she retorted sarcastically. 'But how did you find out my address? It's not in the phone book.'

His eyes searched her face as though trying to make sense of her ill temper. 'Once I explained to the receptionist at the channel about your having left some of your things behind at the Wallaby Creek hotel,' he said, 'and that I had come all this way to return them, she gave me your address.'

'But you didn't come all this way just to return them, did you?' she bit out. 'Look, Ross, if you think you're going to take up where you left off then I suggest you think again. I have no intention of——'

'You're *ashamed* of what we did,' he cut in with surprise in his voice.

Her cheeks flamed. 'What did you *expect*? That I'd be *proud* of myself?'

'I don't see why not... What we shared the other night, Vivien, was something out of the ordinary. You must know how I feel about you. You must also have known I would not let you get away that easily.'

'Oh? And how *does* the legendary Ross Everton feel about little ole me?' she lashed out, annoyed that he would think her so gullible. 'Surely you're not going to declare undying love, are you?' she added scathingly. 'Not Ross Everton, the famous—or is it infamous?—country Casanova!'

His eyes had narrowed at her tirade, their light blue darkening with a black puzzlement. 'I think you've been listening to some twisted tales, Vivien. My legendary status, if one could call it such, has nothing to do with my being a Casanova.'

Now it was her turn to stare with surprise. 'Then what... what?'

He shrugged off her bumbled query, his penetrating gaze never leaving her. 'I *do* care about you, Vivien. Very much. When I woke to find you gone, I was...' His mouth curved back into a rueful smile. 'Let's just say I wasn't too pleased. I thought, damn and blast, that city bitch has just used me. But after I'd had time to think about it I knew that couldn't be so. You're too straightforward, Vivien. Too open. Too sweet...'

He took a step towards her then. Panic-stricken, she backed up into the flat. When Ross followed right on inside, then shut the door, her eyes flung wide.

'Don't be alarmed,' he soothed. 'I told you once and I'll tell you again: I won't ever hurt you. But I refuse to keep discussing our private lives in a damned hallway.' He glanced around the living-room, its emptiness clearly distracting him from what he'd been about to add. 'You're moving out?'

She shook her head. Somehow, words would not come. Her mind was whirling with a lot of mixed-up thoughts. For even if Ross was genuine with his feelings for her, what future could they have together? *Her* feelings for *him* had no foundation. They were nothing but a cruel illusion, sparked by his likeness to Earl.

'Then what happened to your furniture?' Ross asked.

She cleared her throat. 'Earl... Earl took it all.'

'*All* of it?'

Her laugh was choked and dry. 'He left me a single bed. Wasn't that nice of him?'

'Could win him the louse-of-the-year award.'

Vivien saw the pity in Ross's eyes and hated it.

Suddenly, the whole grim reality of her situation rushed in on her like a swamping wave, bringing with it a flood of self-pity. The tears she had kept at bay all day rushed in with a vengeance.

'Oh, God,' she groaned, her hands flying up to cover her crumpling face. 'God,' she repeated, then began to sob.

Despite her weeping, she was all too hotly aware of Ross gathering her into his strong arms, cradling her distraught, disintegrating self close to the hard warmth of his chest.

'Don't cry, darling,' he murmured. 'Please don't cry. He's not worth it, can't you see that? He didn't really love you... or care about you... Don't waste your tears on him... Don't...'

To Vivien's consternation, her self-pitying outburst dried up with astonishing swiftness, replaced by a feeling of sexual longing so intense that it refused to be denied. Hardly daring to examine what she was doing, she felt her arms steal around Ross's waist, her fingers splaying wide as they snaked up his back. With a soft moan of surrender, she nestled her face into his neck, pressing gently fluttering lips to the pulse-point at the base of his throat.

She felt his moment of acute stillness, *agonised* over it. Her body desperately wanted him to seduce her again. But her mind—her *conscience*—implored with her to stop before it was too late.

This is wrong, Vivien, she pleaded with herself. Wrong! You don't love him. What in God's name is the matter with you? Stop it now!

She wrenched out of his arms just as they tightened around her, the action making them both stagger backwards in opposite directions.

'I'm s—sorry,' she blurted out. 'I...I shouldn't have done that. I'm not myself today. I...I just lost my job, and coming so soon after Earl's leaving... Not that that's any excuse...' She lifted her hand to her forehead in a gesture of true bewilderment. 'I'm not even drunk this time,' she groaned, appalled at herself.

Ross stared across at her. 'What do you mean? You weren't drunk the other night. You'd only had a couple of glasses of champagne. Not even full glasses.'

Her sigh was ragged. 'That's enough for me on an empty stomach. I have this almost allergic reaction to alcohol, you see. It sends me crazy, a bit like your brother, only I don't need nearly as much. I'm a cheap drunk, Ross. A *very* cheap drunk,' she finished with deliberate irony.

'I see,' he said slowly.

'I'm sorry, Ross.'

'So am I. Believe me.' He just stood there, staring at her, his eyes troubled. Suddenly, he sighed, and pulled himself up straight and tall. 'Did I hear rightly just now? You've lost your job?'

'Yes, but not to worry. I'll find something else.' She spoke quickly, impatiently. For she just wanted him to go.

'Are you sure?' he persisted. 'Unemployment's high in the television industry, I hear.'

'I have my family. I'll be fine.'

'They live near by?'

'Parramatta. Look, it... it was nice of you to come all this way to see me again, Ross,' she said stiffly, wishing he would take the hint and leave. She had never felt so wretched, and guilty, and confused.

'Nice?' His smile was bitter. 'Oh, it wasn't nice, Vivien. It was a necessity. I simply *had* to see you again before I...' He broke off with a grimace. 'But that's none of your concern now.'

He gave Vivien an oddly ironic look. Once again, she was struck by his *dissimilarity* to Earl. His facial features might have come out of the same mould. But his expressions certainly didn't. His eyes were particularly expressive, ranging from a chilling glitter of reproach to a blaze of white-hot passion.

Vivien stared at him, remembering only too well how he had looked as he'd made love to her, the way his skin had drawn back tight across his cheekbones, his lips parting, his eyes heavy, as though he were drowning in his desire. Immediately, she felt a tightening inside, followed by a dull ache of yearning.

Did he see the desire in her eyes, the hunger?

Yes, he must have. For his expression changed once more, this time to a type of resolve that she found quite frightening. His hands shot out to grip her waist, yanking her hard against him.

'I don't care if you were drunk,' he rasped. 'I don't care if you're still in love with your stupid bloody Earl. All you have to do is keep looking at me like that and it'll be enough.'

His mouth was hard, his kiss savage. But she found herself giving in to it with a sweet surrender that was far more intoxicating than any amount of alcohol could ever be.

The doorbell ringing again made them both jump.

'Are you expecting anyone?' Ross asked thickly, his mouth in her hair, his hands restless on her back and buttocks.

Vivien shook her head.

Their chests rose and fell with ragged breathing as they waited in silence. The bell rang again. And again.

Ross sighed. 'You'd better answer it.' His hands dropped away from her, lifting to run agitatedly through his hair as he stepped back.

Vivien ran her own trembling hands down her skirt before turning to the door, all the while doing her best to school her face into an expression that would not betray her inner turmoil. One kiss, she kept thinking. One miserable kiss and I'm his for the taking...

She was stunned to find Bob standing on the other side of the door, a bottle of wine under his arm, a triumphant and sickeningly sleazy look on his face.

'Hello, Vivien.' He smirked. 'I dropped by to say how sorry I was about the way Mervyn dismissed you today. I thought we might have a drink together, and then, if you like, we could...'

He broke off when his gaze wandered over Vivien's shoulder, his beady eyes opening wide with true surprise when they encountered Ross standing there.

'Oh... oh, hi, there, Earl,' he called out, clearly flustered. 'I thought you were in Melbourne. Well, it's good to know Viv has someone here in her hour of need. I—er—only called round to offer my sympathy and a shoulder to cry on, but I can see she doesn't need it. I... I guess I'd better be going. Sorry to interrupt. See you around, Viv. Bye, Earl.'

Vivien could feel Ross's frozen stillness behind her as she slowly shut the door and turned. He looked as if someone had just hit him in the stomach with a sledge-hammer.

'Ross,' she began, 'I——'

'I'm not just *like* your ex-lover, am I, Vivien?' he broke in harshly. 'I'm his damned double!'

She closed her eyes against his pained hurt. 'Almost,' she admitted huskily.

'God...'

Vivien remained silent. Perhaps it was for the best, she reasoned wretchedly. At least now he would see that there was no hope of a real relationship between them and he would leave her alone. For God only knew what would happen if he stayed.

But what if you're already pregnant by him? whispered that niggling voice.

Vivien pushed the horrendous thought aside. Surely fate couldn't be that perverse?

'I want you to open your eyes and look at me, Vivien,' Ross stated in a voice like ice.

She did, and his eyes were as flat and hard as eyes could be. She shrank from the cold fury his gaze projected.

'I want you to confirm that the main reason you responded to me the way you did the other night is because I'm the spitting image of your ex-lover. You were fantasising I was this Earl while I was making love to you, is that correct?'

*No*, was her instant horrified reaction. *No! It wasn't like that*!

And yet... It had to be so. For if it wasn't, then what had it been? Animal lust? The crude using of any body to assuage sexual frustration? Revenge on Earl, maybe?

None of those things felt right. She refused to accept them. Which only left what Ross had concluded. Perhaps the reason she instinctively rejected that explanation was because her memory of that night had been clouded by alcohol. She recalled thinking the next morning that her pleasure in Ross's lovemaking could not have been so extraordinary, could *not* have propelled her into another world where nothing existed but this man, and this man alone.

'I'm waiting, Vivien,' he demanded brusquely

'Yes,' she finally choked out, though her tortured eyes slid away from his to the floor. 'Yes...'

He dragged in then exhaled a shuddering breath. 'Great,' he muttered. 'Just great. I'll remember that next time my emotions threaten to get in the way of my common sense. Pardon me if I say I hope I never see you again, Vivien Roberts. Still... you've been an experience, one I bitterly suspect I'll never repeat!'

He didn't look back as he left, slamming the door hard behind him.

It wasn't till a minute or two later that Vivien remembered something that challenged both Ross's conclusion and her own. If her responses had really been for Earl, if her memory of that night had been confused by alcohol and her pleasure not as overwhelming as she had thought, then why had she responded with such shattering intensity to Ross's kiss just now? Why?

None of it made sense.

But then, nothing made sense any more to Vivien. Her whole world had turned upside-down. Once, she had seen her future so very clearly. Now, there was only a bleak black haziness, full of doubts and fears and insecurities. She wanted quite desperately to run

## SIMPLY IRRESISTIBLE 69

home to her mother, to become a child again, with no decisions to make, no responsibilities to embrace.

But she wasn't a child. She was an adult. A grown woman. She had to work things out for herself.

Vivien did the only thing a sensible, grown-up woman could do. She went to bed and cried herself to sleep.

# CHAPTER SIX

'WHEN are you going to tell me what's wrong, dear?'

Vivien stiffened, tea-towel in hand, then slanted a sideways glance at her mother. Peggy Roberts had not turned away from where she stood at the kitchen sink, washing up after her husband Lionel's birthday dinner.

Vivien's stomach began to churn. There she'd been, thinking she had done a splendid job of hiding the turmoil in her heart. Why, she had fairly bubbled all through dinner, sheer force of will pushing the dark realities of the past fortnight way, way to the back of her mind.

Now, her mother's intuitive question sent them all rushing forward, stark in their grimness. She didn't know which was the worst: her growing realisation that she was unlikely to land a decent job in Sydney this side of six months, if ever; the crushing loneliness she felt every time she let herself back into her empty flat; or the terrifying prospect that her fear over being pregnant was fast becoming a definite rather than a doubtful possibility.

Her period had been due two days before and it hadn't arrived. Periods were never late when one was on the Pill. Of course, the delay might have been caused by her having forgotten one, but she didn't think so.

Just thinking about actually having a real baby— *Ross's* baby—sent her into a mental spin.

'Vivien,' her mother resumed with warmth and worry in her voice, 'you do know you can tell me anything, don't you? I promise I won't be shocked, or judgemental. But I can't let you leave here today without knowing what it is that has put you on this razor's edge. The others probably haven't noticed, but they don't know you as well as I do. Your gaiety, my dear, was just a fraction brittle over dinner. Besides, you haven't mentioned Earl once today, and that isn't like you. Not like you at all. Have you had a falling-out with him, dear? Is that it?'

Vivien gave a small, hysterical laugh. 'I wouldn't put it like that exactly.'

'Then how would you put it?' her mother asked gently.

*Too* gently. Her loving concern sent a lump to Vivien's throat, and tears into her eyes. Forcing them back, she dragged in a shuddering breath then burst forth, nerves and emotion sending the words out in a wild tumble of awful but rather muddled confessions.

'Well, Mum, the truth is that a couple of weeks back Earl gave me the ole heave-ho, told me he didn't love me and that he had found someone else. I was very upset, to put it mildly, but that weekend I had to go out to that Bachelors' and Spinsters' Ball for work. You know, the one they showed on TV last week. And while I was there I met this man who, believe it or not, is practically Earl's double, and I...well, I slept with him on some sort of rebound, I suppose. At least, I think that's why I did it...'

She began wringing the tea-towel. 'But I also forgot my pill, you see, and now I think I might be pregnant. Then on the Monday after that weekend I was retrenched at the channel and that same day Ross came to Sydney to see me, hoping to make a go of things between us, but he found out how much he looked like Earl and jumped to all the right conclusions, which I made worse by telling him I was sloshed at the time I slept with him anyway. Not that I was, but you know what drink does to me, and I had had a bit to drink and... and... as you can see, I'm in a bit of a mess...'

By this time tears were streaming down her face.

To give her mother credit, she didn't look too much like a stunned mullet. More like a flapping flounder, holding stunned hands out in front of her, while washing-up water dripped steadily from her frozen fingertips on to the cork-tiled floor.

But she quickly pulled herself together, wiping her soapy hands on the tea-towel she dragged out of Vivien's hands, then leading her distressed daughter quickly away from potentially prying eyes into the privacy of her old bedroom.

'Sit,' she said, firmly settling Vivien down on the white lace quilt before leaning over to extract several tissues from the box on the dressing-table and pressing them into her daughter's hands. She sat down on the bed as well, then waited a few moments while Vivien blew her nose and stopped weeping.

'Now, Vivien, I'm not going to pretend that I'm not a little shocked, no matter what I said earlier. But there's no point in crying over spilt milk, so to speak. Now, I'm not sure if I got the whole gist of your story. Ross, I presume, is the name of the man who may or may not be the father of your child?'

'Oh, he's the father all right,' Vivien blubbered. 'It's the child who's a maybe or maybe not. It's a bit too soon to tell.'

Peggy sighed her relief. 'So you don't really know yet. You might not be pregnant.'

'Yes, I am,' Vivien insisted wildly. 'I know I am.'

'Vivien! You sound as if you *want* to be pregnant by this man, this... this... stranger who looks like Earl.'

Vivien stared at her startled mother, then shook her head in utter bewilderment. 'I don't know what I want any more, Mum. I... I'm so mixed up and miserable and... Please help me. You always know just what to say to make me see things clearly. Tell me I'm not going mad. Tell me it wasn't wicked of me to do what I did. Tell me you and Dad don't mind if I have a baby, that you'll love me anyway. I've been so worried about everything.'

'Oh, my poor, dear child,' Peggy said gently, and enfolded her in her mother's arms. 'You've really been through the mill, haven't you? Of course you're not going mad. And of course you're not wicked. But as parents we *will* be worried about you having a baby all on your own, so if you are pregnant you'll have to come home and live with us so we can look after you. Come to think of it, you're coming home anyway. You must be horribly lonely in that flat all on your own.'

'You can say that again,' Vivien sniffled.

'You must be horribly lonely in that flat all on your own...'

Vivien pulled back, her eyes snapping up to her mother's. Peggy was smiling. 'Mum! This isn't funny, you know.'

'I know, but I can't help feeling glad that you're not going to marry that horrible Earl.'

'You never said you thought he was horrible before.'

'Yes, well, your father and I didn't want to make him seem any more attractive than you obviously already found him. But believe me, love, I didn't like him at all. He was the most selfish man I have ever met. Selfish and snobbish. He would have made a dreadful father, too. Simply dreadful. He had no sense of family.'

Vivien nodded slowly in agreement. 'You're right. I can see that now. I can see a lot of things about Earl that I couldn't see before. I don't know why I loved him as much as I did.'

'Well, he could be charming when he chose,' her mother admitted. 'And he was very handsome. Which makes me think that maybe you never loved him. Not really.'

Vivien blinked.

'Maybe it was only a sexual attraction,' Peggy suggested.

Vivien frowned.

'This man you slept with, the one you said looks a lot like Earl——'

'More than a lot,' Vivien muttered.

'Obviously you're one of those women who's always attracted to the same physical type. For some of us it's blond hair and blue eyes, or broad shoulders and a cute butt, or——'

'Mum!' Vivien broke in, shock in her voice.

Peggy smiled at her daughter. 'Do you think you're the only female in this family who's ever been bowled over by a sexual attraction?'

'Well, I . . . I——'

'Your father wasn't my first man, you know.'

'*Mum!*'

'Will you stop saying "Mum!" like that? It's unnerving. I don't mean I was promiscuous, but there was this other fellow first. I think if I tell you about him you might see that what happened between you and this Ross person was hardly surprising, or wicked.'

'Well, all right... if you say so...'

Peggy drew in a deep breath, then launched into her astonishing tale. At least, Vivien found it astonishing.

'I was eighteen at the time, working as a receptionist with a firm of solicitors while I went to secretarial school at night. Damian was one of the junior partners. Oh, he was a handsome devil. Tall, with black hair and flashing brown eyes, and a body to swoon over. I thought he was the best thing since sliced bread. He used to stop by my desk to compliment me every morning. By the time he asked me out four months later I was so ripe a plum he had me in bed before you could say "cheese".'

'Heavens! And was he a good lover?' Vivien asked, fascinated at the image of her softly spoken, very reserved mother going to bed with a man on a first date.

'Not really. Though I didn't know that at the time. I thought any shortcomings had to be mine. Still, I went eagerly back for more because his looks held a kind of fascination for my body which I didn't have the maturity to ignore. It wasn't till his fiancée swanned into the office one day that my eyes were well and truly opened to the sort of man he was.'

'So what did you do?'

'I found myself a better job and left a much wiser girl. Believe me, the next time a tall, dark and handsome man with flashing eyes set my heart aflutter he had a darned hard time even getting to first base with me.'

'You gave him the cold shoulder, right?'

'Too right.'

'So what happened to him?'

'I married him.'

Vivien's brown eyes rounded. 'Goodness!'

'What I'm trying to tell you, daughter of mine, is that there's probably any number of men in this world that you might want as a lover, but not too many as your true love. When that chemistry strikes, hold back from it for a while, give yourself time to find out if the object of your desire is worth entrusting your body to, give the relationship a chance to grow on levels other than the sexual one. For it's those other levels that will stand your relationship in good stead in the tough times. You and Earl had nothing going for you but what you had in bed.'

'Which wasn't all that great,' Vivien admitted.

There was a short, sharp silence before Peggy spoke.

'I gather you can't say the same for the time you spent with this Ross person?'

Vivien coloured guiltily. There was no use in pretending any more that what she had felt with Ross that night had been anything like what she'd felt with Earl. Why, it was like comparing a scratchy old record to the very best compact disc.

Her mother said nothing for a moment. 'Have you considered an abortion?' she finally asked.

'Yes.'

'And?'

'I just can't. I know it would be an easy way out, a quick solution. Funnily enough, I've always believed it was a woman's right to make such a decision, and I still do, but somehow, on this occasion, it doesn't feel right. I'm scared, but I...I have to have this baby, Mum. Please...don't ask me to get rid of it.' She threw her mother a beseeching look, tears welling up in her eyes again.

Peggy's eyes also flooded. 'As if I would,' she said in a strangled tone. 'Come here, darling child, and give your old mother another hug. We'll work things out. Don't you worry. Everything will be all right.'

Vivien moved home the next day. Her pregnancy was confirmed two weeks later.

Once over her initial shock, her mother responded by fussing over Vivien, not allowing her to do anything around the house. Vivien responded by going into somewhat of a daze.

Most of her days were spent blankly watching television. Her nights, however, were not quite so uneventful, mostly because of her dreams. They were always of Ross and herself in a mixed-up version of that fateful night at Wallaby Creek.

Sometimes they would be on the creek bank, sometimes in the water, sometimes back in the hotel room. Ross would be kissing her, touching her, telling her he loved her. Inevitably, she would wake up before they really made love, beads of perspiration all over her body. Each morning, she would get up feeling totally wrung out. That was till she started having morning sickness as well.

Why, she would ask herself in the bathroom mirror every day, was she so hell-bent on such a potentially self-destructive path?

She could not find a sensible, logical answer.

A few days before Christmas, she made another decision about her baby, one which had never been in doubt at the back of her mind. All that had been in doubt was *when* she was going to do it.

'Dad?' she said that evening after dinner.

Her father looked up from where he was watching a movie on television and reading the evening paper at the same time. 'Yes, love?'

'Would you mind if I made a long-distance call? It doesn't cost so much at night and I promise not to talk for long.'

Now her mother looked up, a frown on her face. 'Who are you ringing, dear?'

'Ross.'

Her father stiffened in his chair. 'What in hell do you want to ring him for? He won't want anything to do with the child, you mark my words.'

'You're probably right,' Vivien returned, the image of Ross's furious departure still stark in her memory. He'd made his feelings quite clear. He never wanted to see her again.

But a few months back, she had done a segment for television on unmarried fathers, and the emotional distress of some of the men had lived with her long afterwards. One of their complaints was that some of the mothers had not even the decency to tell them about their pregnancies. Many had simply not given the fathers any say at all in their decisions to abort, adopt, or to keep their babies. Vivien had been touched by the men's undoubted pain. She knew that she would not be able to live with her conscience if she kept her baby a secret from its father.

A dark thought suddenly insinuated that she might be telling Ross about the baby simply to see him again.

Maybe she wanted the opportunity to bring her erotic dreams to a very real and less frustrating fruition.

Pushing *that* thought agitatedly to the back of her mind, she addressed her frowning parents with a simplicity and apparent certainty she was no longer feeling.

'He has a right to know,' she stated firmly, and threw both her father and mother a stubborn look.

They recognised it as the same look they'd received when they'd advised her, on leaving school, not to try for such a demanding career as television, to do something easier, like teaching.

'You do what you think best, dear,' her mother said with a sigh.

'It'll cause trouble,' her father muttered. 'You mark my words!'

Vivien recklessly ignored her father's last remark, closing the lounge door as she went out into the front hall, where they kept the phone. Her hands were trembling as she picked it up and dialled the operator to help her find Ross's phone number.

Three minutes later she had the number. She dialled again with still quaking fingers, gripping the receiver so tightly against her ear that it was aching already.

No one answered. It rang and rang at the other end, Vivien's disappointment so acute that she could not bring herself to hang up. Then suddenly there was a click and a male voice was on the line.

'Mountainview. Ross Everton speaking.'

Vivien was momentarily distracted by the sounds of merry-making in the background. Loud music and laughter. Clearly a party was in progress.

And why not? she reasoned, swiftly dampening down a quite unreasonable surge of resentment.

Christmas was, after all, less than a few days away. Lots of people were having parties.

She gathered herself and started speaking. 'Ross, this is Vivien here, Vivien Roberts. I...I...' Her voice trailed away, her courage suddenly deserting her. It was so impossible to blurt out her news with all that racket going on in the background.

'I can hardly hear you, Vivien,' Ross returned. 'Look, I'll just go into the library and take this call there. Won't be a moment.'

Vivien was left hanging, quite taken aback that Ross's house would *have* a room called a library. It gave rise to a vision of an old English mansion with panelled walls and deep leather chairs, not the simple country homestead she had envisaged Ross's family living in. She was still somewhat distracted when Ross came back on the line, this time without the party noises to mar his deeply attractive voice. 'Vivien? You're still there?'

'Y...yes.'

There was a short, very electric silence.

'To what honour do I owe this call?' he went on drily. 'You haven't been drinking again, have you?' he added with a sardonic laugh.

'I wish I had,' she muttered under her breath. She hadn't realised how hard this was going to be. Yet what had she expected? That Ross would react to her unexpected call with warmth and pleasure?

'What was that?'

'Nothing.' Her tone became brisk and businesslike. 'I'm sorry to bother you during your Christmas party, but I have something to tell you which simply can't wait.'

'Oh?' Wariness in his voice. 'Something unpleasant by the sound of it.'

'*You* may think so.' Her tone was becoming sharper by the second, fuelled by a terrible feeling of coming doom. He was going to hate her news. Simply hate it!

'Vivien, you're not going to tell me you have contracted some unmentionable disease, are you?'

'Not unless you refer to pregnancy in such a way,' she snapped back.

His inward suck of breath seemed magnified as it rushed down the line to her already pained ears.

Vivien squeezed her eyes tightly shut. You blithering idiot, she berated herself. You tactless, clumsy blithering idiot! 'Ross,' she resumed tightly, 'I'm sorry I blurted it out like that. I... I——'

'What happened?' he said in a voice that showed amazing control. 'You did say, after all, that you were on the Pill. Did you forget to take it, is that it?'

She expelled a ragged sigh. 'Yes...'

Once again, there was an unnerving silence on the line before he resumed speaking. 'And you're sure I'm the father?' he asked, but without any accusation.

'Quite sure.'

'I see.'

'Ross, I... I'm not ringing because I want anything from you. Not money, or anything. I realise that I'm entirely to blame. It's just that I thought you had the right to know, then to make your own decision as to whether you want to... to share in your child's life. It's entirely up to you. I'll understand whatever decision you make.'

'You mean you're going to *have* my baby?' he rasped, shock and something else in his voice. Or maybe not. Maybe just shock.

'You don't want me to,' she said, wretchedness in her heart.

'What I want is obviously irrelevant. Does your family know you're going to have a baby?'

'Yes. I'm ringing from their place now. I moved back home a couple of weeks ago.'

'And how did they react?'

'They weren't thrilled at first, but they're resigned now, and supportive.'

'Hmm. Does Earl know?'

'Of course not!'

'Don't bite my head off, Vivien. You wouldn't be the first woman who tried to use another man's baby to get back the man she really wants. In the circumstances, I doubt you'd have had much trouble in passing the child off as his, since the father is his dead ringer.'

Vivien was shocked that Ross would even *think* of such a thing.

'Is that why you're having the baby, Vivien?' he continued mercilessly. 'Because you're hoping it will look like the man you love?'

She gasped. 'You're sick, do you know that?'

'Possibly. But I had to ask.'

'*Why?*'

'So that I can make rational decisions. I don't think you have any idea what your news has done to my life, Vivien.'

'What... what do you mean?'

'I mean that it isn't a Christmas party we're having here tonight. It's an engagement party. *Mine.*'

Vivien's mind went blank for a second. When it resumed operation and the reality of the situation sank in, any initial sympathy she might have felt for Ross was swiftly replaced by a sharp sense of betrayal.

'I see,' she bit out acidly.

'Do you?'

'Of course. You slept with me at the same time as you were courting another woman. You lied to me when you came after me, Ross. You didn't want a real relationship. All you wanted was a final fling before you settled down to your real life.'

'I wouldn't put it that way exactly,' he drawled.

'Then what way would you put it?'

'Let's just say I found you sexually irresistible. Once I had you in my arms, I simply couldn't stop.'

Vivien was appalled by the flush of heat that washed over her skin as she thought of how she had felt in *his* arms. She couldn't seem to stop either. Once she might have fancied she had fallen in love with Ross. Now she had another word for it, supplied by her mother.

Chemistry, it was called, the same chemistry that had originally propelled her so willingly into Earl's arms. Though Earl had had another word for it. *Lust*!

Vivien shuddered. God, but she hated to think her mind and heart could be totally fooled by her body. It was demeaning to her intelligence.

*Men* weren't fooled, though. They knew the difference between love and lust. They even seemed capable of feeling both at the same time. Ross had probably kept on loving this woman he was about to marry, all the while he was lusting after *her*.

'Let's hope you don't run into someone like me after you get married in that case,' she flung at Ross with a degree of venom.

'I won't be getting married, Vivien,' he said quite calmly. 'At least...not now, and not to Becky.'

Vivien's anger turned to a flustered outrage. Not for herself this time, but for the poor wronged woman who wore Ross's ring. 'But...but you can't break your engagement just like that. That...that's cruel!'

'It would be crueller to go through with it. Becky deserves more than a husband who's going to be the father of another woman's baby. I wouldn't do that to her. I've loved Becky all my life,' he stated stiffly. 'We're neighbours as well. I'm deeply sorry that I have to hurt her at all. But this is a case of being cruel to be kind.'

'Oh, I feel so guilty,' Vivien cried. 'I should never have rung, never have told you.'

'Perhaps. But what's done is done. And now we must think of the child. When can I come down and see you?'

'See me?' she repeated, her head whirling.

'How about Boxing Day? I really can't get away from here before Christmas. Give me your parents' address and telephone number.'

Stunned, she did as he asked. He jotted down the particulars, then repeated them back to her.

'Do me a favour, will you, Vivien?' he added brusquely. 'Don't tell your parents about the engagement. It's going to be tough enough making them accept me as the father of their grandchild without my having an advance black mark against my name. However, you'd better let them know about my remarkable resemblance to lover-boy. I don't think I could stand any more people calling me Earl by mistake.'

He dragged in then exhaled a shuddering breath. 'Ah, well...I'd better go and drop my bombshell. Something tells me this party is going to break up rather early. See you Boxing Day, Vivien. Look after yourself.'

Vivien stared down into the dead receiver for several seconds before putting it shakily back into its cradle. Normally a clear thinker, she found it hard to grasp how she really felt about what had just happened. Her emotions seemed to have scrambled her brains.

Ross, she finally accepted, was the key to her confusion. Ross...who had just destroyed the picture she had formed of him in her mind.

He was not some smitten suitor who had chased after her with an almost adolescent passion, ready to throw himself at her feet. He was the man she had first met, an intriguing mixture of sophisticate and macho male, a man who was capable of going after what he wanted with the sort of ruthlessness that could inspire a brother's hatred. He was, quite clearly, another rat!

No...she conceded slowly. Not quite.

A rat would have told her get lost. Her *and* her baby.

A rat would not have broken his engagement.

A rat would not be coming down to see her, concerned with her parents' opinion of him.

So what was he?

Vivien wasn't at all sure, except about one thing.

He was *not* in love with her.

He was in love with a woman named Becky.

Now why did that hurt so darned much?

# CHAPTER SEVEN

'HE's here,' Peggy hissed, drawing back the living-room drapes to have a better look. 'Goodness, but you should see the Range Rover he's pulled up in. Looks brand new. Can't be one of those farmers who're doing really badly, then.'

Lionel grunted from his favourite armchair. 'Don't you believe it, Mother. Graziers live on large overdrafts. Most of them are going down the tubes.'

'Well, I'd rather see my Vivien married to an overdraft*ee* than that overdraft*er* she was living with. Heavens, but I could not stand that man. Oh, my goodness, but this fellow does look like Earl. Taller, though, and fitter looking. Hmm... Yes, I can see why Vivien was bowled over. He's a bit of all right.'

'Peggy!' Lionel exclaimed, startled enough to put down his newspaper. 'What's got into you, talking like that? And don't start romanticising about our Vivien getting married just because she's having a baby. She's never been one to follow convention. Not that this Ross chap will want to marry her anyway. Young men don't marry girls these days for that reason.'

'He's not so young...'

'What's that?' Lionel levered himself out of his chair and came to his wife's side, peering with her through the lacy curtains. By this time, Ross was making his way through the front gate, his well-honed frame coolly dressed for the heat in white shorts and

86

a pale blue polo shirt, white socks and blue and white striped Reeboks on his feet.

Lionel frowned. 'Must be thirty if he's a day.'

'Well, our Vivien *is* twenty-five,' Peggy argued.

'What on earth are you two doing?' the girl herself said with more than a touch of exasperation.

They both swung round, like guilty children found with their hands in the cookie jar.

The front doorbell rang.

Vivien folded her arms. 'If that's Ross why don't you just let him in instead of spying on him?'

'We—er—um...' came Peggy's lame mumblings till she gathered herself and changed from defence to attack.

'Vivien! Surely you're not going to let Ross see you wearing that horrible old housecoat? Go and put something decent on. And while you're at it, put some lipstick on as well. And run a brush through your hair. You look as if you've just got out of bed.'

'I *have* just got out of bed,' she returned irritably. 'And I have no intention of dolling myself up for Ross. He's not my boyfriend.'

'He *is* the father of your baby,' Lionel reminded her.

'More's the pity,' she muttered. Having been given a few days to think over the events surrounding that fateful weekend, Vivien had decided Ross was a rat after all. At least where women were concerned. He'd known she'd been upset about Earl that night, had known he himself had been on the verge of asking another woman to be his bride, one he *claimed* to have loved for years. Yet what had he done? Cold-bloodedly taken advantage of her vulnerability by seducing her, making her forget her conscience and then her pill!

'Vivien,' her mother said sternly, 'it was *your* idea to call Ross and tell him about the baby, which was a very brave and adult decision, but now you're acting like a child. Go and make yourself presentable *immediately*!'

Vivien took one look at her mother's determined face and knew this was not the moment to get on her high horse. Besides, her mother was right. She was acting appallingly. Still, she had felt rotten all day, with a queasy stomach and a dull headache, as she had the day before. She hadn't even been able to enjoy her Christmas dinner, due to a case of morning sickness which lasted all day. If this was what being pregnant was like then it was strictly for the birds!

'Oh, all right,' she muttered, just as the front doorbell rang for the second time. 'You'd better go and let him in. Something tells me Ross Everton is not in the habit of waiting for anything.'

She flounced off, feeling ashamed of herself, but seemingly unable to do anything about the way she was acting. On top of her physical ills, the news of Ross's engagement had left her feeling betrayed and bitter and even more disillusioned about men than she already had. It was as though suddenly there were no dreams any more.

No dreams. No Prince Charming. No hope.

Life had become drearily disappointing and utterly, utterly depressing.

Vivien threw open her wardrobe and drew out the first thing her hands landed on, a strappy lime sundress which showed a good deal of bare flesh. For a second, she hesitated. But only for a second. She had always favoured bright, extrovert clothes. Her wardrobe was full of them. Maybe wearing fluorescent green would cheer her up.

Tossing aside all her clothes, she drew on fresh bikini briefs before stepping into the dress and drawing it up over her hourglass figure. With wry accession to her mother's wishes, she brushed her dishevelled hair into disciplined waves before applying a dash of coral gloss to her lips.

The mirror told her she looked far better than she felt, the vibrant green a perfect foil for her pale skin and jet-black hair. Yet when her eyes dropped to her full breasts straining against the thin cotton, Ross's words leapt back into her mind.

'I found you sexually irresistible...'

The words pained her, as Earl's words had pained her.

'It was only lust,' *he* had said.

Vivien couldn't get the dress off quickly enough, choosing instead some loose red and white spotted Bermuda shorts with a flowing white over-shirt to cover her womanly curves. The last thing she wanted today was Ross looking at her with desire in his eyes. Suddenly, she found her own sex appeal a hateful thing that stood between herself and real happiness.

Reefing a tissue out of the box, she wiped savagely at her glossed lips, though the resultant effect was not what she wanted. Sure, the lipstick was gone, but the rubbing had left her lips quite red and swollen, giving her wide mouth a full, sultry look.

'Damn,' she muttered.

'Vivien,' came her mother's voice through the bedroom door, 'when you're ready you'll find us on the back patio. Your father and Ross are having a beer together out there.'

Vivien blinked. Dad was having a beer with Ross? Already? How astonishing. He only ever offered a beer to his best mates. Perhaps he needed a beer himself, she decided. It had to be an awkward situation for him, entertaining Ross, trying to find something to talk to him about.

I should be out there, she thought guiltily.

But still she lingered, afraid to leave the sanctuary of her bedroom, afraid of what she would still see in Ross's eyes when they met hers, afraid of what she might *not* see.

Vivien violently shook her head. This was crazy! One moment she didn't want him to want her. Then the next she did. It was all too perverse for words!

Self-disgust finally achieved what filial duty and politeness could not. Vivien marched from the room, bitterly resolved to conquer these vacillating desires that kept invading her mind and body. Ross wanted to talk to her about their coming child? Well, that was all he'd ever get from her in future. Talk! She had no intention of letting him worm his way past her physical defences ever again.

She stomped down the hall, through the kitchen and out on to the back patio, letting the wire door bang as she went. The scenario of a totally relaxed Ross seated cosily between her parents around the patio table, sipping a cool beer and looking too darned handsome for words, did nothing for her growing irritation.

'Ah, here she is now,' her father said expansively. 'Ross was just telling us that he's not normally a sheep farmer. He's simply helping out at home till his father gets on his feet again. He flies helicopters for a living. Mustering cattle. Own your own business, didn't you say, Ross?'

'That's right, Mr Roberts. I've built up quite a clientele over the last few years. Mustering on horseback is definitely on the way out, though some people like to call us chopper cowboys.'

'Chopper cowboys... Now that's a clever way of putting it. And do call me Lionel, my boy. No point in being formal, in the circumstances, is there?' he added with a small laugh.

Ross smiled that crooked smile that made him look far too much like Earl. 'I guess not,' he drawled, and lifted the beer to his lips.

'But isn't that rather a dangerous occupation?' Peggy piped up with a worried frown.

'Only if you're unskilled,' Ross returned. 'Or careless. I'm usually neither.' He slanted Vivien a ruefully sardonic look that changed her inner agitation into an icy fury.

'Accidents do happen though, don't they?' she said coldly.

'Now don't go getting all prickly on us, love,' Lionel intervened. 'We all know that neither of you had any intention of having a baby together, but you *are*, and Ross here has at least been decent enough to come all this way to meet us and reassure us he'll do everything he can to support you and the child. You should be grateful that he's prepared to do the right thing.'

Vivien counted to ten, then came forward to pick up an empty glass and pour herself some orange juice out of the chilled cask on the table. 'I *am* grateful,' she said stiffly. 'I only hope no one here suggests that we get married. I won't be marrying anyone for any reason other than true love.'

She lifted her glass and eyes at the same time, locking visual swords with Ross over the rim. But she wasn't the only one who could hide her innermost feelings behind a facial façade. He eyed her back without so much as a flicker of an eyelash, his cool blue eyes quite unflappable in their steady regard.

'Believe me, Vivien,' came his smooth reply, 'neither will I.'

An electric silence descended on the group as Vivien and Ross glared at each other in mutual defiance.

'Perhaps, Mother...' Lionel said, scraping back his chair to stand up. 'Perhaps we should leave these two young people to have a private chat.'

'Good idea, dear,' Peggy agreed, and stood up also. 'Here, Vivien, use my chair. Now be careful. Don't spill your drink as you sit down.'

Vivien rolled her eyes while her mother treated her like a cross between a child and an invalid.

'Will you be staying for dinner, Ross?' Peggy asked before she left.

Ross glanced at his wristwatch which showed five to six. He looked up and smiled. 'If it's not too much trouble.'

'No trouble at all. We're only having cold meats and salad. Left-overs, I'm afraid, from yesterday's Christmas feast.'

'I love left-overs,' he assured her.

Once her parents had gone inside, Vivien heaved a heavy sigh.

'Not feeling well, Viv?' Ross ventured.

She shot him a savage look. 'Don't call me that.'

'What? "Viv"?'

'Yes.'

'Why?'

She shrugged irritably.

'Did Earl call you that?'

'No,' she lied.

He raised his eyebrows, but said nothing.

'Look, Ross, I'm just out of sorts today, OK?' Vivien burst out. 'It isn't all beer and skittles being pregnant, you know.'

'No, I don't know,' he said with a rueful note in his voice. 'But I guess I'm going to find out over the next few months. Something tells me you're a vocal type of girl.'

She darted him a dry look. 'If by that you mean I'm a shrew or a whinger then you couldn't be further from the truth. It's just that I didn't expect to be this sick all the time. I guess I'll get used to it in time. Though I'm damned if I'll get used to my mother's fussing,' she finished with a grimace of true frustration.

'You're going to live here?'

'Where else? I had no intention of staying on in Earl's flat. Besides, I'm unemployed now and I wouldn't have enough money for the rent anyway, so I have to stay here. There's no other alternative.'

'You could come home with me,' he suggested blandly.

Her mouth dropped open, then snapped shut. 'Oh, don't be ridiculous!'

'I'm not being ridiculous. Dad wants to meet you, and I'd like to have you.'

'I'll just bet you would,' she shot at him quite nastily.

Both his eyebrows shot up again. 'You have a dirty mind, Vivien, my dear.'

'Maybe it's the company I'm keeping.'

Anger glittered in his eyes. 'Perhaps you would prefer to be with a man who used you quite ruthlessly then discarded you like an old worn-out shoe!'

Vivien paled. Her bottom lip trembled.

'God,' Ross groaned immediately, placing his beer glass down on the table with a ragged thud. 'I'm sorry, Vivien. Deeply, sincerely sorry. That was a rotten thing to say.'

'Yes,' she rasped, tears pricking at her eyes.

She stared blindly down into her orange juice, amazed at the pain Ross's words had produced. There she'd been lately, almost agreeing with her mother that she had never loved Earl. But she must have, for this reminder of his treachery to hurt so much.

Or maybe she was just in an over-emotional state, being pregnant and all. She had heard pregnancy made some women quite irrational.

With several blinks and a sigh, she glanced up, only to be shocked by the degree of bleak apology on Ross's face. He really was very sorry, it seemed.

Now she felt guilty. For she hadn't exactly been Little Miss Politeness since joining him.

'I'm sorry too, Ross,' she said sincerely, 'This can't be easy for you either. I won't pretend that I'm thrilled at finding out you only looked upon me as a "bit on the side", so to speak, but who am I to judge? My behaviour was hardly without fault. I was probably using you that night as much as you were using me, so perhaps we should try to forgive each other's shortcomings and start all over again, shall we?'

He stared at her. 'You really mean that?'

'Of course. You're the father of my baby. We should at least try to be friends. I can also see it's only sensible that I should come out to meet your family, though I really can't stay with you for my entire pregnancy. Surely *you* can see that?'

'Actually, no, I can't.'

She made an exasperated sound. 'It wouldn't be right. I've never been a leaner. I have to make my own way.'

'That might have been all right when it was just you, Vivien,' he pointed out. 'But soon you'll have a child to support. You have no job and, I would guess, few savings. And, before you jump down my throat for being presumptuous, I'm only saying that because you're not old enough to have accrued a fortune.'

'I'm twenty-five!'

'Positively ancient. And you've been working how long? Four years at most?'

'Something like that...'

'Women never get paid as much as men in the media. Besides, in your line of work you would have had to spend a lot on clothes.'

'Yes...'

'See? It doesn't take a genius to guess at your financial position. Besides, I have a proposition to make to you.'

This brought a wary, narrow-eyed glare. 'Oh, yes?'

'Nothing like that,' he dismissed. 'My father has just come home from a stay in hospital where he's been having therapy. I have engaged a private therapist who specialises in after-stroke care to visit regularly, but there are still times when he needs someone to read to him and talk to him, or just sit with him.'

'A paid companion, you mean?'

'Yes. Something like that. Do you think you might be interested? It would kill two birds with one stone. Dad would get to know the mother of his grandchild and vice versa. And you'd feel a bit more useful than you're obviously feeling now.'

'Mmm.' Vivien gnawed away at her bottom lip. 'I've applied for social security...'

'No matter. You can either cancel it or I'll put your wages into a trust fund for the child.'

She wrinkled her nose. 'I'd rather cancel it.'

'*You would.*'

She bristled at his exasperated tone. 'Meaning?'

'You're too proud, Vivien. And too honest. You must learn that life is a jungle and sometimes the good get it in the neck.'

'Are you saying you have no pride? That you're not honest?'

A shadow passed across his eyes, turning them to a wintry grey for a second. But they were soon back to their bright icy blue. 'Let's just say that I *have* been known to go after what I want with a certain one-eyed determination.'

She gave him a long, considering look, trying not to let his physical appeal rattle her thought processes. It was hard, though. He was a devastatingly sexy man, much sexier than Earl. Oh, their looks were still remarkably similar—on the surface. But Ross had an inner energy, a raw vitality that shone through in every look he gave her, every move he made. Even sitting there casually in a deckchair with his legs stretched out, ankles crossed, he exuded an animal-like sensuality that sent tickles up and down her spine.

'Have you thought up this companion job simply to get me into a position where you can seduce me again?' she asked point-blank.

He seemed startled for a moment before recovering his cool poise. 'No,' he said firmly, and looked her straight in the eye. 'Believe me when I say there will *not* be a repeat performance of what happened that night out at Wallaby Creek.'

He sounded as if he was telling the truth, she realised with a degree of surprise. And disappointment. The latter reaction sparked self-irritation. If *he* had managed to bring this unfortunate chemistry between them under control, then why couldn't *she*?

'Are you two ready to eat?' her mother called through the wire door. 'It's all set out.'

'Coming,' they chorused.

Thank God for the interruption, Vivien thought as she and Ross stood up.

'Vivien?' he said, taking her elbow to stop her before she could walk away.

'Yes?'

'Are you going to take me up on the offer or not?'

She tried to concentrate on all the common-sense reasons why it was a good idea, and not on the way his touch was making her pulse-rate do a tango within her veins.

'Vivien?' he probed again.

Swallowing, she lifted her dark eyes to his light blue ones, hoping like hell that he couldn't read her mind. Or her body language.

'If you trust me in this,' he said softly, 'I will not abuse that trust.'

Maybe, she thought. But could she say the same for her own strength of will? She'd shown little enough self-control once she'd found herself in his arms in the past. What if he'd been lying earlier about why he wanted her in his home? What if he was lying *now*? Men often lied to satisfy their lust. Now that she was already pregnant and his engagement was off, what was to stop Ross from using her to satisfy his sexual needs? How easy it would be with her already under his roof...

'Vivien!' her mother called again. 'What's keeping you?' Her face appeared at the wire door. 'Come on, now, love. I've got a nice salad all ready. You must eat, you know, since you're eating for two. And I've put out the vitamins the doctor suggested you have. Ross, don't take any nonsense from her and bring her in here right away.'

'Sure thing, Mrs Roberts.'

He smiled at the pained look on Vivien's face. 'Well? What do you say? Will you give it a try for a few months?'

A few months...

Something warned her that was too long, too dangerous.

'One month,' she compromised. 'Then we'll see...'

Still looking into his eyes, Vivien would have had to be blind not to see the depth of Ross's satisfaction. Her stomach turned over and she tore her eyes away. What have I done? she worried.

As he opened the wire door and guided her into the large, airy kitchen, the almost triumphant expression on Ross's face sent an old saying into her mind.

'"Will you walk into my parlour?" said a spider to a fly...'

# CHAPTER EIGHT

'WHAT did Mum say to you?' Vivien demanded to know as soon as the Range Rover moved out of sight of her waving parents.

Ross darted a sideways glance at her, his expression vague. 'When?'

'When she called you back to the front gate just now.' She eyed Ross suspiciously. 'She isn't trying to put any pressure on you to marry me, is she?'

'Don't be paranoid, Vivien. Your mother simply asked me not to speed, to remember that I had a very precious cargo aboard.'

'Oh, good grief! That woman's becoming impossible. God knows what she'll be like by the time I actually *have* this baby.'

'Speaking of the baby, are you feeling better today?'

'No,' she grumped. 'I feel positively rotten.'

'Really? You look fantastic. That green suits you.'

Vivien stiffened, recalling how she had argued with her mother over what she should wear this morning. In the end she had given in to her mother's view that she should dress the way she always dressed, not run around hiding her figure in tent dresses and voluminous tops.

But now Vivien wasn't so sure wearing such a bare dress was wise. She hadn't forgotten the way Ross had looked yesterday when she'd agreed to go home with him for a while. The last thing she wanted to do was be provocative.

'I thought you said that you wanted us to start all over again,' Ross reminded her, 'that we should try to be friends. If this is your idea of being friendly then city folk sure as hell are different from country.'

His words made Vivien feel guilty. She was being as bitchy today as she had been yesterday, and it wasn't all because she felt nauseous. When Ross had shown up this morning, looking cool and handsome all in white, she hadn't been able to take her eyes off him. Her only defence against her fluttering heart had been sharp words and a cranky countenance.

Vivien shook her head. Her vulnerability to this chemistry business was the very devil. It played havoc with one's conscience, making her want to invite things that she knew were not in her best interests. Maybe some people could quite happily satisfy their lust without any disastrous consequences. But Vivien feared that if she did so with Ross she might become emotionally involved with him.

And where would that leave her, loving a man who didn't love her back, a man whose heart had been given to another woman? It wasn't as though there was any hope of his marrying her, either. He'd made his ideas on that quite clear.

Still, none of these inner torturous thoughts were any excuse for her poor manners, and she knew it.

'I'm sorry, Ross,' she apologised. 'I'll be in a better humour shortly. This yucky feeling usually wears off by mid-morning.'

He smiled over at her. 'I'll look forward to it.'

They fell into a companionable silence after that, Vivien soon caught up by the changing scenery as they made their way up the Blue Mountains and through Katoomba. She had been the driver during this section when she and Irving had made the trip out to Wallaby Creek, and the driver certainly didn't see as much as the passenger. Oddly enough, the curving road did not exacerbate her slightly queasy stomach. In fact she was soon distracted from her sickness with watching the many and varied vistas.

Despite being built on at regular intervals, the mountain terrain still gave one the feeling of its being totally untouched in places. The rock-faces dropped down into great gorges, the distant hillsides covered with a virgin bush so wild and dense that Vivien understood only too well why bushwalkers every year became lost in them. She shuddered to think what would happen to the many isolated houses if a bushfire took hold.

'It's very dry, isn't it?' she remarked at last with worry in her voice.

'Sure is. My father says it's the worst drought since the early forties.'

'How old *is* your father, Ross?' Vivien asked.

'Sixty-three.'

'Still too young to die,' she murmured softly. 'And you?'

'I'll be thirty-one next birthday. What is this, twenty questions?'

Vivien shrugged. 'I think I should know a little about your family before I arrive, don't you?'

'Yes. I suppose that's only reasonable. Fire away, then.'

'Who else is there at Mountainview besides you and your father and Gavin? I presume you three men don't fend for yourselves.'

He laughed. 'You presume right. If we did, we'd starve. We have Helga to look after us.'

'Helga... She sounds formidable.'

'She is. Came to us as a nurse when Mum became terminally ill. After she died, Helga stayed on, saying we couldn't possibly cope without her. I was twelve at the time. Gavin was only seven. He looks upon Helga as a second mother.'

'And you? Do you look upon her as a second mother?'

'Heaven forbid. The woman's a martinet. No, only Gavin softens that woman's heart. She'd make an excellent sergeant in the army. Still, she does the work of three women so I can't complain. Keeps the whole house spick and span, does all the washing and cooking and ironing, and still has time left over to knit us all the most atrocious jumpers. I have a drawer full of them.'

'Oh, she sounds sweet.' Vivien laughed.

'She means well, I suppose. She's devoted to Mountainview. The house, that is. Not the sheep.'

'Is it a big house? I got the impression it was on the phone.'

'Too damned big. Built when graziers were nothing more than Pitt Street farmers who used their station properties as country retreats to impress their city friends. We don't even use some sections of the house. Dad gets a team of cleaners in once a year to spring-clean. When they're finished, they cover the furniture in half the rooms with dust-cloths then lock the doors.'

'Goodness, it sounds like a mansion. How many rooms has it got?'

'Forty-two.'

Vivien blinked over at his amused face. 'You're pulling my leg.'

He glanced down at her shapely ankles. 'Unfortunately, no.'

'Forty-two,' she repeated in amazement. 'And you only have the one woman to keep house?'

'In the main. We hire extra staff if we're having a party or a lot of visitors. And there's Stan and Dave.'

'Who are they?'

'General farmhands. Or rouseabouts, if you prefer. But they don't live in the main house. They have their own quarters. Still, they do look after the gardens, so you're likely to run into them occasionally. Of course, the place is a lot busier during shearing, but that won't be till March.'

'March...' Vivien wondered if she would still be there in March. She turned her head slowly to look at Ross. In profile, he looked nothing like Earl at all, yet her stomach still executed a telling flutter.

'Do...do you think Helga will like me?' Vivien asked hesitantly.

'I don't see why not.'

Vivien frowned. Men could be so naïve at times. If Helga had been fond of Ross's Becky then she wouldn't be very welcoming to the woman who'd been responsible for breaking the girl's heart.

But *was* it broken? she wondered. Ross had confessed his long love for the woman he'd planned to marry, but Vivien knew nothing of the woman herself, or her feelings.

'Ross...'

'Mmm?'

'Tell me about Becky.'

He stiffened in his seat, his hands tightening around the wheel. 'For God's sake, Vivien...'

She bristled. 'For God's sake what? Surely I have a right to know something about the woman you were planning to marry, the woman you were sleeping with the same time you were sleeping with me?'

'I was not sleeping with Becky,' he ground out. 'I have *never* slept with Becky.'

Vivien stared over at him. 'But... but...'

'Oh, I undoubtedly would have,' he confessed testily. 'After we were properly engaged.'

Vivien could not deny that there was a certain amount of elation mixed in with her astonishment at this news. She had hated to think Ross had behaved as badly as Earl. Not that his behaviour had been impeccable. But at least he hadn't been sleeping with two women at the same time. Though, to be honest, Vivien did find his admission a touch strange.

'I'm not sure I understand,' she said with a puzzled frown. 'If you've always loved this Becky, then why haven't you made love to her? Why were you waiting till you were engaged?'

His sigh was irritable. 'It's difficult to explain.'

'*Try*,' she insisted.

He shot her an exasperated glance. 'Why do you want to know? Why do you care? You're not in love with me. What difference can it possibly make?'

'I want to know.'

'You are an incredibly stubborn woman!'

'So my mother has always told me.'

'She didn't tell *me* that,' he muttered.

'Didn't she? Well, what did she tell you, then? Were you lying to me back in Sydney whe——?'

'Oh, for pity's sake give it a rest, will you, Vivien? We've a tiresome trip ahead and you're going on like a Chinese water torture. God! Why I damned well...'

He broke off, lancing her with another reproachful glare. 'You would have to be the most infuriating female I have ever met!'

Vivien's temper flared. 'Is that so? You certainly didn't find me infuriating once you got my clothes off, did you? You found me pretty fascinating then all right!'

He fixed her with an oddly chilling glance as he pulled over to the side of the road and cut the engine.

'Yes,' he grated out, then thumped the steering-wheel. 'I did. Is that what you want to hear? How I couldn't get enough of you that night? How I wouldn't have stopped at all if I hadn't flaked out with sheer exhaustion?'

He scooped in then exhaled a shuddering breath, taking a few seconds to compose himself. 'Now what else do you want to know...? Ah, yes, why I haven't slept with Becky? Well, perhaps my reasons might be clearer if I tell you she's only twenty-one years old, and a virgin to boot. Convent-educated. A total innocent where men are concerned. Somehow it didn't seem right to take that innocence away till my ring was on her finger. So I waited...

'It's just as well I did, in the circumstances,' he finished pointedly.

Vivien sat there in a bleak silence, her heart a great lump of granite in her chest. Heavy and hard and cold. My God, he had really just spelt it out for her, hadn't he? *She* could be taken within hours of their first meeting. For *she* had no innocence to speak of, no virtue to be treasured or respected. She was little better than a slut in his eyes, fit only to be lusted after, to be *screwed*!

Not so this girl he loved. She was to be treated like spun glass, put up on a pedestal, looked at but not touched, not ruthlessly seduced as he'd seduced her over and over that night.

She pressed a curled fist against her lips lest a groan of dismay escape, turning her face away to stare blindly through the passenger window. Well, at least this would give her a weapon to use against herself every time that hated chemistry raised its ugly head. She would only have to remember exactly how she stood in Ross's eyes for those unwanted desires to be frozen to nothingness. She would feel as chilled towards him as she did at this very moment.

'Haven't you any other questions you want answered?' Ross asked in a flat voice.

'No,' was all she could manage.

'In that case I'll put some music on. We've a long drive ahead of us...'

They stopped a couple of times along the way, at roadside cafés which served meals as well as petrol. Each time she climbed out of the cabin Vivien was struck by the heat and was only too glad to be underway again under the cooling fan of the vehicle's air-conditioning.

Vivien stayed quiet after their earlier upsetting encounter, even though the scenery didn't provide her bleak wretchedness with any distractions. The countryside was really quite monotonous once they were out on the Western plains. Nothing but paddock after flat paddock of brown grass, dotted with the occasional clump of trees under which slept some straggly-looking sheep. Even the towns seemed the same, just bigger versions of Wallaby Creek.

They were driving along shortly after two, the heat above the straight bitumen road forming a shimmering lake, when Vivien got the shock of her life. A huge grey kangaroo suddenly appeared right out of the mirage in front of them, leaping across the road. Ross braked, but he still hit it a glancing blow, though not enough to stop its flight to safety.

Vivien stared as the 'roo went clean over the barbed-wire fence at the side of the road and off across the paddock. Within seconds it had disappeared.

'That's the first kangaroo I've ever seen, outside a zoo!' she exclaimed, propelled out of her earlier depression by excitement at such an unexpected sight. 'I'm glad we didn't hurt it.'

'It'd take more than a bump to hurt one of those big mongrels.' Ross scowled before accelerating away again.

'Why do you call it that?' she objected. 'It's a beautiful animal.'

'Typical city opinion. I suppose you think rabbits are nice, cuddly, harmless little creatures as well?'

'Of course.'

'Then you've never met twenty thousand of the little beggars, munching their way through acres of your top grazing land. The only reason the sheep stations out here haven't got a problem with them at the moment is because there's a drought. Come the rain and they'll plague up, as they always do. The worst thing the English ever did to Australia was import the damned rabbit!'

'Well, you don't have to get all steamed up about it with me,' she pointed out huffily. 'It's not my fault!'

Suddenly he looked across and grinned at her, a wide, cheeky grin that was nothing like Earl would ever indulge in. She couldn't help it. She grinned back, and in that split second she knew she not only desired this man, but she liked him as well. Far too much.

Her grin faded, depression returning to take the place of pleasure. If only Ross genuinely returned the liking. If only she could inspire a fraction of the respect this Becky did...

'What have I done *now*?' he groaned frustratedly.

'Nothing,' she muttered. 'Nothing.'

'I don't seem to have to do anything to upset you, do I? What was it? Did I smile at you like Earl, is that it? Go on, you can tell me. I'm a big boy. I can take it!'

She shrank from his sarcastic outburst, turning her face away. What could she say to him? No, you remind me less and less of Earl with each passing moment...

'Don't you dare give me that silent treatment again, Vivien,' he snapped. 'I can't stand it.'

She sighed and turned back towards him. 'This isn't going to work out, is it, Ross?'

His mouth thinned stubbornly. 'It will, if you'll just give it a chance. Besides, what's your alternative—eight months of your mother's fussing?'

Vivien actually shuddered.

'See? At least I won't fuss over you. And neither will the rest of the people at Mountainview. They have too much to do. You'll be expected to pull your own weight out here, pregnant or not. That's what it's like in the country. You're not an invalid and you won't be treated like one.'

'Do you think that will bother me? I'm not lazy, Ross. I'm a worker too.'

'Then what *is* beginning to bother you? What have I said to make you look at me with such unhappy eyes?'

'I... I really wanted us to become friends.'

'And you think I don't?'

'Friends respect each other.'

He frowned over at her. 'I respect you.'

'No, you don't.'

'God, Vivien, what is this? Do you think I subscribe to that old double standard about sex? Do you think I think you're tainted somehow because you went to bed with me?'

'Yes,' she told him point-blank. 'If you didn't think like that, you'd have slept with Becky and to hell with her so-called innocence. Virginity is not a prize, Ross. It was only valued in the olden days because it assured the bridegroom that his bride would not have venereal disease. Making love is the most wonderful expression of love and affection that can exist between a man and a woman. Yet you backed away from it with the woman you claim you love in favour of it with a perfect stranger, in favour of a "city broad who probably knows more counter-moves than a chess champion". If that sounds as if you respect me then I'm a Dutchman's uncle!'

His face paled visibly, but he kept his eyes on the road ahead. 'That's not how it was, Vivien,' he said tautly.

'Oh?' she scoffed. 'Then how *was* it, Ross?'

'One day I might tell you,' he muttered. 'But for now I think you're forgetting a little something.'

'What?'

'The baby. *Our* baby. It's not the child's fault that he or she is going to be born. The least we can do is provide it with a couple of parents who aren't constantly at each other's throats. I realise I'm not the father you would have chosen for your child, Vivien. Neither am I yet able to fully understand your decision to actually go ahead with this pregnancy. I'm still to be convinced that it has nothing to do with my likeness to the man you're in love with.

'No, don't say a word!' he growled when she went to protest this assumption. 'You might not even recognise your own motives as yet. We all have dark and devious sides, some that remain hidden even to ourselves. But I will not have an innocent child suffer for the perversity of its parents. We're going to be mature about all this, Vivien. *You're* going to be mature. I want no more of your swinging moods or your wild, way-off accusations. You are to treat me with the same decency and respect that I will accord you. Or, by God, I'm going to lay you over my knee and whop that luscious backside of yours. Do I make myself clear?'

She eyed him fiercely, seething inside with a bitter resentment. Who did he think he was, telling her how to behave, implying that she had been acting like an immature idiot, threatening her with physical violence? As for dark and devious sides... he sure as hell had his fair share!

But aside from all that, Vivien could see that he *was* making *some* sense, despite his over-the-top threats. He even made her feel a little guilty. She hadn't really been thinking much about the baby's future welfare. She'd been consumed by her own ambivalent feelings for the man seated beside her. One moment she was desperate for him to like her, the next he was provoking her into a quite irrational anger, making her want to lash out at him. Right at this moment she would have liked to indulge in a bit of physical violence of her own!

Yes, but that's because you simply want to get your hands on him again, came a sinister voice from deep inside.

She stiffened.

'And you can cut out that outraged innocence act too!' he snapped, darting her a vicious glance. 'You're about as innocent as a vampire. *And* about as lethal! So I suggest you keep those pearly white teeth of yours safely within those blood-red lips for the remainder of this journey. For, if you open them again, I swear to you, Vivien, I'll forget that promise I made to you yesterday and give you another dose of what you've obviously been missing to have turned you into such a shrew. I'm sure you're quite capable of closing those big brown eyes of yours and pretending I'm Earl once more. And I'm just as capable of thoroughly enjoying myself in his stead!'

# CHAPTER NINE

IT WAS dusk when Ross and Vivien finally turned from the highway on to a private road. Narrow and dusty, it wound a slow, steady route through flat, almost grassless fields where Vivien only spotted one small flock of sheep, but she declined asking where the rest of the stock was. She wouldn't have lowered herself to make conversation with the man next to her. She was still too angry with him.

How dared he threaten to practically rape her? He might not literally mean it, but she couldn't abide men who used verbal abuse and physical threats to intimidate women. It just showed you the sort of man Ross was underneath his surface charm. As for suggesting that she would actually enjoy it...

*That* galled most of all. Because she wasn't at all sure that she *wouldn't*!

Self-disgust kept her temper simmering away in a grimly held silence while she stared out of the passenger window, her lips pressed angrily together. Eventually, the flat paddocks gave way to rolling brown hills. One was quite steep, and, as they came over the crest, there, in the distance, lay some bluish-looking mountains. But closer, on the crest of the next hill, and surrounded by tall, dark green trees, stood a home of such grandeur and elegance that Vivien caught her breath in surprise.

'I did tell you it was big,' Ross remarked drily.

'So you did,' she said equally drily, then turned flashing brown eyes his way. 'I'm allowed to talk now, am I? I won't be suitably punished for my temerity in opening my blood-red lips?'

His sigh was weary. It made Vivien suddenly feel small. What was the matter with her? She was rarely reduced to using such vicious sarcasm. She could be stubborn, but usually quietly so, with a cool, steely determination that was far more effective than more volatile methods. Yet here she was, flying off the handle at every turn. Snapping and snarling like a she-cat.

It had to be her hormones, she decided unhappily. God, but she was a mess!

She turned to look once more at the huge house, and as they drew closer an oddly apprehensive shiver trickled down her spine. Vivien knew immediately that she would not like living at Mountainview. If she stayed the full month, she would be very surprised. Yet she could not deny it was a beautiful-looking home. Very beautiful indeed.

Edwardian in style and two-storeyed, with long, graceful white columns running from the stone-flagged patio right up through the upper-floor wooden veranda to the gabled roof. An equally elegant white ironwork spanned the distance between these columns, for decoration alone downstairs, but for safety as well between the bases of the upstairs pillars.

Not that Vivien could picture too many youngsters climbing over that particular railing anyway. The house had a museum-like quality about it, enhanced possibly by the fact that only a couple of lights shone in the windows as they drove up in the rapidly fading light.

The Range Rover crunched to a halt on the gravel driveway, Ross turning to Vivien with an expectant look on his face. 'Well? What do you think of it?'

'It's—er—very big.'

'You don't like it,' he said with amazement in his voice and face.

'No, no,' she lied. 'It's quite spectacular. I'm just very tired, Ross.'

His face softened and Vivien turned hers away. She wished he didn't have the capacity to look at her like that, with such sudden warmth and compassion. It turned her bones to water, making her feel weak and vulnerable. Instinct warned her that Ross was not a man you showed such a vulnerability to.

'You must be,' he said as he opened his door. 'I'll take you inside then come back for the luggage. Once you're settled in the kitchen with one of Helga's mugs of tea you'll feel better.'

It was only after she alighted that Vivien recognised the truth of her excuse to Ross. Yet she was more than tired. She was exhausted. Her legs felt very heavy and she had to push them to lug her weary body up the wide, flagged steps. When she hesitated on the top step, swaying slightly, Ross's hand shot out to steady her.

'Are you all right, Vivien?'

She took a couple of deep breaths. 'Yes, I think so. Just a touch dizzy there for a sec.'

Before she could say another word he swept one arm around her waist, the other around her knees, and hoisted her up high into his arms. 'I'll carry you straight up to bed. Helga can bring your tea to your room. You can meet Dad in the morning.'

Suddenly, Vivien felt too drained to protest. She went quite limp in Ross's arms, her head sagging against his chest, her hands linking weakly around his neck lest they flop down by her sides like dead weights. Her eyelashes fluttered down to rest on the darkly smudged shadows beneath her eyes. She felt rather than saw Ross's careful ascent up a long flight of stairs.

'You're very strong,' she whispered once in her semi-conscious daze.

He didn't answer.

Next thing she knew she was being lowered on to a soft mattress, her head sinking into a downy pillow. She felt her sandals being pulled off, a rug or blanket being draped over her legs. She sighed a shuddering sigh as the last of her energy fled her body. Within sixty seconds she was fast asleep, totally unaware of the man standing beside the bed staring down at her with a tight, pained look on his face.

After an interminable time, he bent to lightly touch her cheek, then to draw a wisp of hair from where it lay across her softly parted lips. His hand lingered, giving in to the urge to rub gently against the pouting flesh. She stirred, made a mewing sound like a sleepy kitten that had been dragged from its mother's teat. Her tongue-tip flicked out to moisten dry lips, the action sending a spurt of desire to his loins so sharp that he groaned aloud.

Spinning on his heels, he strode angrily from the room.

Vivien woke to the sound of raised voices. For a moment she couldn't remember where she was, or whose voices they could possibly be. But gradually her eyes and brain refocused on where she was.

Once properly awake, one quick glance took in the large, darkly furnished bedroom, the double bed she was lying on, the moonlight streaming in the open french doors on to the polished wooden floors, the balcony beyond those doors. Levering herself up on to one elbow, she noticed that on the nearest bedside table rested a tray, which held a tall glass of milk and a plate on which was a sandwich, a piece of iced fruit cake and a couple of plain milk-coffee biscuits.

But neither the room nor the food was of any real interest to Vivien at that moment. Her whole attention was on the argument that was cutting through the still night air with crystal clarity.

'I don't understand why you had to bring her here,' a male voice snarled. 'How do you think Becky's going to feel when she finds out? You've broken her heart, do you know that? I was over there today and she——'

'What do you mean, you were over there today?' Ross broke in testily. 'You were supposed to be checking all the bores today.'

'Yeah, well, I didn't, did I? I'll do them tomorrow.'

'Tomorrow... You've always got some excuse, haven't you? God, Gavin, when are you going to learn some sense of responsibility? Don't you know that one day without water could be the difference between life and death in a drought like this? What on earth's the matter with you? Why don't you grow up?'

'I *am* grown-up. And I *can* be responsible. It's just that you and Dad won't give me a chance at any real responsibility. All you give me is orders!'

'Which you can't follow.'

'I can too.'

'No you bloody well can't! Just look at the bores today.'

'Oh, bugger the bores. We've hardly got any sheep left anyway. You sold them all.'

'Better sold than dead.'

'That was your opinion. You never asked me for mine. I would have kept them, hand-fed them.'

'At what cost? Be sensible, Gavin. I made the right business decision, the only decision.'

'Business! Since when has life on the land been reduced to nothing but business decisions? Since *you* came home to run things, that's when. You're a hard-hearted ruthless bastard, Ross, who'll stop at nothing to get what you want. And I know what that is. You want Mountainview. The land and the house. Not just your half, either. You want it all! That's why you were going to marry Becky. Not because you fell in love with her, but because you knew Dad was keen for one of us to marry and produce an heir before he died. That's why you dumped Becky and brought that other city bitch back here. Because she's already having your kid. You think that will sway Dad into changing his will all the sooner. Yeah, now I see it. I see it all!'

'You're crazy,' Ross snapped. 'Or crazy drunk. Is that it? Have you been drinking again?'

'So what if I have?'

'I should have known. You're only this irrational—and this articulate—when you're drunk.'

'Not like you, eh, big brother? You've got the gift of the gab all the time, haven't you? You can charm the birds right out of the trees. I'll bet that poor bitch upstairs doesn't even know what part she's playing in all this. You've got it made, haven't you? The heir you needed plus a hot little number on tap. A lay, laid on every night. I'll bet she's good in bed too. I'll bet she——'

The sounds of a scuffle replaced the voices. Vivien sat bolt upright, her heart going at fifty to the dozen, her mind whirling with all sorts of shocking thoughts. Could Gavin really be right? Was she some pawn in a game much larger and darker than she'd ever imagined? Were she and her child to be Ross's ace card in gaining the inheritance his brother seemed to think he coveted? It would explain why Ross had not made love to this Becky if he didn't really love her...

Shakily, she stood up and made her way out on to the balcony. The night air was silent now, the earlier sounds of fighting having stopped. The sky overhead was black and clear with a myriad stars, the moon a bright orb, bathing everything beneath in its pale, ghostly light.

Gingerly, Vivien looked down over the railing.

Ross was standing there on the driveway next to his Range Rover, disconsolate and alone. While she watched silently, he lifted his hands to rake back his dishevelled hair, expelling a ragged sigh. 'Crazy fool,' he muttered.

Vivien didn't think she made a move, or a sound. But suddenly Ross's head jerked up and those piercing eyes were staring straight into hers. Worried first, then assessing, he held her startled gaze for several seconds before speaking. And then it was to say only three sharp words, 'Stay right there.'

She barely had time to compose her rattled self before Ross was standing right in front of her, his big strong hands gripping her upper arms, his sharp blue eyes boring down into hers.

'How much did you hear?' he demanded to know.

'E—e-enough,' she stammered.

'Enough. Dear God in heaven. And did you believe what that fool said? *Did* you?' he repeated, shaking her.

Vivien could hardly think. 'I . . . I don't know what to believe any more.'

'*Don't* believe what my brother said, for Pete's sake,' Ross insisted harshly. 'He's all mixed up in the head at the moment. Believe what *I* tell you, Vivien. Your presence here has nothing to do with Mountainview. Nothing at all! You're here only because I want you here, because I . . . I . . . Goddammit, woman, why do you have to be so darned beautiful?'

And, digging his fingers into her flesh, he lifted her body and mouth to his, taking it wildly and hungrily in a savage kiss. For a few tempestuous moments, she found herself responding to his desperate desire, parting her lips and allowing his tongue full reign within her mouth. But when he groaned and swept his arms down around her, pressing the entire length of her against him, the stark evidence of a full-blooded male erection lying between them slammed her back to reality.

'No!' she gasped, wrenching her mouth from his. 'Let me go!' With a tortured cry, she struggled free of his torrid embrace, staggering back against the railing, staring up at him with wide, accusing eyes.

'You . . . you said this wasn't why you brought me here,' she flung at him shakily. 'You promised to keep your hands off.'

The sudden and shocking suspicion that he might have been using sex to direct her mind away from Gavin's accusations blasted into Vivien's brain, making her catch her breath. Dear heaven, he couldn't be that wicked, could he? Or that devious?

She stared at Ross, trying to find some reassurance now in his flushed face and heaving chest, as well as the memory of his explicit arousal. That, at least, was not a sham, she conceded. That was real. *Too* real.

But then his desire for her had always been real. That did not mean Gavin wasn't telling the truth. Ross could still be the ruthless opportunist his brother accused him of being, one who could quite happily satisfy his lust for her while achieving his own dark ends.

'I promised there would not be a repeat of what happened that night at Wallaby Creek,' he ground out. 'And there won't.'

'And... and what was that you were just doing if not trying to seduce me?' she blustered, still not convinced, despite his sounding amazingly sincere.

'That was my being a bloody idiot. But I was only kissing you, Vivien. Don't hang me for a simple kiss. Still, I will endeavour to keep my hands well and truly off in future. As for my reasons for bringing you here... I can only repeat it has everything to do with my child, but nothing to do with Mountainview. You have my solemn oath on that. Now go back to bed. You still look tired. I'll see you in the morning.'

Vivien stared after him as he whirled and strode off along the balcony and around the corner.

A simple kiss? There'd been nothing simple about that kiss. Nothing simple at all...

And there was nothing simple about this whole situation.

Though had there ever been?

Vivien lifted trembling hands to push the hair back off her face. God knew where all this was going to end. Perhaps it would be best if she cut her visit short here, if she declined taking the position as companion to Ross's father. There were too many undercurrents going on in this household, too many mysteries, too much ill feeling.

Vivien wanted no part in them. Life was complicated enough without getting involved in family feuds. Yes, she would tell Ross in the morning that she wanted to go back home.

Feeling marginally better, Vivien made her way back into the bedroom, intending to drink the milk then change into some nightwear before going back to bed. But she found herself lying down again, fully dressed, on top of the bed. Soon, she was sound asleep again.

# CHAPTER TEN

WHEN Vivien woke a second time, it was morning. Mid-morning, by the feel of the heat already building in the closed room. Her slim silver wristwatch confirmed her guess. It was ten-fifteen.

With a groan she swung her stiffened legs over the side of the bed and sat up, thinking to herself that she could do with a shower. It was then that she remembered her decision of the night before to go straight back home.

Somehow, however, in the clear light of day, that seemed a hasty, melodramatic decision. She'd been very tired last night. Overwrought, even. Perhaps she should give Ross and his father and Mountainview a few days at least.

As for Gavin's accusations that his older brother was a ruthless bastard intent on using Vivien and her baby to gain an inheritance... Well, that too felt melodramatic, now that she could think clearly. Ross might be a typically selfish male in some ways, but she had sensed nothing from him but true affection and concern for his family. She'd also been impressed by the way he'd handled things with *her* parents. Ross was not a cruel, callous man. Not at all.

Yes. The matter was settled. She would stay a while. A week, at least. Then, if things weren't working out, she would make some excuse and go home. She could always say she couldn't stand the heat. That would hardly be a lie, Vivien thought, as beads of perspiration started trickling down between her breasts.

Feeling the call of nature, she rose and went to investigate the two panelled wooden doors that led off the bedroom. The first was an exit, leading out on to a huge rectangular gallery. The second revealed an *en suite* that, though its décor was in keeping with the house's Edwardian style, was still obviously fairly new.

Vivien was amused by the gold chain she had to pull to flush the toilet, smiling as she washed her hands with a tiny, shell-like soap.

On going back into the hot room, she started unpacking, having spied her suitcase resting on the ottoman at the foot of the bed. A shower was definitely called for, she decided, plus nothing heavier to wear than shorts and a cool top.

Since everything was very crushed she chose a simple shorts set in a peacock-blue T-shirt material, with a tropical print of yellow and orange hibiscus on it. The creases would fall out if she hung it up behind the bathroom door while she had a shower. With the outfit draped over an arm, and some fresh underwear and her bag of toiletries filling both hands, Vivien made for the shower.

The hot water felt so delicious that she wallowed in it for ages, shampooing her hair a couple of times during the process, the heat having made her thick black tresses feel limp and greasy. Once clean, however, her hair sprang around her face and shoulders in a myriad damp curls and waves. In deference to the heat, Vivien bypassed full make-up, putting on a dab of coral lipstick, a minimal amount of waterproof mascara and a liberal lashing of Loulou, her favourite perfume.

Electing to leave her hair damp rather than blow-dry it, Vivien opened the door of the bathroom feeling refreshed but a little nervous. What was she supposed to do? Where should she go?

The unexpected sight of a large grey-haired woman in a mauve floral dress bustling to and fro across the bedroom, hanging Vivien's clothes up for her in the elegantly carved wardrobe, replaced any nerves with a stab of surprise. And a degree of dry amusement.

So this was Helga...

'And good morning to you too,' Helga threw across the room before she could say a word. 'High time you got up. Nothing worse than lying in bed too long. Bad for the digestion. I've straightened your bed and turned on the ceiling fan. Didn't you see it there? It's best to leave the windows and doors closed till the afternoon, then I'll come up and open them. We usually get an afternoon breeze. And leave your dirty washing in the linen basket in the corner.

'I'm Helga, by the way. I dare say Ross has told you about me. Not in glowing terms, I would imagine,' she added with a dry cackle. 'We never did get along, me and that lad. He's not the sort to follow orders kindly. Still, he's turned out all right, I guess. Loves his dad, which goes down a long way with me.'

She drew breath at last to give Vivien the once-over. 'Well, you certainly are one stunning-looking girl, aren't you? But then, I wouldn't expect any different from Ross. Only the best would ever do for him. Fancy schools in Sydney. Fancy flying lessons. Now a fancy woman...'

Vivien drew in a sharply offended breath, and was just about to launch into a counter-attack when Helga dismissed any defensive speech with a sharp wave of her hand.

'Now don't go getting your knickers all in a knot, lovie. No offence intended. Besides, there's no one happier than me that you put a spoke in Ross's plans to marry Becky. I presume you know who Becky is?'

Vivien found herself nodding dumbly. She'd never met anyone quite like Helga. Talk about intimidating! Ross had her undying admiration if he stood up to this bulldozer of a woman.

'Well, let me tell you a little secret about Miss Becky Macintosh,' Helga boomed on. 'She's always hankered after living at Mountainview, ever since she was knee-high to a grasshopper. She's no more in love with Ross than I am. But he's a mighty handsome man and a girl could do worse than put her slippers under his bed every night. When Oliver had his stroke and Ross came back home, Becky saw her chance and set her cap at him. Lord, butter wouldn't have melted in her mouth around him all year. But it's not the man she wants. It's Mountainview!'

Helga snapped the suitcase shut and started doing the buckles up.

'Why are you telling me all this?' Vivien asked on a puzzled note.

A sly look came over Helga's plain, almost masculine face. 'Because I don't want you worrying that you might be breaking Becky's heart if you marry Ross. That little minx will simply move on to the next brother, which will be by far the best for all concerned.'

Vivien bypassed Helga's conclusion that she wanted to marry Ross to concentrate on her next startling statement. 'You mean——'

'My Gavin loves her,' Helga broke in with a maternal passion that was unexpectedly fierce. 'He's loved her for years. But he's painfully shy around girls—unless he's been drinking. He can't seem to bring himself to tell her how he feels. Now, after this episode with Ross, he doesn't think he'll ever stand a chance. He's always felt inferior to his big brother. But if Ross moved far away...'

'I see,' Vivien murmured. 'Yes, I see...'

'You won't want to live here, will you? A city girl like you will want the bright lights. Ross likes action too, not the slowness of station life. You'll both be happy enough well away from here.'

Looking at Helga's anxious face, Vivien was moved to pity for her. She must love Gavin very, very much. As for Gavin... Her heart really went out to him. It couldn't be easy being Ross's brother. Even harder with the two brothers loving the same girl. That was one factor Helga had blithely forgotten. What of Ross's feelings in all this? Or didn't they count?

'I'm sorry, Helga,' she explained, 'but Ross and I have no plans to marry. We're not in love, you see.'

'Not in love?' Helga looked down at Vivien's stomach with a disdainful glower. 'Then what are you doing having his child? Not in love! Well, I never! What's the world coming to, I ask you, with girls going round having babies with men they don't love? It makes one ashamed of one's own sex!'

Vivien's lovely brown eyes flashed defiance as she drew herself up straight and proud.

'I would think you should feel more ashamed of this Becky than me,' she countered vehemently. 'At least I'm honest about my feelings. She sounds like a shallow, materialistic, manipulative little witch, and

I'm not sorry at all that Ross is not going to marry her. He deserves better than that. Much better. He's a... a... And what are you laughing at?' she demanded angrily when Helga started to cackle.

Again that sly look returned. 'Just thinking what similar personalities you and Ross have. Both as stubborn as mules. Lord knows what kind of child you're going to have. He'll probably end up running the world!'

'It might be a daughter!'

'Then *she'll* run the world.'

Helga grinned a highly satisfied grin, stopping Vivien in her tracks. Against her better judgement, she found herself grinning back. She shook her head in a type of bewilderment before a sudden thought wiped the grin from her face.

'Ross doesn't know about Gavin loving Becky, does he?' she asked.

'No,' the older woman admitted. 'Gavin made me promise not to tell him.'

'I see. So you told me instead, hoping I might relay the information. That way you'd keep your promise, but get the message across.'

Helga's look was sharp. 'There's no flies on you, lovie, is there? Now how about a spot of breakfast? You'll want a good plateful, I'll warrant, since you didn't eat the supper I left you. Remember, you're eating for two.'

Vivien only just managed to suppress a groan of true dismay as she slipped on her sandals and followed Helga from the room.

The kitchen was as huge as the rest of the house. But far more homely, with copper pots hanging over the stove, dressers full of flowered crockery and knick-knacks leaning against the walls, and an enormous table in the centre.

'Do you really look after this whole place by yourself?' Vivien asked whilst Helga was piling food on to the largest plate she'd ever seen. She already had a mug of tea in front of her that would have satisfied a giant.

'Sure do, lovie. Keeps me fit, I can tell you. Here, get this into you!' And she slapped the plate down in front of her. There were three rashers of bacon, two eggs, a lamb chop and some grilled tomato, not to mention two slices of toast.

Vivien felt her stomach heave. Swallowing, she picked up the knife and fork and started rearranging the bacon. 'Er—do you know where Ross is this morning?' she asked by way of distraction.

'Right here,' he said, striding into the kitchen and sitting down in a chair opposite her. Vivien looked down, thinking that she would never get used to the way her heart skipped a beat every time she saw him. Of course, it didn't help that he only had a pair of jeans on. Not a thing on his top half. Sitting down, he looked naked.

'You look refreshed this morning, Vivien,' he said, virtually forcing her to look back up at him. She did, keeping her gaze well up. Unfortunately, she found herself staring straight at his mouth and remembering how she had felt when he'd kissed her last night.

'I presume you want a mug of tea?' Helga asked Ross.

'Sure do. And a piece of that great Christmas cake you made.'

Helga threw him a dry look. 'No need to suck up to me, my lad. Your girl and I are already firm friends, aren't we, lovie?'

'Oh—er—yes,' Vivien stammered, which brought a surprised look from Ross.

'I see she appreciates your cooking as well,' he said, and gave Vivien a sneaky wink. She rolled her eyes at the food and he laughed. But laughter made the muscles ripple in his chest and she quickly looked down again, forcing a mouthful of egg in between suddenly dry lips.

'Where's Gavin?' Helga went on. 'Doesn't he want a cup too?'

'Nope. He's out checking bores. Won't be back till well after lunch.'

'Out checking bores?' Helga persisted. '*Today*? But it's going to be a scorcher. Why couldn't he go tomorrow?'

'Because he was supposed to have gone yesterday,' Ross informed her drily.

Helga looked pained and shook her head. 'That boy... Still, you have to understand he's been upset lately, Ross. He's not himself.'

'Well, he'd better get back to being himself quick smart,' Ross said firmly, 'or there won't be anything to do around here except have endless mugs of tea. Sheep don't live on love alone.'

A stark silence descended while Ross finished his tea and Vivien waded through as much of the huge breakfast as her stomach could stand. Finally, she pushed the plate aside, whereupon Helga frowned. Before her disapproval could erupt into words Ross was on his feet and asking Vivien if he could have a few words with her in private.

It was a testimony to Helga's formidable personality that Vivien was grateful to be swept away into Ross's company when he was semi-naked.

'Don't let Helga bully you into eating too much,' was Ross's first comment as they walked along the hallway together.

'I'll try not to. Where... where are we going?' she asked once they moved across the tiled foyer and started up the stairs.

He slanted her a look which suggested he'd caught the nervousness behind her question and was genuinely puzzled by it. 'I need to shower and change before taking you along to meet Dad,' he explained. 'I thought we could talk at the same time.'

He stopped at the top of the stairs, his blue eyes glittering with a sardonic amusement. 'Of course, I don't expect you to accompany me into my bathroom. You can sit on my bed and talk to me from there. Let me assure you the shower is not visible from the bedroom.'

Sit on his bed...

Dear heaven, that was bad enough.

Noting that he was watching her closely, Vivien lifted her nose and adopted what she hoped was an expression of utter indifference. 'I doubt it would bother me if it was,' she repudiated. 'I've seen it all before.'

His features tightened, but he said nothing, ushering her along the upstairs hall and into his bedroom, shutting the door carefully behind them. When he saw her startled look, a wry smile lifted the grimness from his face.

'You may be blasé about male nudity, Vivien, my dear, but Helga is not so sophisticated. Do sit down, however. You make me uncomfortable standing there with your hands clasped defensively in front of you. I had no dark or dastardly plan in bringing you up here, though I appreciate now that my idea of having a normal chat with you while I showered was stupid. Best I simply hurry with my ablutions and then we'll talk.'

Five minutes later he came out of the closed bathroom dressed in bright shorts and a loose white T-shirt with a colourful geometric design on the back and a surfing logo on the sleeves.

It was the longest five minutes Vivien had ever spent. Who would have believed the sound of a shower running could be so disturbing?

'You look as if you're ready to shoot the waves at Bondi,' she commented, mocking herself silently for the way she was openly feasting her eyes on him this time. But she couldn't seem to help herself.

'Dad likes bright clothes. They cheer him up.'

'That's good,' she said, and bounced up on to her feet. 'Most of my clothes are bright.'

'So I noticed.'

'You don't approve?'

'Would it matter if I didn't?'

'No.'

His smile was dry. 'That's what I thought. Shall we go?'

'But you said you wanted to talk to me.'

'I've changed my mind. I'm sure you'll handle Dad OK. You seem to have a knack with men. Follow me.'

She did so in silence, her thoughts a-whirl. What was eating at Ross? Was it sexual frustration, or frustration of another kind? She seemed to be getting mixed messages from him. One minute she thought he admired her, though grudgingly. The next, he was openly sarcastic.

They trundled down the stairs and along a different corridor, towards the back section of the house.

'In here,' Ross directed, and opened a door into a cool, cosily furnished bed-sitting-room. She found out later that it had once been part of the servants' quarters, when Mountainview had had lots of servants. Ross had had it renovated and air-conditioned before his father came home from hospital.

'Dad?' Ross ventured softly. 'You're not asleep, are you?'

The old man resting in the armchair beside the window had had his eyes closed, his head listing to one side. But with Ross's voice his head jerked up and around, his eyes snapping open. They looked straight at Vivien, their gaze both direct and assessing.

'Hello, Mr Everton,' she said, and came forward to hold out her hand. 'I'm Vivien.'

Pale, parched lips cracked back into a semblance of a smile. 'So...you're Vivien...' His eyes slid slowly down her body, then up over her shoulder towards his son. 'Now...I understand,' he said, the talking clearly an effort for him. Vivien noticed that one side of his face screwed up when he spoke, the aftermath, she realised, of his stroke. 'They don't...come along...like her...too often...'

Vivien was slightly put out by his remarks. Why did men have to reduce women to sex objects?

'They don't come along like Ross too often either,' she countered, quite tartly.

The old man laughed, and immediately was consumed by racking coughs. Ross raced to pick up the glass of water resting on the table beside him, holding him gently around the shoulders till the coughing subsided, then pressing the water to his lips. Vivien hovered, feeling useless and a little guilty. She should have kept her stupid, proud mouth shut! The man meant no harm.

'You should let me call in the doctor, Dad,' Ross was saying worriedly. 'This coughing of yours is getting worse.'

'No... more... doctors,' his father managed to get out. 'No more. They'll only... put me... in hospital. I want to... to die here.'

Ross's laugh was cajoling. 'You're not going to die, Dad. Dr Harmon said that with a little more rest and therapy you'll be as good as new.'

'Perhaps,' he muttered. 'Perhaps. Now... get lost. I wish... to talk... to Vivien. *Alone*. You cramp... my style.'

'All right. But don't talk too much, mind?' And Ross lanced his father with an oddly sharp look. 'You'll find me in the library when he's finished with you, Vivien.'

'Call me... Oliver,' was the first thing Ross's father said once they were alone. 'Now, tell me... all about... yourself.'

For over an hour, Vivien chatted away, answering Oliver's never-ending questions. It worried her that he was becoming overtired, but every time she touched on the subject of his health he vetoed her impatiently.

It was clear where Ross had got his determination and stubbornness. Yet, for all his questions, Oliver never once enquired about her feelings for his son, or Ross's for her. He never asked her what she wanted for the future, either for herself or her baby. He wanted to know about her background, her growing-up years, her education, her job and her family. Finally, he sighed and leant back into the chair.

'You'll do, Vivien,' he said. 'You'll do...'

'As what, Oliver?'

His smile was as cunning as Helga's. 'Why... as the mother... of my grandchild. What else? Now run along... It's lunchtime... But tell Ross... I don't want... any.'

Vivien closed the door softly, her mind still on Ross's father.

Oliver Everton didn't fool her for one minute. He was going to try to marry her off to Ross. Not that she blamed him. Death was very definitely knocking at his door and he wanted things all tied up with pink bows before he left this world.

Gavin was accusing the wrong man when he said Ross was trying to manipulate his father. It was the father who was the manipulator, who had perhaps always been the manipulator at Mountainview. Maybe that was why Ross had chosen to follow a career away from home, and why Gavin hadn't. The stronger brother bucking the heavy hand of the father while the weaker one knuckled under.

Now, illness had brought the prodigal—and perhaps favoured—son home and the father was going to make the most of it. Vivien wouldn't put it past Oliver having been the one to insist Ross bring her out here, hoping that the sexual attraction that had once flared out of control between them would do so again, thereby making his job easier of convincing them marriage was the best course for all concerned.

And he'd been half right, the cunning old devil. That electric chemistry was still sparking as strong as ever. She could hardly look at Ross without thinking about that night, without longing to find out if the wonder of it all had been real or an illusion. How long, she worried anew, before her own body language started sending out those tell-tale waves of desire in Ross's direction? How long before his male antennae picked up on them?

He was not a man to keep promises he sensed she didn't want him to keep. He was a sexual predator, a hunter. He would zero in for the kill the moment she weakened. Of that she was certain.

So why stay? her conscience berated. Why tempt fate?

Because she had to. For some reason she just had to...

## CHAPTER ELEVEN

'THERE you are!' Vivien exclaimed exasperatedly when she finally found the library. 'This house is like a maze.'

'Only downstairs,' Ross said, having glanced up from where he was sitting behind a large cedar desk in the far corner. With her arrival, he put the paperwork he was doing in a drawer and stood up. 'You must have really got along with Dad to stay so long.'

'Yes, I did,' she agreed, glancing around the room, which was exactly as she'd first imagined. Leather furniture, heavy velvet curtains and floor-to-ceiling bookshelves. 'I think he quite likes me.'

'I don't doubt it,' Ross muttered as he strode round the desk, his caustic tone drawing both her attention and her anger.

'Do you *have* to be sarcastic all the time?'

'Am I?' There was an oddly surprised note in his voice, as though he hadn't realised his bad manners.

'Yes, you are!'

'You're exaggerating, surely. I think I've been very polite, in the circumstances. Well? What did you think of Dad?'

Vivien sighed her irritation at having her complaint summarily brushed aside. What circumstances did he mean, anyway?

'He's a very sick man,' she commented at last.

'He's as strong as an ox,' came the impatient rebuttal.

'Not any longer, Ross. Maybe you've been away from home too long.'

'Meaning?'

She shrugged. 'People change. Things change.'

'I get the impression I'm supposed to read between the lines here.' Ross leant back against the corner of the desk, his arms folding. 'What's changed around Mountainview that I don't know about?'

Vivien frowned. This was not going to be easy, but it had to be done. 'Well, for one thing...did you know Gavin was in love with Becky?'

Ross straightened, his face showing true shock. 'Good God, he isn't, is he?'

She nodded slowly.

'Who told you that? It couldn't have been Dad!'

'No. Helga.'

He groaned, his shoulders sagging. 'Bloody hell. Poor Gavin...'

'Helga also says Becky doesn't really love you. She says the girl has always coveted Mountainview.'

Ross's eyes jerked up, angry this time. 'Damn and blast, what is this? You've been in this house less than twenty-four hours and already you know more about what's going on around here than I do. Why hasn't someone told me any of this? Why tell you? What do you have that I don't have?'

She looked past his anger, fully understanding his resentment. 'Objectivity, perhaps?' she tried ruefully.

'Objectivity?' His lips curled into a snarl. 'Oh, yes, you've got that all right, haven't you?'

She wasn't quite sure what he meant by that. Maybe he didn't mean anything. Maybe he just felt the need to lash out blindly. 'Ross, I... I'm really sorry.'

'For what?'

'For being the one to tell you that the woman you're in love with doesn't love you back.'

He stared at her, his blue eyes icy with bitterness. 'You don't have to be sorry about that, Vivien,' he bit out coldly. 'Because I already knew that. I've known it all along.'

'But... but——'

'You of all people should know that love is not always returned. But that doesn't stop you from loving that person, does it? Aren't you still in love with your Earl?'

'I... I'm not sure...'

'Real love doesn't cease as quickly as that, my dear,' he scorned. 'You either loved the man or you didn't. What was it?'

'I *did* love him,' she insisted, hating the feeling of being backed into a corner. But if he expected her to admit to not loving a man she'd lived with for nearly eighteen months then he was heartily mistaken. Yet even as she made the claim she knew it to be a lie. She had not loved Earl. Not really.

'Then you still do,' he insisted fiercely. 'Believe me. You still do. Now I must go and talk to my father. If what you say is all true then I have no time to waste. Things have to be done before it's too late.'

'Too late for what? What things?'

His returning look was cool. 'That is not your concern. You've done your objective duty. Now I suggest you go and have some lunch, then do what pregnant ladies do on a hot afternoon. Lie down and rest. Or, if that doesn't appeal, read one of these books. I'm sure there's enough of a selection here to satisfy the most catholic of tastes.'

'Ross!' she called out as he went to leave.

He turned slowly, his face hard.

'Please...don't be angry with me...'

The steely set to his mouth softened. He sighed. 'I'm not. Not really...'

'You...you seem to be.'

The slightest of smiles touched his mouth, but not his eyes. 'It's fate I'm angry with, Vivien. Fate...'

'Now you're being cryptic.'

'Am I? Yes, possibly I am. Let's say then that I'm angry with what I have no control over.'

'But you're not angry with me personally.'

'No.'

'Then will you show me around the house later, after you're finished with your father?'

He stared at her for a moment, his eyes searching. 'It will be my pleasure,' he said with a somewhat stiff little bow.

'I...I'll probably be here,' she said. 'I don't want any lunch. Oh, that reminds me. Your father said to tell you he didn't want any lunch either.'

A dry smile pulled at Ross's mouth. 'Helga *will* be pleased.' And, giving her one last incisive and rather disturbing glance, he turned and left the room.

Vivien stared after him, aware that her heart was pounding. Already, she was looking forward to his return, knowing full well that it wasn't the thought of a tour through this house that was exciting her. It was the prospect of being alone again with Ross.

A shiver ran through her. Oh, Oliver...you are a wicked, wicked man.

Ross returned shortly after two to find Vivien curled up in one of the large lounge chairs, trying valiantly to read a copy of *Penmarric*. The book was probably as good as everyone had told her it was, but she just hadn't been able to keep her mind on it.

Once the reason for this walked into the room she abandoned all pretence at finding the book engrossing, snapping it shut with an almost relieved sigh.

'Finished your business?' she said, and uncurled her long legs.

'For now. Come on, if you want to see the house.'

His tone was clipped, his expression harried. Clearly, his visit to his father had not been a pleasant one. Vivien wished she could ask him what it was all about, but Ross's closed face forbade any such quizzing. Instead, she put the book back and went to join him in the doorway, determined to act as naturally as possible.

But her resolve to ignore the physical effect Ross kept having on her was waylaid when he moved left just as she moved right and they collided midstream. His hands automatically grabbed her shoulders and suddenly there they were, chest to chest, thigh to thigh, looking into each other's eyes.

Vivien gave a nervous laugh. 'Sorry.'

Ross said absolutely nothing. But there was no doubting he was as agitated by her closeness as she was by his. After what felt like an interminable delay, his hands dropped from her shoulders and he stepped back. 'After you,' he said with a deep wave of his right hand and a self-mocking look on his face. See? it said. I'm a man of my word. I'm keeping my hands off.

But did Vivien want him to keep his hands off? So much had changed now. Becky didn't love him, and, while Ross might think he loved her, there was no doubting he was still very attracted to *herself*. And what of her own feelings for Ross? Had they changed too? Deepened, maybe?

She couldn't be sure, certainly not with the chemistry between them still sparking away at a million volts. Vivien would just have to wait a while longer to find out about her feelings. That was what her mother had told her to do. Wait.

'Oh, my God, *Mum*!' she gasped aloud.

Ross looked taken aback. 'What about her?'

'I forgot to ring her, let her know we arrived all right. She'll be worried to death, and so will Dad.'

'Worried?' His smile carried a wry amusement. 'About their highly independent, very sensible, grown-up girl?'

'Who happens to be on her way to being an unmarried mother,' was her droll return. 'That's really surpassing myself in common sense, isn't it? Now point me to a telephone, Ross, or you'll have my mother on your doorstep.'

'There's an extension in the foyer, underneath the stairs.'

Unfortunately, Ross sat on those stairs while she dialled the number, making her feel self-conscious about what she was going to say. The phone at the other end only rang once before it was swept up.

'Peggy Roberts here,' her mother answered in a breathless tone.

'Mum, it's Vivien.'

'Oh, Vivien, darling! I'm so glad you rang. I've been rather worried.'

'No need, Mum. I'm fine. Sorry I didn't ring sooner, but by the time we arrived last night I was so tired I went straight to bed and slept in atrociously late this morning. Then Ross wanted me to meet his father and we talked for simply ages.'

'Oh? And how is Mr Everton senior? Getting better, I hope.'

'Well, he—er—reminded me a little of Uncle Jack a few weeks after his stroke.'

'You mean just before he died?'

'Er—yes...'

'Oh, dear. Oh, how sad. Well, be nice to him, dear. And be nice to Ross. He's a sweet man, not at all what your father and I were expecting. We were very impressed with him.'

'So I noticed.'

'You don't think that you and he—er—might...' She left the words hanging. *Get married*?

Vivien knew what would happen if she even hinted marriage was vaguely possible. She'd never hear the end of it. Yet her mother's even asking the question sent an odd little leap to her heart. Who knew? If Becky didn't love Ross, there might be a chance. *If* she fell in love with him, and *if* he did with her.

That was a lot of ifs.

'Not at this stage, Mum.'

'Oh...' Disappointment in her voice.

'Give Dad my love and tell him not to worry about me. I know he worries.'

'We both do, dear. Do you know how long you'll be staying out there?' Now her voice was wistful.

'Can't say. I'll write. Tell you all about the place. Must fly. I don't like to stay on someone else's phone too long.'

'I'll write to you too.'

'Yes, please do. Bye, Mum. Keep well.'

'Bye, darling. Thanks for ringing.'

Swallowing, she replaced the receiver and walked round to the foot of the stairs. Ross was sitting a half-dozen steps up, looking rather like a lost little boy. Suddenly, Vivien thought of *his* mother. What had she been like? Did he still miss her? She knew she would die if anything happened to her mother. Much as Peggy sometimes interfered and fussed, Vivien always knew the interference and fuss was based on the deepest of loves, that of a mother for her child.

Automatically, she thought of her own baby, and a soft smile lit her face. For the first time, she felt really positive about her decision to have Ross's baby. No matter what happened, that part was right. Very right indeed.

'You look very pleased with yourself,' he remarked as he stood up. 'Anything I should know about?'

'No,' she said airily. 'Not really. Mum's fine. Dad's fine. Everything's fine.'

His eyes narrowed suspiciously. 'You look like the cat who's discovered a bowl of cream.'

Her laugh was light and carefree. 'Do I?'

'You also look incredibly beautiful...'

Her eyes widened when he started walking down the stairs towards her. Perhaps he interpreted her reaction for alarm for his expression quickly changed to one of exasperation. 'No need to panic, Vivien. I'm not about to pounce. I was merely stating a fact. You know, you look somewhat like my mother when she was young. No wonder Dad took to you.'

Vivien did her best to cool the rapid heating Ross's compliments had brought to her blood, concentrating instead on the opening he'd just given her. 'How odd,' she commented. 'I was just thinking about your mother, wondering what she was like.'

'Were you? That *is* odd. What made you think of her?'

'You wouldn't want to know,' she chuckled.

'Wouldn't I?'

'No,' she said firmly, and, linking her arm with his, turned him to face across the foyer. 'So come on, show me your house and tell me about your mother.'

Ross stared down at her for a second before moving. 'To what do I owe this new Vivien?' he asked warily.

'This isn't a new Vivien. This is the real me.'

'Which is?'

She grinned. 'Charming. Witty. Warm.'

'What happened to stubborn, infuriating and uncooperative?'

'I left them in Sydney.'

'You could have fooled me.'

'Apparently I have.'

'Vivien, I——'

'Oh, do stop being so serious for once, Ross,' she cut in impatiently. 'Life's too short for eternal pessimism.'

'It's also too short for naïve optimism,' he muttered.

His dark mood refused to lift, especially when he saw Vivien's reaction to the house. But she found it difficult to pretend real liking for the place. She favoured open, airy homes with lots of light and glass and modern furniture, not dark rooms surrounded by busy wallpaper and crammed to the rafters with heavy antiques. Still, she could see why a person of another mind might covet the place. It had to be worth heaps.

'You definitely do not like this house,' Ross announced as they traipsed upstairs.

'Well, it's not exactly my taste,' Vivien admitted at last. 'Sorry.'

'You don't have to apologise.'

'I like the upstairs better. There's more natural light in the rooms.'

The floor plan was simpler too, all the rooms coming off the central gallery and all opening out on to the upstairs veranda. There were ten bedrooms, five with matching *en suites* and five without. Any guests using the latter shared the two general bathrooms, Ross informed her. Finally, Vivien was shown the upstairs linen-room, which was larger than her mother's bedroom back home.

'My mother,' Ross explained, 'had an obsession for beautiful towels and sheets.'

Vivien could only agree as her disbelieving eyes encompassed the amount of Manchester goods on the built-in shelves. There was enough to stock a whole section in a department store.

'To tell the truth,' he went on, 'I don't think Mum liked this house any more than you do. Or maybe it was the land she didn't like. She was city, just like you.'

'Really?'

'Yes, really. Well, that's about it, Vivien,' he said as he ushered her out of the linen-room and locked the door. 'I must leave you now. I have to check on Gavin's progress with the bores. Perhaps you should have a rest this afternoon. You're looking hot. Dinner is at seven-thirty when we have visitors, and, while not formal, women usually wear a dress. I dare say I'll see you then. *Au revoir*...' And, tipping his forehead, he turned and strode away, his abrupt departure leaving her feeling empty and quite desolate.

Vivien shook her head, wishing she could come to grips with what she felt for this man. Was it still just sex? Or had it finally become more complicated than that?

There was one way to find out, came the insidious temptation. Let him make love to you again. See if the fires can be burn out. See if there is anything else left after the night is over...

Vivien trembled. Did she have the courage to undertake such a daring experiment. Did she?

Yes, she decided with unexpected boldness, a shudder of sheer excitement reverberating through her. Yes. She did!

But no sooner had the scandalous decision been made than the doubts and fears crowded in.

What if she made a fool of herself? What if her second time with Ross proved to be an anticlimax? What if—oh, lord, was it possible?—what if Ross *rejected* her?

No, she dismissed immediately. He wouldn't do that. Not if she offered herself to him on a silver platter. He'd admitted once he'd found her sexually irresistible. He wouldn't knock back a night of free, uncomplicated loving in her bed.

And that was what she was going to offer him.

There were to be no strings attached. No demands. No extracted promises. Just a night of sex.

Vivien shuddered with distaste. How awful that sounded. How...cheap.

Yet she was determined not to go back on her decision, however much her conscience balked at the crude reality of it. Life was full of crude realities, she decided with some bitterness. Earl had been one big crude reality. He'd made her face the fact that sex and love did not always go together. Now Vivien was determined to find out if her feelings for Ross were no more than what Earl had felt for her, or whether they had deepened to something potentially more lasting.

Maybe she wouldn't have been so desperate to find out if she weren't expecting Ross's baby. But she was, and, if there was some chance of having a real relationship with her baby's father, one that could lead to marriage, then she was going to go for it, all guns blazing. Married parents were a darned sight better for a baby's upbringing than two single ones.

Thinking about her baby's welfare gave Vivien the inner strength to push any lingering scruples aside. For the first time in weeks, she felt as if she was taking control of her life, making her own decisions for the future. And it felt good. Surprisingly good. She hadn't realised how much of her self-confidence had been undermined by what Earl had done to her. Losing her job hadn't helped either.

So it was with an iron determination that Vivien returned to her bedroom and set to pondering how one successfully seduced a man.

The practicalities of it weren't as easy as one might have imagined. She'd never had to seduce a man in her life before. Earl had made the first move. So had Ross. Neither was she a natural flirt, except when intoxicated.

Was that the solution? she wondered. Could she perhaps have a few surreptitious drinks beforehand?

It was a thought. She would certainly keep it in mind if she felt her courage failing her.

Of course, if she dressed appropriately, maybe Ross would once again make the first move. Vivien hoped that would be the case. Now what could she wear that would turn Ross on? Something sexy, but subtle. She didn't want to look as if there was a banner on her body which read: 'Here I am, handsome. Do your stuff!'

Vivien wasn't too sure what clothes she'd brought with her. Her mother had packed most of her clothes. And Helga had unpacked them. But she was pretty sure she'd spotted her favourite black dress in there somewhere when she'd rooted around for her toiletries.

Vivien walked over and threw open the wardrobe. First she would find something to wear, then she would have a bubble bath in one of the main bathrooms and then a lie-down. She didn't want to look tired. She wanted to be as beautiful as she could be. Beautiful and desirable and *simply irresistible*.

Vivien walked slowly down the huge semi-circular staircase shortly before seven-thirty, knowing she couldn't look more enticing. The polyester-crêpe dress she was wearing was one of those little black creations that looked simple and stylish, but was very seductive.

Halter-necked, it had a bare back and shoulders, a V neckline that hinted at rather than showed too much cleavage, and a line that skimmed rather than hugged the body. With her hair piled up on to her head in studied disarray, long, dangling gold earrings at her lobes and a bucket of Loulou wafting from her skin, a man would have had to have all his senses on hold not to find her ultra-feminine and desirable.

As Vivien put her sexily shod foot down on to the black and white tiled foyer a male voice called out to her from the gallery above.

'Wait on!'

Nerves tightened her stomach as she turned to watch Ross come down the stairs, looking very Magnumish in white trousers and a Hawaiian shirt in a red and white print. It crossed Vivien's mind incongruously that Earl would not have been seen dead in anything but a business suit.

'Don't tell me,' she said with a tinkling laugh—one she'd heard used to advantage by various vamps on television. 'You've been to Waikiki recently.'

He gave her a sharp look. Had she overdone the laugh?

'No,' he denied drily. 'This is pure Hamilton Island.'

He took the remaining few steps that separated them, icy blue eyes raking over her. 'And what is that sweet little number you've got on?' he drawled. 'Pure King's Cross?'

Vivien felt colour flood her cheeks. Had she overdone *everything*? Surely she didn't really look like a whore?

No, of course she didn't. Ross was simply being nasty for some reason. Perhaps he'd been brooding about Becky and Gavin. Or perhaps, she ventured to guess, he resented her looking sexy when he was supposed to keep his hands off.

Some instinctive feminine intuition told her this last guess was close to the mark.

Knowing any blush was well covered by her dramatic make-up, she cocked her head slightly to one side and slanted him a saucy look. 'Been to the Cross, have you?'

'Not lately,' he bit out, jaw obviously clenched.

'Perhaps it's time for a return visit,' she laughed. 'You seem... tense.'

Vivien was startled when Ross's right hand shot out to grip her upper arm, yanking her close to him. 'What in hell's got into you tonight?' he hissed.

It was an effort to remain composed when one's heart was pounding away like a jackhammer.

'Why does something have to have got into me?' she returned with superb nonchalance. 'I felt like dressing up a bit, that's all. I'm sorry you don't like the way I look, but I won't lose any sleep over it. Now unhand me, please. I don't take kindly to macho displays of male domination. They always bring out the worst in me.'

Yes, she added with silent darkness. Like they make me want to strip off all my clothes and beg you to take me on these stairs right here and now!

'Sorry,' he muttered, and released her arm. 'I...did I hurt you?'

'I dare say I'll have some bruises in the morning. I have very delicate skin.'

'So I've noticed,' he ground out, his eyes igniting to hot coals as they moved up over her bare shoulders and down the tantalising neckline.

Vivien didn't know whether to feel pleased or alarmed by the evidence of Ross's obvious though sneering admiration. There was something about him tonight that was quite frightening, as though he were balancing on a razor's edge that was only partly due to male frustration. There were other devils at work within his soul. She suspected that it wouldn't take much to tip him into violence.

'Did Gavin check all the bores?' she asked, deliberately deflecting the conversation away from her appearance and giving herself a little time to rethink the situation. Suddenly, the course of action she'd set herself upon this night seemed fraught with danger. She wanted Ross to make love to her, not assault her.

'Yes,' was his uninformative and very curt answer. He glanced at the watch on his wrist. Gold, with a brown leather band, it looked very expensive. 'Helga gets annoyed when we're late for dinner,' he pronounced. 'I think we'd better make tracks for the dining-room.'

Vivien would never have dreamt she would feel grateful for Helga's army-like sense of punctuality.

Dinner still proved a difficult meal for all concerned. Gavin, who, unlike his brother, was dressed shoddily in faded jeans and black T-shirt, was sulkily silent. This seemed to make Helga agitated and stroppy. She kept insisting everyone have seconds whether they wanted them or not.

By the time dessert came—enormous portions of plum pudding and ice-cream—Vivien's stomach was protesting. Ross, in the end, made a tactless though accurate comment to Helga about her always giving people too much to eat. Vivien managed to soothe the well-intentioned though misguided woman by saying she would normally be able to eat everything, but that her condition seemed to have affected her appetite.

At this allusion to her pregnancy, Gavin made a contemptuous sound, stood up, and stomped out of the room, having not said a word to Vivien all evening other than a grumpy hello when she and Ross had first walked into the dining-room. Shortly, they heard his station wagon start up, the gravel screeching as he roared off.

'I... I'm sorry, lovie,' Helga apologised for Gavin. 'He's not himself at the moment.'

Vivien smiled gently. 'It's all right. I understand. He's upset.'

'He's not the only one who's upset,' Ross grated out. 'I'm damned upset that people around here chose not to tell me that my own brother was in love with the girl I was going to marry.'

He glowered at Helga, who stood up with an uncompromising look on her face. 'The boy made me promise not to tell you.'

'Then why didn't he tell me himself?'

'Don't be ridiculous!' Helga snapped. 'The boy has *some* pride.'

'Haven't we all,' he muttered darkly. 'Haven't we all...'

'Anyone for tea?' Helga asked brusquely.

'Not me,' Ross returned. 'I think I'll have some port in the library instead.'

He'd asked earlier—and with some dry cynicism, Vivien had noted—if she wanted some wine with her dinner. Vivien had politely declined, whereby Ross had still opened a bottle of claret, though he'd only drunk a couple of glasses. Gavin had polished off the rest.

'What about you, lovie?'

'Er—no, thanks, Helga.' She looked over at Ross, unsure of what to do. Swallowing, she made her decision. 'I might join Ross for some port after we've cleared up,' she said in a rush.

Ross's eyes snapped round to frown at her.

# SIMPLY IRRESISTIBLE 153

'If... if that's all right with you,' she added, battling to remain calm in the face of his penetrating stare.

He lifted a single sardonic eyebrow. 'I didn't think you liked port.'

'I do occasionally.'

Actually, she *did*, though she'd only ever indulged in small quantities before. Earl had always insisted she pretend to drink at their dinner parties, saying people hated teetotallers. She'd usually managed to tip most of her wine down the sink at intervals, but she'd often allowed herself the luxury of a few sips of Earl's vintage port at the end of the evening. It seemed to relax her after the tension of cooking and serving a meal that lived up to Earl's standards.

Vivien considered she could do with some relaxing at this point in time, while she made up her mind what she was going to do. Quite clearly, Ross wasn't going to make any move towards her. Any momentary interest on the staircase appeared to have waned. He'd barely looked at her during dinner.

'I'll see you shortly, then,' Ross said, leaving the room without a backward glance.

Vivien stood up to help Helga clear the table and then wash up. They had it all finished in ten minutes flat. Never had Vivien seen anyone wash up like Helga!

'Off you go now, lovie,' the other woman said, taking the tea-towel from Vivien's hands. 'But watch yourself. Ross is stirring for a fight tonight. I've seen him like this before. He can't stand not having what he wants, or not having things go his way. Oh, he's got a good heart but he's a mighty stubborn boy. Mighty stubborn, indeed!'

Vivien was still thinking about Helga's warning when she opened the library door. So she was startled to see Ross looking totally relaxed in the large armchair she'd been sitting in earlier in the day, his feet outstretched and crossed at the ankles, a hefty glass of port cradled in his hands.

'Close the door,' he said in a soft, almost silky voice. For some reason, it brought goosebumps up on the back of her neck.

She closed the door.

'Now lock it,' he added.

She spun round, eyes blinking wide. 'Lock it? But why?'

His gaze became cold and hard. 'Because I don't like to be interrupted when I'm having sex.'

# CHAPTER TWELVE

VIVIEN froze. 'I beg your pardon?'

'You heard me, Vivien. Now just lock the door and stop pretending that your sensibilities are offended. You and I both know why you dressed like that tonight. You're feeling frustrated and you've decided once again to make use of yours truly. At least, I imagine it's me you've set your cap at. I'm the one who looks like your old boyfriend, not Gavin. Or are you going to tell me you've reverted to the tease I mistook you for that night at the ball?'

Vivien's first instinct was to flee Ross's cutting contempt. For it hurt. It hurt a lot. How could she not have realised her strategy could backfire on her so badly?

But she had faced many difficult foes during her television career. Belligerent businessmen...two-faced politicians...oily con men. She was not about to let Ross's verbal attack rout her completely, though she *was* badly shaken.

'You...you've got it all wrong, Ross,' she began with as much casual confidence as she could muster.

'In what way, Vivien?'

God, but she hated that cold, cynical light in his eyes, hated the silky derision in his voice.

'I...I did try to look extra attractive tonight, but I——'

His hard, humourless laugh cut her off. '"*Extra attractive*"? Is that how you would describe yourself tonight?' With another laugh, he uncurled his tall frame from the chair to begin moving slowly across the room like a panther stalking its prey, depositing his glass of port on a side-table on the way. Nerves and a kind of hypnotic fascination kept her silent and still while he approached. What on earth was he going to do?

Finally, he stood in front of her, tension in every line of his body.

'The dress could almost have been an unconscious mistake,' he said, smiling nastily. 'Despite the lack of underwear under it. But *not* when combined with those other wicked little touches. The hair, looking as if you'd just tumbled from a lover's bed...'

When he reached out to pull a few more tendrils around her face, she just stood there, as though paralysed.

'The earrings,' he went on, 'designed to draw attention to the sheer, exquisite delicacy of your lovely neck...'

Her mouth went dry when he trickled fingers menacingly around the base of her throat.

'The scarlet lipstick on your oh, so sexy mouth...'

Vivien almost moaned when he ran a fingertip around her softly parted lips. She squeezed her eyes tightly shut, appalled that he could make her feel like this when his touch was meant to be insulting.

But at least she was finding out the bitter truth, wasn't she? This couldn't be love—or the beginnings of love. This was raw, unadulterated sex, lust in its worst form, making her want him even while he showed his contempt. His own feelings for her were apparently similar, since he quite clearly hated wanting her nearly as much.

'Close your eyes if you like,' he jeered softly. 'I don't mind. I've already accepted I'm to be just a proxy lover. But believe me, I'm going to enjoy you anyway.'

Her eyes flew open in angry defiance of his presumption.

'You keep away from me. I don't want you touching me!'

His answering laugh was so dark that she shrank back against the door, one hand searching blindly for the knob.

'Oh, no, you don't,' he ground out, turning the key in the lock and pocketing it before she had a hope of escaping. 'And don't bother to scream. This room is virtually sound-proof, not to mention a hell of a long way from the servants' quarters.'

She froze when he coolly reached out to undo the button at the nape of her neck, then peeled the dress down to the waist. When he ran the back of his hand across her bared breasts her head whirled with a dizzying wave of unbidden pleasure and excitement. She didn't have to look down to know that her nipples had peaked hard with instant arousal.

'Bitch,' he rasped, before suddenly pulling her to him, *crushing* her to him, his head dipping to trail a hot mouth over her shoulders and up her throat. Vivien began to tremble uncontrollably.

She moaned when he finally kissed her, knowing that there was no stopping him now, even if she wanted to.

And she *did* want to stop him. That was the irony of it all. But only with her brain. Her body, she had already found out once with Ross, could not combat the feelings he could evoke in her, the utterly mindless passion and need.

'No,' she managed once, when he abandoned her mouth briefly to kiss her throat again.

'Shut up,' was his harsh reply before taking possession of her lips again.

She felt his hands around her waist, then pushing the dress down over her hips. It pooled around her ankles with a silky whoosh. Now only a wisp of black satin and lace prevented her from being totally naked before him. It would have been a humiliating thought, if Vivien had been able to think. As it was she found herself winding her arms up around his neck and kissing him back with the kind of desperation no man could misunderstand. Her naked breasts were pressed flat against his chest, her hips moulded to his, her abdomen undulating against his escalating arousal with primitive force.

Ross groaned under the onslaught of her frantic desire, hoisting her up on to his hips and carrying her across the room, where he lay her back across the large cedar desk in the corner. The cool hardness of its smoothly polished surface brought a gasp of shock from Vivien, almost returning her to reality for a moment. But Ross didn't allow her mad passion any peace. His hands on her outstretched body kept her arousal at fever pitch till she was beside herself with wanting him.

His name fluttered from her lips on a ragged moan of desire and need.

'Yes, that's right,' he grated back with a satanic laugh while he removed the last items of clothing from her quivering body—her panties and her shoes. 'It's Ross. Not Earl. *Ross!*'

Vivien dimly reacted to his angry assertion, wondering fleetingly if he had been more deeply hurt over that Earl business than she'd imagined. But once he had access to her whole body, to that part of her that was melting for him, she forgot everything but losing herself in that erotic world of unbelievable pleasure Ross could create with his hands and lips.

'Yes...oh, yes,' she groaned when his mouth moved intimately over her heated flesh. She groaned even more when he suddenly stopped, glazed eyes flying to his.

'Say that you love me,' he demanded hoarsely as he stripped off his trousers.

A wild confusion raced through Vivien. Dazedly, she saw him smiling down at her, felt his flesh teasing hers. She didn't recognise the smile for the grimace of self-mockery it really was. All Vivien knew was that, quite unexpectedly, a raw emotion filled her heart with his demand, an emotion that both stunned and thrilled her.

'Go on,' he urged, his hands curving round her buttocks to pull her closer to the edge. And him. 'You don't have to mean it. Just say it!'

'I love you,' she whispered huskily and felt the emotion swell within her chest. The words came then, ringing with passion and truth. 'I really, truly love you, Ross.'

His groan was a groan of sheer torture. Quite abruptly, he thrust deeply into her. Vivien felt the emotion spill over into every corner of her body, felt it charging into every nerve-ending, sharpening them, electrifying them. She cried out, at the same time reaching out her arms to gather Ross close, to hold him next to her heart.

For she *did* really, truly love him. She could see it now, see it so clearly. She'd once believed Earl the real thing, and Ross just an illusion. But she had got it the wrong way round. Earl had been the illusion, Ross the real thing. He must have fallen in love with her too, to demand such a reassurance.

So she was startled when he took her hands in an iron grip, pressing them down over the edges of the desk while he set up an oddly controlled rhythm. It was only then that she saw the ugly lines in his contorted face.

Cold, hard reality swept into her heart like a winter wind. Ross was not making love to her. He was making hate, having a kind of revenge. That was why he'd demanded she tell him she loved him. It had been nothing but a cruel parody of what she had begged of him that first night.

'Oh, God...no,' she cried out in an anguished dismay, lifting her head immediately in a valiant but futile struggle to rid herself of his flesh.

'Oh, God...yes,' he bit out and kept up his relentless surging. '*Yes!*'

She moaned in despair when she felt her body betray her, felt that excruciating tightening before her flesh shattered apart into a thousand convulsing, quivering parts. Crushingly, her climax seemed to be even more intense than anything she could remember of that night at Wallaby Creek. She almost wept with the perverse pleasure of it all, but then she felt Ross's hands tightening around hers, and he too was climaxing.

She cringed even more under his violently shuddering body. He despised her and yet he was finding the ultimate satisfaction in her body. It seemed the epitome of shame, the supreme mockery of what this act should represent.

Tears of bitter misery flooded her eyes and she began to sob.

Ross's eyes jerked up to hers as though she had struck him. When he scooped her up to hold her hard against him, his body still blended to hers, she wanted to fight him. But every muscle and bone in her body had turned to mush.

'Leave me...be,' she sobbed. 'I...I *hate* you!'

'And I hate you,' he rasped, while keeping her weeping face cradled against his shirt-front. 'Hush, now. Stop crying. You're all right. It's just a reaction to your orgasm. It was too intense. Relax, honey. Relax...'

Vivien was amazed to find herself actually calming down under the soothing way he was stroking her back. When he moved over to sit down in the huge armchair, taking her with him, she didn't even object. Her legs were easily accommodated on either side on him, the deep cushioning allowing her knees and body to sink into a blissfully comfortable position.

Vivien even felt like going to sleep, which shocked her. She should be fighting him, hitting him, telling him he was a wicked, cruel man for doing what he had just done to her. She certainly shouldn't let him go on thinking that her pleasure had been nothing but sexual, that her crying was merely an emotional reaction to a heightened physical experience.

'You're not going to sleep, are you?' he whispered, his stroking hands coming to rest rather provocatively on her buttocks.

'No. Not quite.'

God, was that her voice? When had she ever talked in such low, husky, sexy tones?

'Tell me, Vivien,' he said thickly, 'was *any* of that for me, or is it still all for Earl?'

Vivien flinched, remembering how she'd momentarily thought during Ross's torrid lovemaking that his resemblance to her ex-lover had affected him deeply. He certainly did keep harping on it. Why care, if it was just vengeful sex he was after? If that were the case it shouldn't matter to him whom she was thinking about.

Vivien's heart leapt. If Ross wanted her to want him for himself, and not for his likeness to Earl, then that could only be because his feelings for her were deeper than just lust. He might not realise that himself yet—she could understand his confusion with Becky still in his heart—but one day soon...

First, however, she had to convince him that Earl was dead and gone as far as she was concerned, then that might open the way to Ross letting his feelings for her rise to the surface.

She lifted heavy eyelids to look up into his face, that face which, though so like Earl's, feature for feature, no longer reminded her at all of the man who'd treated her so badly.

Her hand reached up to lie against his cheek. 'What a foolish man you are, Ross Everton,' she said tenderly. 'You are so different from Earl in so many ways. When I look at you now, I see no one else but you. It was you I was wanting today, you I dressed for tonight, you I wanted to make love to me. Not Earl...' And, stretching upwards, she pressed gentle lips to his mouth, kissing him with all the love in her heart.

He groaned, his hands lifting to cup her face, to hold it captive while he deepened her kiss into an expression of rapidly renewing desire and need. When Vivien became hotly aware of more stirring evidence of that renewing desire, her inside contracted instinctively, gripping his growing hardness with such intensity that Ross tore his mouth away from hers on a gasping groan.

'Did... did I hurt you?' she asked breathlessly, her own arousal having revved her pulse-rate up a few notches.

He laughed. 'I wouldn't put it quite like that. But perhaps you should do it again, just so I can make sure.' And, gripping her buttocks, he moved her in a slow up-and-down motion, encouraging her internal muscles to several repeat performances.

'No.' He grimaced wryly. 'That definitely does not hurt.' He stopped moving her to slide his hands up over her ribs till they found her breasts.

'Lean back,' he rasped. 'Grip the armrests.'

She did so, her heart pounding frantically as he began to play with her outstretched body, first her breasts, then her ribs and stomach, and finally between her thighs, touching her most sensitive part till she was squirming with pleasure. He seemed to like her writhing movements too, his breathing far more ragged than her own.

'Oh, yes, honey, yes,' he moaned when she started lifting her bottom up and down again, squeezing and releasing him in a wild rhythm of uninhibited loving. 'Keep going,' he urged. 'Don't stop...'

After it was all over, and they were spent once more, they did sleep, briefly, only to wake to the sound of thunder rocking the house.

'A storm,' Vivien whispered, and shivered.

'Just electrical, I suspect. There's no rain predicted. You don't like thunder?' he asked when she shivered again.

'I'm just cold.'

He held her closer if that was possible, wrapping his arms tightly around her. 'Want to go up to bed?'

'Uh-huh.'

'I'll carry you upstairs.'

'You can't carry me out of the room like this!' she exclaimed in a shocked tone.

'Why not? No one's likely to see us. Dad's sleeping-pill will have worked by now and Helga will be busily knitting in front of the television. As for Gavin...he's playing cards and drowning his sorrows with the boys down in the shearing shed. Won't be back till the wee small hours.'

'You're sure we won't run into anyone?'

'Positive.'

'If we do, I'll die of embarrassment.'

'Me too. I haven't got any trousers on, remember?'

They didn't run into anyone, despite Vivien giggling madly all the way up the stairs. They both collapsed into a shower together in Ross's *en suite*, which revived them enough to start making love all over again. This time, it was slow and erotic and infinitely more loving, the touching and kissing lasting for an hour before Ross moved over and into her. They looked deep into each other's eyes as the pleasure built and built, Ross bending to kiss her gasping mouth when she cried out in release, only then allowing himself to let go.

Vivien lay happily in his sleeping arms afterwards, feeling more at peace with herself than she had ever felt.

So this was what really being in love was like. She smiled softly to herself in the dark, pressing loving lips to the side of Ross's chest.

'And I think you love me too,' she whispered softly. 'You just don't know it yet...'

# CHAPTER THIRTEEN

THREE days rolled by and Vivien was blissfully happy. Ross was sweet to her during the day, and madly passionate every night. With each passing day she became more and more convinced that he loved her, despite his never saying so. Her own love for him was also growing stronger as she discovered more about him.

Helga had been right when she'd said they had similar personalities. They also had similar likes and dislikes in regard to just about everything. They were both mad about travel and Tennessee Williams's plays and the Beatles and playing cards, especially Five Hundred. It was uncanny. With Earl, she had had to pretend to like what he liked, just to keep him happy. With Ross, there was no pretending. Ever. She'd never felt so at one with a person.

There was another matter that did wonders for her humour as well. She didn't have morning sickness any more. How wonderful it was to be able to wake and not have to run to the bathroom! Her appetite improved considerably once her stomach was more settled, which was just as well since Helga had decided she needed 'building up'.

Yes, Vivien couldn't have been happier. Even Oliver seemed a little better, though he still tired quickly. The couple of hours she sat with him each morning and afternoon were mostly spent with her reading aloud while he relaxed in his favourite armchair. Occasionally they watched a video which Ross brought out from town.

The only fly in the ointment was Gavin, who remained as sour and uncommunicative as ever. He'd hardly spoken a dozen words to Vivien since her arrival, but she refused to let his mood upset her newfound happiness.

He was only young, she reasoned. He would get over his love for this Becky girl, as Ross was obviously getting over his. Every now and then, Vivien found herself puzzling over exactly what sort of girl this Becky Macintosh was to command such devotion.

She found out on New Year's Eve.

Vivien had just finished her morning visit with Oliver. Ross and Gavin were out mending fences. She and Helga were sitting in the kitchen having a mug of tea together when suddenly they heard a screeching of brakes on the gravel driveway. Before they could do more than raise their eyebrows, a slender female figure in pale blue jeans and a blue checked shirt came racing into the kitchen, her long, straight blonde hair flying out behind.

'Where's Ross?' she demanded breathlessly of Helga.

'Down in the south paddocks, mending fences. What is it, Becky? What's happened?'

'There was a small grass fire on the other side of the river. Dad and I put it out, but not before the wind picked up and a few sparks jumped the river. Now the fire's growing again and heading straight for our best breeding sheep. I've rung the emergency bushfire brigade number, but apparently all of the trucks are attending two other scrub fires. They said they'd send a few men along in a helicopter, one of those that can water-bomb the fire. The trouble is the only pilot available is a real rookie. I thought Ross might be able to help.'

'I'll contact him straight away,' Helga said briskly. 'They have a two-way radio with them. I won't be a moment. The gizmo's in the study. I'll send them straight over to your place.'

'Thanks, Helga, I'd better get back. Mum's in a panic. Not that the fire's anywhere near the house. But you know what she's like.'

'Can I help in any way?' Vivien offered. 'Maybe I could stay with your mother while you do what you have to do.'

Vivien found herself on the end of a long look from the loveliest blue eyes. There was no doubt about it. Becky had not been behind the door when God gave out looks. Though not striking, she had a fragile delicacy about her that would bring out the protective instinct in any man. Too bad they never saw the toughness behind those eyes.

'I presume you're Vivien,' she said drily.

Vivien stood up, her shoulders automatically squaring. 'Yes, I am.'

Those big blue eyes flicked over her face and figure before a rueful smile tugged at her pretty mouth. 'If I'd known the sort of competition I had, I would have given up sooner. What odds, I ask myself, of Ross meeting someone like you at that horrid ball? Still, I have more important things to do today than worry over the fickle finger of fate. Yes, you can come and hold Mum's hand. That'll free me to help outside.'

Helga bustled back into the kitchen just in time to be told Vivien was going with Becky. Oddly enough, the older woman didn't seem to think this at all strange. For all her earlier criticisms about the girl's behaviour with Ross, she seemed to like Becky.

It came to Vivien then that there was more worth in this girl than she'd previously believed. That was why Helga wanted her for Gavin—to put some fire in his belly. Becky had a positive attitude and energetic drive Vivien could only admire.

'So when are you and Ross getting married?' Becky enquired while she directed the jeep at a lurching speed down the dusty road that led back to the highway.

'I don't know,' came the truthful answer. 'He—er—hasn't asked me yet.'

Becky slanted a frowning glance her way. 'Hasn't asked you yet? That's odd. When he confessed to me that he'd fallen in love with someone else the night of the ball at Wallaby Creek, and that the girl in question was pregnant by him, I naturally thought you'd be married as quickly as possible.'

Vivien held her silence with great difficulty. Ross had said that? Back *then*? That meant he'd virtually fallen in love with her straight away.

Oh, my God, she groaned silently. My God...

Her heart squeezed tight at the thought of all she had put Ross through that night, especially making him tell her he loved her like that. It also leant an ironic and very heart-wrenching meaning to Ross's statement a few days ago that he had always known the girl he loved didn't love him back, but that didn't stop him loving her. Of course Vivien had thought he meant Becky. But he had meant herself!

Vivien felt like crying. If only she'd known. But, of course, why would he tell her? No man would, certainly not after that day when he'd followed her to Sydney, only to discover that he was the dead-ringer of her previous lover, the man she supposedly still loved. God, it was a wonder his love for her hadn't turned to hate then and there.

Maybe it almost had for a while, she realised, remembering the incident in the library.

But if only he had told her later that night that he loved her, instead of letting her think his feelings were only lust.

And what of you? a reproachful voice whispered. Have you told him you love him? Have you reassured the father of your child that your feelings for him are anything more than just sexual?

She almost cried out in dismay at her own stupidity.

Oh, Ross...darling...I'll tell you as soon as I can, she vowed silently.

'Of course I always knew he wasn't madly in love with me, or I with him,' Becky rattled on. 'But we go back a long way, Ross and I. Gavin too, for that matter. We've always been great mates, the three of us. We love each other, but I think it's been more of a friendship love than anything else To be honest, I wasn't at all desperate to go to bed with Ross. But then...I've never been desperate to go to bed with any man as yet.' She sighed heavily. 'Maybe I will one day, but something tells me I'm not a romantic at heart.'

Vivien only hesitated for a second. After all, nothing ventured, nothing gained. 'Has it ever occurred to you that you might have been looking for passion with the wrong brother?'

The jeep lurched to one side before Becky recovered. She darted Vivien a disbelieving glance. 'You're not serious!'

'Never been more serious. Helga says Gavin's crazy about you. He was simply crushed by your intention to marry Ross.'

'*Really*?'

'Yes, really. He's been as miserable as sin lately because he thinks you're suffering from a broken heart. He blames me and Ross.'

'But... but if he loves me, the stupid man, why hasn't he said so? Why hasn't he *done* something?'

'Too shy.'

'Too *shy*? With *me*? That's ridiculous! Why, we've been skinny dipping together!'

'Not lately, I'll bet.'

'Well, no...'

'Perhaps you should suggest you do so again some time. See what happens.'

Becky looked over at Vivien, blue eyes widening. 'You city girls don't miss a trick, do you? Skinny dipping, eh? Yes, well, I—er—might suggest that some time, but I can't think about Gavin right now. I have a fire to help put out.'

They fell silent as Becky concentrated on her driving. Not a bad idea, Vivien thought, since the girl drove as she no doubt did most things—with a degree of wild recklessness. Or maybe all country people drove like that on the way to a fire. Whatever, Vivien was hanging on to the dashboard for dear life.

Ross and Gavin must have gone across land, picking up Stan and Dave on the way, for all four men arrived at the homestead simultaneously with Becky and Vivien. A plump, fluttery lady raced out to greet them all with hysteria not far away.

'Oh, thank God, thank God,' she kept saying.

'Now, now, Mrs Macintosh,' Ross returned, patting her hand. 'Calm down. The cavalry's here.'

He turned to give Vivien a questioning look, but she merely smiled, hugging to herself the wonderful knowledge of his love for her. Later today, she would tell him of her own love. Not only would she tell him, but she would show him.

'There's the helicopter!' Becky shouted, pointing to the horizon. 'It's a water-bombing helicopter,' she explained to Ross, 'but the pilot's not very experienced. Do you think you might be able to help him?'

'Sure. I haven't exactly done that kind of thing myself before, but it can't be too difficult.'

The dark grey helicopter landed in a cloud of dust, forestalling any further conversation. It was all business. A side-door slid back to reveal several men inside. Stan, Dave and Gavin piled in with them. Ross climbed in next to the pilot, shouting back to Becky to collect some cool drinks and to drive down in the jeep.

Becky didn't look at all impressed at being given such a tame job to do, but in the end she shrugged resignedly. Within minutes of the helicopter taking off, she'd successfully filled two cool boxes with ice and drinks, refusing to let Vivien help her carry them to the jeep.

'You shouldn't be carrying heavy things when you're in the family way,' she was told firmly.

'Where will they get the water from to bomb the fire with?' Vivien asked as Becky climbed in behind the wheel.

'The dam, I guess, though there isn't too much water in it. Maybe the river.'

Vivien frowned. 'But wouldn't that be dangerous? The river's not very wide and there are trees all along the bank.'

'*Dangerous*? For the legendary Ross Everton?' Becky laughed.

'I've heard him called that before, but I don't know what it means.'

'It means, duckie, that you've got yourself hooked to the craziest, most thrilling-seeking chopper cowboy that ever drew breath. Ross prides himself on being able to fly down and hover low enough to open gates by leaning out of the cockpit. He'll heli-muster anything that moves in any kind of country, no matter how rough and wild. Cattle. Brumbies. Buffalo. He's a legend all over the outback for his skill and daring.' She gave Vivien a wry look as she fired the engine. 'Having second thoughts, are we?'

'Of course not!' she returned stalwartly, and waved Becky off.

But a type of fear had gripped her heart. Ross might be very skilled, but hadn't he just admitted he hadn't done this kind of job before? What if he made a mistake? What if the helicopter crashed?

Vivien felt sicker than she ever had with morning sickness. She felt even sicker an hour later while she and Mrs Macintosh stood together on the back veranda of the homestead, from where they had a first-class view of what was going on, both in the far paddocks and in the air. The helicopter had indeed scooped up a couple of loads of water from the dam, but clearly not enough. The grass fire was still growing. Now, the helicopter was being angled around to head for the river. Vivien just knew who it was at the controls.

'Oh, God, no,' she groaned when the machine skimmed the tops of trees in its descent to the narrow strip of water below.

She watched with growing horror when the helicopter dipped dangerously to fill the canvas bag, the rotor blades almost touching the surface of the water before the craft straightened and scooped upwards. 'I can't watch any more,' she muttered under her breath.

But she did, her heart aching inside her constricted chest as she watched Ross make trip after dangerous trip to that river then back to the fire. At last, the flames died, leaving nothing but a cloud of black smoke. Mrs Macintosh turned to hug her when, even from that distance, they heard the men's shouts of triumph.

Vivien couldn't feel total triumph, however. Fear was still gripping her heart. How could she bear Ross doing this kind of thing for a living? How could she cope with the continuous worrying? She wanted the father of her baby around and active when their child grew up. Not dead, or a paraplegic.

Her fears were compounded when the men came back to the house and Ross was laughing—actually laughing!—as the rookie pilot relayed tales of near-missed fences and trees. In the end, she couldn't bear it any more. She walked right up to him and said with a shaking voice, 'You might think that risking your life is funny, but I don't. I've been worried sick all afternoon, and I...I...' Tears flooded her eyes. Her shoulders began to shake.

Ross gathered her against his dusty chest. 'Hush. I'm all right, darling. Don't cry now...' He led her away from the others before tipping her tear-stained face up to him. 'Dare I hope this means what I think it means?'

'Oh, Ross, I love you so much,' she cried. 'I can't bear to think of you risking your life every day. Don't ever go back to doing that helicopter business. Please. I couldn't bear it if you had an accident.'

'I won't have an accident.'

'You don't know that. You're not immortal. Or infallible. No one is. If you love me even a little——'

'A *little*? My God, Vivien, I *adore* you, don't you know that?'

She stared up at him, stunned, despite what Becky had told her. It sounded so much more incredibly wonderful coming from Ross's actual lips. 'You...you've never actually told me,' she choked out. 'Not in words.'

'Well, I'm telling you now. I've loved you since the first moment I set eyes on you, looking at me across that crowded ballroom. You mean the world to me. But you don't understand. I won't have an accident because——'

Mr Macintosh's tapping him on the shoulder interrupted what Ross was going to say.

'Ross...'

Ross turned. 'Yes?'

'Er—Helga just called. I'm sorry, but I have some bad news.'

'Bad news?'

'Yes...your father...'

Vivien closed her eyes as a wave of anguish washed through her, for she knew exactly what the man was going to say. Fresh tears flowed, tears for the man who'd become her friend. More tears for the man she loved. He was going to take this hard.

Mr Macintosh cleared his throat. 'He...he passed away...this afternoon. I'm so sorry, lad.'

Ross's hold tightened around Vivien. Yet when he spoke, his voice sounded calm. Only Vivien could feel him shaking inside. 'It's all right. Dad's dearest wish was that he would die at Mountainview. He...he's probably quite happy.'

Oliver Everton was cremated, in keeping with his wishes, and his ashes sprinkled over the paddocks of his beloved Mountainview. They had a large wake for him at the house, again in keeping with his wishes, and it was towards the end of this wake that Mr Parkinson, Oliver's solicitor, called the main beneficiaries of his will into the study.

Mr Parkinson sat behind the huge walnut desk while Ross and Vivien, Helga and Gavin pulled up chairs. Vivien was perplexed—and a little worried—over what she was doing there. If she was to be a beneficiary, that meant Oliver had changed his will recently. She was suddenly alarmed at what she was about to hear.

'I won't beat about the bush,' Mr Parkinson started. 'It appears that Oliver saw fit to write a new will a couple of days ago without consulting me. Oh, it's all legal and above-board, witnessed by Stan and Dave. Helga had it in her safe keeping...'

Vivien stared at Helga, who kept a dead-pan face.

'But I have to admit that the contents came as a shock to me. I think they might come as a shock to you too, Ross.'

Vivien finally dared to look at Ross, who didn't look at all worried. It crossed her mind then that he knew full well what was in that will. She went cold with apprehension.

'Aside from Ross being left a couple of real estate properties around Sydney and Helga being left a pension trust fund to ensure she won't want for money for the rest of her life, it seems that Oliver has left the bulk of his estate, including the property Mountainview and all it contains, to his second son, Gavin.'

Gavin sat bolt upright in his chair, clearly stunned. 'But that's not fair. Mountainview is worth millions! *Ross*...' He swivelled to throw a distressed look at his brother. 'You must know...I had no hand in this.'

'I know that,' Ross replied equably. 'Dad told me what he was going to do. I fully agreed with his decision.'

Vivien almost gasped at his obvious twisting of the truth. It had been Ross, she realised, who had insisted on the change of will. This was what he had gone to see his father about a few days ago, before it was too late. He knew his father had actually left control of Mountainview to *him*. He had sacrificed his inheritance for love of his brother, for he knew his brother needed it more than he did, in more ways than one.

Gavin was looking even more stunned. 'You *agreed* with my having Mountainview?'

'Yes. I've been made an excellent offer for my fleet of helicopters and the goodwill of my business. I'm going to take it. Believe me, Gavin, I won't be wanting for a bob, if that's what's worrying you. And don't forget about those Sydney properties Dad left me.'

'But they'd be nothing compared to Mountainview!'

'That depends on the point of view. One of them is that penthouse unit at Double Bay Mum inherited.

It's hardly worth peanuts. The other is a substantial acreage Dad bought years ago just outside Sydney on the Nepean River. I've always had a dream to set up an Australian tourist resort, catering for people who want to experience typical Australian country life without having to actually travel out there. That piece of land on the Nepean would be the ideal site.'

'You've never mentioned this before,' Gavin said, clearly still worried.

Ross gave him a ruefully affectionate smile. 'We don't always talk about our dreams out loud, do we, little brother? I thought my duty lay here till I saw you had more heart for this place than I ever would.'

'And what will this tourist resort have in it, Ross?' Vivien joined in, intrigued by the thought of it all.

Smiling widely, he turned to her. 'Lots of things. There'll be a miniature farm with examples of all our animals, shearing exhibitions, sheep-dog trials. Individual cabins for people to stay in. Restaurants that serve typical Australian food. Barbecue and picnic facilities. Souvenir shops. All sorts of things. I think it could be a great success, especially if my wife joins in and helps me. She's a whiz with people...'

She stared back at him, having only heard the word—'wife'. He bent over and kissed her before turning back to face his brother.

'So don't worry about Dad leaving you Mountainview, Gavin. He's put it in the best of hands. And I think there might be a girl somewhere around here who might like to help you and Helga look after the place.'

'Gosh, I don't know what to say.'

Neither did Helga, it seemed. Tears were streaming down her face.

Vivien reached out to take Ross's hand. 'You are a wonderful, wonderful man,' she murmured. 'Do you know that?'

'Yes,' he said, and leant close. 'You will marry me, won't you?'

'You know I will.'

'That's what your mother told me that day. She said if I were patient you'd come around. She said you loved me, but you just didn't know it yet.'

Vivien was astonished. 'Mum said that?'

'Sure thing. She told me her daughter didn't go round having babies with men she didn't love. I should have believed her sooner.'

A lump filled Vivien's throat. Dear heaven... her mother knew her better than she knew herself. But she'd been so right. So very right.

Mr Parkinson coughed noisily till they were all paying attention to him again. 'I have one more bequest to read out. It seems the late Mrs Everton had a sizeable amount of very valuable jewellery which has been kept in a bank vault in Sydney all these years. Mr Everton senior left it all to the mother of his first grandchild, Miss Vivien Roberts. To be worn, his will states. Not locked away. He says it could only be enhanced by Miss Roberts's beauty.'

Vivien tried not to cry, but it was a futile exercise. The tears had already been hovering. She began to sob quietly, Ross putting an arm round her shoulder to try and comfort her. Helga stood up abruptly and left the room, returning quickly with a tray full of drinks. She passed them all around.

'I wish to propose a toast to my employer and friend, Oliver Everton.'

They all stood up.

'May I?' Ross asked thickly.

Helga nodded.

'To Oliver Everton,' he said. 'He was a good father and a good friend. He was a good man. They don't come along like him too often...'

# CHAPTER FOURTEEN

'IRVING! What do you think you're doing?' Vivien remonstrated. 'I asked you to film just the christening, but you've been following me around all afternoon with that darned camera. I came out here on my own back patio to catch a breath of fresh air and up you pop like a bad penny.'

Irving continued filming as he spoke. 'Now, Viv, sweetie, I don't often have such a gorgeous-looking subject to film. You're looking ravishing today in that white dress, especially with that pearl choker round your lovely neck. Have pity on me. I've been doing nothing but film sour old politicians for the channel lately. Of course, if a certain lady journalist would heed her old boss's pleas to return to work then I might get assigned some more interesting jobs... like that one out at Wallaby Creek.'

Vivien's laughter was dry. 'Mervyn can beg till he's blue in the face. I have no intention of ever returning to work for a man who's so stupid. Fancy keeping Bob on instead of me. No intelligence at all.'

'Didn't I tell you? Bob's moved to Western Australia. He's decided the politicians are more interesting over there.'

'Oh, so that's it! Now Mervyn has a hole in his staff and he thinks he can fill it with yours truly. No way, José. I'm very happy helping Ross build this place.' And she swept an arm round to indicate the mushrooming complex. Already their own house was finished on a spot overlooking the river. So was the gardener's cottage. The foundations of the restaurant and shops had been poured that week.

'That's what I told him,' Irving said. 'But he's a stubborn man.'

'Who's a stubborn man?' Ross remarked on joining them. Vivien thought he looked heart-stoppingly handsome in a new dark grey suit. And very proud, with his six-week-old baby son in his arms.

'Mervyn,' she explained. 'You know he keeps asking me to go back to work for him.'

'Why don't you?'

Vivien blinked at her husband. 'But you said——'

Ross shrugged. 'I always believe in letting people do what they want to do, regardless. If you're missing work then by all means go back. You know your mother's dying to get her hands on Luke here, and since your father agreed to quit the railways and take on the job as chief gardener you've got a built-in baby-sitter. Your parents will be living only a hundred yards away.'

Vivien could hardly believe her ears. That was one aspect of Ross's character that never ceased to amaze her: his totally selfless generosity. So different to Earl, who'd been greedily possessive of her time. He'd hated her working.

Thinking about the differences between Ross and Earl brought a small smile to her lips, for they were more different now than ever. Her mother had shown her a picture in a women's magazine the other day, of a couple at the Flemington races. Vivien had not recognised the man till she'd read the caption below the photograph:

Mr and Mrs Earl Fotheringham enjoying a day at the races.

She had stared at the photograph again, then had difficulty suppressing a burst of laughter. For Earl was not only grossly overweight, but he was going bald. In less than a year, he looked ten years older, and nothing like Ross at all. She'd shown the picture to Ross, who'd looked at it, then stared at her.

'And *this* is who I'm supposed to look like?' he said.

'Once upon a time,' she said, trying to keep a straight face.

When Ross had burst out laughing she had too. But from relief, rather than any form of mockery, for now Ross could put Earl's ghost to rest once and for all.

Vivien's father opened the sliding glass doors and popped his head out. 'Is this a private session, or can anyone join in?'

'By all means join us, Lionel,' Ross said warmly. 'Get Peggy out here too and we can have a family shot.'

Lionel looked sheepish. 'Well, actually I was told to bring you all back inside. Your mother says it's getting late, Vivien, and you should be opening the baby's presents.'

They all were soon gathered in the large living area of the modern, airy house, Vivien sitting down on the white leather sofa to begin opening the gifts and cards that were piled high on the coffee-table, while everyone looked on. Irving kept happily filming away. Vivien decided to ignore him as best she could, and began ripping off paper with relish.

There were all the usual christening presents from toys to teddies, clothes to engraved cups, all beautiful and much gushed over by everyone. Gavin, who had become ecstatically engaged to Becky the previous month, had already sent down their excuses at not being able to attend, since they were in the middle of shearing. He'd posted down the cutest toy lamb Vivien had ever seen. The card attached had a small note from Becky.

'What does she mean,' Ross asked, 'about how she's been practising her swimming a lot lately?'

Vivien felt her lips twitching. 'I—er—told her the only way to get good at anything was to practise it.'

Ross frowned. 'Becky practising swimming? That's silly. She's a fantastic swimmer. Why, we used to go...' His voice trailed off as suspicion dawned in his eyes. He gave Vivien a narrow-eyed stare. She busied herself with another present by way of distraction.

'Here's one from Helga,' she announced, feeling it all over before opening it. 'I wonder what it is.' It was quite bulky, but soft.

Ross groaned. 'I have an awful feeling of premonition that Helga's been knitting again.'

Vivien ripped the paper off and everyone just stared. It was, she supposed, a rug of some sort, knitted in the most ghastly combination of colours she had ever seen, not to mention different ply wools. Now she knew why Ross's jumpers had never seen the light of day. Who would think to combine mauve with orange with black with red with purple in a series of striped and checked squares that had no regular pattern? On the card was the following explanation:

I began this before I knew whether your baby would be a boy or a girl, so I decided that neutral colours would be best.

These were *neutral* colours? Vivien stared down at the rug, unable to think of a thing to say.

'What...what is it?' Vivien's mother finally asked.

'A horse blanket,' Ross stated with a superbly straight face. 'For Luke's first pony. Helga's horse blankets are quite famous. Horses love them.'

'Oh,' Peggy said.

'We'll put it in a drawer for him, sweetheart,' Ross said to Vivien. 'Perhaps we should put a special drawer aside in which to save up all of Helga's marvellous gifts.'

'Yes, dear,' she returned with an even better poker-face. 'I think that would be best.'

They were lying in bed that night after Luke had finally condescended to go to sleep, chuckling over the incident.

'I almost died when I first saw it,' Vivien giggled.

'Don't you mean "almost died laughing"? And now, madam, would you like to tell me in the privacy of our bedroom what decadent advice you gave Becky?'

'Decadent advice? Who, me?'

'Yes, *you*, city broad.'

She laughed. 'That's for me to know and you to find out.'

'I think I already have...'

'Then why are you asking? Besides, it worked, didn't it? They're engaged and happy.'

'Not as happy as we are,' Ross insisted, pulling her close.

Vivien lifted her mouth to his in a tender kiss. 'No one's as happy as we are.'

'Too true.'

'Which is why I'm not going back to work.'

'You're not?'

'No. I'm happy doing what I'm doing, looking after Luke and helping you. Maybe some day I might want to go back to television, but not right now. I want to be right here when Luke cuts his first tooth, says his first word, takes his first step. Let Mervyn find someone else,' she went on without any regret. 'I can see I'm not going to be available for at least ten years, till our last child has gone to school.'

Startled, Ross propped himself up on his elbow and stared down at her. 'Our *last* child? How many are we going to have, for heaven's sake?'

'Oh, at least four. Kids these days need brothers and sisters to stick up for them. It's a tough world.'

He shook his head in a type of awed bewilderment. 'You never cease to amaze me, Mrs Everton. First, you bravely went ahead and had my baby when most women in your shoes wouldn't have. Now, after you've just been through a rotten long labour, you tell me you want a whole lot more! I'm beginning to wonder if you're a glutton for punishment or just plain crazy.'

'I'm crazy,' she said, and with a soft, sexy laugh pulled him down into her arms. 'Crazy about you...'

# MILLS & BOON

## By Request

**Bestselling romances brought back to you by popular demand**

# Susan Napier

Secret Admirer

◆

**The Hawk And The Lamb**

Available: July '96            Price: £4.50

*Available from WH Smith, John Menzies, Volume One, Forbuoys, Martins, Woolworths, Tesco, Asda, Safeway and other paperback stockists.*

# MILLS & BOON

# From Here To Paternity

Don't miss our great new series featuring fantastic men who eventually make fabulous fathers.

Some seek paternity, some have it thrust upon them—all will make it—whether they like it or not!

Starting in July '96, look out for:

## Mischief and Marriage
## by Emma Darcy

*Available from WH Smith, John Menzies, Volume One, Forbuoys, Martins, Woolworths, Tesco, Asda, Safeway and other paperback stockists.*

# MILLS & BOON

**For those long, hot, lazy days this summer Mills & Boon are delighted to bring you...**

# *Stolen Moments*

**A collection of four short sizzling stories in one romantic volume.**

We know you'll love these warm and sensual stories from some of our best loved authors.

| | |
|---|---|
| *Love Me Not* | Barbara Stewart |
| *Maggie And Her Colonel* | Merline Lovelace |
| *Prairie Summer* | Alina Roberts |
| *Anniversary Waltz* | Anne Marie Duquette |

'Stolen Moments' is the perfect summer read for those stolen summer moments!

Available: June '96            Price: £4.99

*Available from WH Smith, John Menzies, Volume One, Forbuoys, Martins, Woolworths, Tesco, Asda, Safeway and other paperback stockists.*

# MILLS & BOON

## Royal Affair

## Romancing a royal was easy, marriage another affair!

If you love Hello! magazine then you'll love our brand new three part series **Royal Affair** by popular author Stephanie Howard.

In each book you can read about the glamorous and of course romantic lives of each of the royal siblings in the San Rinaldo dukedom—the heir to the dukedom, his sister and their playboy brother.

Don't miss:

The Colorado Countess in May '96
The Lady's Man in June '96
The Duke's Wife in July '96

*Available from WH Smith, John Menzies, Volume One, Forbuoys, Martins, Woolworths, Tesco, Asda, Safeway and other paperback stockists.*

# MILLS & BOON

# An intriguing family trilogy...

## This summer don't miss Sara Wood's exciting new three part series—True Colours

Three women are looking for their family—what they truly seek is love. A father is looking for his daughter and either one of them could be she.

Things are rarely as they seem in Sara Wood's fascinating family trilogy, but all will be revealed—in True Colours.

Look out for:

*White Lies* in June '96
*Scarlet Lady* in July '96
*Amber's Wedding* in August '96

*Available from WH Smith, John Menzies, Volume One, Forbuoys, Martins, Woolworths, Tesco, Asda, Safeway and other paperback stockists.*

# MILLS & BOON

## Today's Woman

Mills & Boon brings you a series of fantastic romances by some of your favourite authors. One for every day of the week in fact and each featuring a truly wonderful woman who's story fits the lines of the old rhyme 'Monday's child is...'

Look out for Helen Brooks's *Dream Wedding* in **July '96.**

Sunday's child Miriam finds her sunny disposition sorely tried when her firm is hired to cater Reece Vance's sister's wedding. The cynical businessman's outlook couldn't be more different from Miriam's happy go lucky personality but then opposites attract don't they?

*Available from WH Smith, John Menzies, Volume One, Forbuoys, Martins, Woolworths, Tesco, Asda, Safeway and other paperback stockists.*

# *Historical Romance*

**Coming next month**

## AN UNWILLING CONQUEST
### *Stephanie Laurens*
**REGENCY ENGLAND**

Having seen his sister Lenore and brother Jack caught in Parson's mousetrap, albeit willingly, Harry Lester had *no* intention of following their example. Now the news was out that the Lester family fortunes had been repaired, Harry knew the matchmaking mamas would be in pursuit, so he promptly left London for Newmarket, only to find himself acting as the rescuer of Mrs Lucinda Babbacombe, a beautiful *managing* widow, who refused to accept his advice! No matter that he desired her—marriage was out!

## THE COMTE AND THE COURTESAN
### *Truda Taylor*
**FRANCE 1789**

After ten years in Paris under the protection of the elderly Marquis Philippe de Maupilier, Madeleine Vaubonne was well aware that she was mistakenly thought to be his mistress. Even so, it was a nasty surprise when Lucian de Valori, the Comte de Regnay, offered to replace Philippe in her bed! She forcefully refused his proposition, but when Philippe died Lucian was the only one to offer help. Reluctantly she agreed to his escort to her home in Brittany, the start of a journey neither had expected to make...

# MILLS & BOON

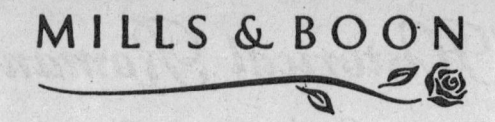

## Next Month's Romances

Each month you can choose from a wide variety of romance with Mills & Boon. Below are the new titles to look out for next month.

| | |
|---|---|
| MISCHIEF AND MARRIAGE | Emma Darcy |
| DESERT MISTRESS | Helen Bianchin |
| RECKLESS CONDUCT | Susan Napier |
| RAUL'S REVENGE | Jacqueline Baird |
| DECEIVED | Sara Craven |
| DREAM WEDDING | Helen Brooks |
| THE DUKE'S WIFE | Stephanie Howard |
| PLAYBOY LOVER | Lindsay Armstrong |
| SCARLET LADY | Sara Wood |
| THE BEST MAN | Shannon Waverly |
| AN INCONVENIENT HUSBAND | Karen van der Zee |
| WYOMING WEDDING | Barbara McMahon |
| SOMETHING OLD, SOMETHING NEW | Catherine Leigh |
| TIES THAT BLIND | Leigh Michaels |
| BEGUILED AND BEDAZZLED | Victoria Gordon |
| SMOKE WITHOUT FIRE | Joanna Neil |

*Available from WH Smith, John Menzies, Volume One, Forbuoys, Martins, Woolworths, Tesco, Asda, Safeway and other paperback stockists.*